A Good Kind of Crazy

By

Majken Selinder Nilsson

Acknowledgements

I dedicate this book to my family, Mans, Lukas, Lena, Helene, and Erik, who put up with me spending countless hours in front of my computer; especially my husband, who never complains about my insanely late nights spent writing and even voluntarily reads what I come up with, though it is not his genre of choice. To my parents, Bjorn and Judy Selinder, for never pushing, but rather encouraging me, my teachers in my small Nevada town, who gave me a top-notch compulsory education, and later those at the University of Nevada, Reno, especially the late Dr. Gary Hausladen, who constantly drilled home the importance of sense of place in any good story. I also thank my late grandmother, Lois Hall, for instilling early in me love for the written word, and my other grandparents who loved and supported me unconditionally through all my endeavors. Then of course, to our amazing Georgia family of friends, especially Ernie and Maytha Smith, for their love and support through all the tough stuff that led me to start writing in the first place.

I appreciate Ms. Rachel March, one of two of my best friends since forever, for her encouragement and support, reading and offering suggestions, and giving me the courage to try, and Charmaine Jerman, the other life- long best friend, who never laughed at my lofty dreams. Then, there are those, Ms. Becky Garfield, Ms. Melinda Jordy, Ms. Loralea Clay, Ms. Maile Enos, and Ms. Sydnie Peck, who graciously volunteered to read my book as beta readers, giving me valuable feedback, as well as authors Ms. Victoria Wilcox and Ms. Tammy L. Grace for their advice regarding the publishing world, and Ms. Kim Lowman for her help securing legal expertise. I also want to extend my thanks to Ms. Kimberly Vancoughnett for volunteering to read through the final product as yet one more pair of eyes, to Majken Longlade for putting in countless hours helping me to produce quality content, and to all those friends who have humored me while I have been writing books.

I am grateful to K.C. Sprayberry, Editor in Chief, at Solstice

Publishing, my amazing editor, Ms. Seana Dombrosky, and all the other people behind the scenes who helped make my dream into reality by first publishing my work. I appreciate all the expertise, guidance, long hours, and hard work that have gone into my manuscript to make it a success. I am also grateful for the incomparable photographic talents of Ms. Lori Collett, whose perfect eye made for an impeccable back cover shot.

Lastly, I am grateful to God for all that I have been given, and for how even the worst of times can produce the most enthralling results. Over and over again, I have been blessed with incredible silver linings for even the darkest of clouds.

Chapter One

Katherine, or Kat, as she was affectionately known to those who loved her, awoke with a start on her forty- third birthday. She glanced around and wondered how she got there: not her bed, nor her house, but her life. She turned her head and looked over at her husband's side of the mattress, finding it empty as usual. He always left at some ungodly hour to beat the traffic in from their suburban neighborhood to his job downtown. She smiled to herself as she thought about him. James had always been a good man and he took his responsibilities of supporting her and their three children seriously. He was a good provider, but as an accountant, he had slowly begun to develop more of the "typical" accountant behaviors through the years. Never very bombastic, he had become even more subdued, almost distant, especially in the last year or so.

Funny how the things that had attracted her most to him when they had met at university—that he was mature and responsible, especially compared to the frat boys on campus—were the things that now made her long for something more. Sure, they had built a good life together. They had a neat and tidy typical suburban home, though it wasn't particularly large. Maybe a little too small even, especially when their three kids were younger. He had been a good, albeit somewhat hands off, father, relying heavily on her to handle the day-to-day minutia of their lives. Of course, he would listen and offer his opinion when she struggled with any big issue, such as if the kids needed braces, which colleges would be the most feasible, or when she was worried about one of their love interests, but he did not get bogged down in the details of their existence. That was Mom's job. All of the doctors' appointments, school meetings, broken hearts, sports, and dance practices fell to her. She was happy that he didn't fight her on much of anything, but sometimes wished he was a little more passionate and involved… with all of them.

Kat rolled over and looked at the clock: 7:30 a.m. it mockingly said. Though she wanted to sleep more, she sat up with a small groan, knowing that she needed to get moving or she would be tempted to stay in bed all day. Then, for a fleeting second, she wondered why. The most exciting thing about her day would be what she made for dinner. She then remembered that it was her birthday and wondered what James had planned. He was far from a romantic, but he always tried to do something he thought she would like on her special day. She had a bit more spring in her step as she walked to the bathroom and turned on the shower. While the water heated up, she stood looking in the mirror, taking stock of how her now forty- three years had treated her physically.

I still have beautiful hair, she thought as she admired her best asset. A little longer than her shoulders, it fell in soft waves around her face. It was a nice chestnut color, shiny and thick. On her last visit, her stylist had recommended that they add some blonde highlights. "Chocolate chip cookie" she had called it, assuring Kat it was the latest thing.

Her eyes caught themselves in their reflection. They were okay. Still a mix between green and hazel, they just looked brown from far away. "Not too many crow's feet," she said aloud.

Her skin was still lightly freckled even as an adult; she couldn't deny her Irish heritage even if she wanted to. However, they weren't terribly noticeable anymore, especially when she put on some foundation. Her lips were still red and full, another of her better attributes. She knew she was lucky in that department. Next, she looked at her chin and neck. Though still fairly taut, she was beginning to see the faintest beginnings of "turkey neck." Her hand flew instinctually to her throat, and she silently wondered what could be done for that. *Surely by now, there has to be some sort of magic cream or procedure, right?*

Her eyes moved downward to her breasts. Still okay too, in her opinion, though a bit saggy from nursing three babies. They definitely looked better in a bra under a shirt, though, that was for sure.

Her hands slipped down to her stomach. Slightly pudgy and lined with a few stretch marks which she absently fingered, she thought back to her three pregnancies and recalled how large she had gotten and how she had wondered if her body would ever go back to the way it was before. It hadn't, of course; bodies never do. No matter how much exercise one does after having a baby, there will forever be physical reminders for every woman who went from maiden to mother.

Her eyes scanned her rear and legs. Definitely more defined than her upper body, they still looked okay, except for some spider and varicose veins: more physical reminders of the three times she had carried another life inside her own body. Still slim, strong, and flexible, her body required very little "leg work" at the gym, when she actually bothered to go.

The shower was steaming now, so she climbed inside. As she was soaping her body, she wondered when her older two kids would call from school. Derrick was studying engineering. Always an overachiever, he was in his last year, having somehow magically done his degree in three years instead of four, and thriving. Olivia was at school, too, though she seemed more interested in gaining her "MRS" than in earning any kind of degree. Kat wasn't even sure what her *major du jour* was this week. As a sophomore this year, Kat hoped Olivia would finally start to pay attention to her studies and not to all the boys around her. But Kat had known since Olivia was small that her focus would be on being a wife and mother. Why that was, Kat wasn't sure. She certainly wasn't like that. She loved her children, but she never recalled having the strong desire to have a family that she observed in Olivia.

Kat shut off the water and her thoughts turned to her youngest son, Andrew. Now a senior in high school, he was such a player: cute, funny, smart, and part of a champion lacrosse team, he had the girls and world falling at his feet. Every day brought a new phone call from some recruiter or another. His grades were excellent and his participation in everything from drama to chess club had pretty much sealed his future. He definitely combined the best of both her and James, Kat thought while drying off.

As she wrapped her towel around her head, the telephone rang. Kat looked at the caller I.D. and saw the L.A. area code. Jen, she thought as she grabbed the phone and said hello. It was only five a.m. on the West Coast, she knew, but Jen's job as a caterer for various Hollywood movies and T.V. shows often meant an early start for her friend. She absently turned on the T.V., having habitually turned it on in the morning for years as background noise to fill the silence of her empty house while listening to Jen talk.

"So, happy birthday, old fart!" Jen blurted. Kat let out a sound somewhere between a grunt and a groan.

"Thanks!" Kat responded wryly. "Just you wait... You're just three months behind me!"

Jen laughed and replied, "Heck, no! I live in LA. It's against the law to get old here."

Kat glanced over at the screen. Some western style drama was on from what she could gather. *Hmmmm... Who is that guy?* she thought as an incredibly attractive, tall actor came on scene with black-brown hair, sparkling eyes, and an infectious grin. *He is yummy! I might just have to start watching this show with eye candy like that!*

"Kat... Kat? Earth calling Kat!" Jen broke into her thoughts.

"Huh? What? Sorry! I got distracted by the T.V. for a second." Kat reached over and hit the mute button on the remote.

"Really? Anything good?"

"Nah... Just some western show. One of the actors is kind of hot, though," Kat replied. "Sorry.... What were you saying?"

"Well," Jen said. "I have a new job but I'm not quite sure what to do about it. It's actually on location in Canada, which would be fine if it weren't for Lucy. I'm trying to see if David would be able to take her full time during filming the season."

Jen and her ex, David, had a good relationship. They shared custody of their seven-year-old daughter, Lucy. However, he also worked in the entertainment industry, so his schedule, like Jen's, could be very unpredictable.

"I hate that I would have to spend such a long time up there during filming, but the off time between seasons is so long, I'd get a nice long break in between if they liked us and wanted us to come back. Plus, the money is good enough, too, that I wouldn't have to work as much during their off season. This is a great opportunity, and I was specifically asked to come. I don't know why they couldn't find someone up there, but apparently, word about me is getting around. If I say no to this, it could really throw me back a step."

Kat knew how diligently Jen had worked to build up her business. She and Jen had worked hard in their teens and in college in the food industry. They decided the summer before college to experiment with a new take on making Southern food healthier as a way to make some extra cash.

Their endeavor had grown steadily before Kat decided to stay in college, close to James, while Jen ventured to try her luck in Hollywood. It had been such a boon to L.A. to have comfort food that the actors could actually eat while maintaining their diets that it gone from an interesting hobby to a booming business within just a few years and was still continually expanding. Other companies had tried to duplicate it, but no one was quite able to get the flavors right. It took true Southern girls to make the recipes taste like home.

"I really need to think about hiring a partner," Jen said. "Hey, you interested?" she asked, only half- joking.

Kat sighed. This conversation was coming up more and more. "You know I would love to help out if I didn't live across the country," she replied.

"I know," said Jen. "But you can't blame a girl for trying!"

Jen started in on telling her all of the latest gossip she was able to glean through her inside track on the L.A. scene. She was a better resource than People magazine and TMZ put together. Apparently, food was not only the way to a man's heart, but also a key to open the mouths of celebrities. Jen not only overheard the deepest, darkest conversations between people on meal breaks, she was also the type of person with whom others felt instantly comfortable, so she often became a confidant, as well, when people would wander over to her for coffee, snacks, and a visit in between scenes and takes. If Kat ever heard anything juicy about a star or a new project, all she had to do was call Jen and she would get the real lowdown long before the details were public knowledge.

"So… what's Mr. Boring doing for your birthday today?" Jen asked, moving the focus back to Kat.

Kat smiled to herself. Jen had never really gotten over Kat's decision to stay home rather than going with her to Los Angeles. Even though the reason she stayed wasn't all about James and their relationship, Jen had forever held a grudge against him for ruining her dreams of running a successful business with her best friend since seventh grade.

Kat burst out laughing. "Nice… Mr. Boring? Come on! Are you ever going to let go of the fact that I married him instead of chasing our teenage dreams?"

"Nope! He's the reason that you didn't come with me so that we could meet Johnny Depp. I'll never forgive him for that."

"Jen, didn't you meet him years ago now?" Kat asked.

"Sure. But that still doesn't change the fact that you weren't here with me when I did," Jen replied. "Too bad, too. He's actually pretty cool."

Kat rolled her eyes. "I'm sure he is. Is there anyone you haven't met there?"

Returning to the original subject, Kat continued, "I honestly haven't got a clue what James has planned this year. He was gone before I woke up this morning and he didn't say anything last night when he finally came through the door after eleven."

"*Wow!* Eleven?" Jen asked incredulously. "Why was he out until eleven?"

"Some work thing. It has been happening more and more since the merger last year. Traveling a lot more, too; more clients to woo, new bosses to impress. In general, just a lot more work to do, I guess. You know the drill," Kat replied.

"Weird," said Jen. "I would have never guessed being an accountant would be so… adventuresome."

"Yeah, I guess. It's really only an issue about once a month when they have their corporate meetings with the executives from New York. Honestly, I don't mind. Gives me some time to binge watch all of my 'girl shows' without any guilt," Kat said. "Like this one. Wow, that guy is really good looking! I may have to add this show to my queue…"

"What is it called?" Jen asked.

"I don't know. Don't have time right now to figure it out, either—I've got to run. But let me know what you decide about Canada. Sounds like a great opportunity."

"Okay," Jen said. "Enjoy your birthday. Hope Mr. Boring doesn't disappoint! I'd love to have you come out for a visit soon. It's been too long"

"I know, I know. I'll try to come again soon. You know, just with it being Drew's final year of high school, things are crazy."

"Man, the last year of high school for your baby! Where has the time gone?" Jen asked sadly. "There's no way we are old enough to have kids in college already."

Kat laughed, "Well, no… Not if you are thirty-six when you have your first baby."

"Only baby," Jen corrected. "Better than twenty-one, my friend! At twenty-one, I couldn't even imagine taking decent care of myself, let alone another human being. When you had a husband and a baby, I was still having nights at the club that resulted in one-night stands. I couldn't even keep a plant alive back then!" Jen retorted.

Suddenly, it sounded like Jen was out of breath. "I need to run now. I didn't realize it was already five-thirty. I have to be on set in forty-five minutes and I haven't even showered yet. Wait... Why did you have to get off the phone before?"

"Oh! Nothing, really. I'd just gotten out of the shower and was in my towel when you called. I was getting cold," Kat responded lamely, not wanting to admit she had sought to get off the phone so she could ogle the handsome actor without distraction. "I'll let you go. Watch that crazy traffic. Love ya!"

She clicked the off button on her phone and stood up to get dressed, and her cell immediately starting to ring again.

"Hi, Mom!" Derrick said from other end of the line. "Just running to class and wanted to tell you happy birthday and that I love you. Hope Dad has planned something nice for you. Gotta go. I'm going to be late!"

"Wait! Derrick…," Kat heard the phone click off.

Well, at least he remembered, she thought ruefully.

She got up off of her bed and started to straighten the covers when she accidentally hit the mute button on the remote and sound blared like a foghorn through the silent house. Her eyes were once again drawn to the T.V. just as the actor had a close-up.

Wow! Kat thought as she settled back on the bed's decorative pillows. *It's my birthday and I can indulge myself with a little eye candy for a few minutes.*

Thirty-five minutes later, she realized she was hooked. The story based in a Western gold mining town in Colorado at the turn of the century had captured her attention. The scenery was breathtaking, and the acting was decent. The writing was also pretty good, though a bit sappy and corny. The lead male character who had initially caught her eye was adorable as the town's sheriff with his western twang, and his female counterpart, the unmarried town seamstress, was gorgeous. Their chemistry was undeniable. She checked the menu to find out what she was watching. *Western Skies* it read.

I haven't enjoyed a western show like this since I was a kid watching Little House on the Prairie she laughed to herself. *Kind of an old-school, feel-good show. Of course, whoever that guy is certainly helped!*

Kat hurried up to finish getting ready for her day before heading downstairs, and the usual boring chores were soon done. There was a time when she didn't have enough hours in the day to keep up with all the tasks revolving around being a stay-at-home-mom. Now, she seemed to have too many to fill.

She looked around the room and decided that since she had nothing better to do, she might as well hit the gym, so she grabbed her bag and headed out to her car. As she fought her way through the morning traffic, she blasted her music loudly. A young man pulled up beside her and started laughing at her obvious singing along. At first, she was mortified, but then remembered that one of the great things about being over forty was that she really didn't care what people thought anymore. She threw her hand up next to her head in an awkward sort of salute and speed off as soon as the light changed. *I may be old,* she thought, *but I'm not dead yet!*

Chapter Two

Kat sat at home on the couch waiting for James to come home. She hadn't bothered to start cooking, as she figured that he would be taking her out somewhere for her birthday dinner. When she glanced up at the clock, it read 6:30 p.m. It wasn't unusual for him to not be home yet even on one of his "normal" days, especially since traffic could be so incredibly terrible; she hardly went anywhere between the hours of three and eight every evening if she could help it.

Drew was off doing who knows what. After lacrosse practice, he would often go to friends' houses to study and hang out. Given he had just over two more months under their roof until he graduated and the fact that he was a good kid, James and Kat were letting him do his own thing more often than not, so she really didn't have any guess as to what time he would walk through the door. Kat smiled wistfully as she remembered all the years she had spent chauffeuring the kids to and from their activities, how many times she had put the Raffi CDs on repeat or Disney movies in the DVD player. Now that her children were making their own way in the world, she realized she seemed to have worn out her usefulness.

She turned on the T.V. to the evening news. Finding it boring and mundane, full of the typical reporting of goings on in any large metropolitan city in the U.S., she quickly flipped over to one of the nightly entertainment programs. Talk of some awards show from the past weekend hardly kept her attention as she scanned through the T.V. guide on the lower portion of the screen until she saw *him*: the guy from that morning's western was on the screen. Walking the red carpet with his costar on his arm,

he was smiling and waving as they walked into the building. He was giving her his rapt attention as he put his hand on the small of her back, demonstrating a sort of proprietary protectiveness as he guided her.

Ah! That would explain the obvious chemistry they have. They must be a couple, Kat realized.

The reporter mentioned that *Western Skies* had started out as a small production, not expected to last more than one season. It was a "filler show."

"Little did anyone know that it would explode the way it had," she continued to gush, "and it was mostly because of middle-aged housewives everywhere crushing on the male lead, Ian Gregory."

Ian Gregory, Kat committed to memory. *Never even heard of him before today. I wonder where he has been hiding. I'll have to ask Jen if she knows him.*

She continued to watch as other costars of the show made their way up the red carpet. They all seemed to have a laid-back camaraderie between them that suggested they were friends off screen as well as on.

Lydia Swan, who was also an unknown and played the female lead, was gorgeous. Even on T.V., Kat could see the eyes of men burning holes into her. She was the type of woman who could light up an entire room. Her blonde hair fell in soft waves around her face and down her back, accentuating her big blue eyes. Her red dress clung to her every perfect curve and her lipstick was the exact same shade as her dress. *Bet* she *has no stretch marks or sagging boobs,* Kat thought ruefully.

She glanced at the clock. It was now almost seven. James should be coming through the door any second. Kat turned the T.V. back to the news to check the traffic. No major delays on any of the roads James traveled were reported, so she sat back and waited as the evening darkened around her.

After a few minutes of listening to the following sports report simply because it was on, Kat recalled the entertainment reporter saying there were two seasons of *Western Skies,* so she flipped her T.V. to Netflix and searched for the show. Sure enough, it popped up. She debated if she really wanted to start watching it, but she figured it couldn't hurt to just see the first episode and find out if it was worth her time, or if her enjoyment of the episode she'd caught earlier was a fluke.

Adapted from a book, the story was of a young single mother named Sarah, who after having lost her husband to influenza, decided to cut her losses and travel across the country to her sister and brother-in-law's family in the small Colorado mining town he'd been transferred to because of his position with a railroad. Determined to escape the memories of her late husband that had become too much to bear, she knew with her sewing skills she would be able to support herself and her young son.

What Sarah hadn't counted on was the young town sheriff, Joe, who simultaneously infuriated and fascinated her. He had taken it upon himself to make sure she knew the dangers of being one of only a handful of single women in the dusty town and more importantly one of the even fewer who didn't engage in "immoral activities" to earn her living. Embarrassed and a bit insulted that he seemed to think she was too naïve to watch out for herself, the young woman struggled to find a balance between her need to feel independent in her new life and his determined protective behavior toward her.

Forty-five minutes later, the first episode ended. Looking up at the clock again, Kat wondered what was keeping James and if she should start another. She reasoned that she could simply turn it off when he came home and pick it up again tomorrow, so she might as well.

Once again, time flew by. By this point, it was a little after eight-thirty and James still had not appeared. She called his cell, but it went straight to voice mail. Generally, he was pretty bad about using his phone and her texts and calls to him often went unanswered, so she didn't think too much of it. Still, it meant there wasn't any reason to not start the third show in the series, which she proceeded to watch until James finally made it through the door.

It was nine-thirty when he finally walked in.

Engrossed in his phone as he stepped into their entryway, he quickly shoved it in his pocket when he saw Kat and said,

"Hello."

"Hi!" said Kat. "You're later than normal tonight."

"Yeah, traffic"

Kat cocked her head as she looked at him. *That's funny, there were no reports of anything major happening when I checked the news earlier.*

But remembering her Netflix binge, she shook her head. Maybe something had happened between when he left the office and the two plus hours she had been watching the show.

"What's for dinner?" James asked her. "Did you already eat, or?"

"Ummm… No. I thought we would be going out tonight," Kat told him.

"Why would we do that? It's the middle of the week in the middle of the worst quarter to be an accountant," he replied grumpily.

Kat stared at him. *He can't be serious. He's just messing around with me. He wouldn't have forgotten my birthday, right?*

He looked up at her and said, "Why are you looking at me like that? Sorry. I've had a long day. I see now that you didn't cook anything. What should we do? Open a can of soup, or?"

By now, it was clear to Kat that this was not some romantic farce James was playing: he truly did not remember that it was her birthday. She balked at him for a few seconds before responding, "Well, seeing as how it's my *birthday* today, I figured we would be going out. But I guess it's too late now."

"Yes," said James. "Tomorrow will be another early one. Wait… What? It's your birthday today? Are you sure?"

"Yes. I am absolutely sure that my birthday is today. Just like it has been for the last forty-three years…"

"Oh, crap! I can't believe that I forgot. I'm so sorry. I'll make it up to you this weekend, all right?" James quickly loosened his tie and placed a kiss on her cheek as he walked past her. "Right now, I just want out of these clothes and into my sweats. Can you find something for us to eat?"

Seriously? Kat fumed as James headed up the stairs. *That's it? Not even a "Happy birthday?" Just an "Are you sure it's your birthday?" I cannot believe it! Though, what should I expect from Mr. Boring?*

She mentally admonished herself for the last thought. She knew that his work was crazy and stressful right now after the recent merger.

Wandering into the kitchen, she opened the cupboard doors. She found some tomato soup and started to make grilled cheese sandwiches. By the time James had come back down, the food was ready. Taking his with a "Thanks," he walked over to the couch and plopped down. Flipping the T.V. on to some sports show, he began to eat, his eyes never leaving the screen.

Kat had already accepted it was spring: time for news of college football signings. Southern women knew that this was the "other" football season, when men relived their glory days of playing ball, hoping to be picked up by some school or other, or if they hadn't had a chance, then having had someone else from their school chosen was good enough. Of course, James was never particularly athletic, but he was still an avid supporter of his alma maters.

Kat was just thankful it wasn't the fall. Their devotion was even worse then, as every weekend was spent on the couch in front of the T.V. or at the stadium with the guys. Every housewife worth her salt in the South knows that fall is the high point in any Southern husband's year, so much so that they would all joke about being "football widows". It was as if Christmas lasted a whole semester; more, if your team managed to make it into a bowl game.

Every house had the colors of Clemson, Auburn, UGA, etc., flying outside, and everyone inside had at least one article of clothing to represent "their" team. It was all just part of the modern Southern Gentlemen's Code.

Kat took her bowl and sat down at the table in the breakfast nook. On her way, she picked up her cell and casually glanced through her text messages. Olivia had sent her a *Happy birthday, Mom!* text, complete with a little smiley face emoji. She responded back with a quick *Thanks. Love you!*

Next, she read Jen's text: *Sorry I had to get off the phone so abruptly this morning. Hope you and Mr. B. had a great night.*

Kat stared at the screen. She generally tried to protect James from Jen's critical eye, but tonight, she was too hurt. She hit reply and typed furiously: *No! Nothing! Mr. B. is sitting on the couch watching sports news. Meanwhile, I'm sitting at the table alone, eating my canned tomato soup and grilled cheese. I'll call you tomorrow.*

Unexpectedly, her phone vibrated on the table, shaking Kat out of her pity party. Jen had responded: *WTH? Seriously? Oh, that man! I'm SO sorry. Talk to you tomorrow. I have Lucy tonight. Happy birthday, sweetie!*

Kat cleaned up the kitchen and walked into the family room. She looked to James, who did not even glance up from the T.V. as he handed her his plate and said, "Thanks, babe."

She put his dishes in the dishwasher and turned it on before turning off the lights in the kitchen and telling James that she was heading to bed. He nodded without even looking in her direction and said, "Fine. I'll be up in a few. I just want to watch a little more."

Just when Kat had finished her nightly routine and was about to climb into bed, Drew knocked softy and stuck his head through her bedroom door.

"Hi, Mom! I'm home. Happy birthday! Sorry I missed dinner. Big chem test tomorrow and I have to pass. Hope you and Dad did something fun, at least."

She walked over to him and gave him a hug. "Yeah, it was fine, thanks. Good luck on that test tomorrow. I love you!"

"Love you, too, Mom," Drew said as he backed out of the room and shut the door gently behind him.

She was in bed reading by the time James came into their room. He brushed his teeth, changed into his pajamas, and then crawled into bed beside her and sighed.

"Kat, I'm really sorry. It's just that work is crazy, and I'm really stressed. We have that meeting in Las Vegas soon and I have to get everything done before we go. I promise, we will go out to dinner this weekend and then we will have a good time in Vegas. Okay?"

Kat smiled tightly at him and said, "Sure. It's fine. I know. Don't worry about it."

She turned out her light and rolled over on her side. Before long, James' arm was over her waist with his hand creeping up over her rib cage underneath her pajama top.

Are you kidding me? she thought as his hand cupped her breast. *He is such a guy. Sex is the ultimate birthday present to them. I'd rather have a root canal tonight given how I currently feel about him.*

But being the good girl she'd been raised to be, she let him continue. He rolled her onto her back and lifted her pajama top. A few mechanical kisses on her lips, breasts, and neck, and he was ready, so he pulled down her pajama bottoms and climbed on top of her. She lay there as he moved over her, willing it to be over quickly, so she could just get to sleep and forget about her bad day. Just as she started to get more into it, though, he abruptly finished with a groan and rolled off of her. He kissed her cheek and said, "Thanks! That was nice. Happy birthday! Goodnight."

Kat lay there looking at the ceiling for a long time. James was fast asleep, and she was incredibly frustrated. Though he was not the most attentive lover and their times together often ended with him enjoying it more than she had, she couldn't believe that on her birthday he had been so selfish. She grabbed her phone and opened her Netflix app. There he was again—Ian Gregory—his face staring at her from the screen, beckoning her to press play.

As she watched him, Kat wondered what kind of lover he would be. He was so kind and gentle on screen, yet still rugged and confident, and so considerate to the character played by his costar. *Surely, he has to be as attentive and considerate in real life, too? No one could actually play someone that nice if they weren't, right?*

He had kind eyes and a quick smile that seemed so genuine and spontaneous that even the best script could not invent it. She shook her head and tried to concentrate on the story line.

The next morning when Kat awoke, she looked immediately to James' side of the bed. As usual, he was gone, leaving crumpled bedding in his place. She got up and got into the shower; as the water rained down on her, she was consumed by thoughts of her horrible day the day before. Afterward, as she walked down the stairs, she looked around and thought about how her day today was essentially just the same as yesterday and the one before that. She squared her shoulders slightly to shake off her feelings of disappointment and anger before grabbing her gym bag and keys and heading out the door.

Kat's mom called as she was stopped at a light, and she debated whether or not to pick up. Though she loved her mother, she was the epitome of a Southern Belle, and didn't seem to grasp that life had changed dramatically since she'd been a young woman. In her mind, everything was still "Yes, ma'am" and "Yes, sir", Sunday suppers with the family after church, and sweet tea under the ceiling fans of the front porch in the summer.

Feeling guilty, Kat picked up the phone. "Hello?" "Oh, hi, sweet pea," her mom drawled. "Just thought I should call and wish you a happy birthday. Hope you had a good day yesterday! Sorry I didn't call, but I just had a million things to do durin' the day, and then last night I figured that James would've taken you out somewhere anyways."

"Oh, hey, Mama. No problem. It was okay. The kids called or texted, but James got home late. We had tomato soup and grilled cheese."

Kat didn't want to get into how James forgot about her birthday. Her mom thought that all women should be happy being the doting wife and forgive men for their "indiscretions," which seemed to be Southern for all the stupid and insensitive things men did. She would have just reminded Kat that he was tired from working so hard to support his family and she should be grateful for that fact.

"How's Daddy?" Kat asked.

"Well, he is doin' a bit of all right. Feelin' better this week. Took a turn on the golf course yesterday afternoon. He's at the market right now. He told me to tell you happy birthday and that he loves you."

"Aw… that's sweet. Tell him I love him, too."

Kat and her father were very close. Being the only girl of four kids, and the baby at that, she had always been her daddy's little princess. Her brothers had also been very protective of her growing up and they still had a decent relationship, but they had scattered all over the U.S. after graduating. Now she only saw them once a year if they were all lucky enough to be able to get together. Thanksgiving seemed to be the holiday of choice, which meant that the women all stayed in the kitchen cooking while the men communed around the T.V., watching football.

"Everyone else doing okay? The boys are good and their kids?"

"Yes, dear. Everyone is doin' just fine. How are those sweet grandbabies of mine?"

"They're fine, Mama. Just busy with school. You know how it is."

"I sure do. Well, sugar, I'm goin' to get off the phone. I'm havin' lunch with the ladies. Have a good day now, and I'm so glad your birthday was good."

"Thanks. Have a good day. Love you."

Kat hit the end button on her hands free and bit her lip. She couldn't believe how insensitive and out of touch her mom could be sometimes. It didn't matter whether Kat was happy or not, just as long as she did her part to uphold the image of a strong, Southern, Christian family. She wished she could talk to her mom about what she really felt and thought but knew that it would never be well-received. A part of her deep Southern roots, she knew, was her duty to put on a smile and be sickeningly sweet to everyone she met, regardless of how her day was or how she felt inside.

At the gym, she stepped up on one of the ellipticals and got set in her workout. Looking up at the T.V. hanging on the wall across the room, there he was again on some sort of daytime talk show! Ian Gregory's smiling face loomed as he responded to the interviewers. Suddenly, he looked down at the floor in the studio with an endearingly shy smile and blushed a lovely shade of pink. She could not hear what any of them were saying, but she could read the closed captioning. Because of the few seconds' delay between spoken words and the text at the bottom of the screen, Kat saw that Ian had been responding to a question about his personal life; more specifically about whether or not he and Lydia Swan were in a relationship.

"She's fabulous," is how he had replied. Kat realized that he was careful not to give anything away, but smart enough to keep them guessing.

She looked away from the giant screen and glanced around the room. Based on the rapt attention the women around her were paying the T.V., she clearly was not the only one who found Ian Gregory attractive.

A few seconds later, she heard one of the women drawl, "Oh, my, I certainly wouldn't kick *him* outta bed for eatin' crackers."

She has to be from Alabama, southern Georgia, or Mississippi, Kat thought to herself. *No one else under fifty around here drawls like that anymore.*

"Me, either," said another.

"Don't bother. He's involved with that Lydia girl. You know… his costar. I heard they're living together now," replied a third.

Kat rolled her eyes. She decided she owed Jen a phone call and she would ask her if she knew anything about this Ian Gregory guy, rather than rely on some gossip between women she didn't know.

When she got back in her car, she hit the voice recognition button and dialed Jen. Though it was now a little past nine a.m. out West, she hoped that the set her friend was working with this week was done eating and now shooting so Jen would have a few minutes to talk. Her phone rang a few times before Jen picked up.

"Talk to me," she said.

"Uh? Hi? Jen?"

"Yeah? What's up, Kat?"

"Did I get you at a bad time? I can call back."

"No. Just a sec."

Kat heard Jen yell over her shoulder, "Hey, Melinda? Can you take over here for a few? Thanks!"

"So, what's up today, Jen?"

"Oh, you know. The usual drama: the coffee isn't properly sourced, the organic oranges didn't come on the backs of camels across the sea from Israel, that sort of thing. Good Lord, this can be a thankless job sometimes! How about you? Still mad at Mr. B?"

"Yeah. It gets better. Apparently non-gratifying sex was my birthday gift."

"Nice! Though I have to say I thought any sex with Mr. B. would be non-gratifying."

Kat sat in stunned silence for a second. "You really don't like him, do you?" she asked quietly.

"No, not really. Sorry. I never have. He is the epitome of a Southern Boy and exactly what I fought so hard to avoid. He's a Mama's Boy! Probably was called 'Bubba' growing up! And he never really seems to care about *you*, just about how you make him look. The beautiful Southern Belle on his arm, maintaining his home, raising his kids. He never really had any room in his life for you as a person. Truly, I could replace you with the neighbor down the street and he probably wouldn't notice, as long as she makes good snacks for his football game."

"Wow, Jen. Tell me what you really think."

"I'm sorry, Kat. But I can't abide by his treatment of you."

"You can't abide by? Are you kidding me? Who's the Southern Belle now?"

"Honestly, Kat. You played by the rules. He was nice and steadfast. He had manners and was getting a good education. He was decent looking, and his family was established. Basically, he was everything we had been told to look for in a man.

"But what he lacked, and still does, is passion: for you, for the kids, for anything. You could've come with me out here and played fast and loose, but you chose to play it safe and boring. You fell right into the trap that Southern women have fallen into since the beginning of the Antebellum. That man is a dud. He treats you like crap, and frankly, you let him."

"Oh. Wow. Okay, then. I don't even know how to respond to that one."

"Look, I'm sorry. I've had kind of a bad morning. I'm getting all kinds of pressure to do this thing in Canada. I don't know what to do about Lucy and I'm sick to death of all of the divas around here. But I shouldn't be taking it out on you. Please come out here. Maybe if you aren't there for a week, he might notice you are gone."

Kat snickered in spite of herself. "You know I can't this spring. Drew has so much going on. Derrick's graduating from university. I just can't get away right now," Kat said sadly.

"Okay, I understand. I just don't want you to fade into the background, Kat. You're fabulous. I feel like you think your job is done, like you have no more value to give anyone anymore. But the kids are grown, and your life should just be beginning. Now is the time to start living for yourself a little. Not your husband, not your kids."

"Thanks. I know. I'll come out soon, I promise. Just let me get through May. Hey, that reminds me. James has that conference in Las Vegas next week. Would you be able to make it over there? We are staying for four days."

"I don't know right now. Depends on how much longer I'll be on this movie set. However, if I have to deal with Little Miss Diva much longer, it won't be very long, but you may have to come bail me out of jail! I've got to go. Love ya!"

"Love you, too, Jen."

Kat hung up the phone and thought about what Jen had said. Fading into the background: that was exactly what was happening. She had worked so long and hard raising her family that she didn't even know who she was anymore. She didn't know how to spend her free time. She had put her own wants and needs so far on the back burner, she didn't even know if the gas was still on. No one looked at *her* anymore. She was only James' wife or Derrick, Olivia, or Drew's mom. She herself had become a non- entity.

She pulled into her driveway and began to think about her and James' upcoming trip to Vegas. They had been there once before, years ago when the kids were little, and they had really enjoyed themselves. The food was fantastic, they had gone to shows, and the sex had been great. It was like a second honeymoon and had been fabulous for reconnecting. She found herself hoping that this would be exactly what they needed to get back on track and remember the things that had made them fall in love with each other in the first place.

Chapter Three

By the time Friday rolled around, Kat had pretty much gotten over the pain of James forgetting her birthday. She had rationalized it by accepting he was just busy and stressed from the dust of the merger still settling and preparing for the upcoming conference. Therefore, she was surprised when he asked her on Thursday night if she wanted to go to dinner the next day to celebrate.

"Yes! That sounds great. Thank you!" she called over her shoulder as she walked out the door to pick Drew up from a friend's.

The next evening, Kat headed over to the high school for Drew's game. As much as she loved watching her youngest on the field, she had really begun to dread sitting in the bleachers with the other mothers. She looked around at the group of women above her as she started up the stairs. It was easy tell which women were born and bred in the South versus the ones who were Northern transplants. The Southern girls had their hair done and makeup perfect. They wore blinged out jeans and T-shirts with tall boots and had their container of sweet tea or a bottle of Diet Coke beside them. The other women wore yoga pants and body-hugging fleece hoodies over T-shirts, with their hair pulled back in ponytails, and sunglasses covering their eyes as the evening sun set. Their faces looked to be bare of any makeup, except possibly some mascara or lip balm. Some wore hats with their ponytails stuck through the hole at the back. They held their Starbucks cups and pushed their Ugg boot-clad feet underneath their seats.

It's like there's a fashion Mason-Dixon Line going on here she thought, as she climbed the stairs.

Kat smiled and waved back at the women who looked up at her, saying "Hi!" as she passed. She found a seat next to Holly and sat down.

Unfortunately, Holly was in the middle of a conversation

with Ashley, whom Kat really couldn't stand, but as their husbands worked for the same company and their boys had grown up together and played on the same sports teams since forever, she was forced to interact with her on a regular basis. She much preferred Holly and her New York candor to Ashley's down home, sickeningly sweet demeanor. Holly was her "Jen away from Jen," as she liked to call her.

Her friend held up her hand in greeting as she listened to some inane drivel pouring out of Ashley's mouth. She glanced back over her shoulder at Kat and winked at her, letting her know that she was enjoying conversing with Ashley about as much as Kat did, so Kat sat silently staring out over the field, watching the boys play until Ashley's voice cut through her thoughts like a knife.

"So, Kat, are y'all ready for Vegas next week?"

Kat looked over at her. "Sure, I guess. Just have to pack a few things and get on the plane."

"Have you bought anythin' new to wear to the dinner on Saturday night?"

"No, not yet... Wasn't really planning on it, honestly."

Ashley looked over at her and exclaimed, her South Georgia accent becoming more pronounced in the process, "But, honey! You just *have* to get somethin' nice. It's black tie, for goodness' sake. And it *is* the first conference since the merger. It's our duty to make our husbands look good for the new managers."

Kat looked up at Holly, who had an amused smile playing on her lips. "Don't worry, Ashley. I was planning on wearing the red formal I wore to the Christmas party a few years ago. It will be fine."

"Oh, sweetie," Ashley proclaimed, "You cannot possibly wear that old thing! I mean it was nice and all, but everyone has seen you in that before. Is it a money issue? Because if it is, I would be happy to give you some. I know it has to be hard to make ends meet with two in college and another headin' out soon, especially on what little money James makes. They sure do underpay that poor man."

Holly quickly turned to Kat, her jaw dropping, the shock over what Ashley had just said written all over her face. Kat raised her eyebrows slightly and looked past Holly to Ashley with a sly smile turning up the corners of her mouth.

"No. No, thanks, Ashley, that won't be necessary. You see, it isn't an issue of money. I just don't have to be decorated like a wedding cake to make James look good. I'm lucky that way. Anything I have is fine."

Holly snorted with laughter while taking a drink of her coffee as Kat spoke, which she quickly covered with a cough. "Sorry! I swallowed wrong," she explained.

Ashley looked at Kat and just shrugged. She then stood up quickly and walked over to another mother, calling, "Hey, Diana. How *are* you? I just *love* that color on you!"

Holly turned to Kat and shook her head. "I will never get over you Southern women. It's like a beautifully choreographed cat fight. It's the most incredible thing I've ever witnessed. You're all sweet like sugar, but it's laced with arsenic."

Kat shrugged. "Yeah, welcome to Southern living. Nowhere else are women able to seemingly compliment you, all the while driving that knife in just a bit further. Not my preferred way of doing things, but I learned how just to keep up."

"Man, I'll take the rudeness and brutal honesty of New York women over that anytime. I cannot believe it."

"You haven't lived here long. You'll learn. It's eat or be eaten alive down here, and these natives have been born and bred to protect their territory with a smile."

Holly just looked up at her. "God love me then, because so help me, if one of them tries anything like that with me, I'll lay them out flat."

Holly then changed the subject. "So, you're going to Las Vegas next week?"

"Yes, James' company is having a conference there; the first since the merger, like Ashley said. I'm looking forward to getting away and reconnecting with him. I know he's an accountant and all, but lately, he's been even more subdued than normal. I think this whole merger is freaking him out a bit, honestly. He says his new boss is something else and his coworkers are cutthroat."

"Like Ashley's husband?" Holly asked with a grin. "No, not him. He's actually a pretty nice guy, at least as far as I can tell. He's an attorney who handles contract negotiations, hence the comment about James and his poor CPA salary."

"Wow. I still can't believe that. You were so calm."

"Well, it took every fiber of my strict Southern upbringing to not smack that woman. But you get more flies with honey than vinegar, right?"

"You would know, growing up here. Sugary-sweet seems to be the method of choice with which to drown your opponent."

"Sure! Because you get to save face by looking like a lady. It's all about appearances down here, sugar." Kat thickened her accent and gave Holly an exaggerated wink. "Speaking of that, could Drew stay with you while we are gone? He's a good kid, but an empty house to himself for five days would be too much temptation for any kid."

"Not a problem at all," Holly assured her. "Just remind me to stock my pantry. Those boys can pack it away, especially after a game."

They continued to watch the game in companionable silence, cheering when their team won, and then headed off in their opposite directions. "See you Wednesday, if not before," Kat called back over her shoulder.

Later that night, James took her to her favorite Italian bistro. He was trying hard to make up for his forgetting her birthday, but he still kept looking at his phone and texting.

"What's going on?" Kat asked. "You never look at your phone when we're out like this."

"Nothing; just texts from my coworker about our presentation next week. We're trying to get a few last-minute details figured out. Sam's persistent, to say the least."

"Okay. Well, I'm shocked that there would be this much to discuss on a Friday night, but whatever. I know you keep saying that you have to work extra hard to keep up with this new group."

"Sure do. I'm really hoping it's temporary. I'm looking forward to this trip and being done with this pace for a while." James took her hand and stroked his thumb over the top of it. "I've missed you lately."

"Aw… that's so sweet. I've missed you, too. It feels like I hardly get to see you anymore. I'm looking forward to this trip; to reconnect with you like last time we were there. Remember that?"

James' phone started buzzing on the table. He nodded at her, putting up his finger to signal her to hold that thought as he jumped up and answered while he walked out of the dining room.

Their plates were served, and Kat watched him engrossed in what seemed to be a pretty intense conversation with his hands moving in the air to emphasize whatever he was explaining to the person on the other end of the call while their food got cold. After about ten minutes of waiting for him to come back to the table, she finally picked up her fork.

James returned to the table five minutes later. "Intense conversation?" Kat inquired.

"Yes. You can say that. Sorry. Sam can really be a ballbuster sometimes." He gave her a wry smile over the table and began to eat.

"So, tell me about this Sam," Kat told him.

"Not much to tell. Harvard educated, lives in Manhattan. Works like a dog. Nothing much else to report, honestly."

"Must be a pretty lonely life, working so much."

"I guess…" James trailed off, obviously not wanting to continue the conversation about Sam.

"You ready to fly out on Thursday?" he asked her.

"I suppose. Just the last-minute laundry and packing. Holly agreed to let Drew stay with them while we're gone, by the way."

"That's a relief. Even though he's a good kid, leaving him alone may be asking for it," James said, reiterating what Kat had said earlier to Holly.

They continued their meal while talking about their goings-on. Kat kept up the conversation without much effort as her life seemed to have more details than his. He nodded along and listened, commenting every once in a while, as she continued to report about the kids, their parents, the neighborhood association, and the car that needed to be serviced.

As the meal ended, he rose from the table and asked if she was ready to go. She reached for his hand when they were walking out of the restaurant and he took it, but only for a few seconds until he reached into his pocket to grab his key fob. They drove home in silence, each absorbed with their own thoughts, while Kat happily thought that after close to twenty-three years of marriage, it was wonderful that they were comfortable enough around each other to just be.

When they walked in through the door, Kat turned to him and said, "I'm heading up to bed. Don't be too long, okay?" She gave him a wink.

He pulled out his cellphone and told her, "Don't worry. I'll be up shortly. Just have to take care of this one last thing."

Kat was under the covers when James made it up the stairs. She switched off the T.V., not wanting to watch the news any longer. Feeling a bit lonely and invisible after her recent conversation with Jen, she was looking to James to reassure her. When he came out of the bathroom and climbed into bed, she rolled over to him and started running her hand over his chest.

"That feels good," he said.

"Good," she purred. "I've been worried about you lately. All work and no play." She looked seductively at him.

"Yeah, it has been tough. I'm really tired. Do you mind if we just go to sleep? I promise we'll catch up in Vegas."

"Oh! Okay! I'm sorry. Have a good sleep." Kat gently kissed his forehead and rolled over.

In the morning, she got up before James and headed downstairs. His phone was still on the charger from the night before and as she walked past, it lit up. Even though it was locked, she saw a text message visible on the screen.

Thinking it might be important, she entered in his pass code and saw that it was from Sam: *So looking forward to this week! Thanks for all of the reassurances that everything will turn out fine. I really need you to keep saying it. We will get through this together. We have a lot more to discuss once we see each other.*

She thought it was a strange message, but she couldn't really discern what was off about it. As she put the phone back on the counter, Drew walked into the kitchen.

"Hey, Mama," he said as he reached for the cereal. "How are you?" he asked through his yawn.

"Fine, thanks. All ready for your game today?"

"Yes, ma'am! It should be a good one. Both teams are coming in undefeated so far this year. They are the team to beat at this point."

Kat leaned over and handed him the milk, planting a kiss on his cheek in the process. "I'm sure you will all do great. You always do."

"Thanks. I'm a bit nervous. Coach says that there may be some more scouts there."

"Why are you nervous? Honestly, kid, it seems like at this point, you could pretty much go wherever you want. Pretty soon you're just going to have to commit."

"I know. I just get nervous knowing that there are people there who are watching my every move. It's intimidating. Besides," he said with a crooked grin, "I'd rather have my choice between all the schools, not just some of them. I'm thinking I maybe want to go far away to college, not just stick around here."

Kat shook her head at her boy. She had loved them all, of course, but Drew was her baby. Not just because he was the youngest, but because he was the one who really stole her heart. Married at twenty, she had Derrick at twenty-one, Olivia just two years later, and then Drew came along just after she turned twenty-six. She had been so busy that her head spun, but Drew was born right when Derrick was going to Kindergarten and

Olivia started preschool. She and Drew had more time to be by themselves and bond than she had had with the other kids. He was also her snuggler; the one who would sit on her lap while watching T.V. and find his way into their bed every night until he was almost five. He would still hold her hand in public until he turned ten. Even now, he would often give his mom a kiss on her cheek before running out on the field to play. His actions made all the teenage girls swoon and the other mothers jealous.

Kat ruffled Drew's hair, telling him to have a great game and that she loved him. "Are you sure you are okay with me not going to the game today?"

"Yes, ma'am, that's fine. I know that you need to go and get all gussied up for your trip so Dad can have a hot piece of eye candy on his arm." He winked at her.

"Gussied up? Seriously? How old are you? One hundred and twelve?" Kat laughed.

"Nope, just turning on my Southern charm. I heard it attracts the ladies," he said with another wink, and then gave her a quick hug before grabbing his gear on the way out the door. "Love you!"

A few minutes later, James made it down the stairs. He scratched the stubble on his chin and grabbed a coffee cup. While he was pouring, Kat said, "Hey, you got a text from Sam."

The coffee mug crashed down on the floor, breaking into a million little pieces, spilling its contents all over the white cupboards. Without a word, Kat looked at James and handed him the rag from the sink.

"Sorry about that," he said. "I guess I'm not all the way awake yet. Did you say that I got a text from Sam? How would you know that?"

She watched him as he bent over and wiped off the cupboard doors. "I was just walking past your phone when it lit up. I saw the name Sam, so I picked it up and saw the text message notification on the locked screen. I figured it must be pretty important, so I unlocked it and read it. Is that okay?"

"Sure," James coughed. He peered at her for a few seconds

and then said, "Why wouldn't it be?"

"Okay, just making sure. You seemed a little shocked when I brought it up. Is there something you need to tell me about you and this Sam character?" she joked as she wrapped her arms around his waist from behind.

James spun out of her arms and looked intently at her for a second before returning the rag to the sink and replied, "No, nothing at all. I was just surprised that Sam would text on a Saturday morning. I guess I had better go and see what the deal is."

He picked up his phone and left the room as Kat grabbed the broom and dustpan from the closet and began to sweep up the broken shards of ceramic. Shaking her head, she wondered what in the world was making James so jumpy. *The stress must really be really getting to him.*

Chapter Four

Thursday morning came quickly, with Kat and James were in a hurry to get to the airport. James had been so busy the past few days that they had hardly had time to talk to each other. He would walk in the door between nine and ten each night, and be on his computer and cellphone until coming to bed at one a.m. He would then get up at five-thirty and be out the door by six. Kat had taken Drew to Holly's the previous night, and then they had packed in companionable silence, only speaking to ask about necessary items for the trip.

Jumping into the car, they hit the interstate and prepared to wind their way through downtown to the airport. On a good day, the drive could take a little bit over forty minutes. But there weren't really any "good" traffic days anymore, not since the South had exploded as the new "it" place to move.

They hit the inevitable traffic jam about three miles out from downtown. James drummed his fingers on the steering wheel and kept checking his watch, while Kat stared straight ahead and wondered why James was so antsy. They had left in plenty of time, planning for this to happen, as the city center had seemed to be in a constant state of gridlock for at least the last five years.

"James," she started.

"What?" he curtly responded.

"What's the matter?"

"Traffic. Always this stupid traffic."

"Yes, but there's always traffic nowadays. Not like when we were kids. We have plenty of time, so why are you so nervous?"

"I don't know. I'm stressed, okay? A lot is riding on this trip, and I have to get there and get settled. Speaking of that, I have a meeting tonight, so do you think you could find some other wives to have dinner with?"

Kat looked over at James, shocked. "Really? You have a meeting tonight? Isn't tonight the 'meet and greet' reception?"

"Oh, yeah. I forgot about that. I guess you can just go to that and eat."

"Where will you be? Don't you have to go to that, too?"

"I told you already. I have a meeting. I'll come and find you when we are done," James said.

"Um, well, I don't really feel like going to that by myself. It would be a little awkward, don't you think?"

"No. Ashley and Tom will be there. Can't you just hang out with them for a while?"

Kat looked at James incredulously. "You must really be stressed if you are suggesting that I willingly spend time with Ashley. I'd really rather be left for dead in the Nevada desert without food and water than spend an evening with that woman, especially if you aren't there.

"Honestly, though, I don't know many of your coworkers from here and no one from New York. It'll be pretty hard to stand around and explain to everyone that I'm James' wife when James isn't even there."

"Well, just tell them I'm at a meeting, then. They'll understand. Will you just MOVE!" James shouted at the traffic.

Kat decided that it was best to drop the subject for now. James was already tense and stressed and she didn't want to make things worse. She pulled out her phone and started texting Jen:

Hey. What's up? Heading to the airport. Are you going to be able to come over and see us?

Jen: *Not sure yet. Want to. Just waiting for this infernal movie to wrap. I'll know tomorrow if we have another day of catering on set Saturday or if I'm free.*

Kat: *Okay. James is so stressed out. I don't dare talk to him right now.*

Jen: *Why? What's up with him?*

Kat: *Work. Normally, we engage in a little "stress relief," if you catch my drift, before something like this. But he always said he was too busy, so we didn't this time.*

Jen: *Ewwww... I really didn't need to read that.*

Ding. The phone sounded as Jen's last message came in.

James looked over at Kat and exploded.

"Jesus! Can't you turn off the sound on the damned thing? Seriously. Who are you texting, anyway?"

"Oh, sorry!" Kat responded. "I can silence it. I'm just texting Jen to see if she can make it to Vegas on Saturday to hang out for a while during your meetings."

"I hope not!" James muttered under his breath.

"What was that?"

"Nothing. You know I can't really stand Miss Free Spirit. Living in L.A., hobnobbing with the stars, thinking she's all that."

Kat just looked at him, perplexed. "You knew when you married me that it was a package deal with Jen."

"Yeah, I realize. Little did I know how much I would live to regret that. She's a bad influence on you."

"Bad influence? What are you talking about?"

"She's always filling your head with all of these stories about the famous people she 'supposedly' works with and how you could have had that life, too, if you hadn't married me." James made air quotes with his hands just above the steering wheel, emphasizing the "supposedly."

"Honestly, I think she makes three-quarters of that stuff up. She probably doesn't even have a catering business; she works at some café and lies to you."

Kat laughed, "You've got to be kidding me, right? Of course, she has a legitimate business! I've been there and seen her setup with my own eyes, remember? Even if you didn't believe her, her ex would confirm it. Besides, she just got a really great offer to go to a set of some T.V. show in Canada. She's considering it, if he will take Lucy while she is up there."

"Well, that's another thing. What kind of mom would leave her kid for three months? Especially at what is she now? Seven years old?"

"Um… you do realize that she's leaving Lucy with her dad, right? She isn't leaving her with some homeless guy on the corner. She's as much his responsibility as hers."

"See? Right there. That's what I mean. What kind of woman would put her career above her husband's and just take off? What's he supposed to do with the kid?"

"Her ex-husband, actually, and I guess he'll have to do the same thing she has to do for Lucy. Find a decent babysitter and do the best he can."

"It's just not right. A woman should be in the home and taking care of the kids if at all possible."

"Whoa. Where is this coming from? You do realize that this isn't the 1950s, right?"

"Of course! But that's the reason that they didn't stay married. She wouldn't put her life on hold for him. Not like you did. How else is he supposed to be successful?"

Kat looked out the window at the planes flying overhead as they approached the airport. His words resonated deep within her: *She wouldn't put her life on hold for him. Not like you did.*

Kat closed her eyes and felt the tears forming against her lashes. That is exactly what she had done. She had put her life on hold to let him be the man of the house. She had given up her dreams the minute he put that rock on her finger. At the time, she thought it was what she wanted. She had been so young and idealistic, but now she had to wonder who she really was and if she had done the right thing.

She took a deep breath, squared her shoulders, and looked up in an attempt to stop her tears. An old trick of her grandmother's, it had saved her many times from situations just like this through the years. She flipped down the visor and opened the mirror, running her fingertips under her eyes and grabbing her lipstick out of her purse, applying it expertly and smacking her lips together. Closing the visor, she turned to James and smiled just as he pulled into a parking spot in the multi-story car park. He merely looked her over as he turned off the car and opened his door. Popping the trunk, he pulled out their suitcases, then hit lock on his key fob and just started walking toward the terminal without a word. Kat had to start out at a bit of a run to catch up as they crossed the drop off lanes and made their way inside the busy building.

At the ticket counter, they waited in line until their turn came, then James grabbed his bag and marched up to the counter, once again leaving Kat behind. She picked up her bag and followed him just in time to hear the agent ask him about his traveling companion.

"Here I am!" Kat told her, with a smile plastered on her face. "My husband's just a little excited to get out of town for the weekend."

Or maybe he just would rather get away from me, she pouted to herself, indulging in a moment of self-pity.

The agent took their luggage, gave them their boarding passes, and told them to have a good trip before they headed over to the TSA security check and observed the insanely long line.

"Great," James complained. bitterly "This is going to take all day."

"It seems to be moving, dear," Kat replied tersely.

Putting his carry-on onto the floor, he began taking off his shoes to go through the line, and then turned to her expectantly to do the same.

"Oh, yeah! I always forget about this part," Kat exclaimed.

"Well, hurry up, so we don't hold everybody else up. That's why this thing always takes so damn long!"

"Okay! Sorry! Here! Can you please hold my purse for a second?"

James took the bag from her with a dramatic sigh and made a big production of holding it, ensuring everyone around them knew that it was her purse, and he was such a gentleman for taking it for her. Appearances were not only important for women to maintain in the South.

They walked toward their gate and saw Ashley and Tom. Kat slunk behind James and grabbed his hand, trying to steer him to the other side of the room, but he looked down at her and shook his head. Just then, a voice rang out across the hall.

"Yoo-hoo! Well, hello, y'all! We were wonderin' when y'all were goin' to make it here. We made sure to save some seats.”

“Good morning, Ashley. Aren’t you sweet to think of us?” James drawled, beaming his most charming smile in her direction.

“Come on, Kat. Why don’t you sit here right next to Ashley while Tom and I take a little walk? I need to catch him up on the finer points of the presentation for Saturday.”

“Sure thing, honey,” Kat said as she flashed him a pained smile and sat down beside Ashley.

“I’m just so excited y’all are comin’ on our flight with us. Las Vegas! What an incredible place! I haven’t been there in a few years. You?”

“No, Ashley. We haven’t either. Not since the kids were small. I think Drew was about three. It was nice.”

“Well, you know what they say about Vegas: what happens there, stays there,” giggled Ashley.

Oh, my Lord, thought Kat. *This woman actually giggled. This is going to be a long weekend.*

“So, what are we goin’ to do first, Kat? Want to go shoppin’, or the pool, or the spa and salon? Oh, yeah. The salon! You could use a little sprucin’ up. It’ll be fun!”

“Actually, I just went to my stylist on Saturday. I’m good.”

“Really? Hmm... I’ll have to give you the number for my gal when we get home. I can’t tell that you have done anythin’ different in years.”

“I just got some highlights put in a few weeks ago,” Kat defended herself.

Great. Why did I just say that? I don’t have to explain myself to this woman.

“Well, okay. Maybe we could just go for a mani-pedi, then. Your nails need some help, sugar.”

Kat only gaped at Ashley in shock, unsure of how to even dignify her comment with a response. Ashley got the hint and sat back, looking at her phone.

Pulling out her own phone, Kat discretely typed to Jen: *Help! I’m stuck next to Southern Girl Barbie, and I can’t escape!*

One word came back: *Ashley?*

Kat: *Yes, ma'am. However did you guess? In the span of forty-five seconds my nails and hair have been disparaged and I'm also not any fun because I don't want to go shopping or to the spa. Save me! Please, please, please come on Saturday!*

Jen: *Look, doll, I'll try. Meanwhile, buck up. Reach deep into that Southern heritage. "Tomorrow is another day" and all that crap.*

It was time to board the plane by the time the men came sauntering back to their wives. Gathering up their bags, they made it to business class and sat down, Kat and James two rows behind and across the aisle from Tom and Ashley.

Ashley turned around and said, "Aww! That's too bad that y'all are stuck all the way over there! I was lookin' forward to some more girl time." She actually stuck out her bottom lip.

Kat simply smiled and shrugged as if to say, "What are you going to do?"

She settled back in her seat and looked out the window at the tarmac. She went to reach for James' hand like she always did on flights. Not the world's bravest flier, she counted on him to keep her calm, especially during take-offs and landings. He took her hand and gave her a small smile, until his phone sounded off that he'd received a text. Trying to be helpful, since she was smaller than he was, Kat reached down into his bag and pulled it out for him, entering his passcode as she did. It didn't work. Trying it again, his phone still didn't unlock while he watched her. She handed it over to him with a shrug and looked out the window again. He furiously typed for a few minutes, then turned off his phone and put it in his bag.

"Everything all right?" Kat asked him.

"Yeah, sure. Just confirming the info for my meeting later today."

She nodded, then asked, "Hey, why didn't your passcode work?"

"Huh? Oh! I got a new phone from work the other day. My old one had a glitch or something."

"Oh," said Kat. "It looks just like your old one. You'll have to give me the new code."

"Yeah. Okay. Fine. Remind me when we get there," James told her as the plane pushed back from the gate. As it began to taxi, he pulled out his laptop.

Their plane started revving its engines in preparation for take-off and Kat instinctually reached for James' hand again. She looked up into his eyes and he gave her another small, reassuring smile. Looking out the window, she watched the scenery go by faster and faster before they were airborne.

James immediately dropped her hand and wiped his on his pants. He then opened his laptop and began to work on some boring looking Power Point presentation.

Realizing that this was not going to be a carefree flight, Kat turned on her iPad and pushed in her ear buds. She opened Netflix and pressed play for the fifth episode of *Western Skies*. As they cruised at 30,000 feet, she caught up with the lives of Sheriff Joe McIntyre and seamstress Sarah Johnson.

About halfway through the flight, James stood up and went to the restroom and Ashley seized her opportunity, jumping into his empty seat. Kat sat completely still for a second, hoping that Ashley would get the hint that she was in the middle of a show and would leave. Unfortunately, that did not happen, and Kat sighed as she paused her program and pulled out her ear buds.

"Hey, sugar. Whatcha watchin'?"

"Oh, this show called *Western Skies*. Ever heard of it?"

"Sure! I watch it all the time. I can't wait until the next season. Sheriff Joe is just as sweet as a peach! But ssshhhh! Don't tell Tom. I don't want him thinkin' that he has any competition," Ashley replied with a wink. "Did you just discover it? Where have you been, honey? Livin' under a rock?"

"Yeah. I just stumbled upon it by accident about a week ago when my friend Jen called. It's a pretty decent show. A little corny at times, but sweet. It reminds me of simpler times."

"I know. And that Ian Gregory and Lydia Swan are just made for each other, aren't they? They make the sweetest couple," Ashley threw out.

"Really? Are they a couple? I hadn't heard that they had confirmed or denied that rumor," said Kat defensively.

Wait, this is crazy! Why am I defending that they are not a couple and what do I care if they are in a relationship or not?

"Well, no... Of course, they'll never confirm or deny it! They like to keep things interestin'. Good for their publicity to keep everyone guessin', I suppose."

"I need to ask my friend, Jen. She's a caterer in the business and knows just about everyone in Hollywood worth knowing. Maybe she can give me the lowdown. If there's a story to be told, Jen has been told it!"

"Well, let me know," Ashley sang as she saw James making his way back up the aisle to them. "Enjoy your show!"

James sat down and fastened his seatbelt. "What was all that about?"

"Oh, Ashley and I were just bonding over some show. Apparently, we do have one thing in common after all. Maybe she isn't all bad."

"Hmm… that's nice. Back to the grind."

James slipped in his ear buds and pulled up pages and pages of complicated Excel spreadsheets.

Kat eventually closed her eyes and fell asleep.

She awoke abruptly as the plane touched down at the McCarran International Airport in Las Vegas when her iPad shot off her lap as the brakes came on. She bent down instinctually to grab it up off the floor and on her way up, she looked up at James with a shocked expression on her face and asked him why he hadn't woken her when he knew they were landing. He gawked back at her for a second before answering her with a look of disgust.

"Sorry! I guess I was just so busy working on stuff, we were already descending when I looked up. I didn't want to wake you up when you were sleeping."

"Okay, but it would have been nice to at least maybe grab my iPad, don't you think?" she snapped back at him.

But it was no good. James was already taking off his seatbelt and getting ready to stand as the plane pulled up to the gate. As soon as the door opened, he grabbed their bags from the overhead compartment and started toward the door. Kat, on the other hand, still had to gather her purse and put her shoes back on. Meanwhile, James was looking back at her with an exasperated expression.

"Come on!" he chastised. "Hurry up! I'm blocking the aisle waiting for you!"

Kat glanced up at him from putting her iPad in her bag and told him he could just move back into the row of seats beside him and let people pass, but instead, he took his bags and headed off toward the open door, saying he would wait for her inside.

She picked up her bag and stayed stooped over under the overhead bins, waiting for her chance to exit the plane. Finally, a sympathetic guy took pity on her, letting her step in front of him as they were all filing out. Once in the lobby, she saw James standing with Ashley and Tom, and as she walked up, she heard him say, "…can always be counted on to be at the tail end, bringing up the rear in any situation."

Kat glared at him for a second before closing the gap between them and taking his arm.

"Well, the tail has to make sure that the ass hasn't left anything behind!" She smiled sweetly up at him as they all stared at her.

Tom cleared his throat. "Ahem! Well, we'd better go find a shuttle or something to take us to the hotel."

They had all started to move toward the baggage claim signs when James grabbed her arm and pulled her back.

"What the hell was that?" he hissed at her.

"What do you mean?"

"You know exactly what I mean. Why did you call me an ass in front of my colleague and his wife?"

Not wanting to fight, she sighed. "I don't know. I don't know what came over me. I'm sorry."

James considered her for a second and said, "That was really humiliating. How will it look if word gets around that my wife disrespects me in public?"

His comment made her bristle in response. "Is that all you care about? How you look to your colleagues? How about your wife? You can't seem to get away quick enough from me lately and I'm just tired of it, I guess."

"How many times do I have to tell you that I'm completely and utterly stressed about this conference before you get it through your thick head that it has nothing to do with you, alright?" he retorted.

Kat thought long and hard before she responded. She had so much more she could have said, but was it worth it in the middle of the airport?

"Fine! You're right. I'm sorry. It was uncalled for, and I shouldn't have started out our trip like this. I apologize." Kat's shoulders hung down and she looked defeated.

"Good!" James replied. "Please don't ever do that to me again."

Gathering up their luggage, they headed out to the shuttle with Tom and Ashley. They said nothing to each other as they looked out the window while the shuttle lumbered toward the Strip. When it pulled to a stop in the driveway of the casino where they were staying, James grabbed her bag, along with his and stalked off without a word, making a beeline for the reception desk.

While he was checking in, Ashley came up to Kat. "Oh my, sugar. What was that all about?" she asked her.

Kat glanced over at her and mumbled, "I don't know. Just tired from the trip, I guess. Maybe just tired in general. James has been so busy preparing for this conference that I've hardly even seen him in weeks. Before that, he was doing late nights and monthly business trips for almost the whole year since the merger."

"Well, honey, you can't just say things like that to your husband, especially in public. It just doesn't look right! My word, I bet your mama would've been fit to be tied if she'd seen that! I know she brought you up better than that."

"I know. I was just frustrated and took it out on James in front of you and Tom. I'm sorry you had to see it."

Just then, Tom and James walked up with their keys and joined Kat and Ashley, heading toward their room.

When Kat and James walked up to their door, Tom and Ashley kept walking.

"See y'all tonight," Ashley sang as James put the key card into the lock and the door flew open.

Chapter Five

"Wow! Nice room!" Kat said.

James walked over to the window and looked past the Strip to the mountains in the distance. "It is. Nice view, too. It's funny to be able to see so much at one time. At home, you can't see the forest for the trees."

Kat took his comment as an unmentioned truce and moved over to him in front of the window and wrapped her arms around his waist. They stayed that way for a few minutes, their eyes scanning across the valley. The sun shone brightly, and a slight breeze ruffled the fronds of the palms on the Strip below.

"Want to go out and look around?" Kat asked James.

"No, thanks. I have to unpack my suit and get ready for the meeting this afternoon before I step into the shower."

James gathered his toiletries and shut the bathroom door. As she heard the water flow, she sat down on the side of the bed and began to think. Why *had* she said that to James? What was she hoping to gain? Where had that even come from? She reached back into her deepest subconscious and searched for answers. She had sounded so disgruntled, hurtful; completely unlike herself and contrary to how she was raised. Ashley was right: her mama would have had a coronary if she had heard what Kat had said.

The opening of the bathroom door dragged her out of her reverie. James stepped into the room to let Kat know that he was actually going to have to go to the meeting right away, since the participants had all made it into town.

"Really? Already? It isn't even three o'clock yet. When will you be back?"

"I don't know. It may very well take a long while. Just head on down to the reception at seven and I'll find you, okay?"

"I guess," Kat sighed. "Have a good meeting. Hope it's productive. Love you."

She made a kissing sound into the air, and James responded

with a small, tight smile on his way out the door.

Kat picked up the towel James had discarded on the bed in his haste to get to his meeting. She put it up to her face and noted the familiar smell that all hotel towels seem to share: a slight hint of bleach mixed with the smell of fresh linen. She had always wondered how she could replicate this smell at home. It reminded her of family trips, past conferences, and her honeymoon. It was the smell of vacation and being able to relax and let go.

Deciding she wasn't going to just stay in the room, she changed out of the skirt and blouse she had worn for traveling and pulled on some yoga pants and a T-shirt. She threw her hair up into a ponytail as she took stock of herself in the mirror. *I look like a Northerner,* she laughed at herself.

Kat shut the door to the room behind her and headed toward the elevators, thinking she would go walk on the Strip. She strolled onto the casino floor, where the sights, sounds, and smells immediately overwhelmed her senses in the seemingly labyrinth of neon. Quickly becoming disoriented and over-stimulated, she was clueless about where to even begin to look for an exit. Wandering aimlessly through the rows of slots until she found herself at the poker tables, she watched for a while as men threw chips down and laughed with each other, drinks by their side.

Kat kept moving until she stumbled upon the gift shop. As she meandered through the shelves of cheesy souvenirs, she grabbed a few postcards for their parents and kids and grabbed each of the kids a key chain that was shaped like a slot machine with Las Vegas scrolled across it. She thought they would get a kick out of receiving the exact same thing their parents had brought them fourteen years before. After making her purchase, she found the elevators by accident and headed back to the room. It was just barely four-thirty, and she couldn't think of anything to do for the next two and a half hours until she could head downstairs.

Once cloistered back in the safety and quiet of the room, her phone began to vibrate. She picked it up and saw it was Jen calling her.

"Hey, doll. I hate to do this, but it looks like I won't be able to make it on Saturday after all. I'm so sorry. Madame Diva decided she didn't like the lighting in one of the scenes, so they have to reshoot it."

"That's too bad," Kat answered sadly.

"How's Sin City?'

"Boring!"

"What?! Boring? Are you sure you're in the right place? Las Vegas, *Nevada*?"

Kat thought carefully before responding, "Yeah. James is already at his meeting. I wandered around for a while on the casino floor, but it's just smoky and dark down there. I didn't come here for Vegas. I came here to try and reconnect with him."

"That's going to be hard while he's at meetings."

"Yeah, that's the problem. Just biding my time now until I go down to the 'meet and greet' in a few; the reception where I'll be simply 'James' wife.' Do I even have a first name in the real world anymore?"

Kat said good-bye, set her phone down, and turned on the T.V., but nothing was enticing. She flipped aimlessly through the channels until an old movie caught her attention, settled back into the pillows on the bed, and closed her eyes, promptly falling asleep given her early morning in order to get to the plane.

She awoke with a start two hours later. Sitting up and orienting herself to her surroundings, she glanced at the clock and saw that she only had forty-five minutes to get ready and get down to the reception. Groaning as she rolled over, she punched a pillow in her dissatisfaction with how this trip was going so far. But regardless, she felt she owed it to James to look her best that night and dragged herself off the bed and into the bathroom.

After applying her makeup and fixing her hair, she then went to her suitcase, finding the new lacey black underwear and bra she had bought just for this trip. Dropping her dress over her head, she then shook out her hair, thinking she would leave it down for the night after she glanced in the mirror to make sure it hadn't gotten out of control when she had put her clothes on. She then strapped on her high-heel sandals and ran some lipstick across her lips. A few dabs of perfume on her neck and wrists, and she was ready to go.

Winding her way to the second-floor conference rooms, her nametag was waiting on the table just outside the door with many others: Katherine Anderson. Resigned, she picked it up, pulled off its backing, and slapped it on her chest just above her left breast.

Katherine Anderson she mused. *I haven't been called Katherine in I don't even recall how long. Probably at our wedding.* Taking a deep breath, she walked into the huge room and looked around.

A dance floor with a DJ had been set up in the far corner of the cavernous space. There were two large buffet tables set up with finger food and two bars, as well. Tables covered with white cloths and candles on top were in the center of the room, seating six people apiece, many of the seats already occupied. Feeling vulnerable, Kat stood by herself and felt clueless about what to do. She didn't see anyone she knew, so she wandered around aimlessly for a while before finding the bar.

"A red wine, please," Kat told the bartender as she thought, *Maybe some alcohol could make this bearable.* As he handed the glass to her, he smiled shyly at her. The man, several years younger than she, made her heart flutter for a second until she realized he was just trying to make her feel good for a better tip. She grabbed a folded-up fiver and placed it in the glass at the side of the bar with a, "Thanks."

As she stood off a little to the right of the bar, a woman started walking over to her. About ten years older than Kat, she had a kindly smile. She came up and grabbed Kat's free hand and shook it while saying, "Hi, there. I'm Susan Jones. In which location do you work?"

Kat looked into her eyes for a second before replying, "Oh, I don't work. I'm James' wife."

She saw the look of confusion pass over the woman's face before she rearranged it back into a smile.

"Oh! That's so great! Nice to meet you." She walked off before Kat even had a chance to respond.

She found herself at an empty table toward the outside of the grouping nearer to the back. She put down her wine glass and pulled out a seat.

Great, she contemplated, *what am I supposed to do now? I can't carry my clutch, my wine, and get myself a plate of food.* She quickly decided the best thing to do would be to put her wine glass down, shove her purse under her arm and walk to the buffet tables, hoping that the busboy wouldn't see the half empty glass on a barren table and just discard it.

She picked up a few things and was snaking her way back to the table when a boy around Olivia's age reached for her glass. "Wait!" she called. "I'm still drinking that."

Kat quickened her step to close the distance between herself and her table, breathlessly apologizing, explaining that she was just getting some food.

The kid looked her up and down and said, "Are you sitting here all alone?"

"For now, yes. My husband will be joining me shortly."

"Whoa. *Awkward*!" he said as he shifted the basin full of used dishes on his hip and moved on.

Kat sat down and looked around when out of the corner of her eye, she caught a glimpse of blonde hair. Ashley saw her at the same time and threw her arm up in the air, waving across the room at Kat. She smiled weakly back at her as Ashley turned to Tom and leaned in to tell him something. He looked up at Kat and gave a slight nod of his head, as his hands were full of his plate and drink. They started coming toward her as Kat wished the floor would just open up and swallow her whole.

"Lord, give me strength!" she prayed under her breath.

The couple meandered over to Kat's table, stopping every few feet to say hello and chat with the people they met along the way. When they finally arrived, Tom pulled out Ashley's chair and she sat herself down while Tom, still standing, asked what they would like to drink.

"Oh, I want me one of those frou-frou drinks. You know? The kind with an umbrella and some fruit on the side?" Ashley purred.

"Kat?" Tom turned to her. "Nothing, Tom, thanks. I'm good."

"Are you sure? It's no trouble. James asked me to make sure you had all you needed until he's able to get down here."

"Well, okay, then. I guess I'll have another glass of merlot."

Tom took off in the direction of the bar, while Ashley and Kat sat together, looking out over the crowd of people, and not saying a word. After a few minutes, Ashley swung around in her seat and said, "So, where's that man of yours, anyway?"

"He had a meeting this afternoon. He left around three."

"This afternoon? Honey, it's almost seven-forty- five in the evenin'. Where could he be?"

"I don't know. It was some meeting about the big presentation tomorrow."

Just then, Tom arrived back with the drinks. As he sat down, Ashley turned to him and asked, "What's the deal with this big meetin', sugar? How come you didn't have to go? Seems like it's a pretty big deal if it has been goin' on for over four hours."

"I don't know anything about it," Tom answered truthfully. "I wasn't invited so it must not have anything to do with me and my role in the project."

"Okay, darlin'. Just checkin'," Ashley trilled.

At that moment, James walked into the room. He stood backlit in the doorway and looked around a little bit.

He looks so handsome, Kat thought as she admired him. He had put on a nice suit and tie and looked more relaxed than she had seen him look in months. Just as she was wondering if she should go to him so that he could find them, she heard from right beside her, "Yoo-hoo! Oh, James? Here we are, honey!"

Half the room turned and looked at them sitting at their table. Kat could feel her cheeks reddening as she hung her head in complete mortification. She quietly slipped from her chair and slinked over to where James was standing and touched his arm. He followed her back to their seats and looked around the room.

"Hi!" said Kat. "You look nice! Did you just take a shower?"

"Yeah. We were finished about forty-five minutes ago, so I decided to go upstairs and wash some more red clay from home off myself."

He gave her a wink and put his arm across her shoulders. Kat smiled up at him and leaned back into the crook of his neck. He sat with her like that for a second before he straightened up in his chair and put his arm back down at his side.

The evening wore on and people would come and go from their table, conversing with both Tom and James. The names and faces became a blur, and it was very obvious that everyone was more interested in talking shop with the guys than actually socializing. After another hour or so, Tom looked up and said, "The place is beginning to thin out but it's not even nine-thirty yet. Y'all want to go do something else?"

Ashley giggled at him and clapped her hands together, "Sure thing, sugar! There's that famous nightclub here. Y'all know the one where all the stars make an appearance when they are here? They bring in the guest DJs and everythin', too."

Kat looked up at James and caught his expression. He met her eyes and rolled his upwards toward the ceiling.

But Tom jumped in with, "Hey! That sounds like fun. What do y'all say?"

James was then stuck. He didn't want to say anything that could be construed as negative to his colleague and so he responded that yes, it could be fun. He put his fingertips in the small of Kat's back, making her shiver, while guiding her toward the door on their way out.

Several hours and many drinks later, Kat and James were on the dance floor. They had long since lost track of Tom and Ashley among the throngs of people smashed together in the hot and steamy club. As Kat danced around James, he laughed at her and swept her up into his arms. She threw her head back and he began kissing her neck. She stopped suddenly and grabbed his face between her hands and gave him a long, passionate kiss on the lips. She moved her body up against him and rubbed her calf up and down his leg. He groaned, then leaned over and whispered seductively in her ear, "Come on. Let's get out of here," as he grabbed her hand and pulled her back toward the entrance.

She kicked off her heels and swung them on her fingers as they ran through the casino floor, laughing like kids. James pushed the elevator button and stood beside Kat, holding her hand. Another couple got on the elevator with them, and they all stood staring straight ahead.

Suddenly, though, Kat felt James' fingers tickling her butt. She turned to look at him, but he kept staring at the doors and didn't even react. Only the small hint of a smile that was playing on the corners of his mouth indicated he had any idea of what going on. The elevator stopped and the other couple walked off. When the doors shut, James was instantly kissing Kat, shoving her up against the back wall. He kissed her with a passion she had never seen from him before. She was more than willing to meet him halfway and wrapped her leg around his as their kiss deepened. The doors flew open on their floor, startling them both. James gave her another quick peck on the lips and grabbed her hands.

"Let's go!" he said, and they took off running down the hall.

When they reached their room and James began fumbling in his pocket for the key card. Kat reached up around his back, hooking her arms through his and resting her hands on his shoulders. She covered his neck and ears with small kisses, and he trembled. He flipped around and Kat pressed him up against the door, kissing him as her fingers tried desperately to loosen his tie and work on the buttons of his shirt. James reached behind him without breaking their kiss and pushed the key card into the lock. The door flew open, and they tumbled inside.

They looked up at each other and started to giggle.

Kat immediately dropped her shoes and reached around

James' neck, lunging at him, her lips squarely meeting his. All of the pain and loneliness she had been feeling over the last little while spilled out of her as her kisses became more frantic and intense, and he was more than enabling her in her endeavor.

He reached up behind her back and yanked on the zipper of her dress. Once it flew open, he grabbed the bottom and ripped it over her head, only waiting the split second she needed to raise her arms above her. Kat then began working on his belt, pulling it open with such force that she pulled the whole thing out from around his waist. His hand went to her bra, and he fingered the delicate lace.

"This is nice," he whispered while he cupped his hand around her breast.

She felt exposed, standing there in the room wearing nothing but her bra, panties, and hose. Bending down to pull off her pantyhose, he suddenly grabbed her hands.

"Let me," he whispered to her.

He grabbed the waistband and pulled it down over her hips. He put his warm fingers between the material and her outer thighs, rubbing her legs all the way down while sliding them off. He then stood up with a sheepish schoolboy grin and a glint in his eye.

"My turn," she cooed as she reached once again for the buttons on his shirt. She took her time opening each of them as slowly as she could, kissing her way down as she did. James' head rolled back, and he let out a series of small moans as she got lower and lower, nearer to the button on the waist of his slacks. She pushed his shirt off his shoulders and ripped it down his arms and back. She lifted his undershirt over his head and then began kissing his lips, moving ever downward again to his stomach and just a little below. Grabbing her hands, he stared intently at her for a few seconds before dropping them down at her sides and freeing the button on his pants from its hole. He shoved them down his legs and stepped out of them, leaving him standing exposed in only his boxer briefs.

Unable to help herself, her eyes were immediately drawn to

the bulge between his legs.

"Oh, my!" she gasped.

He saw her admiring him and laughed. Grabbing her hand, he brought her over to the bed. Pulling back the covers, he gently pushed her back onto the mattress and placed the bedding over her. He then turned to the window and opened the curtains wide before walking back over to the bed, pulling off his underwear and sliding in next to her.

She asked if he wanted her to be naked.

"*No!*" he replied, his voice deep and rough with passion. He moved her panties to one side and soon they were loving each other completely under the glow of the Strip's neon lights.

***

The sun came flooding into the room the next morning, shinning directly into Kat's eyes. She woke up, squinted, and rose up on her elbows to look over at James' sleeping form before rolling over to spoon against him. He soon rolled over onto his back in response, lifting his elbow up and out as he did, opening his eyes slowly.

"Good morning," Kat whispered.

He smiled a slow, sleepy smile at her and whispered, "Good morning."

"How did you sleep?"

"Well. Really well! How about you?"

"I did, too!" she said giddily.

"What are your plans for today while I'm in my presentation?" he asked her.

"I don't know yet."

She started to sit up and the room began to spin a bit. Putting her hand up to her forehead, she immediately noticed the slight ache behind her eyes. She lay back down on the bed for a moment before asking, "How much did we have to drink last night?"

"I don't know. I think I lost count after about four for me. You had more. You and Ashley were laughing about the 'frou-

frou’ drinks for a while before we got separated from them. Why?”

“I think I might be a bit hung over,” she responded. “I have a headache.”

“I’m sorry,” James said, as he reached up and stroked her forehead with his fingers. “You okay? Can I get you anything?”

“No, thanks. I think I’ll be okay. That’s what I get for drinking without eating much. It’ll pass once I get up and get moving. But you shower first. I need to lie here for a bit longer, I think.”

James rose out of the bed and reached for his underpants. He pulled them on before walking around the corner of the mattress and starting to laugh.

“What’s so funny?” asked Kat.

“This!” he said as he pointed at the line of clothing trailing all the way across the room to the door.

Kat smiled at him and said, “Yeah, we were a little too preoccupied last night to worry about hanging things up.”

He walked over and gave her a kiss on the forehead and then continued into the bathroom, whistling a tune. Kat heard the shower turn on and the sound of him drawing the curtain back over the tub while she lay looking out the window, squinting slightly at the bright morning Las Vegas sun reflecting off the thousands of windows around them. She absently ran her fingertips over her stomach and thought about how great last night had been. Images came flooding back as she remembered how James had kissed her, held her, loved her. She smiled as she wondered why in the world they had not made connecting like that more of a priority for a long time.

James came out of the bathroom and pulled on a pair of pants and a button-down shirt. He said, “All yours!” as he pointed toward the bathroom.

Reluctantly, Kat stood up and journeyed down the hall. She turned on the water as James came in and fixed his hair.

“That was really awesome last night,” she said over the sound of the water.

"It sure was!"

"I can't wait for tonight," she peeked her head around the edge of the curtain, meeting his eyes in the mirror. "I'm hoping for a repeat performance!"

James broke their gaze and looked down at the counter. "Yeah. Me, too."

He turned around and walked over to the shower. Pulling back the curtain, he puckered his lips. Kat reached out with her own and they made contact.

"I'll see you later, okay? Have a good time this afternoon," he said before walking out the door.

Kat finished her shower and contemplated what she wanted to do for the day. A whole day without James loomed before her but she honestly didn't want to do anything other than have him back in their bed and in her arms.

Instead, she looked out at the sun and thought that a day by the heated pool might be just the thing.

She put on her swimsuit and tied her sarong around her waist before grabbing her hotel key and heading out the door. Winding her way down to the entrance of the pool, once there, she lowered herself into a lounge chair and put on her hat and sunglasses. Looking around the area, she noticed all the truly beautiful people who had come out to enjoy the unusually warm weather. Thin women with large breasts in skimpy bikinis sauntered past while guys in the pool leaned over their arms at the side, following them with their eyes, sometimes whistling or making comments. Free drinks abounded and the atmosphere was reminiscent of her one spring break in college along the Florida coast before she married James. She looked down at her own one piece and noticed the fact that no one even glanced her way. She was invisible. Suddenly, she felt old and washed up. Then, she thought back to the time that she and James had shared the night before. It had been like their honeymoon all over again twenty-three years later.

How lucky am I that I have such a wonderful husband, she said to herself as she closed her eyes and soaked up the rays of the warm Las Vegas day.

56

Chapter Six

At around two o'clock, Kat sat up and realized she was starting to get a little too pink in the strong desert sun and it was aggravating her headache. Her stomach was also rumbling, and it dawned on her that she ready hadn't had much to eat since Wednesday night before they left home. She quickly gathered up her things and headed back inside. On her way to her room, however, she passed by the spa, and on a total whim, she walked into it and booked a massage.

Several hours and many spa services later, Kat strutted back to her room, feeling beautiful and refreshed. She hadn't felt so sexy in years. She had even had a Brazilian wax for the first time in her life in preparation for what she hoped would be another amazing night between the sheets with James. Giggling, she pointed her toes while she slid on another new bra and lacey panties set. Her red dress slipped on, and she zipped it closed, admiring how it hugged her curves in all the right places. She'd had the spa do her makeup as well, so all she had to do was wait for James to return. Antsy with anticipation, she grabbed her iPad and started the next episode of *Western Skies*.

It was almost over when she heard James putting the key card into the door. She turned off her device and waited for him to walk in and see her, his tuxedo laid out beside her on the bed. He walked in the door and started talking.

"Hey, Hon. I am so glad that is over! I…"

He looked up and caught his first glimpse of Kat. "Whoa!" he said, stopping short. "You look gorgeous!"

"Thanks! I took Drew's advice and got all 'gussied up' for the dinner tonight."

"You most certainly did!" He walked over to the bed and leaned down and kissed her. He went to lay her back when she exclaimed, "No! Wait! Watch my hair!"

James righted her and sighed. "Then I guess I'd better put on my monkey suit now."

"Probably a good idea. We're expected downstairs at dinner in about twenty minutes. I'm very much looking forward to later tonight, though."

She lifted her skirt up just enough to give him a glimpse of her lacey panties. He turned to bend and put his face on the bed with a groan.

When he was finished dressing, they left for the conference room, found their table assignments, and found themselves quickly engaged with a group of James' colleagues.

Halfway through dinner, Kat excused herself and stood up to go to the restroom. When she walked into the stall and sat down, she heard the door open again and someone enter a stall a few doors down. Kat was standing, attempting to pull up her pantyhose while holding her clutch and making sure that hem of her dress hadn't gotten stuck, when the restroom door opened again, and two women walked in.

"So, is he here?"

"Yes, he is. I saw him all yesterday afternoon. It was fabulous!"

"I can't believe you were that reckless, Samantha. I thought you said he brought his wife."

"He did," Samantha replied nonchalantly.

Kat ventured a look out the gap between the stall walls and the door. She could see two beautiful women in what had to be their late twenties or early thirties standing by the mirror, applying their lipstick. They both looked sleek and stylish in their black dresses and had posh, educated accents.

This oughta be good, thought Kat.

"He did? She still doesn't have a clue?"

"Nope! What do you expect? She's just some middle-aged, stupid, uneducated Southern Belle. She doesn't even have an inkling that I've been screwing her husband for almost a year! He tells her that the team is having monthly meetings and comes up to see me. We stay either at a hotel or at my apartment. Let me tell you, the sex is beyond hot, even if he is older."

Suddenly, Kat felt like a hot knife had been shoved into her gut. She took a deep breath and panicked. *No! It can't be. It has to be a coincidence.*

"Oh my God!" the second girl exclaimed. "I think I saw her last night. She was a total bleach blonde and loud and had the *worst* Southern drawl. Made my skin crawl. Sounded like a total hillbilly. She yelled out across the room at someone, and she actually said 'Yoo-hoo.' Who does that? So, when he's going to tell her, then?"

"James says he'll tell her in the late spring, after their oldest son graduates from college and their youngest is done with high school. He says it'll make things easier once all of those family obligations are out of the way."

Oh, God! Oh, no! That's *Sam!*

Kat felt like she was going to faint. She braced herself between the two cold walls of the stall and inhaled deeply. The younger women looked up and back toward the bank of metal doors behind them at the sound of Kat's hands slapping the cold, unyielding metal. How could she have been so stupid?

Shrugging her shoulders, Samantha turned her attention back to her reflection. Leaning over slightly, she shook her breasts to push them up a little higher in her dress.

"It's so incredibly hot to know that he's here with her and she isn't even suspicious."

She grabbed her phone out of her bag and lifted up bottom hem of her dress. Spreading her legs, she bent forward slightly, and Kat heard the distinct click of a camera shutter as she saw a flash.

"What are you doing?" the second girl exclaimed. "I'm taking a picture for James. No panties. He totally gets off on these. I text them to him and it drives him insane."

"Wow! You text him those on his phone? Isn't that a little risky? Guess the old guy doesn't need Viagra with you around."

Samantha and her friend grabbed their bags and walked out of the bathroom. Kat took another deep breath and rolled her eyes up to the ceiling, using that old trick of her grandmother's once again. She straightened her shoulders and opened the stall door, went to the sink, and started to wash her hands. While the water washed away the soap, a few stalls down, the toilet flushed, and the door opened. Kat raised her head and caught Ashley's eyes in the mirror as she came up behind her. Ashley just stood frozen in place for a second, looking at her. Then, she walked over to Kat and enveloped her in a big hug. Kat clung to her for a few seconds and then Ashley held her out at arm's length.

"Oh, sugar. Bless your little heart. I'm so sorry. What are you goin' to do?"

Kat raised her glance and looked into Ashley's face. "I don't know," she whispered.

"Well, hon, I told you that you should have gotten a new dress...."

Chapter Seven

Kat opened the door with such force that it crashed and bounced against the wall. She marched back to toward their table, coming up beside James' chair, standing there for a second while he finished his sentence, and then she leaned over, telling him, "I'm going back up to the room right now and you need to come with me."

James smiled at the man he was speaking to and said, "Excuse me."

He leaned over to Kat as she stooped down and asked her, "Are you okay? What's going on? Are you sick?"

Kat just glared at him. She whispered quietly between her teeth, "I don't want to get into it here. Not unless you would like me to cause a scene."

She then stood up straight and smiled gracefully at the people around the table. Ever the lady.

James put his napkin down on the table and excused himself. He took Kat's elbow and walked her over to the door and out into the hall.

"What the hell is going on, Kat? Are you sick? Is it the kids? Did something happen to one of our parents? Come on. I'm getting worried here. You have to talk to me."

Kat didn't say a word as she continued her march toward the elevators. She punched the button and stood tapping her toe impatiently. Concerned, James put his hand on her arm, and she whirled around as hissed into his face, "Don't you touch me!"

James recoiled in shock. The elevator doors opened, and they stepped inside. For the entire ride, James kept taking sideways glances in her direction, his confusion very obvious. On their floor, the doors opened, and Kat stomped down the hall to the room. She jammed her key card into the lock and threw open the door.

"Get inside!" she growled.

"Kat? Kat! What the hell is going on?"

"Give me your phone, James!"

"My phone? What? Why do you want my phone?"

"Just do it!" she hollered.

James, always afraid to cause a scene, stared at Kat with big eyes. He saw she meant business, so he slowly pulled his phone out of his pocket and handed it to her. Kat snatched it, holding it in her hand. She then looked at him and said, "Tell me again about Sam."

"Well, I told you. Harvard educated, hard-working, lives in Manhattan. Where is this all coming from?"

"Is there anything you're leaving out, James? Anything you need to tell me?"

"You're talking nonsense!"

"How about this, James? Is Sam per chance Samantha?"

His eyes widened for a second as the color drained from his face. He took a breath and shook his head. "What? Why are you asking me this?"

"Give me the passcode to your phone."

"Ah, Kat. Come on. I don't want to do this. I'm tired. Can't we just go to bed like we did last night? That was nice. This is so not how I envisioned our evening."

"Give me the damn code! *Now!*" she roared.

"Okay, okay, Kat. It's thirty-six twenty-two."

"Why did you change it, James?"

"I told you! I had to get a new phone! It was the code that came with it! Please, Kat. What is going on?"

"Really? It came with the phone, huh? The funny thing is, James, that I may just be a 'stupid, uneducated Southern Belle,' as your lovely tramp just called me, but even I know that you choose your own personal passcode. So, I repeat. Why did you change it, James?"

"Please, Kat. I don't understand. Why are you so angry? Please! Can we talk about this?"

Kat was typing in the passcode as he was talking.

She pressed on his text icon and there it was.

She turned to James and said, "You want to talk? Do you?"

He just nodded his head uncertainly.

"Really? Are you sure, James? Okay, then. Let's talk. You can start by telling me why you have some other woman's crotch shot on your phone!"

Kat shoved the phone into his face.

James gasped and reeled back. "What? Where did that come from? Kat, I swear that wasn't there earlier!"

Kat just glared back at him. She pulled the phone back and started scrolling through the other texts from and to "Sam". She saw some very sexually explicit messages, complete with other pictures of a breast or crotch, some legs in garters and hose, and then she stumbled upon a shot of his erect penis.

"Really, James? This one just showed up and you haven't got any inkling how it got there? Do you really think I'm that big of an idiot? These texts go back way more than just a week. I can't even scroll through all of them."

Suddenly, something dawned on her. "You didn't get a new phone, did you, James? This is your old phone, and you just changed the code."

She looked again at the phone. "Seriously, James? Really? You had to send a picture of your penis? *Classy.*"

"Kat," James pleaded. "Please."

Kat turned her back and he saw her shoulders rise. She let out a heartbreaking sob as her whole body shook.

James, feeling guilty, decided he needed to try another tactic.

"How do you even know that is my penis?"

Kat pivoted back so she was facing him. "Are you kidding me? I have seen your penis nearly every day for the last almost twenty-three years. I know what it looks like!" She spun back around.

"They look different?" James was obviously getting flustered. He walked over to her and tried to put his hand on her shoulder.

"Get your hands off of me! And, no, not necessarily. However, the mole on the left side of your stomach, right above your pubic bone, is pretty distinctive."

James backed away from her like she was about to combust and watched helplessly as she sobbed. Sounding resigned, he finally conceded. "Okay, Kat. Let's talk about this. I owe you the truth, at least."

Kat turned back around to face him and sat down on the bed. He took a deep breath.

"Her name is Samantha. I call her Sam for short. We met when the merger first took place. She's twenty- eight years old. I told you that she was Harvard educated and lives in Manhattan. That part was all true."

Kat sighed. "Twenty-eight? James, she's just five years older than Derrick! Seven years older than Olivia. They could be friends!"

"How did you find out?"

"I overheard her. She and another girl came in while I was using the restroom. I was even there when she took that latest picture. Isn't that great? I had a front row seat, literally, as my marriage blew apart before my eyes."

"Oh my God, Kat, I'm so sorry you had to find out this way."

"Please, James. Save it. You aren't sorry I found out this way. You're just sorry I found at all. If you weren't worried about me finding out, you wouldn't have been doing her behind my back for almost a year."

James just hung his head, his shoulders drooping down. "You're right. What can I say?"

"Tell me, James, do you love her?"

He looked down at the floor and took a few seconds before answering. "I don't know," he whispered.

"You don't know?"

"No, I don't. I know I love you, Kat. I love the life we have built together. But this girl… this girl… she does something to me."

"What do you mean, James? Like sexually, or what?"

"Yeah, Kat. She does stuff. Stuff I never even dreamed

about. Stuff I can't talk about, let alone ask you to do. Dirty stuff. Fantasy stuff. I'm sorry."

"So, she performs sex acts with you that are too sordid to do with your wife?"

"Yeah. Pretty much. Kat… Kat, she makes me feel alive, like I'm seventeen again."

"Why are you telling me all of this?"

"Because Kat! You're my best friend. For twenty-four years, I've told you everything. It has been killing me keeping this from you, but it's too good to give up."

Suddenly Kat had a thought. It was so vile, so repulsive, her stomach heaved, and she almost threw up. "So, yesterday… your 'meeting'. You were screwing her, weren't you?"

"Yes."

"And then you came up here a few hours later and made love to me like nothing was wrong?"

"Yes." He hung his head.

"Well, I guess I should be happy at least that you had the common decency to shower in between your interludes. How was it, James? Did you take notes to compare? I bet it has never happened that you had both of us back-to-back before, huh? Hell, you could have even saved time and had a threesome!"

He wrenched up his head in surprise to look at her, having the nerve to check her expression to see if that would have ever actually been a possibility. Kat glowered at him.

"It's different with you. You're a lady. My wife. You are refined; sweet. I can't ask you to do these things. I'm ashamed of myself, but it feels too good."

"So, you have your wife for your sweet sex and your twenty-eight-year-old whore for your tricks?"

James' head jerked up again. "Don't call her that."

"Okay. What else should I call her? Your floozy? Your tramp? Your sex toy? Please, enlighten me on the proper terminology for a woman who screws someone else's husband, who gets off on knowing that I have no clue what is going on. But she doesn't just have sex with you. Oh, no. She has to be a goddamned porn star.

"You know, I overheard her telling her friend that you were with her at her apartment and sometimes a hotel. How come I never saw these charges on the bill? She said you were lying to me about how the monthly meetings were for work, so obviously the company didn't pay for the travel."

"Because I got myself a card," James said.

"You *what*? You opened a secret credit card? How did you pay for it?"

"Come on, Kat. You know I pay all of the bills. It wasn't hard."

"Oh, I know. But, contrary to popular belief, I'm not an idiot. I do have access to our online banking, and I've never noticed another credit card payment."

"I know," he said quietly.

"How do you know?"

He mumbled something into the back of his hand. "I'm sorry, James. I didn't quite catch that. Could you please repeat it?"

James cleared his throat and said, "Because I opened another bank account in only my name. I got a substantial raise a few months after the merger and split the direct deposit, so the old amount still went into our joint account every paycheck and the difference went to my new account."

Kat just stared at him. She couldn't think of anything else to say. She was exhausted. They had been at this for what seemed liked hours and she couldn't take anymore.

"Get out," she ordered calmly.

"What? Kat? Come on! Where am I going to go?"

"I don't care. Just get out of my room. Go find your whore."

"I can't," James whined. "She went clubbing with some friends."

"*Get out*!" she screamed at him. "I am giving you exactly sixty seconds to gather your stuff and get out of this room. After that, I cannot be held responsible for what I do to you."

"Okay… okay… I'll go. Kat, I love you. I didn't want this

to happen this way. I am so sorry."

"No, you wanted to have your cake and eat it, too. Now, seriously, you have thirty-five seconds left."

James grabbed all of his clothing and shoved it into his suitcase. Running into the bathroom, he grabbed his razor and toiletries. He seized his jacket and headed toward the door. When he was almost about to turn the handle, Kat told him to stop.

He turned around with a smile on his face. "Does this mean we can work through this? Please, Kat."

"No. I just need to ask. Did you at least use protection with her?"

He held her gaze for a long time before answering, "No. Not always. She's on the pill. I'm sorry!"

Kat bent over and took off her shoe. She looked right at him and held up her arm, readying to throw her stiletto at him.

"Get *out*, you son of a bitch!"

James turned quickly and exited to the hall, the door slamming shut just as her shoe made contact. Kat stood alone in the center of their room, hair sliding out of its up- do, makeup running down her face. She didn't know what to do. She couldn't even think straight. So, she did the first and only thing she could think of. She grabbed her phone and started dialing.

Chapter Eight

"Hello?" came the sleepy voice on the other end of the line.

"Jen?" was all Kat could manage before the sobs began.

"Kat? Kat? Is that you? What the hell? What's going on? It's twelve a.m. Are you crying? Why are you crying?"

Kat couldn't do anything but sob into the phone for almost ten minutes. Jen didn't know what to do. All she could think of was to continually murmur "It's okay, Kat. I'm here. No matter what it is, we will get you through it."

Finally, Kat was able to gulp and take in a big breath before she was able to speak. "It's James."

"Oh my God. What's happened? Is he hurt? Is he sick? Kat, what happened?"

"He… He… has… been… screwing… his… twenty… eight… year… old… colleague… for… close… for close… to a year!" Kat managed to choke out.

"Oh my God. What did you say? James has been screwing his twenty-eight-year-old colleague?"

"Yes." She hiccoughed.

"Oh, Kat. I am so sorry. I don't even know what to say. Did he tell you why?"

"Oh, yes. Because I'm a lady and he said he has fantasies he can't ask me to play out with him. This girl sounds like a porn star. Hell, that's probably how she put herself through Harvard!" she added with a sniffle.

"How did you find out?"

"I overheard her talking to her friend in the restroom tonight. I was in a stall and heard the whole thing. Jen, she even took a crotch selfie and sent it to him!"

"Wow. Classy."

"I know. And that is not even the worst part…"

"Oh, God. It gets worse?"

"Yes, Jen, so much worse. Ashley was in another stall and heard the whole thing, too." Kat wailed.

The phone went silent for a second. "Oh, no, Kat. I can't believe it. What did she say?"

"She told me she was sorry and then said that she told me I needed to get a new dress."

All of a sudden, Kat started laughing hysterically.

Jen sat on the other end of the line and just listened.

Finally, she broke in, saying, "Kat! Kat! You've got to calm down."

"What am I going to do, Jen? I'm three thousand miles away from home. I have no job, no money of my own. I can't get on the plane on Monday with everyone. Jen, please come here and get me! Please!"

"Oh, honey, I so would, but I have to be up in four hours to finish that job. But we *will* figure something out. I've got to make some calls. Just hang out and I'll get back to you soon. Okay, Kat? Please? Don't do anything stupid. We will get you squared away."

"Okay," Kat whispered. "I'll talk to you soon."

Kat sat on the bed with her head in her hands. How dumb was she? What had she been thinking? Dropping out of college at twenty years old to get married? Sam was right. She was just a stupid, uneducated Southern Belle.

After about thirty minutes, her phone rang. "Okay. Here's the deal. I talked to my sister. She managed to get you a Buddy Pass. Go to the airport first thing in the morning. Go to her carrier's counter and tell them that you have a Buddy Pass waiting for you and you need to get to Hartsfield-Jackson. You'll have to fly standby but being early on a Saturday morning in Vegas will probably work to your advantage. When you get a spot on a plane, call your father. Tell him to meet you at the airport and then go back with him to their house. I don't want you to go home by yourself. Okay? Kat, are you there? Are you listening?"

"Yes, I'm here. Okay."

"Give me Holly's number. I'll text her and ask her to keep Drew a few more days."

"No, Jen. Thanks. I'll call her when I get in. Thank you. And thank Kristina, too. I know she probably doesn't want to use one of her Buddy Passes on me."

"No, Kat. She loves you, too. She said to tell you she's so sorry this happened to you."

"Okay. Thanks."

"Kat?"

"Yeah?"

"Try to get some sleep. I know it'll be hard, but it will be a long day tomorrow. Try to fall asleep for at least a little while until you can leave for the airport. Kristina says the counter will be open by five. Okay?"

"Okay."

"Love you! I'll talk to you soon. You *are* going to be all right. I promise."

Kat hung up the phone. It was now close to one a.m. What was she going to do to pass the time? Jen had told her to sleep, but she knew that wasn't going to be possible. So, she packed up her things and, too numb to think, she sat on the bed looking out the window toward the Strip until the clock on the bedside table said it was 4:30. She got up and grabbed her things, the slamming hotel door behind her, representing the end of life as she had known it for the last twenty-three years.

Chapter Nine

True to Jen's word, Kristina had a Buddy Pass waiting for Kat at the counter. She was also right about getting onto a plane at six a.m. going east not being a problem on a Saturday morning in Vegas. As soon as she knew her spot was confirmed, Kat took a deep breath and called her father's cell.

"Daddy?"

"Yes? Kat? Is that you? Honey, aren't you supposed to be in Vegas? What time is it there?"

"Yes, Daddy, it's me. It's five-thirty in the morning here. I'm at the airport. I need you to please meet my flight at Hartsfield-Jackson. My flight number is thirty-four eighty-six, and I'm landing at one this afternoon."

"Why sure, sugar. You bet I'll be there! Don't you worry. I love you now, you hear? You fly safe and I'll see you soon. I'm goin' to go tell your mama what's happenin'. You take care!"

That right there, Kat thought to herself. That was the perfect example of why she loved her father so much. He trusted her implicitly. Whenever she needed something, he was always there. He never asked any questions, just helped her in any way he could.

Kat boarded the plane and sat back, waiting for take-off. Out of the silence, her phone dinged and lit up with a text.

James: *Kat. Please. Where are you? We can work through this. Please, Kat! I went back to the room, and you were gone. Where are you? I'm worried.*

Kat turned off her phone and then threw it into her purse in disgust. How dare he write to her and act like he cared about her? If he loved her, why was he sharing his most intimate self with someone besides her?

She pondered how at no other time does a person become truly connected with another human being without fear or inhibitions than when making love. Literally physically connected, joined together, not just on an emotional level.

How could this have happened? How could she have been so trusting? So ignorant? When she thought about the whole picture, the signs were there: his sudden attachment to his cell, his multiple business trips on which no one else she knew seemingly needed to go, his indifferent treatment of her, forgetting her birthday and being so short tempered, his definite drop in desire for her. He had blamed it all on stress and she was naïve enough to believe it.

The plane touched down a little after one o'clock. Kat grabbed her bags as she called her dad and told him to drive up from the cellphone lot to get her. Within a few minutes of her arriving on the sidewalk, his car slid up beside her. She opened the back door, threw her bags into the car, and moved up the front seat before opening the door, slipping in, and putting on her seatbelt. Her dad pulled away from the curb and drove out toward the freeway.

"Hey, baby doll. Wanna talk about it?"

"Not right now, Daddy. But thank you for coming to get me."

"Anytime, sugar. You know I'd move heaven and earth for you."

Kat gave her father a grateful smile and leaned back in the seat. After about twenty minutes, she spoke up.

"Daddy? James has been stepping out on me. I found out last night. His mistress is someone he works with, and she was there at the conference. I overheard her talking to her friend in the restroom about it."

"Oh, sweet Jesus. baby girl, I'm so sorry that happened to you. No one deserves somethin' like that."

"Thanks, Daddy. What am I going to do?'

"Well, for now, you'll come home with us. You can stay as long as you need to, okay?"

"Okay. Thank you."

"It's not a problem at all, honey. Just relax and let us take care of you until you get your feet back under you."

They drove the rest of the way in silence. Her father always knew the right things to say and how to say them. He never tried to solve her problems or tell her that she was wrong. He just listened to her and gave her a sounding board to work through her thoughts and emotions.

When they got into the house, Kat's mom came running up to her before embracing her.

"Well, look what the cat dragged in! Hello, sugar! What a surprise to hear you were comin' home. I thought you were in Vegas until Monday afternoon."

"No, Mama. Change of plans," Kat said as she leaned over and kissed her mother's cheek. "I need a quiet place to think for a while, away from any distractions."

"Well, okay, darlin'. You know you're always welcome here. Come on into the kitchen. Can I get you somethin' to eat?"

"No, thank you, ma'am. I'm just really tired. Can I go upstairs to my room and sleep, please?"

"Absolutely. I'll have Daddy bring up your bags for you. You just rest now. We will catch up when you wake up."

"Thank you, Mama. I love you."

"I love you, too, sugar. You get some rest now."

Kat slunk upstairs to her old bedroom. She threw her purse on the floor in the corner and then sat down on her bed. Looking around her room, she remembered the night before her wedding to James. How excited and hopeful she had been, knowing that her time in this room, in her childhood home, was coming to an end. She recalled how she thought she was going to be a grown, independent woman and her life would be glorious. She scoffed at herself now. *Sure. How independent am I? I went from my parents taking care of me to James. I have no money, no education. What am I going to do? Work at Walmart? Become a waitress at Waffle House?*

She flopped back on to her bed and stared at the ceiling.

***

When Kat woke up the next day, the sun was streaming through her window. She looked over at the clock and realized that she had been asleep for nearly twenty-four hours straight.

How is that even possible? she wondered.

Then, it hit her like a freight train: all the memories from the trip came flooding back.

She sat up and rubbed her eyes. Her father had at some point brought up her bags and someone had spread a blanket out over her, too. She grabbed some clean clothes and stepped out into the hallway. Walking down to the bathroom, her mind started racing.

Now what am I going to do?

She turned on the water for the shower and, stepping in through the clouds of steam, she began to hash out what her next steps should be.

Okay. Today is Sunday. James won't even be back until Monday night. I can ask Daddy to run me up to the house and I can get my car and my stuff. Drew is set with Holly until Tuesday afternoon after practice, so I don't have to worry immediately about him. I have my ATM card and can pull out $500 a day until at least Tuesday before James even realizes it. I have our two credit cards. Since I don't have a job, I don't think he can kick me out of the house. Since he obviously has the means to pay for a hotel and I don't, that's what I'll demand he does.

Making it back into her room, she was already feeling a bit better knowing that she at least had a plan for the next few days. Grabbing her phone, she turned it on. She gaped as the millions of texts from Jen, James, and even Ashley came rolling in. She began to read through them, getting angrier and angrier as she read those from James:

Kat? Come on. Please? Let me know you are all right.

Please, Kat. Don't be like this.

Okay, Kat. It is eleven am here and still no sign of you. Are you with Jen?

I know you don't want to talk to me right now. But please, at least text me back and let me know you aren't lying dead in the middle of the Nevada desert somewhere, okay?

Soon after, James' texts went from being concerned to hostile:

Come on, Kat. Quit acting like a child. This is ridiculous!

Kat, I'm getting mad now. If you don't stop this and let me know you are okay, I'm going to cancel your credit cards and call the bank and tell them you are missing, so they will close down your debit card.

Did you know that your little trip to the spa here cost me $600?

You will talk to me, do you understand?

Then, he backed off again: *Please, Kat.*

And finally: *I called Jen. She finally told me you went home to your parents. Stay there and we will talk when I get home on Monday, okay?*

Kat realized that James must have been desperate and worried to have called Jen. Next, she began to read the texts from Ashley:

Hey, Hon. Just checking to make sure you are okay.

Sugar, it isn't the end of the world. You can work through this, I'm sure.

James is worried about you. Don't do this to him.

He feels terrible and wants to know you're okay. I understand that you don't want to have to deal with him right now, but please text me back so I can tell him you are okay. Please?

Wow! Kat thought. *It must be bad when Ashley is showing some genuine concern.*

Next came the texts from Jen:

Did you make it home?

Hey, let me know you got there.

I'm so sorry I couldn't come and get you. Please don't be mad. Okay?

James just called. I finally had to tell him where you went. You would be proud of the hell I put him through first, though. Of course, I let him know several times that he is a complete S.O.B. and a snake, and that he never was or ever will be good

I just called your Mama. She said that you made it home and have been sleeping. Call me when you wake up.

Kat began dialing. Jen picked up on the second ring. "Hey. How are you?"

"I don't know."

"What do you mean you don't know?"

"I feel like I'm living in a horrible nightmare. What just happened? How did I go from being happily married for close to twenty-three years to living in my childhood bedroom again in the span of forty-eight hours?"

"Because of James. This is all his fault. He is a pig!"

"Jen, I don't know what to do next! What do I do? Do I go home and just pretend this never happened? Do I go home and kick him out? Do I get a job? Where am I going to get a job? I have no education, no skills. What do I tell the kids? Oh, Jen, how could I have been this stupid? Why didn't I listen to you when you told me to at least finish college before marrying James? Ah, hell! Why didn't I just run away to L.A. with you?"

"I don't know, Kat," said Jen. "But it is never too late. I can still use a partner."

"Oh, Jen! You don't know how tempted I am to say yes and just jump in the car and go. If I didn't still have Drew at home, I probably would."

"I know, I know. But you aren't without options. You could always just come out here for a week or two until you get through the shock of it all."

"Okay. Thanks. I had better get downstairs and face my mama. This isn't going to be pretty."

"Oh, Lord! No, it is not. Godspeed! Call me later if you need to."

"Thanks, Jen, for everything. You saved the day."

"Not a problem. Talk to you soon."

Kat hung up and stood up from her bed. She took a few deep, calming breaths before she opened the door to go downstairs and face her mother. As she had told Jen, this was not going to be pretty.

Kat walked into the kitchen and found her mother sitting at the table in the breakfast nook, reading the paper. She looked up and asked said, "Hi, sweet pea. How are you doin' today? Daddy and I were gettin' worried, wonderin' if you were going to just keep sleepin' all day. Can I get you, anythin'? Maybe some coffee or sweet tea?"

"No, thanks. I'll grab a glass of tea myself. You just sit there."

"Kat, honey, your daddy told me what happened. I'm so sorry, sugar."

"Thanks, Mama. I just can't believe it."

"Well, honey, you have had quite the shock. You can just stay here until James gets home. Then, he can pick you up here and y'all can start pickin' up the pieces and get back on track."

"Mama?"

"Yes?"

"You know that it isn't going to be that easy, right?"

"Well, sure I do, sugar. But time heals all wounds. You can go home with him and start to talk and see if y'all can find some common ground."

"I'm not sure I'm going to go home with him. I…"

"Oh, sweet pea," her mother interrupted, "you can't mean that. You have to go home with him! Where else would you go? You are his wife!"

"But, Mama, he was stepping out on me. I don't know how I can just move on from that. How…"

"Oh, honey. It happens! People move on from it all of the time."

"Oh, really? Women get over their husbands sleeping around all of the time, do they?"

"I don't like your tone, young lady. But yes, this happens all of the time, and people work through it. Many of my friends have dealt with this exact situation. Honey, it's just sex, not love. You will move on."

"It wasn't just sex, he was having an affair. He was…"

"Well, I don't see what the difference is."

"He was …"

Her mother interrupted her again. "Now, enough of this feelin' sorry for yourself, young lady. You need to stop your whinin' and cryin' and carryin' on, pull yourself together, and put on a little makeup, then prepare yourself to save your marriage! I'll call Pastor Jack to see if y'all can get in with him for some marriage counselin'. I know y'all can get back on track. Everythin' just went a little cattywampus."

"Mama!" Kat countered. "Things did not just go 'a little cattywampus'! It isn't that simple. This isn't going to be an easy fix."

"Well, now, I know that, sugar. It will take some time and a lot of work on your part."

"What do you mean a lot of work on my part? What about James? Why is this…"

"Well, now, James is just a man, darlin'. They are weak. They're often tempted by the flesh and have these little indiscretions. It's just what they do."

With that, Kat lost her last shred of patience. "Indiscretions? Really, Mama? This wasn't 'an indiscretion!' He was fucking another woman for ten months and kept it hidden from me. That isn't an indiscretion. That is a whole goddamned firestorm!"

"Katherine Elizabeth Curtis! What did you just say? You'd better not have said what I think you just did."

"It has actually been Katherine Elizabeth Anderson for nearly a quarter century, and yes, Ma'am. I said exactly what you think I said, and I will say it again. He was *fucking* another woman for ten months and still coming home to me!"

Her mother stared at her for a few seconds, too stunned to speak. Finally, she said, "I will not have my daughter sayin' that filthy word! How dare you speak that word in my house? You are a good Christian woman and words like that should not even be in your vocabulary."

"You just don't get it, do you? I can't just turn a blind eye and get over it. Would you have? Would you have just turned a blind eye if you had discovered Daddy had been stepping out on you? Do you even know what this feels like? Did Daddy ever step out on you?"

"I wouldn't know, sugar. I've never asked, and he has never told me. If he did, then he was gentlemanly enough to keep his weaknesses hidden from me. That was James' biggest mistake."

"Mama… Oh, Mama. I can't…. I just can't believe that you would honestly think that James' biggest mistake was letting me find out. What about me? Aren't I entitled to someone who loves and respects me?"

"Oh, but honey, he does respect you! You're the one wearin' his ring, not her."

"Not for much longer," Kat mumbled.

"What was that?" her mama asked her.

"I said 'not for much longer'. I'm going to file for divorce."

"Kat! Oh, no! You can't do that! How would it look?"

"How would it look? It would look like I deserve better than to put up with his crap. It would look like I have some dignity and self-respect. You know what he told me, Mama? He told me that he wasn't ready to give her up. That she does things to him that he could never ask me to do as his wife."

"Well, there you go, then, sweetie pie. He said it himself: men have needs. He loves you and respects you enough that he doesn't want to soil you with his more animalistic desires. He can meet his physical needs in any old place. He can only get your love from you."

"I can't believe you would really accept that. So, it's okay for him to have sex outside of marriage when it's something he feels is too tawdry for me? As long as it's something he can do with a common whore, he shouldn't bother me with his requests?"

"Yes. That is exactly what I'm sayin'. Men are intimate with their wives. For their more primal needs, they sometimes don't want to burden them. You're a lady, Kat, and he's just treatin' you as such. Sex is not love, honey. It's just sex. It's just physical, not emotional. He makes love to you. He comes back home to you. For the emotional part, you are the only one who can fulfill his needs."

"And you know this how? Have you been witness to every aspect of our marriage all these years? And besides, I just can't agree to that. I won't be put on a pedestal and treated like I'm some delicate flower that needs to be preserved. He either wants all of me, or he gets nothing. He doesn't have the right to decide what is too primal for me or not. That is my choice!"

"Kat, stop! Listen to me. He loves you. He wants to protect you from his more aggressive, brutish side. He wants you to be his safe haven."

"Well, I'm not going to let him. Mama, this discussion is over. I love you, but I cannot sit here another minute and be told that this was not only inevitable but okay. I'm going to ask Daddy to take me home now!"

"Kat! Kat? Come back here…."

Kat stormed out of the kitchen and found her father sitting in his easy chair, watching golf on T.V.

"Daddy?" she said. "I'm ready to go. Please take me home now."

He looked into her eyes and held her gaze for a second. Nodding slowly, he reached for the remote and turned off the T.V.

"Okay," he said. "If that's what you want to do, I'll take you. Go pack your stuff and I'll bring it down for you."

As Kat started heading up the stairs, she heard her father go into the kitchen. She stopped and looked back when she heard his voice. "What did you say to that poor little girl? I told you not to make an issue of it. She's in shock. She needs time to process what happened before you start tellin' her that she has to forgive him."

"Have you ever stepped out on me?" her mother responded quietly.

"I am too much of a gentleman to even dignify that question with an answer. However, if I had, I would not have been stupid enough to let you find out like that idiot James."

And with that, he turned and left the room.

81

Chapter Ten

By Monday night, Kat had moved all of James' belongings into the spare room in the basement. She had worked hard all of Sunday evening after her father had dropped her off at her empty, dark house and all-day Monday, too. Now all she could do was sit and wait for the inevitable.

She heard his key in the lock and braced herself for whatever might be coming through the front door. The door swung open, and he stood still for a second, his eyes adjusting from the light of the evening to the darkness in the entry hall.

"Kat? Kat? Are you here?"

Kat said nothing as she sat on the couch in the family room. He walked further into the house and put down his bags. Then, after switching on the hall light, he found his way to where she was.

"There you are! I was so worried about you," he said. "I called your parents', and all your mama did was cry and your father told me that he didn't want to speak to me right now. Did you tell them, Kat?"

She finally looked up and met his eyes. "*Of course,* I told them!"

"Oh, Kat, why did you have to tell them? It's bad enough that Jen and Tom and Ashley know!"

"Don't forget Kristina, the person who was able to get me home. I told them because they are my parents and I needed to explain to them why I flew to the other side of the country at six a.m. two days ahead of schedule!"

James stood planted in place, simply staring at her.

She held his gaze for a few seconds, daring him to challenge her. He finally broke contact and looked off to the side. He grabbed his bags and started toward the stairs.

"Oh, no! No way in *hell*! You're in the basement."

"What! Really, Kat? You're banishing me to the basement?"

"Yes. And you're incredibly lucky that I don't kick you out altogether!"

"You can't kick me out of the house that I pay for!" he retorted.

"Really? Do you really think a judge is going to make me leave *my* home because of *your* antics? Because I would expect that the judge would make us sell the house and split the profits, but let me stay here in the meantime, while you would have to find another place to live."

His eyes widened in shock as her words washed over him. "The judge would make us? What are you saying, Kat? You want a divorce?"

"You bet your ass I want a divorce!" she countered. "The sooner the better, in fact. Oh, and too bad, but the alimony you will most certainly have to pay me until I can get through the rest of my schooling is going to cut into all of your spending money for your trips to New York. I'll see to that."

"Kat, look… I told you. I don't love her! I love you!"

"James, I'm not discussing this again. Put your stuff downstairs."

"Did you make any dinner?" he asked.

"Yes, I did, and it was delicious. I don't know what you're going to find to eat, however. That's your problem now."

With that, she rose from the couch and ascended the stairs to their bedroom. From the top, she heard him finally reach down to grab his bags and open the basement door.

***

By Tuesday afternoon, Kat was resolved in what she was going to do. She had talked to a lawyer and had determined that her predictions about what would happen with their divorce had been, for the most part, accurate. Her only hang up now was telling the kids. Since Drew was coming home that night, she figured she would start first with him.

He walked through the door and gave Kat a kiss on the cheek.

"Hi, Mama! How was the trip?"

"Well, it was interesting, to say the least. I need to talk to you."

Drew looked at his mother, concern evident on his face. "What's up? Everything all right?"

"No, Drew. It isn't. Your dad and I have decided to separate. I'm so sorry that this happened now, with you being so close to graduating and in the middle of the lacrosse season, but it needs to happen."

"Why? What happened?"

"Let's just say that your dad and I discovered that we have different desires."

Drew looked at his mother and slowly shook his head. "What do you mean? Mama, I can't believe this. Everything was fine when y'all left last week and now this? What happened?"

"Drew, I will have to let your father explain things further. I've said all I'm going to say on the subject. We both still love all y'all very much and we will still work together to make sure y'all have what you need. But we won't be married any longer."

"What's going to happen? Are we selling the house? I can't move schools in the last few months of my senior year!"

"Yes, Drew, the house will be sold. The attorney said that we can probably wait until you and Derrick are graduated and sell this summer. You can live with either your father or me until you leave for college."

"What are you going to do for money? You don't work."

"I know, sweetie. But it'll be okay. Dad will have to pay me alimony for a few years until I get up on my own two feet. I'll probably go back to school."

"Mama, I can't believe this. I thought our family would be the one to make it. So many families are broken up by this point in school. It is really sad to see what happens. I don't want y'all to not even be able to stand being in the same room together." His face was sad, reminding her of the little boy he'd been not so long ago.

"Drew, I promise you that I'll act like a grown up and treat your father with respect when we are all together. As for him, I can't say. That's his decision to make."

Drew slowly nodded his understanding before he hugged Kat and then went up to his room. She looked around sadly at all of the pictures and memories of their family and the life they all had built together. As much as it broke her heart, though, she knew for her sanity's sake that she couldn't stay in this relationship anymore. It wasn't fair to her, and it wasn't a good example to set for the kids. She was still sitting on the couch, sorting through her memories, when Jen called.

"How are you?" Jen asked.

"Okay, I guess. I just told Drew that James and I are getting a divorce. He took it as well as could be expected, I suppose. He was mostly just upset because he thought we were going to make it. He said he thought we were going to be together for the rest of our lives. I'm just so glad that they were all older when this happened. I can't imagine how much harder this would have been if they were still younger."

When Jen didn't reply, Kat realized she had maybe spoken out of turn.

"Oh, sorry, Jen! That wasn't meant to be directed toward you and y'all's situation."

"No offense taken… It hasn't always been easy, but David and I are so much better as friends. Nothing happened that was a betrayal. We just weren't compatible, and we decided to go our separate ways. We are both too busy to date, so that is not an issue, and we're able to co- parent Lucy very amicably. I just hope that it continues as she gets older."

"Jen, I still don't know what I'm going to do. The attorney said that I'll have to do something. The alimony and half of the proceeds of the house will keep me afloat for a little while, but I'll have to go back to school or get a job. I haven't done either since I was twenty-one years old."

"Well, you could always come here. Seriously, please consider it! You and I could be partners again. Even if you don't want to do it long term, at least come to Canada with me for this contract. It will get you away from everything and give you time to think. It's supposed to be gorgeous up there, too."

"I would, Jen, but I can't with it being so close to Drew's graduation. It's crunch time for college and finals and all of the things that this last year entails."

"Kat, you've done everything for so long; let James take some responsibility in this. Let him be his dad. Even though I despise the man, I do know he loves his kids. Give him the chance to step up to the plate. He may just surprise you."

"I don't know, Jen. I just don't know. So much is up in the air right now…"

When their conversation drew to a close, Kat hung up, then went upstairs to her room, grabbed a suitcase, and started packing. She grabbed her favorite clothes and shoes and made sure that she threw in her passport for good measure.

This doesn't mean I'm going, she rationalized with herself. *It's just to make me feel better, like I have options.*

She took her bag and put it in the back of her car. She then managed to pretty much avoid James on Wednesday and Thursday. He was back to going in early and staying out late at the office. When he came home, he went straight to the basement. The few times he had tried to text her or speak with her, she had simply not responded.

Perhaps it could be construed as a juvenile way to handle the situation, but she really didn't feel that there was anything left to be said. She went ahead and had her attorney start the process of drawing up the divorce papers, but she just couldn't quite bring herself to have him actually file them.

On Friday morning, she was surprised to see James sitting at the breakfast nook table drinking his coffee when she came downstairs. It was well past eight a.m., and it threw her for a loop to have to deal with him.

"What are you still doing here?" she asked, shocked.

"I've taken the day off. We need to talk, Kat."

"I really have nothing left to say to you, James. I'm sorry that it has ended up like this, but I'll remind you it's of no fault of mine. I actually have honored the marriage vows that we declared in front of all of our family, friends, and God."

"I'm sorry Kat! I am so incredibly sorry. I'm through with Sam. Can we please just go to counseling and try to make it work? I love you, and I don't want this to end."

"I just don't know. I am way too hurt and angry right now to think clearly."

"Please, Kat. I know I screwed up. It was the stupidest thing I have ever done. I know you owe me nothing, but you're my best friend. I miss you! I miss talking to you. Please don't throw away twenty-three years of what we had together because of my one indiscretion."

And there it was. That terribly simplistic word again: indiscretion. James' declaration had begun to move her, but she bristled the moment he uttered that one word.

"No, James. An indiscretion would have been spending all of our money in Vegas on the slots. It would have been not talking with me before you bought a sports car. Hell, it even— maybe—could have been a one-night stand when you were traveling. Had too much to drink and had sex with a stranger, never to hear from her again. As my mama said, sex doesn't always equal love. But James, screwing your twenty-eight-year-old colleague for close to a year does not count as an indiscretion. It counts as a complete and utter betrayal, and I don't know how I would even begin to get past it.

"I've told Drew we are separating. I haven't told Derrick and Olivia anything. Somehow, I can't bring myself to tell them that their father was having sex with someone who was basically their own age. Something tells me it will freak them out. So, how about you deal with that? I spared Drew the intimate details of your complete and total failure as a husband since he is still technically a kid; whether you chose to fill him in or not is up to you. But you will tell Derrick and Olivia everything. I deserve that much."

James nodded his head slowly before he spoke, reaching simultaneously for her hand.

"I talked with your mama the other day. Pastor Jack has agreed to give us marriage counseling. Kat, I want to try it. I'm begging you, please let's try again."

In that instant, Kat simply felt worn out. The stress and pain of the last few days washed over her like a tidal wave. She didn't want to do this anymore. She felt like a deflated balloon and just wanted things to go back like they were.

"Is it really over with Sam?" she asked James.

"Yes! It's really over. I ended it with her. I told her I loved and wanted you."

Kat took a deep breath. "I guess I owe it to you and our children to try again, as long as you promise me it's truly over with that woman. But there will be stipulations. You will give me full access to your computer and phone at any time I ask. You will also tell your company that they will need to send someone else on your team on any overnight trips. What excuse you give them is up to you, because I'm sure that you don't want to tell them it is because you can't keep your penis in your pants, and you were involved in a clandestine relationship with a colleague. I also demand that you cancel your credit card and cut it up in my presence and that you change your new bank account today, putting it in my name only, and give me the debit card now so that if this ever happens again, I'll have access to money you can't touch. Understand?"

"Okay! Yes! Whatever you say! I'll do all of that. Thank you! Thank you so much! I'm so incredibly sorry. I guess I was just having a midlife crisis. My mortality started looming in front of me and I didn't know how to handle it. And then Sam, a beautiful young woman, came on to me and, well, it felt like she was the one who could make it all go away and make me feel young again."

James made an awkward attempt to hug Kat, but she just stood still and stiff, with her arms at her sides.

"When can I move back up to our room?" he asked.

"I'm nowhere near ready to discuss that yet. You will have to remain downstairs until I feel ready to invite you back into my bed."

"Okay. I guess I deserve that. But Kat, I keep thinking about that night in Vegas. I want to relive that with you. Please?"

"James, I have errands I need to run. I've got to go."

"Oh, okay! I guess I'll just work from home, then. Maybe we can go out to dinner tonight? I'm really looking forward to getting us back on track."

"Drew has a lacrosse game. After that, I may be willing to have dinner with you."

As Kat ran her errands, her thoughts were consumed with what she had just agreed to. Though she was still incredibly angry and hurt, it just felt easier to give in. This was all new territory for her, and she was scared. She had never lived alone, and she had let James handle so many of the financial details of their lives that she wasn't even sure how to pay a bill at this point. She had rarely even pumped her own gas. He took care of all of that for her and the thought of being thrown into world of managing completely by herself was overwhelming.

"This is for the best." She said the words out loud, though there was no one else in the car but her.

Chapter Eleven

In the warm Southern spring evening, Kat drove to Drew's game. She wanted to make sure to try and keep his life as normal as possible and had made every effort to maintain their regular routine. As she got out of the car, she stood in the parking lot and took a deep breath. She was praying that Ashley wouldn't say anything to her about what happened, valiantly hoping that the woman's upbringing would mean she had the ability to just gloss over everything and not make a public scene. She had just about convinced herself it would all be okay when she reached the bleachers.

As Kat started her ascent, however, she quickly noticed that no one would make eye contact with her and several of the other mothers were passing knowing looks between each other. She was beginning to feel very uncomfortable—paranoid even—as she meandered over to Holly and sat down.

"Hi," Holly said, not looking her in the eye.

"Hi! How are you?"

"I'm good. How about you?" Holly still wouldn't look at her.

"I don't know… I'm feeling paranoid, like everyone is trying to avoid me."

"Ashley told us all what happened. I'm so sorry. I don't even know what to say and I'm sure that the other women feel the exact same way. They are probably all amazed that you are even here."

"Everyone knows that my husband had an affair?"

"I'm afraid so."

At that moment, Ashley pranced over to them and tried to give Kat a hug. "Well bless your heart, sugar. I didn't expect to see you here. How are you doin'?"

Kat looked at her for a few seconds and said, "I'm doing as well as can be expected, I guess. I was a little surprised to see that so many people seem to know what happened."

"I'm sorry about that, Kat. Word travels fast, I guess."

"Yes, I suppose it does, especially when the bearer of it can't keep other people's business to themselves. But it's okay. James and I've decided to stay together. He promised that he broke it off with her and that he loves me."

Ashley cocked her head to the side and looked at Kat with a pitying expression. "Honey, I was just worried about you and Drew. I figured that all this would affect Drew's game. I wanted to tell the other mothers so they could tell their boys that Drew may be off his game for a little while."

She paused for a few seconds and narrowed her eyes before continuing, "But, Kat, what do you mean that James broke it off with Samantha? Honey, she dumped him! I guess havin' him available twenty-four/seven suddenly made him a lot less appealin'. I think that she cared more about the excitement that comes with the risk of gettin' caught than anythin' else."

Ashley babbled on, seemingly forgetting that Kat was the subject of this conversation's wife and not just another mother with whom to gossip.

"Ashley!" Holly admonished. "Are you kidding me? What the hell is wrong with you? Do you think Kat really wants you talking about her life like it's a soap opera? This is her family you're talking about! And, on that note, how dare you share that very personal information of Kat's with others? No one needed a warning about Drew's 'dropping the ball' so to speak. He's obviously doing just fine down there. You're just a mean-spirited, gossipy, attention-hogging, busybody who isn't happy unless she has everyone focused on her. You make me sick!"

"Well! I don't have to listen to this!" Ashley stood and with a flip of her hair, walked away and sat down with another group of mothers.

"Thanks," Kat mumbled, dejectedly.

"Don't mention it," Holly replied. "I have wanted to tell that woman off for a good long time. I can't stand her!"

Kat nodded and then turned her attention back to the game. She sat quietly and watched, trying desperately to hold back the tears that were threatening to come. She didn't know what to say or what to think. Suddenly, she stood up.

"I have to go," she told Holly. "Can you please drive Drew home?"

"Sure, not a problem. Where are you going, Kat?"

"I just have to go…"

Kat hurried down the bleachers and made it to her car before she started to cry. She sat in the driver's seat, sobbing and screaming, hitting the steering wheel with the palm of her hand a few times. Then abruptly she stopped. Pulling out her phone, she texted her kids: *I'm leaving. I love you.*

She threw her car in drive and left the parking lot. Before she knew it, she was in Nashville after hooking up with Interstate 40. She hit the hands free and had her car dial Jen.

"Hello?" Jen said.

"Hi."

"Kat, what's up? What's going on?"

"I left."

"What do you mean, you left?"

"I left! I went to the lacrosse game, and no one would look at me. Finally, Holly told me Ashley had told everyone what happened. Ashley then came over and told me that James had lied to me once again and that he didn't dump Sam; she dumped him. I couldn't take it anymore! I got up and I left. I'm in Nashville and I'm coming to you. I'll see you in a few days."

"Wait… What? You're coming here? Kat, I'm *so* excited! Oh my God, please tell me you brought your passport? We leave for Canada in a week."

"Yes, I did. I packed a bag a few days ago and threw it in my car—I've been driving around with it like a security blanket—and I made sure I put my passport in there. I want to go to Canada."

"Okay, great! Drive safely and I'll see you when you get here! Please be careful. That's a long drive to do by yourself."

"I know. I'll get there as soon as I can."

Kat continued rolling down the I40, stopping only to get

gas and energy drinks or coffee. When she got tired, she pulled off the road and slept for a few hours and then started again. She sang along to the music on the radio and took the time needed to process what she had done. Of course, the texts and calls were coming in fast and furiously from James, her kids, and her parents. Even James' mom tried to call one time. Kat just ignored them all and continued heading west.

When she hit Oklahoma City, her radio was on a local country station. All of a sudden, Miranda Lambert's "Mama's Broken Heart" began to play. Kat reached over and turned the volume up all the way and sang at the top of her lungs. How aptly the lyrics applied to Kat's polite Southern upbringing. It wasn't about what was on the inside, as long as the outside looked perfect. Her soul could be shriveling and turning black, but she had better not let it show. It was always all about appearances.

Soon, the landscape was getting drier. Across Texas, through New Mexico, into Arizona and then, not long after, the exit for Las Vegas. She started thinking about how crazy it was that she was now right back where her life had begun to unravel just a little over a week ago. The memories of that horrific night kept running through her mind over and over until she thought she would scream: Sam's words in the bathroom, the look on James' face when she'd asked him if Sam was really Samantha, her throwing her shoe at him as he walked out the door. Tears rolled down her cheeks and clouded her vision as she drove.

***

Kat had never been so happy to get to the California state line. Taking a deep breath, she told herself that there was no more looking back, only forward. She was excited about going to Canada with Jen, where it would be like the old times when they had had such a great time working together. She wondered where in Canada they were going, what it would look like there, and if it would be cold. As she cruised into the San Fernando Valley and to Jen's house, she got more and more excited.

When she pulled up in front of Jen's bungalow, the door

flew open. Jen ran up the front walk until she and Kat came together in a hug. Arms around each other, jumping up and down and screaming, the neighbors all probably thought that they were crazy. Jen put her arm around Kat's shoulders as they walked back inside.

"How are you? How was the drive? I bet you are dog-tired!"

"Yeah, I'm pretty tired. It was good. Made good time; I hardly stopped at all. I just wanted to get here. Can we go to the beach tomorrow?"

Jen laughed at her friend. "Of course, we can! At least for a while. In the morning, I need to get the last things together for Melinda and Gerard before they start on down the road with the truck and R.V."

"R.V.?"

"Yup. Where we're going is really remote. Everyone will be staying together in R.Vs. It could get really interesting. Just the crew, the actors, and us all together up there with nothing more than the trees and bears."

"Holy cow! Where are we going?"

"To some property the network or production company owns in the Canadian Rockies, near Calgary. By the way, I hope you brought some warm clothes. It'll still be cold up there this time of year."

Kat looked incredulously at Jen. "Uh, no. I live in the South, remember? I don't even own a real winter coat."

"Well, then. It looks like a little shopping is in our future. Do you still have your credit cards? Seems like James owes you a bit of a shopping spree!"

"I do! I don't know when he'll close them, though. They were still open long enough for me to get gas on the way here, but he threatened when I left Vegas that if I didn't tell him where I was, he was going to shut everything down and report me missing."

"Well, regardless, I've got money. You'll also be earning a wage up there."

"Wait, no! Jen! I can't accept that."

"You can and you will! Girl, you're going to earn it, believe me. This is not going to be an easy gig, all of us together on a couple acres for a few months. Calgary is like an hour and a half away. You well remember how it was to be on your feet cooking all day, to boot. You'll earn every last penny I pay you!"

"We're all going to stay in one R.V.? You, me, Gerard, and Melinda?"

"Yes, we'll all be sharing. It'll be fun, like summer camp, only colder! On the weekends, I'm sure that some of the crew will head back down to Calgary if they don't have to film. The actors will probably fly home when they can, at least every once in a while. The rest of us poor folks will be staying there, though, poking around Calgary if we're lucky. The weather up there can be really unpredictable this time of year, so I've been told that this will pretty much be a seven day a week job for the whole three months, even longer if needed," said Jen.

Kat wasn't so sure: being in such close quarters with others, two of whom were practically strangers, when she was still so fragile sounded like it could be a recipe for disaster. Jen had said that she and Kat would share the big bedroom which would help, but at worst she figured she could always fly out and go home if she needed to.

The next morning was spent making preparations for the trip. There were several locations in Calgary from which to purchase organic produce and meat, but many of the Southern delicacies would have to be trucked in with them in amounts that would only last through the beginning of the shoot. After that, they would have to be shipped to the location to be restocked. It sounded like it was going to be a lot of work to make this adventure come together, but Jen was composed. Every time Kat would start to ask questions, which would then intensify to near hysterics, her friend would tell her all would be fine. Jen had always been the calm one.

They spent the afternoon at the beach in Malibu, and Kat could not remember a time when she felt so relaxed. The women spent the day reminiscing about the past and giggling like schoolgirls. As the day got later, however, the talk got more serious.

"Kat?"

"Yeah?" Kat groaned, lifting her arm from shading her eyes and rousing herself from her punch-drunk, warm, sun-induced sleepy state.

"Why didn't you come with me when I first came out here?"

"I don't know. I was scared, I guess. I was engaged to James, and I didn't want to disappoint anyone or make anyone look bad. I really did love him, you know."

"I know you did. What I never figured out was why."

"I honestly don't know. I think it was because he seemed so grown up and focused. He acted so much more mature than the other boys we went to school with. I figured he was what I was expected to marry and have a family with. Mostly, I think, I fell for him because he was there. He paid attention to me, loved me. No one else gave me a second glance, but he was incredibly devoted and serious about me. He made me feel special."

"I can understand that, I guess. I just always felt like you were settling. It felt like you went with the first man you met. I can't help feeling that maybe you didn't think you would ever find anyone else; someone, I don't know, better."

"I think you're right. There never really was anyone else who was interested in me. Maybe I figured that he was my only shot."

"I can't help but wonder what would have happened if you'd come out here with me. I've met so many different people. I've experienced all kinds of men. And when I say experienced, I mean *experienced*! I've dated everyone from busboys waiting for their big break to producers and directors, studio execs, and even actors. No one super famous, but I did have a few really good one-night stands.

"By the time David and I got together, I felt like I had sown my wild oats. And he's a good man. I've just discovered that I'm better off by myself. I'm selfish and I don't want to have to answer to anyone. I love being Lucy's mom, but I couldn't handle any more kids. It sounds terrible to say, but I'm actually really glad that she goes to her dad's a couple of days a week, so I can have some time to myself."

"That's the total opposite of me. Maybe this split is my fault. I focused so much on the kids and their needs, I forgot my own and most likely neglected James', too. I forgot that we would still have a marriage when the kids were gone. I think he felt lonely and scared about getting older and felt like he was the one who was fading away.

"I'm still really hurt that this has happened, but my anger is lessening a bit. I think, in our own ways, we were each struggling to find a new purpose in our world that was going to change so drastically in just a few months. I don't think we even knew who the other one was anymore, let alone ourselves."

"Wow. You really can't think that you're responsible for any of this?"

"No, not all of it. Not most of it, honestly. I mean, I was struggling with where I fit in, but I didn't have sex with someone else! But I remember that I did love James very much, or at least I thought I did, and all of the good times we had. He is a good dad. Not the most attentive, but he was present in their lives, and they know he loves them. That's better than a lot of kids. Lucy is lucky like that, too. Even though you and David don't live together anymore, she still has both y'all in her life."

"Do you want to go back to James?"

"I can't say right now. I am hurt, but what makes me most upset is the betrayal. Even more than the fact that he was sleeping with someone else, what hurts the most is that he lied to me. We were best friends. No offense."

"None taken," said Jen. "I never felt threatened by him."

"I miss the friendship we had; that focus on the common goal we shared. I feel sort of like I'm floundering in the abyss now. I also feel lonely. It's hard to be with someone pretty much every day for so long, and then suddenly they are gone. It feels weird to go to bed alone and to not have someone there beside me when I wake up in the morning."

"I can respect that," Jen replied. "Even though James is far from my ideal man, I can understand how it must be to suddenly lose someone who had been such an integral part of your daily life."

"Jen, it's funny... I miss the mundane conversation you have when you're comfortable with someone. I mean, I talk with you, but it's still different. It's almost like having someone listening while you share your internal dialog. We would talk about the dry cleaning, putting out the can on garbage day, what was for dinner, that sort of thing. We'd converse when we were brushing our teeth in the morning. It wasn't the conversation that was important; it was that there *was* conversation, someone there to listen. I feel weird having to be quiet all of the time, but talking to one's self is generally not seen as a good thing." Kat gave Jen a rueful smile.

***

A few hours later, Kat and Jen gathered up their stuff and headed back to the house. Melinda and Gerard were due at six o'clock to go over everything one more time before they hit the road the next day. As David wasn't able to take Lucy until four days later due to a work obligation, Kat and Jen would fly up then. Given it would take that long for Jen's employees to drive to up there and start to get set up anyway, they wouldn't be missed on location.

When Gerard drove up, Kat read the side of the truck and started laughing.

"Oh, no! You didn't!" she exclaimed.

"I most certainly did! I wanted to surprise you!"

"*Southern Comfort Food, aka, Kat in the Jen House.* I cannot believe you did this!"

"I wanted to go back to our roots, to what we called our venture so many years ago. Of course, the official name of *Southern Comfort Food* hasn't changed, but I figured we could have a little fun."

"Thank you, Jen. I can't believe it. That seems like a whole other lifetime ago."

"Well, I figured it was good luck then, so it will be now, too!"

They did a final check of everything before going over the route to the location and then sent Melinda and Gerard home, all set to start out in the morning.

After that, they spent the next few days buying clothes for the climate up north. Neither of them, given where they lived, was prepared to face the cold, wind, fog, rain, and snow Jen had been warned would be possible.

They went to outdoor stores and tried on coats and boots, and bought hats, scarves, gloves, and cold rated sleeping bags, laughing the entire time about how they looked like the Abominable Snowman or the Michelin Man when they were all bundled up.

The night before they were scheduled to leave, they tried to pack the stuff into their suitcases and laughed even more hysterically when they were so stuffed with fluff that they couldn't close them. David had already come and gotten Lucy, so Kat and Jen were drinking wine, which made the funny situation into a downright raucous one.

They went to bed ready and excited for their flight to Calgary the next day. Kat's final thoughts as she drifted to sleep were how much fun she was having and how she hoped it would continue when they got up there.

Sometime in the very early morning, Jen gently shook Kat's shoulder.

"Kat? Kat? Wake up! Something's happened."

Kat sat up with a start and blinked a few times when Jen switched on the lamp on the bedside table.

"It's Lucy," Jen said. "She had a seizure. David had to call 911. I've got to get to the hospital."

"What? A seizure? Has she had them before?"

"Yeah, remember that she had a few if she got a fever when she was little? We were told it wasn't abnormal and they were the type she would most likely outgrow. But David said this one was really bad. He thought she stopped breathing, so he called the paramedics. They took her to the children's hospital at UCLA."

"Okay, let me get up. I'll go with you."

"No, you stay here and sleep. One of us has to be with it enough tomorrow to get us to Calgary. I'll head over now and hopefully we'll know more in a few hours. I'm hoping that this is just a fluke and that I'll be ready to fly out tomorrow afternoon."

"Are you sure? I really don't mind coming."

"I'm sure. You're already jetlagged from coming West and it'll be even worse tomorrow when we change time zones again. You stay and go back to sleep. I'll call when I know more."

Jen turned off the light and Kat rolled over. She felt guilty about not insisting she go with Jen, but she'd also felt she had enough of drama in her own life right now; she couldn't handle someone else's, too. She knew Lucy was in good hands and her mother and father would take good care of her. There really wasn't anything Kat could do at the hospital anyway that would make a difference one way or the other.

At 8:00 a.m., her cell rang. Waking up and thinking it was Jen, she picked it up without looking at it first.

"How is she?" she asked.

"What? Hello? Kat?"

Oh, crap, it's James! Kat realized with horror. *Why didn't I look at the caller ID before I answered?*

"Kat, where are you? Everyone's been calling you for over a week. I called the credit card companies and they said that your cards were last used in Los Angeles. Are you with Jen?"

"Yes."

"Oh, thank God! When are you coming home?"

"I don't know."

"What do you mean you don't know?" James was clearly getting exasperated.

"I don't know. Not yet anyway. I'm flying out to Calgary this afternoon with Jen to work on location for a T.V. show. I don't know how long I'll stay and when, or even if, I will even be coming home."

"Calgary? Isn't that in Canada?"

"Yes. Alberta, Canada to be exact."

"Why are you going to Canada?"

"Because that's where the show is being shot."

"But why Canada?"

"Because, according to Jen, the producer is from Alabama, and he wants some Southern food up there. He's a friend of a friend who recommended Jen to him. He likes her food and wants to give her a shot."

"Okay, but why Canada?"

"I don't know and frankly, right now, I really don't care. I just need to go and do something completely different."

"Different? Kat, come on. I thought we were going to work on this. I didn't have any idea where you were. You texted the kids you were leaving, and Holly brought Drew home. That was the last time any of us has heard a thing from you. We're all worried sick!"

"I'm fine."

"Well, I know that now. Kat, what's happening? Aren't we going to give this another shot?"

"I wanted to, James. I was all set to. But when I got to the game, Ashley came over and talked to me. She had opened her big mouth to all the other mothers on the team in case Drew was out of sorts, or so she said. But then she also informed me that you had not broken it off with Sam; she had broken it off with you."

There were several seconds of silence. "Stupid Ashley!" James muttered

"James, it's not Ashley's fault. I was all ready to try and work things out, but then you lied to me again."

"So, you're just going to take that woman's word over mine?" he then asked.

"Yes. As crazy as it is to say right now, yes, I am. I have lost all faith in you. If you hadn't lied to me about so much else, maybe I wouldn't have believed her. But you have woven a web so complex and deceitful, I can't trust a single thing you say anymore. Did Sam break it off with you?"

Again, there were several seconds of silence before he replied faintly, "Yes."

"Well, I appreciate you finally being honest with me, James, but it's too little, too late. You said you loved me and wanted to try again, but then in the next breath, you lied to me yet another time. I'm going to Canada. I need this. I have to get away."

"What about Drew? What about his and Derrick's graduations?"

"Those are both a few months away. Who knows if I'll even stay up there that long? So, I'll cross that bridge when I get there. There are planes that fly in and out of Calgary every day. I'm sure I can make it back for both of them."

"What are you going to do for money? I won't be paying for it."

"Jen's paying me."

"You're working with Jen again?"

"Yes."

With that, it was like the air went out of James' sails, all his arguments exhausted.

"Did you bring your passport?" he asked weakly, obviously resigned to the fact that Kat would not be changing her mind. It hurt, though, that after everything that had happened, he cared enough about her to check that she was prepared.

"Yes."

"Well, okay then. I guess there's nothing I can do to change your mind. I love you, Kat, and want you to come home. But I understand why you aren't, and I'm sorry I hurt you. Please be careful up there. Many people love you down here."

"Thank you. Please tell the kids I'll be in touch. I need to get up there and get settled, but I'll talk with them soon."

"Okay. Goodbye then, Kat. I love you!"

"Goodbye, James. Take good care of yourself and Drew."

She ended her call and took a deep breath. That had gone so

much better than she thought it would. She was happy that James finally seemed to accept their new normal. They had taken a first step toward healing, and it felt good.

A few minutes later, Jen called.

"Hello?" She sounded worn out and dejected.

"Hey, how's it going?"

"Not well. She's being admitted. They want to run some more tests."

"Oh, no! I'm so sorry, Jen."

"Thanks. David and I are exhausted."

"I can only imagine."

"Kat?"

"Yes?"

"I can't leave today. I can't leave David to deal with this alone."

"Okay. What do I need to do to reschedule our flights?"

"Nothing. Kat, I need you go without me. They are starting the shoot tomorrow and we *have* to be there, ready to go. I can't be, so you have to."

"Jen, it's been years since I've done catering! Especially for something that really matters. This is your livelihood. What if I screw it up?"

"You won't. It isn't that different than what we did in college. Melinda and Gerard will be there to help. They've done this a million times before and will be great support. Please, Kat!"

"Well, how long do you think it'll be before you can get up there?" Kat didn't want to disappoint Jen or stress her out further.

"I don't know. It depends on what they find. As soon as I can, I promise."

Kat took a deep breath. "Okay, Jen. I'll try. I can't make any promises that I'll be able to do it, but I will try."

"That's all I can ask. How can I ever thank you?"

"You have done so much for me already! Just consider this a small payback."

Chapter Twelve

Kat arrived in Calgary at eight that evening. Gerard found her standing at the curb, exhausted, waiting to be picked up. She was surprised to see that he was driving a car.

"Hey, there. I don't know what I was expecting, but it wasn't a car. Though I suppose I didn't think you would be coming in an R.V., either."

Gerard smiled at her, saying, "Yeah. We rented a car yesterday when we got up here. Makes it easier to run errands up and down these mountain roads."

Gerard was a very sweet man, but one of few words. As they drove out of Calgary and headed up toward the mountains, he and Kat were silent, each in their own worlds. It was dark so Kat couldn't make out much of anything at all and she soon fell asleep after her long flight and interrupted slumber the night before.

She woke when they arrived. At the location, all she could see was trailer after trailer, far too many to count.

Gerard pulled in next to theirs and turned off the car. "Holy cow, it's cold up here!" Kat said as she stepped out of the car.

"Yup. Spring in the Canadian Rockies means something completely different than it does in Los Angeles. Or where you're from, too, I expect."

"You're right about that. I don't think I've ever felt it so cold in my life. And that wind!"

"Yeah, it can howl up here and it comes right off the crest. It'll make setting up harder for the crew, for sure."

He pulled her luggage from the trunk and carried it into the R.V. where they found Melinda reclining in one of the push-out bunks, reading a book. After a few minutes of exchanging pleasantries, Gerard put her bags in her bedroom and sat down at the table. Knowing that they must be expecting some sort of direction, Kat then addressed the two of them,

"Okay. Well, as y'all know, there's been a big change of

plans. Jen will be up here as soon as she can, but things are still very much up in the air with Lucy, so she's asked me to run the show. I haven't done this in years and never with this much at stake, so I'm counting on y'all to help me out and make this work. I know the producer is taking a big gamble with this kind of food while not really knowing Jen and what all she can do."

Melinda and Gerard nodded.

"Do either of y'all know what time they start shooting tomorrow morning?"

"At eight a.m.," Melinda answered, "They need the sun to get up in the sky a little bit. They won't shoot many night scenes for a while, as it's still too cold and there will be too much steam from the breath of the people and animals."

"Okay. So, we need to have everything up and ready by about six I would assume, so that the crew and actors have enough time to eat and then get to where they are going. So, that means we need to get up at about four. Does that sound about right?"

"Yes, that should work," Gerard replied amicably.

"Well, it's almost ten-thirty now. I suggest we get some sleep. Four in the morning is going to come awfully early."

***

The alarm ripped through Kat's head after what felt like only a few seconds of sleep, and she groaned in response. It was pitch black outside, stars still filling the sky. Rolling over, she reluctantly got out of bed and went to her bag to get her clothes. She honestly didn't know it was possible to be so cold, and thanks to nerves and exhaustion, she was already shivering uncontrollably. She also didn't know where they were going to set up. It had been so dark last night, she hadn't been able to see anything and hadn't thought to ask. Throwing on some warm clothes, she opened the door. On the other side, Melinda and Gerard were both dressed and were putting on their big parkas, hats, and gloves.

"Oh, boy! This doesn't look good. Just how cold is it out

there?"

"According to my phone, it's minus two Celsius, so about thirty degrees Fahrenheit," Gerard replied.

"Okay. Well, that's doable, I guess. Let's suit up and head out."

The location hosted a number of buildings designed and set up to look like an old Western town with one low, dark building situated just off to the side. Their small group headed toward the outlier. Inside, it looked like a dining hall at a summer camp with round tables and chairs, a kitchen fronted by a large cutout, and a buffet station in between. It was a perfect set up: people in the line could clearly serve themselves, so the caterers could focus instead on keeping everything stocked. Gerard had mentioned that the studio had built this kitchen and dining room after the winds coming down off the mountains kept ripping up the tent they used during the filming of the first season. It had finally been decided that it was cheaper and saved time just to construct a building, seeing how the property could be used for many productions. They all put on their aprons and quickly got to work.

By six a.m., the first people had begun to wander in for breakfast. Kat barely looked up as she continued to prepare for the onslaught. She recognized no one, so she figured that they must be the crew: makeup artists, camera men, wardrobe, etc. The three caterers worked well together and soon the majority of the first wave had cleared out. A little later, Kat was vaguely aware that more people had come into the building and were getting into line. She had just come out with a big tray of food and was concentrating on changing the pan in the buffet server when she overheard a very irritated male voice.

"What the bloody hell are grits?"

Her head snapped up and she found herself face to face with *Ian Gregory*. She inhaled sharply and tried to think straight. As he looked at her, she scrambled to think of something, anything, to say.

"Well?" he demanded. "Hello, I'm waiting!"

"Oh my God, you're Irish!" Kat exclaimed before she had even realized that she had spoken.

"Wait! I am?" he said sarcastically, looking at her like she was crazy.

Kat heard the laugh of a woman to his left and glanced over to see Lydia Swan.

"You still haven't answered my question. What the hell are grits?"

"Um… Well, it's like oatmeal made out of corn…" she replied. "Organically sourced corn," she quickly added.

"Oatmeal made out of corn? Why not just have oatmeal made out of oats? I'm partial to Irish oatmeal myself!" he said with a cocky grin.

"We don't eat much oatmeal in the South. We eat grits."

"Why are we having food from 'the South'? 'The South' of what?"

"The Southern part of the United States," she answered tersely. Kat was starting to go from shocked to exasperated. She had plenty to do other than get into a discussion about geography and regional cuisine.

"Why are we having food from the Southern part of the United States when we are in the mountains in Canada?" he pressed her.

"Ian, behave!" Kat heard a drawl from much further down the line. "I chose the caterin' company. I'm from Alabama and I'm sick of the crap they served us up here for the last two seasons. I mean, what in the hell is back bacon and why are french fries served with gravy and cheese curds? I want bacon bacon! I decided I wanted me some real down home cookin' this time: grits, fried chicken, okra, greens, black eyed peas. Y'all don't like it, y'all can go down to Calgary for all y'all's meals."

"I don't know if I like it," Ian retorted. "I don't even know what any of that is. Greens? Like the color?"

"Ian," Lydia took his arm, "It's okay. It isn't that bad. Hurry up and grab something. We need to get to makeup."

"I don't want oatmeal that is made of corn, that's for sure.

What else have you got?"

"We also have cheese grits made with a nice English cheddar, gluten and dairy free waffles, and biscuits and gravy with free range, hormone and antibiotic free turkey sausage. The gravy is made with coconut milk."

"*Cheese* grits? You mean you take oatmeal made out of corn and put cheese on it?"

"No. We mix the cheese in with it," Kat replied coolly.

"So, you ruin oatmeal by making it with corn and then you make it even worse by adding cheese? What the hell is the matter with you people from the South?"

"Um… nothing? It's just how we eat."

Kat was really starting to get irritated now, though her upbringing kept her from showing it.

"Do you have anything else? I see some fruit down there. Is a banana still a banana or an orange still an orange in your 'South,' or is it like the corn oatmeal?"

Kat was completely flustered by this point. He was being relentless, and she didn't have any idea what to say to this man. She was still disconcerted by the fact that he was Irish and, honestly, that he was there, in person, standing right in front of her. Her temper got the best of her, however, and she told him in her best mom voice, "It's pretty simple, actually. If you don't like what is being served, then don't eat!"

She then looked directly into his eyes and defiantly held his stare until he eventually dropped his gaze to the floor.

Lydia smiled and then playfully hit Ian in the butt with her hand before telling him to take his banana-orange and go sit down so the rest of them could eat.

Wow! What a jerk! Here I thought he seemed like such a nice guy. Obviously, appearances can be deceiving.

Once the breakfast rush was through, Melinda, Gerard, and Kat all sat down to eat their breakfast. Kat looked at both of them and asked, "Are we on set for that show *Western Skies*?"

Melinda swallowed the food she had in her mouth and answered, "Yes."

"But I thought that show was supposed to be in Colorado?"

Gerard studied her for a second and answered, "It's set in Colorado; it's filmed in Canada. It's as close to Colorado as they can get without being there, I guess."

"Why?"

"I don't know; maybe because it's cheaper? Or easier? No one ever told me, and I've never bothered to ask. As long as I get paid, I can work anywhere."

"But… How could you not tell me?" she cried.

"Because you didn't ask?" he answered simply.

"Oh."

They finished eating and cleaned up the mess. Kat sat down with a cup of coffee and picked up her phone. She dialed Jen.

"Hey. How's Lucy?"

"Okay. Still in the hospital. It looks like she has type one diabetes. They want to do more testing today. How's Canada?"

"Oh my gosh, that's so sad! I'm so sorry to hear that. As for Canada, I'm so incredibly mad at you!"

"Mad at me? Why?"

"Why didn't you tell me that we were working on the set of *Western Skies*?"

"I don't know. You didn't ask, I guess. Why? Does it matter?"

"No. Only that the hottest guy on the planet is on this show and he doesn't like grits."

"What?"

"Ian Gregory! He doesn't like grits."

"Who doesn't like grits?"

"I don't know. An Irish actor, apparently. Actually, I don't know if he doesn't like grits. He didn't try them. In fact, my interaction with him was reminiscent of Dr. Seuss' *Green Eggs and Ham* mixed with Abbot and Costello's *Who's on First*."

"It couldn't have been that bad."

"Oh, it could. It was. Bad. Very bad! It took the producer *and* Lydia Swan to get him to back off. She knew how to handle him, that's for sure."

"That's really surprising. For most shoots in town, the assistants come the majority of the time to get the food for the actors, but on location, everyone usually ends up interacting a lot more because they are together so much. They become a sort of dysfunctional family. But from everything I've heard, Ian's really a nice guy; funny, talkative, not at all pretentious. The crew, producers and even past caterers have all said he was a breeze to have on set. None of that normal Hollywood B.S. a lot of actors dish out. Maybe his new-found fame finally got to his head."

"It must have, and now I'm really nervous. He's the star of the show! What happens if he doesn't like what we are serving, Jen?"

"Then we deal with it. It wouldn't be the first time that I've had to work around someone's dietary idiosyncrasies. I have had the strangest requests. One person wouldn't eat any type of oil. That was a fun shoot!"

"Okay. How do I go about finding out what he wants to eat instead, then? I could hardly form a coherent sentence when he was standing in front of me. I don't know if I could actually have a conversation at this point."

"Ah! You're star struck. Don't worry; it happens to all of us at first until you realize they're people, just like us. Most of the time, they all end up being really nice. It's just a bit of an adjustment period until you get comfortable. I promise by the end of the shoot, you'll able to hang out with everyone on set and feel completely fine. Besides, it's the producer we have to please, so don't worry about anyone else. Of course, the actors can influence the producers, but they still have the ultimate say."

"That's what the producer said. He said that if anyone didn't like his choice of caterers, they could go and eat in Calgary."

"Well, there you have it. We make three separate entrées a meal, plus we are also handling craft services, so we have extras, like scones, fruits, and vegetables. Therefore, everyone should be able to find something. No one has ever starved yet on my watch."

"Okay, then. I guess I'd better get back to it. Lunch is coming up soon and I have to make sure that Melinda and Gerard have it handled."

"I promise they do. They are the best in the business. I'll update you on what's going on with Lucy when I know more. Until then, just keep on doing the best you can and stay warm!"

Lunchtime passed in a blur. For this first day, with everyone just getting back into the swing of things, the producer had asked for sandwiches, fruit, and other foods that were more grab and go and able to be eaten as everyone had time. It was an easy prep and clean up, and soon it was time to start dinner.

Gerard, Melinda, and Kat worked on preparing the catfish, okra, and greens for the main entrée. They also had oven-baked 'fried,' free range, antibiotic and hormone free chicken with panko breading, potato salad with extra virgin olive oil mayonnaise, and red beans and rice for the vegetarians. Gerard's specialty was Cajun food, and every night there would be something on the menu with a Louisiana flare.

After a long day of shooting, the set wrapped, and people began filtering into the dining hall. It became loud and boisterous with everyone letting off steam from the stress and worry about the first day of the new season, and it wasn't long before Kat was once again face to face with Ian Gregory.

"Hello," he said.

"Hello," Kat replied and then swallowed nervously.

"So, what have we got here? Let's see… catfish. Is this another trick food like the corn oatmeal? If I actually ingest this, will I be eating cat or fish? Because I have to say I am quite morally opposed to eating cat." He looked down at her with a completely deadpan expression.

Kat returned his look and squinted her eyes. "It's fish," she replied archly.

"Fish? Then why do they call it 'cat'?"

"Because the fish have these little whiskers on their faces…"

Abruptly, she stopped talking and looked up, meeting his eyes. She thought there might have been just a slight twinkle in them, like he was maybe messing with her a little bit, but she couldn't be sure.

"Would you like some?" she asked him.

"Thanks, but I think not. I think I'll stick with this fried chicken. It's just called chicken. I think it's safer than some sort of hybrid creature."

"Ian, stop torturing the poor woman and just grab some food! I know it isn't what you are used to, but my God. It's food. People in another part of the world eat it and they survive." Lydia admonished from right behind him.

Ian glanced over his shoulder at her with a mock pout. "I don't want to merely survive. Eating cat seems like something I would have to do to survive. Besides, isn't a catfish a bottom feeder? I should think that I'd have to be really hungry to eat that!"

"Seriously… Eat, don't eat… It's all the same to me!" Kat snapped before turning her back to him and, still fuming, straightened the utensils that didn't need straightening.

Once he'd taken some chicken and strolled toward a table, Kat turned back around to Lydia who looked up at her with a sympathetic expression. "Don't mind him. He's just messing around. He can be unrelenting. He'll get used to it and be fine in a few days."

Kat just nodded her thanks and went back to making sure that the food was attractively plated and warm.

The rest of the evening went off without a hitch.

The producer came over and thanked them for the wonderful down-home meal, saying it tasted as good as what his Meemaw had cooked when he was a child and that he was so grateful that he finally had some food he could stomach.

As he was talking, Ian walked over to them, complaining, "Okra is gross. It's slimy! Why do you people want to eat slimy veg? What's wrong with where you both come from? Is there a food shortage there or something? Corn oatmeal, hybrid animals, slimy veg. What's wrong with some meat and potatoes? I'm Irish! I have to have potatoes! It's a rule."

"You watch your tongue, Ian." The producer punched him playfully on his upper arm. "This is how I want to eat and I'm still in charge, you know. I hired you and I can fire you."

"For not liking slimy veg?"

"Yes."

"Well, that's complete bollocks!" Ian grumbled.

"Maybe, but my set, my rules!" George retorted with a determined look on his face.

Ian quit fussing with a scowl and Kat breathed a sigh of relief, grateful to get back to the rest of the evening's work.

After the meal finished and everything was cleaned up and prepped for the early morning the next day, Gerard, Kat, and Melinda headed back to their R.V. Kat's feet and back were killing her. She hadn't been that beat in she didn't know how long. They had been up at four in the morning, and it was now close to ten at night. All she wanted to do was to fall directly into bed. As she pulled her sleeping bag up around her, though, she began to worry that she was really messing up and that this Ian guy could cause a huge problem, maybe even convince the producer to find someone else. Her last thought as she drifted off to sleep was that she would have suck it up, find him tomorrow, and ask him what he wanted to eat.

Chapter Thirteen

The next morning, Kat decided to wait until after breakfast to look for Ian. She had purposely stayed back when he came through the line because she just didn't feel like getting into another conversation where he had the upper hand. As he walked by her to leave, he gave her a quick smirk, shook his head, and kept on walking.

Midmorning, she stepped out of the dining hall and walked over to the rows of buildings that created Main Street in the fictitious Colorado town of River City. All kinds of people were roaming around, and she was surprised to see how much attention to detail the set builders had added. It truly looked like a frontier town with the uneven, worn-looking wooden sidewalks and the fake second story facades that were often used for signage in the Western towns of old. Hitching posts for horses were stuck in the ground and spittoons were outside the doors of fabricated businesses. The realistic setting made the large stands of lighting and tracks where the camera operators could move with the actors walking down the street all the more incongruous. Kat had never really thought before about what all went into making a T.V. show or movie. It always looked so natural, like it was happening in real life, with no real indication of all of the activity and equipment behind the scenes that made it happen.

Looking down Main Street, she saw that Lydia and Ian were in the middle of a scene. Lydia's character, Sarah, was upset with Ian's character, Joe, because she felt he was treating her like a child, always checking up on her. They exchanged rapid fire dialogue in what seemed like a very heated argument which culminated in Sarah slapping Joe's face and walking away.

As soon as the scene was over and the director had yelled "Cut!", Lydia and Ian came together, and he wrapped his arm around her shoulders. She looked up at him with adoration as he leaned over and kissed her on the cheek. They walked together like that until they were far off to the side of the set, when Kat overheard Lydia ask if she had hurt him. She caressed the red mark on the side of his face with a gentle hand, apologizing for underestimating the distance between them when she went to do her stage slap which had actually ended up making hard contact. Ian just laughed and gave her a hug, saying "Not a problem, love. I'm fine," before they separated, each heading back toward their respective trailers.

Now's my chance! Kat quickly walked to intercept him so he would be forced to stop and talk with her.

"Um, Mr. Gregory? Hello? Can I talk to you for a second?"

He glanced at her, his expression flat. "If you make it quick."

"I just wanted to check with you and see if there was anything specific you would like me to make for you since you don't seem to like the food?"

He stared down at her for a second and said, "I don't have time for this," before starting to walk away from her.

"Okay, then. Well, please be sure to tell me if there is..." she continued to speak to his departing back, her voice trailing off from her feeble attempt to save face.

For the next week, Kat continued making the menu that she and Jen had discussed. She also made sure to try to stay out of Ian's way as much as possible. She let Melinda and Gerard handle the set up and refilling and managed to find something else to do whenever she saw Ian coming in to eat. He would always have everyone at his table and beyond nearly rolling on the floor laughing, talking a mile a minute very animatedly, but every time he and Kat interacted, he was never so sociable; he seemed to really dislike only her.

As she walked around the set during her downtimes, however, Kat couldn't help studying him. Often he would be reading his script, pacing back and forth as he muttered his lines to himself, moving his free hand around in a circle as he talked. He could also be found sitting on one of the porches, or on a bench with Lydia, reading lines together or talking and laughing with each other. They were obviously very close and had an intimate relationship. Other times, she would find him getting his makeup touched up or talking with the director about a particular scene. Every once in a while, he would glance up and catch Kat looking at him and slightly tip his head in greeting of sorts, at which point she would quickly look down at the ground and continue on her way.

It turned out that there was as much speculation about if Ian and Lydia were indeed a couple on set as off. While very affectionate with each other, they maintained their separate trailers and never engaged in public displays of affections that would confirm they were romantically involved. Every day, the rumors oscillated between them just being really good friends to that their engagement was imminent. Ian was always very attentive and would help Lydia stand up or put her hand in the crook of his arm as she negotiated her voluminous period-appropriate skirts while they negotiated stairs or walked down the street. One time, he was even seen scooping her up and carrying her over a mud puddle, her arms locked around his neck and her head thrown back in laughter. Ultimately, the one thing that everyone could agree on was that they were adorable together and every time they were observed sharing a tender moment, there was a collective "Aw" heard on set.

***

At the end of that first week, Kat was walking down the road, away from the set. She needed some air to clear her head, but the forest was thick around her, and she was a little too intimidated to venture into it very far, as she was scared she might get lost. As she was walking, a Fed Ex truck pulled up and the driver jumped down.

"Hey, lady? Is this the set of that T.V. show, *Western Skies*?" he asked her.

"Yes, it is. Can I help you?"

"Yes, please. I have this envelope for a Mr. I. McGregor. Could you please direct me to him?"

116

Kat didn't have a clue who I. McGregor was. There were so many people on location that she hadn't even begun to learn the names of any others besides Ian, Lydia, and George, the producer.

"I honestly don't have any idea. The set is a bit further down the road though. If you drive further in, you'll probably find someone who knows more than me."

The young driver sighed and started heading back to the truck. Kat heard him mumbling about how he had been driving for an hour and a half to a place in the middle of nowhere, and how he would ever find one particular person on an active set and then his way back to town before dark. He didn't look to be much older than Derrick, and she felt her motherly instinct take over.

"Hey!" she called out. "Give it here. I'll take it with me, and when I walk back, I'll ask around and see if anyone knows who he is."

"Thanks, lady," the kid answered gratefully. He got into his truck and sped away.

Kat walked back toward the set while wondering who she could ask about who this guy was. She wasn't really comfortable talking with anyone other than Melinda and Gerard yet but tucked the envelope under her arm and headed toward a bunch of the crew standing around.

"Hey! Do any of y'all know who a Mr. I. McGregor is?"

She heard a shocked murmur ripple through them.

"What? What did I say? Who is he?"

One of the boom operators replied "Well, uh, that's actually Ian Gregory. His real name is Ian McGregor."

"Oh, of course! Why didn't I realize that? Great! Thanks! Where could I find his assistant or whoever would be able to give this to him?"

"Well, I haven't seen his assistant in a while. But we just finished shooting a scene and I saw Ian heading to his trailer. He's done filming for a little while, so I think that he probably is taking a break."

"Okay, thanks. I guess I'll walk over and see if I can find his assistant along the way."

Heading for the line of trailers, Kat kept one eye open for Ian's assistant as she walked along. Not seeing him, she found herself standing directly in front of Ian's trailer. She thought about dumping the package on the top step and making a run for it, but it had begun to rain lightly, and not knowing what the package contained, she was worried it would get wet and ruined. She took a deep breath and knocked on the door.

"Just a minute!"

She stood there and waited, stepping back so she wouldn't get hit by the door when he swung it open.

Hearing his footsteps come closer, she took a deep breath as he opened the door.

"Oh. It's you," he said dryly. "The caterer."

"Uh, yes. That's me. Sorry to disturb you; I couldn't find your assistant anywhere. I have a package for you." She held it out for him to take.

"So, you are a delivery driver on the side? Don't we pay you enough?" he sneered.

"No! No, not at all! I was out walking, and the poor driver seemed a little overwhelmed by all of this. I told him I would take it to him. I mean you: I. McGregor. I didn't know that I. McGregor was you, or that you were him." Why did he always turn her into a bumbling idiot when she was around him?

"Okay. Thank you, I suppose," he responded.

He took the package and said good day to her as he shut his door.

"Well, that wasn't *so* bad, I guess," she thought as she headed back toward the dining hall.

Chapter Fourteen

As production got under way and people were on a more reliable schedule, Kat found her groove and got more comfortable with what she was supposed to be doing. Jen still needed to be in Los Angeles with David to learn how to navigate Lucy's new diagnosis and didn't know when she would be able to get up to the set to take over, but Kat assured her that things were going better, and that people seemed to be enjoying their specialty cuisine.

She also had more time to herself now that she had gotten her legs under her and had begun to trust that Jen was right: Melinda and Gerard truly were the best in the business. Kat would give them direction to start preparing the evening meal, and then go out on a run in the early afternoon. She had more time to explore and loved to hit the trails around the set. It was a good way for her to burn off stress and think.

After being on location for about two weeks, Kat headed out as usual, pondering her recent conversation with James. He had called her the night before to check in and see how she was doing.

"I'm okay... Getting the hang of things up here. I'm remembering why I loved to do this so long ago! People really do open up around food. And I'm enjoying how much fun happens around here as everyone comes together for meals. From the actors to the crew to the interns, around the table they're all equals, simply enjoying each other's company."

"So, I take it that means that you aren't coming home anytime soon?" James asked dejectedly.

"You'd be correct. Jen's still down in L.A. Lucy has type one diabetes and managing it involves a steep learning curve. Her assistants are marvelous, however, and they really are running the show."

"That's good, I guess, but we all miss you."

"Thank you."

"Don't you miss us?" James asked.

"Of course, I miss everyone. I'm just so busy that I don't actually have time to think about it much. I really miss the kids. We've texted back and forth here and there, but it sounds like everyone is doing all right."

"They are. Everyone here says hello."

"Well, thank you again."

There was silence at the other end of the phone before James said, "Kat, what's going on? What are we going to do? I don't like being in limbo."

"I'm sorry, James, but this is my life, too. Right now, I'm thinking through what I want and how to move on from here. I'm sorry it isn't to your timetable, but this is something I have to do for me."

Kat had ended her call and evaluated how she was feeling. Of course, she truly did miss everyone, but for the first time in as long as she could remember, she was not responsible for anyone's happiness but her own, and it was lovely.

Kat was still deep in thought on the trail when, not seeing a tree root, she tripped, twisted her ankle, and fell down hard on her side. She stood up and tried to put weight on her foot to see if she could walk, but it buckled underneath her, and she fell back down with a grunt. Sitting up, she brushed herself off as well as she could on the ground and looked around at the forest, which seemed to be getting darker and more isolated by the minute. She had been running for quite a while and hadn't told anyone in what direction she was going. For that matter, she hadn't told anyone she was heading out for a run, so no one would even know to look for her until much later, when they realized she was missing.

Suddenly, the idea that she may have to stay out all night hit her. She was not dressed for a cold spring night in the Canadian Rockies. Though the days were warming up, the nights were still below freezing, and she wasn't sure how she would keep warm. She grabbed her cell and decided to try calling Melinda so that maybe someone would be able to find her before it got dark, but then realized that she had taken several turns as she ran, so other than her initial heading from set, she couldn't give any clear information about where she was now. Figuring it was still worth a shot, though, she quickly discovered she didn't have reception where she was among the trees.

Kat had been sitting where she fell for about thirty minutes, trying not to panic, when she heard something. Fearing that it might be some sort of wild animal that would find her sitting basically defenseless on the forest floor, she looked frantically around. She had been warned, like the rest of the set, that while not common, there were still moose, bears, and mountain lions in the area and to be careful.

Another few minutes passed as Kat squinted into the darkening forest, the sun dropping still lower in the sky. She could still hear something approaching, but the trees and the breeze obscured the direction from which it came. A minute or so later, she could just make out the shape of a horse and rider coming around the curve of the trail a bit ahead of where she sat.

Not wanting to spook the horse, she sat patiently until they got close enough to her that she could call out, "Help!"

The horse and rider came closer, and Kat saw it was Ian Gregory.

Of all of the rotten luck.

"Why are you sitting on the ground?" he asked, surprised to see her there.

"Because I tripped over this tree root while I was running, and I've twisted my ankle."

"Can you walk?"

"Not very well. Certainly not all the way back to the set."

"Well, then, I guess it's a good thing I came upon you. I can be your knight in shining armor and rescue you. Would you like a ride back?"

It irritated her no end that he looked so smug, literally perched up high on his horse.

"Seeing as I have no other option, yes, please."

Ian jumped down off of his horse and helped her to her feet.

"Have you ever ridden before?"

"Yes. My grandparents owned a horse farm in Kentucky when I was a kid. But," she paused, looking warily at the saddle, "I've never ridden Western before."

Ian gave her a cockeyed grin that emphasized his dimples. "Well, I had never been on a horse before in my life when I auditioned for this part, but I've learned a lot. I lied when they asked me if I rode, and for the first few episodes it was completely obvious I was clueless about what to do. I've gotten better, though. Are you ready? Can you get up there?"

"I think so. He's tall! I think if I can just get this foot into the stirrup, though, I should be able to put enough weight on this foot to lift myself up."

Suddenly his hands were around her waist as she put her foot into the stirrup, and he lifted her up off of the ground. Once she was situated, he swung up easily behind her. She sat perfectly still as his arms went around her and took the reins to control the horse. Mere inches from his body, she felt like she could barely breathe. With his face right over her shoulder, he quietly said near her ear, "I'd better hold him. He's a good boy, but he's used to me."

"Oh! Okay! That's fine. Thanks for the ride."

They rode together in silence for the few miles back to the set. The horse swaying, the throbbing of her ankle, and the warmth of the horse beneath and Ian behind her all combined to make Kat feel very sleepy. She had to work hard to stay focused on the trail and hold herself upright rather than lean into Ian, until they reached the dining hall.

"Wait up there until I get down and I'll help you, so you don't put any weight on that foot." He jumped down effortlessly and reached back up as she started her descent. Once more she felt his strong hands around her hips as he guided her to the ground.

"Can you walk now?" he asked her.

She tried to take a step and winced. "Not really," she said with a grimace and trying not to whimper in pain. "It hurts too much."

Ian had her put her arm across his shoulders and he supported her as she hopped inside the building. Helping her ease down into a chair, he told her to sit tight while he disappeared back into the kitchen. He returned a few minutes later with a bag of ice wrapped in a towel.

"Thanks," she told him as he placed it over her ankle. He bent down and began to unlace her running shoe and took it off before rolling down her sock and feeling along the edges of her ankle where it had begun to swell.

"That doesn't look so good," he told her, seeing the swelling and bruising. "I'm going to go find one of the medics to come and take a look at this." With that, he got up, turned on his heel, and left her alone.

As she sat there, she could not believe that in the span of four weeks, she had gone from seeing this man for the first time on her T.V. to having him put ice on her injured ankle in the middle of the Canadian Rockies.

A short time later, Ian came walking back in with a medic from the crew. The medic adeptly moved her foot around and declared that he thought it was just a sprain, but that she should probably go have it x-rayed down in Calgary, just to make sure.

Kat inhaled sharply and said, "I can't do that! I have all of these people to feed in just a few hours. Not only that, but I also can't drive."

The medic looked at her and shrugged his shoulders. He turned to Ian and asked if there was anyone who could drive her down the mountain. Ian looked at him and then at Kat before declaring, "I can."

Kat locked eyes with him. "What?" she asked, incredulously.

"I can," he repeated. "I'm not filming for the rest of the day, which was why I was out for a ride. I don't really have anything else to do for the rest of the afternoon actually."

"Well, thank you—that's really kind—but I can't go. I have to feed everyone."

"I saw your two assistants back there when I went to get the ice and they seem to have everything under control. I think they can get along without you for one meal."

Kat looked at Ian and then the medic. "Is it really necessary?"

"I think it would be for the best, yes."

Kat finally nodded. "I guess I have to, then. Are you sure, Mr. Gregory, that you don't mind?"

"Please, it's Ian, and if I minded, I wouldn't have offered. I'm kind of selfish like that," he grinned at her.

"What about Lydia? Won't she be mad?" Kat asked nervously.

"I don't think so. We have all had our spills up here. She'll understand. I think the medical community in Calgary is pretty well prepared for our group by now when they know we're filming."

With Kat's permission, Ian and the medic raised her up onto her good foot and then Ian once again put her arm around his shoulders and supported her as she hopped to the door. Leaving her resting against the doorjamb, he ran off to grab a car. A few minutes later he pulled up to the door, parked, and ran around to open the passenger door before returning to help her get in. As he leaned over and fastened her seat belt she hardly dared to breathe, but she could faintly smell his aftershave. He shut her door, climbed in himself and they drove away from the set.

Kat couldn't think of anything to say so finally, she turned to him and simply said, "Thanks."

"Not a problem! I'd do the same for anyone on set. That was a nasty spill. I'm just glad that I found you or you would have had a very rough night. There's a storm rolling in and it's going to get cold and snowy."

"I appreciate all your help. Thanks for knowing what to do."

"It's my Scout training," he said with a wink.

"You were a Boy Scout?"

"I was!"

"I didn't know there were Boy Scouts in Ireland. Or at least

I had never thought about whether there were Boy Scouts in Ireland or not," she said with a grin.

"Ireland was one of the first countries outside of the U.S. to have Scouting. The first meeting was held there in 1908."

Kat looked over at him, impressed, as he focused on the curving mountain road before them. "How do you remember that?"

He shrugged. "We had to learn it at some point, and I guess it just stuck. I've always had a good memory, I suppose. Helps with my career—it doesn't take me long to learn my lines."

"My boys did Scouting for a while."

"Your boys?"

"Yes. I have two boys. One is twenty-two and the other is seventeen."

He quickly glanced over at her. "How is that possible? Were you twelve when you had your first?"

"Bless your heart! No, I was twenty-one. I also have a daughter who is twenty now herself, though I can't imagine her having a baby right now."

"I can't believe that you have three kids!" He shook his head in disbelief.

"Well, believe it, because I do. Derrick, my twenty- two-year-old, is an engineering major and is graduating in May. Olivia is a sophomore at university, and Drew, my youngest, will be graduating high school also in May. How about you? Any kids?"

He threw his head back and laughed. "None that I know about, anyway," he answered.

"Um… I guess that's good?"

He just grinned at her in response.

When they arrived at the hospital, Ian went inside to grab a wheelchair and helped to settle her in the seat. He then pushed her into the waiting room and went to explain why they were there. After he returned, he reported that there shouldn't be too much of a wait.

Kat was indeed called back shortly, with Ian pushing her

into the exam room. He then proceeded to sit down in one of the armchairs set out for patients' families. Kat, feeling uncomfortable, looked over at him.

"Thanks. You really don't have to stay. I can call and ask Melinda or Gerard to come and get me. I'm sure this will take a while and one of them can just drive down here after dinner."

"Don't be ridiculous," Ian scoffed. "I don't have anywhere else to go and I'm already here, so I'll just wait with you until you are done."

"Well, okay, but you really don't need to wait right here with me. You might be more comfortable waiting out in the waiting room. "

Ian cocked his head to one side. "Are you trying to get rid of me?"

"No! No, not at all! But I can't imagine sitting in here with me is all that thrilling."

"It's fine. I'm sort of enjoying the company. Better than waiting out there by myself without anyone else to talk to. Or worse, surrounded by people who recognize me and then having to talk to everyone. Here I can hide out and feel comfortable."

Kat glanced over at him. He was sitting, leaning forward with his feet planted flat on the floor, his elbows resting on his knees, and his hands clasped in front of him. His hair, usually slicked back off of his face for his role, was flopping onto his forehead. His dark blue eyes suddenly looked up at her sitting on the gurney, and he smiled when he caught her looking at him. She felt her heart stutter for a second: she still couldn't believe that she was sitting there, two feet away from him.

He broke the silence. "So, your name is Katherine?" "Yes, but I don't go by that. Everyone just calls me Kat."

"It didn't dawn on me until they called you out there in the waiting room that I didn't even know your name."

"Yeah, I guess it's because you're used to everyone knowing yours."

"You didn't," he grinned.

Kat became flustered and blushed. "Well, no not your given

126

name. I meant your stage name.”

“Don’t be embarrassed. It was an easy mistake.”

“It isn’t like it’s so incredibly different.”

“No, but how many actors do you know who don’t use their given names?”

“Point taken,” Kat agreed.

The doctor came in and asked what had happened. Ian and Kat began talking over each other, each giving their own versions to the story. Finally, Ian looked at her and said, “So sorry. Why don’t you tell him?”

The doctor examined her foot and ankle and confirmed what the medic on set had said, that it was most likely just a severe sprain, but that they would take an x-ray just to be sure. He then left the room and left Kat and Ian alone again.

“So… You’re Irish,” Kat said.

“I am. And you’re American. Southern American.”

“Yes, yes I am,” Kat laughed. “What brought you to the States? Or, Canada, I guess, as the case may be?” she continued.

“Well, I started out in Ireland as a young lad in commercials, which led to walk-on parts and eventually smaller roles in the U.K. I got full of myself and decided that I should make my way to Hollywood on a three-month tourist visa waiver to see if I could get cast anywhere. I did and started once again with commercials and small parts. It wasn’t much, but it allowed me to stay. Eventually I started to get larger parts, and even had a couple of shows which lasted a full season before they were canceled. It had started to wear on me though, and so I was thinking about going back home, when on a whim I auditioned for this little production my agent had heard about. As I told you back on the trail, I completely lied about my horsemanship. I think I may have even said that I played polo back home!” He chuckled and winked at her. “By the grace of God, I was cast for the part. I came up here for the first season, fully expecting that it would be another stop gap. Little did I know that people would like it so much and that it would take off. What about you? How did you end up here in the backwoods of Canada?”

"It's a long and boring story," she stated with a sigh.

"I can't believe that. Everyone has an interesting story."

"Hmm… Where to start, then? My friend Jen and I decided to start a catering business after high school. We had worked for a caterer before graduation on the weekends to make some extra cash. The guy was the most inept businessperson ever but he managed to make money, so we figured it would be a good way to pay for our post- secondary school. Two years later, though, I was married at twenty, had my first baby when I was twenty-one, and then had two more in quick succession while Jen had gone to L.A."

She took a deep breath and continued, "I'd been married almost twenty-three years when I recently discovered my husband was having an affair. I thought I would be able to stay and work it out, but one day, I just got into my car and drove to Jen in L.A. She had just gotten this gig and was very excited. She'd been bugging me forever to be a partner, but obviously I couldn't, being married with three kids and living all the way across the country from her. I needed to escape though, so I did. I drove cross country to join her. Right before we came up here, however, Jen's daughter had a seizure. She had to stay in L.A. with Lucy and her ex-husband to be there for the tests and such, so I came up here by myself with her two assistants. And here I am." Kat gave him a weak smile.

"Your ankle still hurting?" he asked her.

"Yes, a little. Mostly, I'm just really tired and want to get back to the trailer and into bed."

At that moment, an orderly came to take her down to x-ray. Ian stood to go with her when the man turned to him and said, "I'm sorry, sir. Patients only. You can wait here for your wife."

Kat's head shot up. "Oh! He's not my husband!" she began to explain.

"Oh, so sorry. My mistake. You can stay here and wait for your… whatever," he corrected, grabbing the handles of Kat's wheelchair, and pushing her toward the hallway. Kat turned back and looked at Ian and mouthed, "I'm sorry!" as she was being wheeled away. He just looked at her and shrugged, as if to say, "What are you going to do?"

Several hours later, Kat was told she was soon to be the proud owner of an orthopedic boot and crutches.

Though she had not broken a bone, the doctor had informed her that she had a nasty sprain and needed to stay off of her feet for a few days. When she heard the news, Kat told him, "I can't do that! I'm the head caterer on the *Western Skies* set up in the mountains. I have to be able to walk."

The doctor scowled at her in annoyance and told her that he still wanted her to rest and elevate her foot as much as possible, to which Ian replied, "We'll make sure she stays off of that foot. Thank you, doctor."

"Wait here for your boot, crutches, and discharge paperwork," he said as he exited the room. Kat looked at Ian and sighed.

"What?"

"How are you going to keep me off my foot? I have to prepare meals three times a day for almost a hundred people."

"I can help."

"Really? You can help? In case you don't remember, you have a job already. It's called being the lead actor in a T.V. program. Somehow, I don't think the producer will take too kindly to your sudden desire to change your career focus."

"I'm not in every scene. I'll just make sure that I come and help when I can."

Kat eyed him suspiciously before asking, "Why are you being so nice to me all of a sudden?"

"Honestly, I don't know," he admitted. "I guess I must like you."

There was that crooked grin again, making her heart skip a beat.

"Like me? You don't even know me!" she exclaimed.

"You're right. I don't. But there's something intriguing about you, Kat. I feel comfortable when I'm around you, like I can be myself. It's not something that actors are generally able to do, at least not right away. Everybody always seems to want a pound of flesh."

"I don't really understand why you would feel that way. You've never even spoken to me before today, except to complain about my food."

"Oh, yeah. Sorry about that. I can be quite the sarcastic *eejit* sometimes." He looked down at the floor. "Usually when I'm nervous. And stressed," he added the last bit quickly.

"Why would you be nervous?"

"Because I'm actually quite shy," he replied, with a smirk.

"Yeah, sure you are. Okay. Why were you stressed, then?"

Ian instantly became serious. "Because my mother is sick and I'm trying to purchase a house in Los Angeles for her. That's what the Fed Ex driver delivered the other day: the mortgage paperwork. I'll live there too, of course, when I'm not up here. Northern Ireland is too cold and rainy, and she's getting too old to be there by herself. I visit on breaks when I can, but it's not enough. At least if she's in Los Angeles, I can get back to her relatively quickly."

"Oh. I'm so sorry!" Kat told him. "But what about your father?"

"My father died when I was just a lad."

"Oh, my gosh! I'm so sorry!"

"Thank you. It was a long time ago."

"What happened, if you don't mind me asking? Was he sick?"

"You know… February 28, 1985?" he asked her.

Kat looked over at him and shrugged. "No. I don't recall anything specific about that date. Should I?"

Ian was quiet for a moment. "I supposed you wouldn't, with you being American. Well, it was the day of the worst attack ever carried out by the I.R.A. There was a mortar attack on a constable station."

"Oh, my gosh! Your father was killed by the I.R.A? Constable… was he a policeman?"

"He was indeed a policeman, but he wasn't killed at that

130

station. His was the other tragedy that day, at least for my family. My father was on duty and stabbed by a man he was just trying to get home from the pub. The guy was really pissed and not in his right mind."

"Oh, wow! I'm so sorry. I don't know what to say… That's terrible! Why was the guy so angry? That must have been really hard to grow up without your father," Kat said remorsefully.

Ian laughed. "Pissed back home means something very different than in the States. The guy was, how should I say, blind-assed drunk." He continued, "It was awful. I was only seven at the time. My ma was a nurse and she worked hard. My sister and I were on our own a lot. We had our grandparents and our neighbors who all pitched in, but Ma was often still lonely and tired. It's the least I can do for her to take care of her now."

"Wow. She's really lucky to have a son like you. And you have a sister?"

"I do. She's a solicitor in London. She works in the City there."

"Is she older or younger than you?"

"Two years younger. She's married to another solicitor, and they have a two-year-old little girl. We aren't close. We like each other and all, but we don't have a lot in common. She went into law enforcement, of sorts, like my father, and I play a sheriff on T.V. Not exactly the same thing, but kind of coincidental, don't you think?" Ian smiled.

"So, you're still in your thirties, then?"

"I am."

"Oh, wow. I feel so old." Kat shook her head.

"Why? How old are you?"

"I just turned forty-three a few weeks ago."

"I guess that would make sense, since you have a twenty-two-year-old. Which I still can't fathom, by the way."

"So, yeah, I'm almost six years older than you," Kat sighed.

"And? What's the big deal? Age is just a number."

Kat studied him for a few seconds. Was he flirting with her? Something in his tone of voice made her wonder if perhaps he was more telling himself than her that age didn't matter. She then quickly admonished herself for being so stupid. Of course, he wasn't flirting with her! He was with Lydia, that much was abundantly clear.

The nurse came into the room, gave them Kat's discharge instructions, and told them they could leave. Kat tried to navigate the crutches they had given her, but when they reached the exit, she saw it was snowing lightly.

"Oh, great. Now I'll break my neck!" she cried, exasperated.

Ian told her to wait there and took off, sprinting across the snowy parking lot to the car. Having gotten her in and settled, he patted her leg as he stood up, shut the door, and returned to his place behind the wheel. Soon, they were heading back out of town and up into the mountains.

They hadn't talked as much since getting in the car. Ian was watching the road intently as the spring snow swirled around them, and Kat didn't want to disturb him when he was concentrating so hard.

After a while, though, he laughed and said, "Honestly, you're brave to ride with me. I'm still not one hundred percent comfortable driving on this side of the road, especially when I'm tired and there isn't anyone coming at me from the other direction to remind me. So, if I start to drift over, please say something!"

"Oh, gosh! I didn't even think about that. Are you okay to drive in this?"

"Well of course, being Irish, I can drive in the dark and rain pretty well. This much snow has taken some getting used to, but it's supposed to be Colorado, after all. We'd get some at home, but nothing compared to this. After being up here for the last two seasons, though, I've gotten pretty good."

They fell back into silence, listening to the radio playing softly as they wound their way up to the location.

By the time they made it back to the set, it was late enough that dinner was over, and people were heading back toward their respective trailers to sleep in preparation for the early morning.

Following her directions, Ian found her trailer and parked in front. The snow was considerably deeper here, so he told her to sit tight before getting out. He then knocked on the trailer door before flinging it open without waiting for a response. When he came back to the car, he opened her door, reached inside, and then lifted Kat up easily into his arms.

"What are you doing?" she exclaimed, shocked that he would do such a thing.

"I'm carrying you into the trailer so that you don't slip and fall," he responded, like it was the most natural thing in the world.

He took her up the stairs and put her down on the couch and then ran back outside to get her crutches, before looking to Melinda and Gerard.

"The doctor said she has to stay off of this ankle for a few days. Can you manage without her?"

Both Gerard and Melinda assured him that they would be fine, and that Kat could take the time she needed to recover. With that, he gave them all a salute and walked out the door. As soon as the door shut, Melinda turned to her and proclaimed in light-hearted envy, "Lucky bitch!"

Kat looked up, surprised. "Why would you say that?"

"I swear I would maim myself in order to have that man carry me anywhere. You just also spent all afternoon and evening with him- alone. He carried you back on his horse, ran to get the ice and the medic, drove you to the hospital, drove you home, and carried you inside. As I said, lucky bitch!"

Kat looked sheepish but then gleefully cried out, "It was kind of worth maiming myself! He even buckled my seatbelt for me. Twice!"

Melinda just shook her head. "Don't even go on. It will just make me hate you. Every woman on this set was wishing she were you."

"Well, they can take this stupid sprained ankle, then. Besides, what about Lydia?"

"What about her? Even if they are together, a woman can

enjoy a little attention from a man without being romantically involved."

"Yeah, I guess so. I just don't know why he was being so nice, especially when he was so nasty earlier."

"That's just the kind of guy he is," Melinda replied. "He likes to help others and is really personable."

"He wasn't that way with me. He was quite the jerk!"

Gerard suddenly looked up from his crossword puzzle. "Maybe he likes you," he declared simply.

Chapter Fifteen

The next afternoon, still in costume, Ian came to visit Kat. Having knocked before entering, he wiped his muddy boots and carefully made his way back to the bedroom, where Kat was lying with her foot propped up on some pillows. Leaning against the doorjamb, arms crossed, he asked how she was doing.

"I'm okay," Kat said. "The foot is a little tender, but I guess that's to be expected."

"I should say so!"

Kat looked at him and said, "Would you like to come in? You don't have to stay there in the threshold."

Ian moved inside and sat down on the edge of her bed. "Can I get you anything? Have you eaten? Need a drink?"

Kat shook her head. "I'm fine. Thanks, though."

"My pleasure. Let me know if that changes and I can help."

They sat in silence for a few minutes and then both glanced up at the same time, their eyes meeting. Kat held his gaze for a few seconds before he cleared his throat and looked away.

"I'm glad that you are doing a little better."

"I am. Thanks! I really appreciate all that you did for me yesterday. I still can't believe that the star of a T.V. show would take me to the hospital and sit with me for hours, and then take me home through a snowstorm."

"I certainly hope, Kat, that you consider me more than just a T.V. star. In fact, that's what I like about you. You stood up to me, treated me like I was everyone else. Most of the time, women get all soppy and weird around me when they first meet me, not argue about what grits are. They can't seem to separate Joe from Ian and it's as if they get the vapors! You seemed to see me as Ian, the man, and not Joe, the sheriff of River City."

"I guess I just hid it better than most then, because I was in shock and felt like I couldn't think straight," Kat heard herself admit. She was then horrified to hear herself continue, "Then again, while some of it was you, most of it was that it dawned on me at that moment that I'd come all of the way up here to work on a show and had never even bothered to ask which show it was! Goes to show you how desperate I was to escape my current situation at the time."

She cocked her head to the side and asked, "By the way, I have to ask: how come you sound so American on screen when you sound so Irish when you're not?"

"Didn't you ever mess about with different accents when you were a kid?"

"We did, of course. We'd try to be British or French or German. Sounded terrible, obviously, with our Southern drawls, but we still did it."

"Well, we did that, too, only with American or Canadian pronunciations. Most of the popular movies and T.V. shows come from this side of the pond, and we all wanted to sound like you."

She grinned. "Not like me. If you sounded like me, you would have said, 'We all wanted to sound like all y'all'."

"I said we practiced American English, not Southern," he quipped back. "Here, let me try it. 'How're y'all doin'?' Hmm… That is definitely an accent—actually a language—unto itself. I think you have to be born into knowing how to speak that way."

Kat laughed at him. "You're probably right. You do an American accent really well, but—sorry to break it to you— Southern not so much."

"Hey, give me a break! That was my first time! And I've had some help with my accent. Some sounds are just a little too different for me to manage on my own so I'm grateful I had such a good diction coach. If you noticed, I really try to not break character when I'm on set, so I don't mess up and we don't have to re-shoot. That's why I use Joe's accent even when the cameras aren't rolling: if I don't, I can fall right back into my Irish brogue." He winked at her.

The two of them spent a few hours together talking. Building on their conversations from the day before, they compared their childhoods in their respective countries and their families. Kat eventually shared that she had three brothers, and he looked shocked.

"So, I should worry about speaking to you, then?" he asked with a grin.

"No, I think as long as you are not James, you're safe."

"Who's James?"

"Oh! He's my... Well... He's my James. He was my husband. Still is technically, I guess, but as I said, he cheated on me, and so he is now just... my James. I don't know what to do with him, honestly. So, I ran away."

"Are you going to divorce him?" Ian asked.

"I'm not sure. I think so, but then I get nostalgic about the history we share, which makes it harder. I figured I'd be growing old with him. Having our grandchildren come over while we sat on the front porch, sipping lemonade."

"It must be hard to have the rug ripped out from under you like that. You had your life all set, or so you thought, and then it got all turned upside down and inside out." Ian stated, while looking at her with so much intensity it made her forget to breathe.

"It got all cattywampus," Kat practically whispered.

"What is 'cattywampus'?" Ian asked her with a look of utter confusion on his face.

Kat managed to pull herself back together. "It's an old Southern term. You know... that language unto itself? It means when something goes completely, utterly off track or wrong."

He laughed. "That is honestly the craziest word I've ever heard! And that's saying a lot since I'm from Great Britain, the home of Gaelic and Welsh!"

"It sure is. I'm from the South and *I* still think it's a crazy word!"

"Kat, I learn something new from you each time we talk. I enjoy it. You bring me back to reality and remind me I still have a lot to learn, regardless of my fame."

Kat blushed a lovely shade of pink and shrugged her shoulders. "Thanks."

Ian stood up and ran his hands down the front of his pants to straighten them. "Well, I need to get back to the set to discuss tomorrow's shoot."

"Of course. Have a good night!"

Ian leaned over and kissed her on the forehead. "Good night, Kat," he said as he headed out the door. "I'll see you tomorrow."

Kat lay in her bed and stared at the ceiling. They had only really known each other for a few days, but he made her stomach feel like it was full of butterflies. Not like when she had seen him on T.V., but like a schoolgirl seeing her crush. She couldn't believe that she was developing feelings for him, feelings she knew she shouldn't be having, but she couldn't seem to help.

I am a married woman, a mother of three. He is six years younger than me, together with Lydia, and an actor. He is just playing another part. I'm stupid to think that there is actually anything to this! she reasoned with herself. And with that, she rolled over and fell asleep.

Chapter Sixteen

When Kat woke up early the following morning and moved her ankle around, she discovered it felt considerably better, so she gingerly swung her feet over the edge of the bed, put on her boot, and stood up.

Definitely better Kat thought to herself as she took a few steps toward the door on her way to the bathroom.

She got dressed and ventured outside onto the wet ground with her crutches and carefully hobbled toward the dining hall. There were still patches of snow in the shady spots and she was terrified that she was going to slip. When she had made it about halfway to her destination, she saw Ian step out from between two trailers. As soon as he saw her, his face lit up with a smile and he hurried over to her.

"You're up and about! How are you feeling?"

"Okay, thanks. Better. Scared to death I'm going to slip on this ice, though."

"How about I walk with you to make sure you get there?"

"You don't have anywhere else to be?" Kat asked.

"The good thing about being the lead is that they can't start without me." He said as he glanced at her sideways, looking cheeky.

"Nice. So, I'll be the one who gets into trouble, not you."

"You are the Magic Chef of Southern Cuisine! George wouldn't dare fire you or he might starve to death." Ian declared. Kat smiled wryly, hoping fervently that it was true.

They continued together in silence. Every few seconds, Kat couldn't help herself, and would glance up at Ian's profile. She still couldn't believe that she was here, and with *him*! At one point, she sneaked a peak at him again and they locked eyes, and while Ian grinned at her, Kat quickly looked down and blushed. Kat was flustered and didn't know what to say, though she felt she had to say something. "Thanks for walking with me."

"Not a problem. Hey, after lunch, would you like to go

horseback riding with me? I know that you can't walk too far yet, but maybe you've got cabin fever and would like to get out for some fresh air and sunshine?"

"I'd like that."

"I'll tack the horses and be here around two, if that works?"

"It should. We can touch base at lunchtime, if that's okay?"

"Sounds great! Well, you made it, so I'll take my leave."

He leaned in, kissed her on the cheek, and then held the door open for her. She lurched inside and found Melinda and Gerard already elbow deep in the breakfast prep. They sat Kat down to do the chopping and stirring and anything else that would keep her as immobile as possible. From her seat further back in the kitchen, she watched everyone coming in and saw Ian come up to the buffet with Lydia and get his plate. Lydia turned and looked into his eyes as she said something to him.

Kat couldn't hear what she had said, but she saw Ian's head tip back and she heard him laughingly respond. "Lydia, I love you!" He then bent over and kissed the top of her head. Kat's heart sunk.

What was that?

Just as quickly, though, she told herself she was being ridiculous, that Ian was just a friend and that she was crazy to read anything more than that in their interactions.

He feels responsible for me since he helped me in the woods. That's all! He's just trying to be a nice guy. He and Lydia are obviously a couple.

Kat returned her attention to the tasks at hand. The rest of the morning and the lunch rush flew by, so she was surprised when a few minutes after two o'clock, Ian walked in and asked if she was ready to go. She checked quickly with Gerard and Melinda that it was okay if she left before she hobbled to meet him. Outside, his large black horse was tied up, and beside him was a beautiful brown mare with a white starburst on her forehead. Kat cried out in delight when she saw the gorgeous creature standing in front of her and while balanced on the crutches under her arms, clapped her hands like a delighted child.

"Oh, she's so beautiful! I haven't ridden since I was a girl."

"She's Lydia's horse."

He stepped behind her to again grabbed her hips and lifted her so she could find the stirrups and get into the saddle before hopping onto his own horse.

"She's really gentle. Lydia didn't have any real experience riding horses either, except as therapy animals. Unlike me, though, she didn't lie about it, so they gave her this gentle girl. I got the feisty one."

"Therapy horses? Did Lydia work with them, or...?"

Ian looked sternly at her. "I shouldn't have said that. In fact, please forget I said anything about it." His expression and body language made clear that he was unwilling to say anything more.

"Okay," Kat agreed, nonplussed.

They rode a trail that wound through the trees. After they had gone about three miles away from the set, Kat heard the trickle of water. She looked to the side and saw that they were following a stream. She was just about ready to comment on it when the trail turned to the right, and they stepped into a beautiful meadow bordered on the far side by a small lake. Beyond that, the mountain tops reached ever heavenward, topped with snow remaining from the winter storms.

Kat gasped. "Oh, my word! This is the most gorgeous place I have ever seen!"

"It's beautiful, for sure. Nothing can beat these mountains. I love my Irish landscapes but being here next to these peaks and under this big, blue sky, I feel small; insignificant. And, as I said yesterday, it isn't a bad thing for an actor to be reminded that the world doesn't revolve around them and that not everyone will just fall at their feet," he stated matter-a-factly. "It reminds me out here to stay grounded and true to who I am. Everybody in Los Angeles is so caught up with appearances. They're always trying to look younger, skinnier, more ripped... Out here it's obvious we're all but a speck in time. It's a true reality check. Our existence doesn't mean anything in relation to the amount of time these mountains have stood, regardless of who we are.”

“That was beautiful.”

“That’s me: a bloody poet!” He grinned sheepishly.

“You’re certainly nothing at all like I imagined.”

“You imagined me? Hmm… I’m intrigued.”

Kat felt her cheeks grow hot as she looked straight ahead. “Well, you know when you see someone on T.V., you don’t know who they are. You only see their character. You have no idea if the person who plays that character is anything like them in real life, or completely different.

“With Jen doing this for so many years, she’s told me stories. People think certain actors and actresses must be so nice because of the role they play, but in reality they can be real pains.”

“You mean like how you thought I was when you first met me?”

Kat was quiet for a minute. She wanted to think about her answer rather than just blurting something out.

“Well, yes, I did think you were a bit of a jerk when I first met you,” she admitted. “It felt like you thought you had something to prove, like an alpha male marking his territory.”

“I’m sorry about that. I honestly don’t know what came over me. I was flustered, nervous.”

“Because it was the first day on the set for the new season?”

“Not at all. This isn’t work to me. It’s fun. I get paid to dress up and be someone else. I was nervous… well… I was nervous because of you.”

“Me?”

“You!”

“Why were you nervous about me?” Kat was dumbfounded.

“I don’t honestly know. There’s something about you, Kat. I think it was the way that you talked to me like I was a regular person. You weren’t trying to impress me, like so many other people do. You had a confidence about you that made me feel like I was just like everyone else in that room, not the star of the show. It threw me for a loop, as you say. I kept waiting for you to offer to make me something else, but you didn't. You didn't let me intimidate or boss you into submission."

"Wow. I really had you fooled then because I was completely intimidated, and I was terrified you were going to have us fired. Jen had left all of this in my hands, and I was mentally running through how I would tell her that I had ruined everything on the first day!"

They stopped the horses on the far side of the lake and Ian helped Kat down before leading the horses to a tree to tie them up. Kat sat on the grass, watching while he picked up some rocks and started to throw them toward the water in an attempt to skip them.

Kat observed him for a few minutes, before she called, "Give me those!"

She took the rocks and managed to skip the first one four times before it plunged into the water with a final dramatic splash.

"Hey! How did you do that so well?" Ian was shocked.

"Practice. Years and years of practice. I had three brothers growing up, remember? And then I had two sons. I was surrounded by boys who liked to get dirty and wet."

"I like to get dirty and wet."

Kat turned her head to look at him, wondering if he had really just said what she thought she heard. It wasn't so much his words, but how he had said them. When he saw her gaping at him, he chuckled.

"Just seeing if you were paying attention."

Kat turned back toward the lake and set her eyes far across the water. She was once again analyzing everything he said, wondering if she was hearing propositions that weren't there or making more of what he said than what he meant. Much like with his interviews regarding Lydia, she Kat realized he was very good at saying just enough to leave a question hanging in the air. As soon as she had convinced herself that she was indeed making too much of things, he made her wonder all over again with his next flippant comment.

"So, tell me about 'your James,' as you call him. How did you meet, that sort of thing?"

"He and I met in college in the library. We had an anthropology class together and I had noticed him across the room, but never thought he'd even looked in my direction. He came over to me, though, and asked if he could borrow my notes from the last class. Of course, I let him. It wasn't until a few days later that it dawned on me that I had seen him in class that day. We started dating soon after. He made me feel unique and special when no one had really even given me the time of day before. I felt so lucky that he was interested in me. He was, and still is, a very good-looking guy. He's tall, with nice brown eyes and blonde hair. Not very athletic, but still in decent shape.

"Anyway, he was almost done with his accounting degree and seemed to be everything I ever wanted. And for twenty-three years, he was: he worked hard, did things with the family, and seemed to love the life we had built together. I think that is why his cheating was such a shock. I never had any indication that he was feeling unfulfilled."

"That must have been rough."

"It was. It still is. And I need to decide soon what to do about the situation. I had an attorney draw up the documents to file for divorce when I found out, but I chickened out before actually filing them. I don't know why. He cheated on me. His actions told me that I wasn't good enough. So, why am I struggling when I think about ending it? I don't think I love him anymore, but I can't tell if that's really it or if his actions hurt me so badly and made me so angry that they are blinding me from my true feelings."

"I can understand that. Giving up the dream of a perfect family is sometimes the hardest thing of all," Ian said simply.

"That's exactly it! I really don't think I love him anymore. I think I was comfortable. I thought that he would be my life. It never even dawned on me that we even could, much less would, change course."

"I hope you realize that this is not your fault," Ian said. "I hope you understand that it was his choice and there isn't any excuse for it."

"I know. But I still can't help but wonder if I could have done something better. Something different that would have made all this heartache unnecessary, you know?"

"I know that he must be a fool to give you up," Ian remarked.

There it was again, his saying things that made her heart skip a beat.

"You are a good and caring woman, Kat. I'm a good judge of character—blame my dad's being a cop— and I can tell that you are supportive and unassuming. Most of all, I can tell you are loyal, both to yourself and to others. You're true to form, you don't falter. And believe me when I say that steady, calm women tend to be a rarity in my line of work!"

"Thanks. So, um, now that I've poured out my heart to you, what's your story? Any sordid past love affairs, any telling history?"

"Not really. I've never really been interested in women."

"Oh!" Kat exclaimed in surprise, wondering how her reading of him had been so completely off.

Ian sat quietly for a second, then threw his head back and started laughing when he saw her expression. "Well, no, *that's* not what I meant. I like women; I've just never had a lot of interest in having a serious relationship. I think it's because I don't really know who I am or what I want out of this life yet. But, more importantly, I can't know what a woman wants out of me. Will she really love me for me? Or only for one of my characters, my growing fame, or for my money? It's my worst nightmare that I'll wake up next to someone after having been married for a few years and realize that the only thing we had going for us was her infatuation with me that I interpreted as love."

"You don't have to worry about that with Lydia, though, right?" Kat tried fishing for information.

"No, I don't have to worry about that with Lydia," Ian agreed. With that, he stood up and offered to help Kat up. He went back to grab the horses and led them back to her. His demeanor made it clear that no matter what was going on between him and Lydia, he was not willing to talk about it.

Chapter Seventeen

A few days after her accident, Ian came into the kitchen around two o'clock again. He smiled when he saw Kat perched on a stool, chopping vegetables for the night's meal. Walking over to her, he exclaimed, "Looks like fun!"

Kat looked up and smiled back.

"It is! At least seeing your face will be after I tell you we're having—what did you call them? Oh, yeah, 'slimy veg.'"

Ian reached over and grabbed an okra.

"How can something that looks so much like a miniature zucchini be so misleading? It looks innocuous enough, but when you cook it… Yuck!" Ian made a face and shook his head.

"You remind me of my kids when they were little and had to eat their vegetables. How old are you again, Ian?"

"Old enough to know that I don't *have* to eat slimy vegetables if I don't want to!" he retorted with mock haughtiness.

"Yes, Ian. You're a big boy. You can choose to eat what you want. I won't make you clean your plate or even try a bite. But I'll tell you that they will be hand-breaded and fried in peanut oil."

"Does that make it better?"

"Ian, when is something breaded and fried in peanut oil *not* better?" she asked incredulously.

"Okay. I'll try one bite to prove to you that peanut oil can do nothing for this sorry excuse for a veg. What else is on the menu for tonight?"

"For the main course, I'm doing mock ham hock and beans, served with mustard greens. Fried apples will complete the meal. I say mock ham hock because some people on set don't eat pork for various reasons, so we are actually using smoked turkey ham."

"Sounds completely foreign and scary. Why don't you ever make anything Irish?" he said.

"I tried to ask you what you wanted me to make the second day up here and you walked away from me, saying, if memory serves, 'I don't have time for this.' You lost your vote that day!"

"Oh, yeah. I remember that. I'm sorry I was rude."

He took another knife and began to chop okra alongside of her.

"That's okay. After the whole grits/catfish debacle, you'd already established that you were rude."

When he started to protest, she cut him off. "Therefore, your actions did not surprise me one bit. Par for the course and all that stuff. It was at that moment that I decided I would give you a wide berth. In fact, if it weren't for Jen, I think that wide berth would have extended back to Los Angeles!" She smirked at him.

Ian chopped in silence for a while before sighing, putting down his knife and turning toward her. "I shouldn't have said that. The truth is that I didn't want to talk to you."

"You didn't want to talk to me? Why ever not."

"Because I was embarrassed about how I'd acted the day before. I came across like everything I despise about Hollywood: entitled, spoiled… Whatever the male equivalent of a diva is. Then when you came up and were trying to ask me what you could do to make it better even though I knew that I had been the one who behaved so poorly, I became even more annoyed. I didn't want you to start fawning over me when I didn't deserve it, especially when I'd been so impressed by the fact that you hadn't the day before. I didn't want to give you the chance to change my perception of you."

"True, but I just figured you were a stereotypical Hollywood star. I guess I'd expected the poor treatment, so it was no biggie," Kat told him.

"What's next?" Ian changed the subject.

"You're in luck! There are potatoes in this meal! How are you at peeling?"

"'How are you at peeling potatoes?' she asks the Irish man," he echoed sardonically.

"I take that, then, to be a confirmation that you are prepared to peel and chop the mountain of potatoes over there. You think you're Irish enough to handle it?"

"Challenge accepted," he said as he marched to the sink. He pulled a garbage can over and got to peeling.

Melinda and Gerard were clearly amused by the two of them joking and laughing with each other, with Ian asking questions about the food and Kat answering. When he saw the pile of mustard greens, he was shocked at the sheer volume of them. She told him that they may look like a lot right now, but they would shrink considerably once they were cooked, though he still looked incredulous.

"I sure hope so," he said, "Because I'm beginning to feel like Seymour in *Little Shop of Horrors*!"

He sat on a stool and watched Kat carefully wash each leaf and stem and then chop them into manageable strips. Seeing that it was almost time to set everything out for dinner, she grabbed a large sauté pan and put in some oil and garlic. Next, she added the greens and stirred them around, adding salt and pepper. Once the leaves were wilted, she added some free-range chicken broth she had made the day before with leftover chicken bones, having made Brunswick Stew with chicken instead of rabbit. She reduced the heat and allowed the greens to simmer for another five minutes and then added ground mustard right at the end. Ian was mesmerized as he watched her move around the stove.

"Wow, I never would have guessed the leaves would shrink so much!"

"I told you so!" Kat gloated.

He rose and moved closer to her. Resting his hands on her shoulders, he looked over her into the pan. "Smells good!" he said.

"It is! Would you like to taste?"

"I gather I could try," he answered somewhat reluctantly.

"Grab me that fork over there and you can."

Kat put some of the greens onto the utensil and lifted them out of the pan. She placed her hand under the fork to catch any drips and stretched her arms out toward his open mouth. He took a bite, chewed for a second, and then his eyes lit up.

"Hey! These are actually really good! The best color I ever ate."

Kat began to laugh as she remembered that first day when he had argued with her and George about Southern food, asking what greens were, and if Southerners ate colors. Thoroughly amused, she asked, "Do you have a lot of experience eating colors, Ian?"

"I'll have you know that I was the top crayon eater at my nursery school!" he declared proudly.

"I would hope that my greens taste better than crayons!" She made a disgusted face.

"They most definitely do!" he affirmed.

The door opened and people started coming into the dining hall. Ian leaned over and kissed Kat's cheek, thanking her for the nice afternoon before he walked out of the kitchen. When Kat looked up, she saw that Lydia was eyeing her and she suddenly felt a wave of nervousness wash over her. She smiled weakly back, but the actress just continued to stare at Kat like she was sizing her up. When Ian walked over to her and put his arm around her, she gazed up at him adoringly and said something that made him laugh. Ian got his food and they headed over to a table with their costars and began to eat.

Kat tried to tell herself not to worry; that Lydia didn't seem angry or upset that she had seen Ian with her in the kitchen. She seemed more interested in *why* he was there than that he was. Still, she had to wonder if she was getting uncomfortable with the amount of time Ian and Kat spent together. Lydia seemed to be as possessively protective of Ian as he was of her.

For the rest of the night Kat was deep in thought and didn't even notice when Ian and Lydia left for the evening. She cleaned the kitchen with Melinda and Gerard, saying very little as she pondered what Ian and Lydia's relationship truly was. As much as they interacted, it seemed more that they were just very close, almost like twins. They were in tune with each other, holding each other in very high regard and gave off a definite "Us against the world" vibe that was undeniable. But while they clearly cared about each other very deeply, there seemed to be something that was missing. Though not openly demonstrated by public displays of affection, anyone could see that there was a level of physical intimacy between them that was stronger than normal for friends, but it was still less than what was common for a romantically involved couple. She simply could not wrap her head around what Ian and Lydia shared.

As she strolled back toward the trailer later that evening, she stopped and looked up at the sky. It was a crisp night with a slight breeze blowing in from the mountains. The stars were so prolific, she couldn't remember a time in her life when she had seen so many of them. As she walked further away from the lights of the set, she saw the Milky Way. She stood in awe at the beauty and peace surrounding her. Thinking back to Ian's comment about the mountains, and how when looking at them he had felt inconspicuous and small, like his life would not mean much in the scope of the existence of the universe, she felt sad and disappointed that she didn't have someone with whom to share this experience. Even with all of the campouts, boating trips, and cruises she had been on with her family over the years, she had never experienced something as truly remarkable and humbling as she was just then, standing there looking at the heavens. It felt like a weight lifted off her and she could finally breathe.

Having finally made it into her room, she grabbed her phone and texted her kids that she loved them very much and hoped that they were doing well. She spent the last minutes of the day reading their responses that they loved her and missed her, too.

Chapter Eighteen

In the little over three weeks they had been there, Kat and Ian had fallen into a sort of routine. Every day, when he was on break or didn't have to film, he would come and prepare food with her, or he would come get her and they would take the horses out or walk somewhere together, always talking. Their conversations were long and varied and Kat began to feel that she was holding nothing back; that she was completely exposed. She had never felt so vulnerable, yet so comfortable with another person in her life, except for Jen.

Kat was telling Ian things that she never would have dreamed of sharing with anyone else. Her thoughts about that he was the one asking all the questions kept creeping back to her, though. Whenever she would ask him much of anything, he would divulge very little about his personal life or private self, so she decided one night to Google him. She couldn't find much other than his name, his age, his height, a list of the shows he had done and his nationality. He was on Facebook, Instagram, and Twitter, but his posts were generic, mostly pictures and status reports of the happenings on set. There were a few pictures of him on his horse, or at the beach, but mostly everything was strictly professional. Certainly, Kat found sites that claimed the types of rumors that always surround celebrities—that he was gay or secretly married to Lydia—but even they were few and far between. On a whim, she decided to look up Lydia, too. Her online presence was exactly like Ian's, only there was even less available about her. Curious, Kat determined to ask Ian about it all the next time they saw each other.

***

Ian came by the next day around two o'clock to pick Kat up. She felt badly about leaving Gerard and Melinda so often, but when she brought it up with them, they both emphatically insisted she go. Kat, being her typical self, then worried whether it was because they had it all under control or that they just didn't want her around.

She and Ian rode their horses to the meadow and then let them run through the grass around the lake, sometimes together, sometimes drifting apart. When the horses were tired, Ian and Kat tied them to a nearby tree and sat down next to the lake, contentedly staring out over the water, not talking. Kat had her legs out in front of her and her arms stretched back behind her, her elbows propping her up, with her head tilted toward the sun and her eyes closed. She righted her head and slowly opened one eye, glancing at Ian. She found him looking at her with his legs crossed as he absently picked blades of grass in front of them and ran them through his fingers.

"Enjoying the sun?" he asked her.

"Immensely. At home this time of year, the weather is warming to the low eighties and the sky is blue with big, puffy white clouds. The humidity of the summer is still a few months away and the trees and flowers are blooming. Here, it seems like spring is about two months behind schedule."

"I've been spoiled myself by Los Angeles," Ian told her. "That's why I want to buy a house there. I lived with rain and cold and damp for so long, I feel like I'm molding."

"Ian?"

"What is it?"

"This is going to sound really weird… Don't think I'm a crazy stalker or anything, but why can I not find much about you and Lydia online?"

"Oh. That."

"Yes. That. I'm curious. I found a lot of speculative gossip about how you and Lydia are secretly married, or even that you are gay. I just find it strange that in this day and age actors can be as private as y'all are."

"We spend big money to make sure that our personal lives stay off the web."

"What do you mean?"

"I mean we don't want people to know our personal

business, so we pay companies to search for any mention of us and take care of it. The normal publicity stuff is okay, but as for our families, relationships, and backgrounds, we keep it very private," he said unapologetically.

"Why? No offense, but I thought actors kind of got off on being in the limelight."

"Not all of us, okay?" He looked out across the lake in a not-so-subtle attempt to let her know that as far as he was concerned, this conversation was over. This time, however, Kat wasn't about to let him shut her out again.

"Ian, you know just about everything there is to know about me. Other than that night we talked about your father passing, you haven't told me much of anything personal. You aren't afraid I'm going to go to the paparazzi or anything, right?"

He was quiet for several seconds before answering her.

"No, I don't think you would go to the paparazzi," he finally answered.

"Then what is it? Were you a serial killer back home, or what?" She thought she could perhaps break the tension with a joke.

Ian smiled at her and shook his head. "It's nothing like that. I'm not a serial killer. I'm just a private person."

"Okay, I can respect that. But what about Lydia? Is she also that way?"

"Look, Kat, I can't speak for Lydia. She and I just have an agreement that we keep ourselves to ourselves. That's all I am going to say on the subject."

"Okay. I'm sorry if I'm making you uncomfortable. I just feel like you are getting to know me and, well, I still know very little about you."

"I know."

"Are you in love with Lydia?" There. She had finally gotten up the nerve to ask him.

"I care about her very much," he said, again with his signature evasiveness.

"That doesn't really answer my question. Are you in love

with her? Are you in a relationship with her? Because if you are, I think that we are spending too much time together. I don't ever want anyone to feel about me the way I feel about my husband's mistress."

"Lydia knows that we're friends. She's not upset about the time we spend together."

Ian was picking at the blades of grass again. "She isn't jealous?"

"Should she be?" he asked, looking up and meeting her eyes.

Ouch, that hurt! There was her answer to whether or not he was interested in her.

"No. Not at all. I just don't want to… I can't… Never mind."

Kat didn't want to get into it. How could she ask Ian if the reason why Lydia wasn't jealous was because he thought of Kat as a friend, and she had been misinterpreting the signals she thought he had been giving her?

"I'm sorry," she said.

"It's fine. Have you thought any more about what you are going to do about your divorce?"

It bothered her that Ian was just so damned adept at changing the subject, always bringing the focus back to her.

"Yes. I think I'm ready to have the attorney file the paperwork. I haven't talked to James much lately, but I think we both need to get this behind us and move on. I've come to the conclusion that I don't love him anymore. I don't think I could ever get that back, either. The damage has been done. I can handle a lot of things but lying and being deceitful are definitely not two of them."

"I'm sorry you are going through this, Kat."

Ian reached over and took her hand. He brought it up to his lips and gave her a kiss on her knuckles. It was yet another one of those mixed signals he was so good at giving. She sighed, resolving herself to the fact that he was a kind and empathetic person and felt sorry for her pain.

"We'd better think about heading back," he told her.

He stood up and offered his hand to Kat to help her get up

on her feet. They got on their horses and headed toward the set.

"Thanks for the ride," Ian said with a smile as they walked back together toward the dining hall.

"Thank you, too. That lake is so beautiful. I'm glad you showed it to me."

"Any time," he told her, as he leaned over and kissed her cheek, leaving her standing in the door in a state of utter confusion.

After he left her, Kat became more and more mortified the longer she thought about the questions she'd asked him. She took her embarrassment out on the food she prepped as she chopped and stirred for the evening meal, and started to wonder if Ian thought of her more as a mother figure than someone to be romantically interested in. The more she analyzed it, the more likely it seemed, and she felt stupid for ever thinking that he could possibly be remotely attracted to her as anything more than a friend.

Face it, Kat. You are old and worn out. How could anyone like Ian ever be interested in you? You just projected your feelings onto him.

After dinner that night, Kat called Jen. They had both been so busy that they hadn't been communicating all that much, but Kat missed her. She wanted someone to bounce her humiliation off of and to tell her it was all okay in response. Jen answered on the second ring.

"Hello?"

"Hey, Jen. It's me. How are things? How's Lucy?"

"Oh! Hi! Lucy is good, thanks. We're slowly getting the hang of this stuff. David is more reluctant and worried than I am at this point, so until he's more comfortable with everything, I'm stuck down here. Everything okay?"

"Sure," Kat said.

If you don't count humiliating myself by thinking a T.V. star six years younger than me was interested.

"Kat? What's going on?"

"How do you know that anything is going on?'

"Really? Do you even have to ask? I've known you forever. I can tell when something is bothering you. Now spill it."

"I'm a fool. I made a complete ass of myself," Kat blurted out to her sadly.

"Why's that? What happened?"

"I've been hanging out with Ian. A lot! Ever since I sprained my ankle and he found me in the woods, we have spent just about every afternoon together."

"I know. I've been talking with Melinda. How does that make you a fool, though?"

"Oh, God! Melinda's been talking to you? Is she complaining that I'm not doing my share, or…?"

Jen laughed. "No, Kat. She was just mentioning how lucky you were to have hurt your ankle because Ian has been so attentive. She was saying that if it were her, she would be milking it for all it was worth. But she also said it was nice to see you coming out of your funk, and that you were enjoying yourself and feeling more comfortable with everything."

"Oh, good! I've been worried that they think I'm a slacker. She's right. I have been spending a lot of time with him and I'm coming out of my funk. But this afternoon, I did something stupid. I told him that I had Googled him and Lydia and asked why I couldn't find much about either of them, and then he proceeded to give me a lecture about how they choose to keep their private lives private."

"And?"

"I asked him, Jen… Oh, God… I asked him if Lydia was jealous about how much time he and I were spending together and he responded, 'Why? Should she be?'"

"Ouch!"

"I know!" wailed Kat. "How could I have been so stupid to think that his attention was anything but friendly? I've been out of the dating scene for so long, I've obviously lost it. Not that I had a ton of experience before, either, but now I don't even know which things are signals and which aren't."

"What kind of signals are you thinking you're

misinterpreting, Kat?" Jen asked her, patiently.

"He's just so attentive. He talks to me, asks me all kinds of questions, all while making me feel like he's looking through my eyes into my soul. You know how he looks at Lydia on screen? That's how he looks at me. He's always kissing me on my cheek or forehead at the end of everything we do together, and today, when he asked me if I had decided what I was going to do about James and the divorce, he was holding my hand and brought it up to his lips and kissed it! Who does that? Is this normal friend behavior between men and women nowadays?"

"Well, yes, sort of. People are way more physical than they used to be, even just friends. But those are some pretty confusing signals. Maybe not the hugs or even the kisses, but the thing with the hand? That's weird."

"Jen, I began to panic that he thinks of me as a mother figure. He knows I have three kids. He keeps talking about how comfortable he is with me. Maybe he's just hanging out with me because I'm fulfilling his need to be mothered? I don't know…"

"I wish I knew what to tell you, Kat. He is very private. No one knows much about him, or Lydia, for that matter. Usually there's someone, somewhere who pops up from a famous person's past at some point, but that hasn't happened yet with them. I have a pretty good beeline for the town gossip, but everyone is tight-lipped about those two."

Kat continued, "He's very affectionate with Lydia, too. He often holds her hand or wraps his arm around her shoulders and kisses her both on the cheek and the top of her head sometimes. They're always very proper, but ever since I saw them together on T.V. at some awards show, I thought that he was very protective of her and that they were very intimate. They just don't admit anything to anyone.

"But, come to think of it, he's that way, even though it's to a lesser degree, with all of the women he interacts with regularly on set. I'm different, though. I don't do his makeup, fit his costumes, or run his errands. I'm just a caterer. That's why I'm confused. He doesn't even have to acknowledge me, but he does."

"Kat, you're very likable. You are intelligent, calm and you do give off that 'mommy' vibe. You make people feel comfortable around you and you take care of those you love. It's very apparent."

"Jen, I asked him if he loved Lydia."

"Oh, God!"

"I know!" Kat wailed. "He answered, 'I care for her very deeply.' It was so awkward! Then he proceeded to tell me that he and she have some agreement to keep their private lives private, but he wouldn't go into why they are so adamant that they do so. See? Total mixed signals."

"I agree. It is weird. Maybe he's gay."

"I thought of that. But he then he made a comment before that he likes women. Long story…," Kat said quickly.

"Anyway, I'm being ridiculous, regardless. I've only known him one month. I'm just using him as a crutch to get over my marriage ending, I guess. Someone to focus on so I don't have to think about the pain, maybe? So, why do I care?"

"I don't think that's it. I think if anything, it's because he's paying attention to you. He's making you feel relevant when James made you feel like you were yesterday's garbage. We all want to be wanted. His attention makes you feel like you aren't disposable or worthless and that you have something to offer people even when James' actions claimed that you didn't. There's nothing wrong with that, either. Enjoy it! Bask in it! You aren't going to marry the guy. You aren't even going to properly date him. So, enjoy that a gorgeous, kind man, who just about every woman in the world who has seen him lusts after, wants to spend time with you and let that tell you that you have so much more to offer than James led you to believe."

"Thanks, Jen. I guess I just feel stupid for thinking that he could be attracted to me. I'm so mortified… I even told him that I didn't ever want to be the reason that a relationship broke up! What was I thinking?"

"You were thinking that you wanted to spare Lydia the

same heartache you're going through. There's nothing embarrassing about that, my friend. It's noble. Maybe a bit forward of you, but even if you're just friends, it shows that you are a conscientious person to be worried about how someone's partner would feel about him spending so much time with you. I bet he didn't even notice, though, at least in the way you meant it," Jen explained. "Totally changing the subject, what are you doing for the spring holiday break in the schedule?"

"What?" Kat was confused.

"There's going to be a break for Passover and Easter when the set shuts down for ten days. It allows people to get back home for their respective religious activities. Are you going to come back down here? I can't imagine you'd want to go home."

"No, I don't want to go home. What about Melinda and Gerard?"

"Gerard's flying home to Louisiana to be with his family. You know, big Catholic mass, etc. Melinda is meeting a friend in Vancouver or Seattle; I can't remember which."

"Well, maybe I should just stay here. Keep an eye on things."

"Kat, I don't think that's a good idea. You'll be the only person on the set for ten days, more than an hour outside of Calgary and miles from anyone. I think you should just fly back down here and hang out with me."

Kat gave up. "Okay. If you insist, I will."

"Yes, I insist! If something were to happen, you'd be up there all alone. Not only that, it would also give you too much alone time in your head which I don't think is a good thing for you right now."

"Okay, okay! I'll come. I'll buy my ticket this week and come on down."

"Sounds good. I've got to run. I have to go check Lucy's blood sugar now. Good talking to you, though. And Kat?"

"Yes?"

"Don't beat yourself up about this. You're testing the waters after being away from the pool for a very long time. It'll be a lot like how it was in junior high and high school, with all of that awkwardness, until you get your bearings, and that's okay."

"All right. Thanks, Jen! Love you!"

"Love you, too, doll. Talk to you soon."

Kat hung up the phone and thought about what Jen had said. Was she so starved for attention and reassurance after her husband's affair that she was seeing things that weren't there? Was she inventing scenarios to make herself feel desirable and lovable? Kat decided that this was the most logical explanation and that the only solution was to back off her feelings and treat Ian like a friend, not a potential love interest. And it worked, at least for a while.

Chapter Nineteen

Kat went out of her way the next few days to avoid Ian. She was always polite but professional whenever he came to get his food and she made sure she was always too occupied with the next meal prep to go with him when he came by during any of his free time. She was still mortified about the presumptions she had vocalized by the lake and blushed whenever she saw him, so she treated him like she treated James' college buddies: respectful, but not familiar. At first Ian looked at her quizzically but then just shrugged his shoulders and walked out when she told him she was too busy to go for a walk or ride.

She had just finished cleaning up from lunch and decided to head back to her trailer. Her ankle had mended significantly but since she was standing so much more now it was aching again. Getting it elevated with ice seemed exactly the thing she needed before the dinner rush.

She had been relaxing at the trailer for about thirty minutes when a knock came at the door. Not knowing who was there, she called from her position on the bed for them to come inside. The door opened, and Ian stepped through.

"Good day, Kat."

He sounds particularly Irish today, she thought, though she wondered if it was just that she hadn't spoken with him very much in the last few days.

"Hello. How are you?"

"I'm okay. I just wanted to ask you something."

"Okay. What is it?"

"Lydia has a bad cold, and her voice is practically gone. She's been ordered to go on vocal rest for three days, which means she can't talk much. But we always rehearse our lines together in the evenings, and I don't really know who else to ask. Would you mind helping me tonight?"

"I guess that would be fine. I'm not done with cleaning up after dinner until nine-thirty or so, though, and Melinda and

Gerard go to bed pretty early since we have to be up so early in the morning, so we can't do it here. Want to come into the dining hall or…?"

"We could do that. Or we could go to my trailer. Whichever is fine with me, though we might be more comfortable there than in that big room."

"Sounds good," Kat confirmed.

"Great! Wonderful! Thanks so much. I'll come by and get you at about nine-thirty, and we'll go from there, okay?"

"I'll see you then."

Ian left, and Kat lay back on her bed and wondered why he was asking her. *Couldn't his assistant do it? The producer? Anyone other than the caterer?* She shrugged and got up to go begin the dinner prep.

When Lydia came into the room to get her food, she smiled sweetly at Kat, but didn't say a word to anyone, so Kat figured that Ian hadn't been exaggerating earlier.

At nine-thirty on the dot, a few minutes after Gerard and Melinda had said goodnight and headed back up to the trailer, Ian walked inside. He was still in costume from an evening shoot, looking like a cowboy sheriff and smelling faintly of horses, hay, and fresh mountain air. He walked over to Kat and asked if she was ready to go.

He held her hand in the crook of his elbow, as was proper for the era in which the show was set, while they walked to his trailer. He opened the door and Kat stepped inside. She didn't know what she'd been expecting, but it felt very intimate to enter his highly personal space. It looked like a regular trailer and was very tidy inside. He had a few scripts from other episodes lying around, but other than that, it was pristine.

He showed Kat to the small sofa and handed her a script before sitting down beside her and telling her which page she needed. She found it and saw it was a heated scene between Joe and Sarah. She looked at Ian expectantly, not quite knowing what he wanted her to do.

Suddenly he spoke, his Irish accent gone, a Western

American twang taking its place. Kat stared at him for a second, still amazed by how he could turn his accent off and on like that. He sounded confident and rugged with his deep voice, like he had spoken that way for his entire life.

When he finished his line, he looked up at Kat, waiting. She gazed at him with admiration for a second, mesmerized by the man before her, forgetting what she was supposed to be doing. She saw his eyes widen slightly as he realized she wasn't reading Sarah's line. Kat quickly looked down and tried to find where to begin, trying to hide the reddening of her cheeks.

Sarah: *Joe, I don't understand. Why do you treat me like a child? I am a grown woman, with a child of my own. I was married, for goodness' sake. You don't have to follow me around like a guard dog in order to keep me safe.*

Joe: *I'm sorry, Sarah. I just care about you… a lot. I don't want to see you get hurt.*

Sarah: *There are several single women in this town. I know some of them may not have the best reputation, but I'm sure they warrant as much protection as I do, probably more so, given their profession. I'm just a simple seamstress. No one bothers with me. No one even looks in my direction when I walk down the street.*

Joe: *Sarah, that's not true. I'm a man, and I see how other men look at you. You're young and attractive. There are a lot of single men here working the mines and not an overabundance of women, especially a nice woman like you: someone they could marry and take home to meet their mother. I worry about you. You're innocent and trusting. These guys are rough, sometimes a little desperate, and always a lot drunk. Please just promise me that you won't go out alone at night unescorted, anymore.*

Sarah: *All right, Joe. I'll listen to your advice. But as for anyone wanting to marry me and take me home to meet their mother, that's not going to happen. Who would want me? I'm a twenty-three-year-old widow with a young son. Who would want to take that on?*

Joe: *I would, Sarah. I would like to take that on, if you would let me.*

Kat looked up at Ian and caught his eye. A small grin spread across her lips as she realized that she was privy to information about the series before just about anyone else. Joe was finally explaining to Sarah how he really felt about her for the first time in two and a half seasons. Ian smiled back at her and nodded at the script.

Sarah: *Pardon me?*

Joe: *I said that I would like to take that on. I want to inform you of my desire to court you and, hopefully, to marry you one day soon. I want to be a father to that little boy and any other children we may have together. I want to come home to you every night and wake up with you every morning. Sarah, I can't do this anymore. I have to tell you how I feel. It has been consuming me. I hope and pray you feel the same way.*

Kat looked at Ian, under the spell of the words he had just spoken. Even though they were beautiful, what really got her was how he said them, so full of love and emotion. Kat's eyes filled with tears, thinking about how she would love to have a man say those things to her in that manner. She would give anything to hear a man proclaim his devotion to her like Joe was doing with Sarah, to feel that passion, to feel so special. She had never had that before. Sure, James had been kind and told her that he loved her, but he had never poured his heart out like that.

She wondered, though, if any man really would, or if it only happened in fairytales, this one set in a dusty mining town in late 1800's Colorado. Ian studied her face for a second before taking his hands and placing them on her cheeks. With his thumbs, he carefully swiped away the tears that had spilled over as he smiled at her.

"Oh my gosh, I'm so sorry!" Kat said, very embarrassed.

"Don't be," Ian told her.

"It's just there's so much emotion in this scene. The words he says to her. That only happens on T.V., doesn't it? But it's every woman's dream to feel that loved and desired."

"We have good writers," he said with a shrug. "Mostly

women," he added.

"Ah. Now it makes sense," Kat replied with a sheepish smile.

"Shall we continue?" Ian asked her.

"Yes, I think I have my emotions under control… It's just after everything that has happened with James, I feel like no one will ever want me again. I feel like Sarah. Who would want to take me on… Oh my gosh, why am I telling you all of this?" Kat was mortified she had poured her own heart out, but couldn't stop the words from tumbling out, anyway.

Ian just smiled kindly at her and pointed to the script.

Sarah: *Joe! Where is this coming from? What are you saying?*

Joe: *I'm saying that I love you and that little boy, and I want to marry you. I waited a year for you to grieve your husband. I waited another year to for you to like me. I can't wait another year to let you know how much I love you, desire you.*

Sarah, I can't breathe when you are near me. I can't think straight. I have to have you in my life. I already love that little boy as if he were my own flesh and blood.

Please say I may court you and allow me to eventually ask for your hand in marriage.

Kat looked up at Ian and saw him looking at her with his famous intensity. An electric spark ran through her body as her eyes met his. She was the one who suddenly couldn't breathe, couldn't think straight. Looking back down at the script, she softly spoke the next lines to him.

Sarah: *Yes, Joe. I want you to be my husband. I've loved you for a very long time, but never allowed myself to dream that you might feel the same for me. I will allow you to court me, of course, but I'd also say yes if you asked me to marry you right now. If I have learned anything, it's that life is too short to waste time on frivolous things.*

Kat read the stage direction and saw that Joe was supposed to lean into Sarah, take her face in his hands and kiss her passionately. She looked up in surprise at Ian as he raised his right hand to her face and put his mouth on hers, caressing her cheek. Her eyes popped open in shock; Ian Gregory was kissing her. Surely, it was only because it was in the script, right?

Her mind was racing a million miles an hour until she finally stopped thinking about anything and just responded to his lips on hers. The kiss deepened and grew more intense. She allowed herself to melt into him, her hands running up his back onto his shoulders, digging her fingers into his flesh. He pressed into her, pushing her gently back onto the couch as his hands moved to her shoulders and down. He squeezed his hands around her arms and his lips traced a line from her mouth to her neck as Kat threw her head back and arched her torso into him. She had a fleeting thought that this was most certainly not in the script and immediately another that she didn't care. Even if it was in the script, she was still thrilled to have this gorgeous man kissing her like that.

After a few minutes, he pulled himself up. He looked at her shyly. "Sorry."

"I'm not! That was incredible!" Kat blurted, surprising herself. She immediately clapped her hand over her mouth in shock. After a few seconds of silence, she added, "If this is method acting, I'll take it!"

Ian looked down at the floor. "Kat, this isn't acting. Well, the script was, but the kiss was real. I've never met anyone like you before. I don't know what it is, but you enchanted me from the second I met you, listening to you trying to explain what grits were. I never meant to kiss you like that, to push you into something when I know what you've been through, but after I saw your tears I knew for sure that you're special. You are everything I thought you were and more. You make me feel comfortable and safe. I feel like you wouldn't care if I acted another day in my life; that you would love me for me and nothing else."

With his declaration, Kat lunged at him, throwing herself in his arms, meeting his lips with an intensity she had never before known. She kissed him, deeper and deeper, until she was sitting in his lap, one of her hands tangled into the hair at the base of his head, her other arm around his waist. They sat like that, embracing for a long time, enjoying each other. Kat didn't know if this was a fluke—a one-night stand in the making—but in that moment, she didn't care. She vowed she was going to see it through to the end, whatever that meant.

Ian slowly stood up, picking her up in his arms as he did so. He carried her back to his bedroom and kicked the door open. Laying her on the bed, he climbed up beside her, before beginning to kiss her lips, her neck, her collarbone and then lower. He straightened up and gently stroked her cheek with his thumb before leaning down to kiss her again, and their desire for each other grew until it was nearly feverous.

Kat heard herself moan as Ian slid his tongue in along hers and moved over her as he began to caress her mouth more fully with his own. Unable to process anything else that was happening, she felt like she was under a spell and that her body was no longer her own, that he was controlling it. She began to claw at his shirt, trying to pull it out from the waistband of his jeans.

He took hold of her wrists and whispered, "Slowly. What's the rush?"

Kat just looked at him and whimpered in both frustration and desire. She began to fumble with the buttons on his shirt anyway and soon she was rewarded by running her hands over his smooth chest. He rolled over onto his back relaxing into the sensation of her soft hands roaming up and down his torso, until Kat worked her fingers into his belt buckle in an attempt to remove it. She couldn't believe how bold she was being, how uninhibited. She had never been like this before in her life. Just when she managed to open the buckle and start on the top button of his jeans, he grabbed her hands and gasped, "We can't."

"Why not?" she whined breathlessly at him.

"Because," he told her between kisses, "because I don't want it to happen this way. You're not like anyone else. You deserve special and incredible, not a trailer in the middle of nowhere.

"Besides, you're still married, and I won't be the reason you become like your husband. I can wait until your divorce is final and you're truly free, so that you won't regret it because you will know that you honored your vows." He gave her a sly grin. "I truly am a nice Catholic boy at heart."

"I don't care about that," Kat argued eagerly. "As far as I'm concerned, I'm divorced. He left me. I'm perfectly okay with how this is going. Please!" She couldn't believe that she was actually, literally, begging for it.

"I'm not. Kat, you need to be able to respect yourself and know that you did nothing to tarnish your expectations or reputation. However," he said with a wink, "that doesn't mean that we can't enjoy ourselves while getting awfully close."

Kat groaned softly as she rolled over onto her back and put her forearm across her eyes. She knew Ian was right. In that regard, he already knew her better than she knew herself. He understood that if she had succumbed to her desires after having been so angry and hurt by James, she would beat herself up for, in essence, doing the same thing.

"Ugh," she moaned again. "Why do you have to be right?"

"Kat, there's time. I promise you. There isn't any rush. Now that I've found you, I won't let you go. Let's do this right. File for divorce; then let's move on. For now, let's just enjoy each other as much as we can, while saving the best for last."

He lifted his arm and she rolled up next to him, tucking her head between his head and shoulder. Wrapping his arm around her, he stroked the hair off her forehead and kissed her there.

"Stay," he murmured sleepily after several minutes.

"What?"

"Stay with me tonight. Please?"

"I thought you said…"

"Please just stay with me. Just like this. I promise; this is enough. But please don't go."

There would be no argument from Kat. She fell asleep in his arms and as she drifted off, she couldn't remember a time when she had ever felt so comfortable.

Chapter Twenty

Kat woke up early the next morning and was surprised to see where she was and that it had not all been a dream. She couldn't believe that there she was, in Ian Gregory's trailer—in his bed—until she looked over at him sprawled out on his stomach across his side of the mattress, the blanket they had thrown over them across his waist, his strong back exposed by the shirt bunched up his torso. He looked so relaxed, like a little boy. She quietly extricated herself from the blanket and got off the bed, praying it wouldn't creak as she did. Walking out of the bedroom, she gathered her shoes and coat from the night before and quietly let herself out the door.

Just barely five a.m., the set was just beginning to stir as people prepared for another long day of filming. Kat tried to be as inconspicuous as possible, but by the looks people gave her, it wasn't hard to imagine that they knew exactly why she was there and probably from where she had come. She felt her cheeks grow hot as people began to look and then whisper to each other about what the caterer would be doing coming from the direction of Ian's trailer before dawn, and what would Lydia say about it?

Kat grabbed her phone out of her pocket and typed a text to Jen: *Doing the walk of shame back to the trailer. Isn't that what this is called nowadays?*

Not even thirty seconds later, Jen responded: *WHAT?!?!? Do you know what the walk of shame is? What are you doing? WHO are you doing?*

Kat: *Ian.*

Jen: *WHAT!?!?*

Kat: *Not doing. Just… not doing. Just enjoying?*

Jen: *OMG, I'm calling you!*

Kat's phone rang a few seconds later. She slid her finger across the screen to answer as she continued walking back to her trailer, but she veered off into the trees a little way.

"Hello?" she said in a hushed tone, not wanting to be

overheard.

"Oh my God, Kat. What's going on?"

"I don't know, Jen. He asked me to run lines with him last night because Lydia is sick and on vocal rest. We read a really intense part of the script, and then Joe and Sarah were supposed to kiss. Next thing I know, he was leaning over and putting his lips on mine!

"It was an intense kiss. It was an awesome kiss! Melt your knees kind of kiss, like nothing I have ever experienced before. After a few minutes of that, he carried me to his bed and then we kissed some more. Things started to heat up and I was more than ready to continue, but then he stopped me, telling me that he didn't want it to be this way for me; that I deserved better and that he knew I needed to be divorced from James or I would regret it. I tried to argue because by that point, I wasn't thinking straight or caring, but he insisted."

Kat took a breath and continued, "But then he asked me to stay. So, the last thing I remember was putting my head into the crook of his shoulder with his arm wrapped around me. I must have fallen asleep, because the next thing I knew, I was awake. It was morning and he was sprawled out, half naked, next to me on the bed. I didn't know what to do, so I panicked, grabbed my shoes, and left."

"Oh my God! Kat!"

"I know! Isn't this crazy?"

"No, Kat. This is bad. *Very* bad. If this gets out and Lydia and he *are* together, you will get us fired. What were you thinking?"

Kat was quiet for a second. She hadn't even considered that.

"Oh, my Lord, Jen, I didn't think about that. I'm so sorry. I was selfish and stupid."

"It isn't good, that's for sure."

"What are we going to do?"

"Well, you are going to get into that kitchen and make breakfast like nothing happened. Hopefully, it's early enough that no one saw you. Pretend that everything is normal, and this never occurred."

Kat didn't have the courage to remind Jen that she was an hour ahead of her in Los Angeles, so some of the crew had seen her and from where she had come.

"Okay. I'll do that. I'm so sorry, Jen."

"It's okay, Kat. You didn't know," Jen sounded exasperated. "But you need to understand that this happens a lot on sets. One of the actors gets a little curious and starts to mess around with someone else in the cast or on the crew. The girlfriend/boyfriend/spouse finds out and all hell breaks loose. I should have warned you. Actors are notorious for scoping out fresh meat and getting a little action on the side."

"Oh, God!" Kat cried. "I had no idea! So, I was just his little piece on the side? His conquest?"

"Most likely, yes," Jen said bluntly.

"How could I have been so stupid?"

"Remember how I said that you were testing the waters of the dating pool again? Well, girl, you just jumped off the high dive. I hope it was worth it, too, because this could cost us a ton of money."

"Jen, I really am so incredibly sorry… I didn't think. It won't happen again. If by some miracle this doesn't get out, I'll stay away from him from now on."

"Sounds like a good plan. I'll talk to you later."

Kat ended the call and shook her head. How could she not have seen this coming? Of course, he wasn't interested in her! He was just playing games, seeing what he could get. As Jen had said, he had probably seen how vulnerable she was, making her an easy target. He'd probably done this with half the crew already by this point.

And how could Lydia be so blind? she thought with disgust.

As she walked, her humiliation grew, and tears streamed down her face. But as she walked into the kitchen, she had to admit to herself that his kisses had been worth every penny her recklessness may have cost them. She walked directly to the back and threw on her chef's jacket, hoping to hide the fact that she was still in yesterday's clothes.

When Melinda walked in a few minutes later with Gerard, Kat didn't even look up as she greeted them.

Melinda and Gerard looked at each other questioningly, clearly noticing that Kat was wearing the exact same clothes from the day before, but rather than confront her, they just got to work. Never the most vocal bunch, especially first thing in the morning, they worked together like a well-oiled machine and soon breakfast was ready.

The crew and actors began to filter in and fill their plates, before sitting down. Kat felt sure that many of them were looking at her suspiciously, but she just tried to tell herself that she was being paranoid; that no one could have possibly known what went on last night between her and Ian.

The dining hall had just about cleared out when he walked in with Lydia. They didn't say much to each other as they got their food, but Kat reasoned that if Lydia was still on vocal rest, this would not be unusual. They sat together and ate, not really interacting, but just being.

Eventually, Ian touched her hand and held it for a second. Then he jerked his head toward the kitchen and Lydia studied him for a long moment before giving him a slight nod of her head. He stood up and wandered into the room, stopping in front of Kat.

Here it comes: the kiss off. She cringed, bracing herself for what she was sure to come next.

"Good morning," Ian said to her. He leaned over and kissed her cheek. "Sleep well?"

He had his back to everyone, facing her, and he winked.

"Ummm… Yeah. Good morning. I slept pretty well, thanks."

"Glad to hear it."

Kat glanced up and out into the dining area at Lydia. She was still sitting at their table, looking at her blankly. Kat couldn't tell if she was angry, curious, or indifferent. All she knew was that she felt like she was under a magnifying glass and Lydia was the sun.

"What are you doing today?" Ian asked her.

"The usual, I guess. Why?"

"Want to come and look around the set with Lydia and me this afternoon?" he asked. "I know you haven't seen too much of it, at least inside. Since Lydia still can't talk yet, I don't have a long shoot today and they're filming most scenes at the mine."

Kat panicked. Why did they both want to spend time with her this afternoon? But she tried to play it cool as she told him, "Okay. Sure. That could be interesting."

"Wonderful!" he said. "I'll come by at the usual time, then?"

"Yes. That should work fine."

Ian smiled at her and leaned over to give her a hug and stealthily kissed the top of her head. "It's a date then, love."

He walked back to Lydia, and he wrapped his arm around her shoulders as they walked out the door.

Kat worked herself into a frenzy for the remainder of the morning. What was going on? What game was he playing? How could he be so affectionate with Lydia after what he had said to her last night? After what they had done? If he only wanted a piece of action on the side, then why did he tell her to wait, to slow down, and that he would wait for her until her divorce was final?

Oh, God, she suddenly thought to herself, horrified, *maybe they like threesomes!*

Gerard and Melinda hadn't said anything to her for hours, but finally Melinda apparently couldn't take it anymore.

"So, Kat. How'd you sleep last night? I never heard you come in."

"I slept fine, thanks."

"I'm normally a really light sleeper, so I'm surprised that I didn't wake up when you came in. You must have been very quiet."

Kat knew she was being painted into a corner, but she wasn't willing to admit her guilt, so she just didn't respond. Her upbringing had taught her to avoid any kind of confrontation and to always save face, so she figured silence was her best option at that point.

Gerard looked at Kat and said, "He must have had a lot of lines to study last night."

"Um, yeah, it was a fair amount," Kat responded noncommittally.

Kat was really worried that Melinda and Gerard would be furious if they lost their jobs because of her actions. She made a resolution right then and there that she would not admit to anything, no matter what.

Nothing really happened with Ian, anyway, she rationalized. They had not had sex. They had spent the night talking and maybe making out just a little, but she tried to convince herself it was still pretty much a platonic relationship.

Then it hit her that maybe this was what Ian was saying about not letting them go any further and that he wanted her to maintain her reputation. Perhaps he knew that people would find out and he wanted her to know that she had done nothing wrong, not really. But why would he toy with her emotions like that and not want to go any further? If he'd only wanted a one-night stand, he could have just had one—she had clearly been more than ready and willing, so why had he stopped and claimed to care about what she and others thought if he was just after his own pleasure?

By the time two o'clock rolled around, Kat was sure that Ian and Lydia were coming to tell her that he had had a lapse in judgment the previous night, however that it didn't mean anything; that this happened all the time, but that they were still together and very much in love. Therefore, when the door opened, she felt her knees buckle and she had to grab onto the counter to steady herself.

"Ready?" Ian called to her.

Not trusting her voice, all Kat could do was nod. She took off her chef's whites and hung them on a nearby hook before walking toward them like a child approaching their parents after being naughty. Not only mortified that she had let things go so far, but she also felt terrible that she had potentially caused Lydia a lot of pain. Having been on the receiving end of that pain, she knew she wouldn't wish it on her worst enemy.

When she reached them, they turned and left, Ian holding the door for the two women. They walked together down Main Street of the fictitious River City, and Kat was soon once again fascinated by all of the attention to detail. It felt as though she had stepped back in time with the buildings having been weathered slightly to make them look old and the store fronts filled with period merchandise.

Ian stopped in front of the jail and stepped inside. There, Kat found herself looking at a jail cell, complete with cot, blue and white stripped mattress, and quilt. The bars, though only three years old, were meticulously weathered to look like they had been there a long time. The wooden desk that stood in the corner was made of oak and stained with what looked like old-fashioned furniture varnish, as it lacked the added gloss of modern polyurethane. The calendar was set to October 2, 1897, and an old-fashioned rifle hung on pegs on the wall. The set looked so much like a museum exhibit that Kat was afraid to touch anything for fear of disturbing it. Instead, she merely strolled around, studying everything. Except for the modern necessities of filming, there was not one thing that looked like it had been made in the current century.

"This is incredible! I cannot believe the attention to detail. Is all of this stuff old or…?"

"Some of it is old. Some of it is reproduction. We have a really great props team who takes their job very seriously. Most people don't realize that many period shows and movies have historians who work with them to ensure that everything is as close to historically accurate as possible," Ian explained.

Kat glanced over at Lydia, and she gave Kat a small smile as Ian moved over to the door and opened for the women to step out. The next stop was the dress shop Sarah owned. In the show it looked so small and quaint that Kat was surprised how much bigger it was in person and said as much.

Ian nodded. "The cameras, lighting, and sound equipment actually take up a lot of space, so what you see on T.V. is generally about three quarters the size of the room that is actually needed."

Kat ran her fingers over the bolts of calico fabric and lace trimmings in Sarah's establishment and admired the hats that were displayed in the windows before she turned and saw the vintage sewing machine. Laughing delightedly, she walked toward it.

"Does this really work? I see Sarah using it in almost every episode, but are you really using it?"

Lydia looked up at Kat, smiled, and nodded her head before looking expectantly at Ian.

"They brought someone in to show her how," he said.

"That is so incredible. I've always wanted to see how these things actually worked. May I?"

Lydia walked over to the machine and sat down. She showed Kat how to work the treadle and thread it, then got up and handed Kat an old scrap of fabric. Kat perched on the stool and began to move her feet, amazed at what such a relatively simple piece of machinery from that time period was capable of producing.

She got up and thanked Lydia who just smiled sweetly back at her again.

The next stop was the saloon with its old player piano. Kat smiled when Lydia turned it on, and music began to play. It was reminiscent of every Western movie she had ever seen as a kid. The polished oak bar gleamed and had a footrest made from solid brass pipe. The bottles lined up behind it on the shelf looked authentic and glasses sat at the ready. The rest of the space held five tables with chairs around them which also looked so perfect she could imagine herself a resident here in this room, watching her fellow citizens on any given day in 1897.

They exited the saloon and began walking to the livery. Not only for the show, the horses were also housed there throughout filming. Kat reached up and petted the muzzle of Lydia's horse, smiling as she remembered childhood visits to her grandparents' farm.

The trio spent the rest of the afternoon wandering around the remainder of the buildings, including the characters' homes and offices in the show. The diligence required to make sure every piece was where it belonged was amazing. Kat had never realized there was so much involved in staging an authentic looking period production. Though not individually noticeable, each small element added to a sense of time and place that created a unified whole, making it seem the viewers were truly immersed in the lives of the characters from over one hundred years ago.

When it was finally time for Kat to go back to the kitchen, Lydia and Ian walked her back. Even though it was strange that Lydia had said nothing all afternoon in an attempt to preserve and heal her voice, she felt that the woman was kind and gentle. Kat was unsure of why they felt the need to show her around together, but she had appreciated that they both took the time to share a part of their world with her.

Leaving Kat at the kitchen of the dining hall, they both leaned over and kissed her cheek before turning and walking away while Lydia tightly gripped Ian's arm. Kat shook her head and wondered for the millionth time what the true story was with the two of them.

If they were together and Lydia was okay with Ian spending time with her, then that must mean that Ian wasn't interested in her. But then why did he kiss her? If Lydia was in a relationship with Ian, then why was she seemingly okay with another woman spending so much time with him, and even wanting to join them? Things just weren't adding up in Kat's mind, and she was driving herself crazy spinning her wheels.

She was still deep in thought during the final touches of the meal prep, ruminating over what had happened between her and Ian the night before. Eventually, she concluded that it had merely been an accident. They were rehearsing an emotional scene; maybe he was just feeling lonely and so was she. He was perhaps interested in seeing if she was attracted to him. Kat reworked every scenario she possibly could in order to convince herself it was all just a fluke and finally resolved to enjoy it for what it was.

She wasn't too worried that he or Lydia were going to go to the producer about her behavior, because why, then, would they want to spend the day with her? She still couldn't shake the feeling, however, that Lydia had been sizing her up today. What she couldn't determine was why.

While Kat analyzed everything upon her return to the kitchen, she was lost in her own private world. She said very little and moved around Gerard and Melinda as if they weren't even there. At times, she looked distressed. At other times, she seemed to have come to some sort of realization. She was so deep in thought that when Ian came in to get his food, Kat didn't even look up, though he smiled and waved inconspicuously to her.

Watching Kat's behavior, her coworkers continued to get apprehensive about what was truly going on between with her and Ian, and if her pensive mood had anything to do with the fact that she had not come back to the trailer the night before. No strangers to the inner workings of Hollywood, they both knew what a dangerous line Kat was walking and, most importantly, what it could potentially mean for all of their jobs.

A while later, Kat looked up when Melinda hesitantly approached to tell her Ian had asked for her. Once he caught her attention, he asked softly, "Same time, same place tonight?"

She shook her head. "I don't think that is a good idea."

"Oh… all right, then. Thanks for the food. This stuff is growing on me. Goodnight."

Kat stayed with Melinda and Gerard until the kitchen was spotless and everything was set up for the morning rush. Kat then told them they could go ahead and leave, and that she would finish shutting off the lights and closing up for the night. She had most of the lights already off when she turned around to leave and saw Ian standing in the doorway, letting out a small scream.

"I'm so sorry for frightening you!" he exclaimed.

"That's okay. I just wasn't expecting anyone. Why are you here?"

Ian stared at her for a second before speaking. "Because I felt that there was some awkwardness between us today and I wanted to make sure you were doing all right."

Kat took a deep breath and sighed. "Honestly, Ian, I don't know what to think. I'm incredibly confused. Last night you seemed to be just as much into what was happening as I was, but then you just stopped. Then today, you take me on a tour of the set with Lydia, with whom everyone says you are involved. What's going on?"

"I just thought it'd be nice for you and Lydia to spend some time together, to get to know each other better."

"Ian, I'm sorry, but that's really weird. What is really going on between y'all? I'm sorry, but I can't continue to spend time with you unless you come clean about what exactly your and Lydia's relationship is. I feel like I'm being toyed with, and I don't like it. Are y'all in an open relationship? Or into threesomes?"

He laughed when she said that. "No, we're definitely not into threesomes, and we don't have an open relationship. But I did want you two to spend some time together. It's time you know the truth about Lydia and me, but it isn't only my story to tell. Hopefully, tomorrow she'll be able to speak again, and we can talk in the evening. Would that work?"

"I guess that could work. Meanwhile, I have to know. What happened last night? Did we just get carried away because of the scene? Were you just using me for your own amusement?"

"Kat, no. I told you. It was and continues to be real. It's also true that I didn't want you to do something that you would regret. I know the situation with your husband hurt you deeply because you've expressed to me more than once that you don't want to come between anyone else's relationship."

"But why me, Ian? Is it because I'm here and am willing? Because I'm an easy mark? A lonely, dumped, middle-aged woman who seems sad and desperate? You're surrounded all day, every day, by younger and beautiful women. I don't understand what exactly is making you seemingly feel an affinity for me?"

He sighed before saying, "I don't know, honestly. Because you are you? You are real, down to earth, grounded, and you give me what for? You're right that I'm surrounded every day by beautiful women. They are gorgeous, young, and God knows they are willing. But they are also calculating, shallow, and vain.

"Believe me when I tell you that it's a really bad idea for two actors to be in a relationship together. I've been there and done that and it *never* works. We need constant attention and reassurance that we are attractive and good at our craft. We know how to act a part, so it's hard to separate reality from fiction. We also fight over the bathroom!" He chuckled. "Honestly, though, Kat, what I am trying to say is that actresses are just as neurotic as actors. Our whole livelihood relies on our looks and our ability to exude a persona to the world. It can be a shallow, egotistical, almost narcissistic, existence. It really doesn't work to have two people like that in a relationship."

"But surely you could find someone else who has more to offer than me. I'm a middle-aged mom. I have a mom body, for goodness' sake! I'm far from being anyone's ideal of beauty."

He looked quizzically at her for a second before answering. "Kat, you know I have a mother, right? I mean, I know what a mother's body looks like. It isn't some defect that needs fixing. You carried life. That's obviously going to change you, but it's truly not the negative thing that women are led to believe. But beauty isn't the most important thing to me. I could have my pick of many beautiful women, but what they all are seemingly missing is fortitude. Experience in the real world, knowing what it is to care for someone more than themselves.

"It's hard work to be what society considers beautiful and it's very high maintenance. But I guarantee you if my makeup artists and stylists got their hands on you, you would look just as stunning and glamorous as any famous actress. It's mostly just a lot of smoke and mirrors.

"Regardless, at the end of the day, I want a woman who will ride horses with me and get covered in grass and mud while not caring that the wind tangled her hair. I want a woman who can be perfectly okay with rolling out of bed in the morning after rolling around in it with me all night and going for a hike or to the shops without taking three hours to get ready. I want a real life, not a fake Hollywood one. It's like what I said to you the other day: you treat me like everyone else. You're genuine."

"I still can't believe that you could be even remotely attracted to me. My husband certainly went for someone younger and more beautiful than me."

"Why is it so hard to believe that there are men out there who think that confidence and substance are attractive? Looks fade, Kat. Especially when they are enhanced and reworked into something that's not real. What's constant is someone's soul, and yours is a good one."

"I'm really struggling to believe all this, Ian. It genuinely sounds like what a man would say just to get a woman into bed, but I was already willing to do that with you."

"Kat, contrary to what the media says, there are men who like curves. Some men don't care about imperfections. We all have them; some of us are just better at hiding them or are genetically blessed to have them show up later rather than sooner. We all age. Every scar, every pound, every wrinkle just shows you lived.

"What's brilliant about you, Kat, is that you don't only get your affirmation from the attention of others. It's rare to find someone like that, especially in the entertainment industry. Let's be honest- the majority of the longest running relationships in Hollywood are those where the other partner has little or nothing to do with industry.

"Many of those spouses aren't drop dead gorgeous, but they have something that shows from the inside: devotion, caring, confidence. Never underestimate the power of someone's inner beauty."

"Are you sure you haven't just been out in the middle of nowhere for so long that you're forgetting what beautiful women look like?"

Ian smiled. "I'm sure. In fact, I like coming to the middle of nowhere to forget about what gorgeous women look like so that I can concentrate on what I want out of my life. Now, please, let's call it a night and we will talk with Lydia tomorrow, if she's up to it."

"All right, Ian. That sounds good. Have a good night."

Ian leaned over and took her in his arms. He hugged her tight and kissed her on the lips. "You, too, Kat. You, too."

Chapter Twenty-One

Late the next night, Ian, Lydia, and Kat all walked to Ian's trailer. He opened the door and gestured for them to go inside, and once they were seated, he turned to Kat.

"What we are about to tell you is very personal and private. We tell very few people. In fact, we have an agreement to that effect. Before we tell anyone anything, we both have to meet them and agree it's okay."

"Oh my gosh!" Kat joked. "Are y'all CIA?"

Lydia laughed quietly and said, "No, we aren't."

Ian walked over and sat next to Lydia on the couch, grabbing her hand and leaving Kat to sit alone in a chair. He looked at Lydia and gave her a soft nod. She took a deep breath and began to speak quietly in an effort to not strain her still-fragile voice.

"Kat, as Ian said, we are both very quiet about our personal lives. This is mostly because of me. I've asked Ian to help me."

"Okay…"

Lydia sighed and slapped her hands on the tops of her thighs. "Here goes. When I was a kid, I lived with my parents in New Jersey. It was a terrible existence. They were both drug addicts and abusive to me and each other. I don't have many memories, but I recall I spent many days with nothing to eat, living in a freezing cold apartment.

"When I was about six, I was playing on the playground near our apartment building, and I was approached by a cop. He asked why I wasn't in school, and I didn't know what to tell him. I remember I only stood there blinking at him. He noticed that my clothes were completely inappropriate for the weather outside and took me home. When we got there, he found my parents high, with paraphernalia all around them. He called back up and social services, and I was taken from my home and placed in emergency foster care."

"Oh, my gosh, Lydia. I'm so sorry!"

"Thanks. Anyway, over the years, I was bounced from

house to house. There were several attempts made to get my parents to get clean and reunify me with them, but it didn't last long. By the time I was a teenager, I had been in seven foster homes. I'd been physically, emotionally, and sexually abused by the other foster kids in the house, or once by a foster family themselves. I was a real handful and was finally sent to live in a group home.

"My only true escape was acting. Completely as a fluke, I got into drama in high school and loved it. I could be whomever I chose, and no one could say anything. It truly saved my life. The minute I was eighteen, I left the group home with my stuff in a black plastic garbage bag and took off. I hitchhiked across America, using sex to pay for whatever I needed along the way."

Lydia took a deep breath and continued. "When I arrived in Los Angeles, I was clueless about what to do or where to go. I was extremely lucky to find an organization that assisted teen runaways and soon had a job and was able to support myself, while auditioning for parts. I changed my appearance as much as I could. I was a lot like Ian in that I got a few commercials, local at first, but then national. Then, I started getting cast in plays, then as extras on T.V. shows and in movies.

"One night, the lead of the play for whom I was the understudy got sick, so I took over the part. An agent was in the audience. He liked what he saw, so I signed with him and he had me audition for this part on *Western Skies*. Luckily, I got it."

"Wow, Lydia, I had no idea."

"And that is exactly the point, Kat. I don't want anyone to have any idea. I'm not the girl I left behind in New Jersey at eighteen. The only good thing I ever got from my parents was my looks, and with that I got to come here and reinvent myself. I changed my name and made myself as invisible to my old life as I could. I wanted a clean break, a new opportunity."

"I'm so sorry, Lydia. I cannot imagine someone putting a child through all of that horror. You are amazingly resilient."

Lydia looked over at Ian and he smiled happily at her with a slight nod of his head. "I told you had nothing to fear by telling her."

"Yes, Ian, you did. I've since made some discrete inquiries into the whereabouts of my parents. They're still in New Jersey, still addicted to drugs. Honestly, I was surprised that they're even still alive. I know that if my true identity were discovered, they would come out of the woodwork, find me, and I'd be burdened by what happened in the past. It would be Pandora's Box. I know for sure they would try to exploit me financially. Quite frankly, I'd rather that the personal and professional repercussions of reintroducing that relationship into my life are simply never issues I have to deal with."

"I can understand that. Why would you want to open up old wounds?" Kat responded.

"Exactly!" Lydia stated emphatically. "Not only that, once my past is discovered, I will forever be fighting off the complications of other aspects of my life I'm not proud of, such as exchanging sex for what I needed to survive, having been in trouble with the law, and the dealings with some of my past foster families. It's a history I do not care to revisit in any form."

"Well, surely you know that people will understand these issues, given your background, right?" Kat asked her.

"If only it were that simple. I'm the co-star of a family-friendly show that has been adopted by fans who are largely members of the Christian Right. I highly doubt they would be too willing to overlook that I was hooking for my own survival not that long ago.

"All of that aside, I don't want to be scrutinized and I don't want people's pity, either. The person I am now is light years different from the person I was then. That girl is dead and buried, only good for being forgotten. I want to be known for my talent, my compassion, and my enthusiasm, not my sordid and tabloid-worthy background."

Kat sat quietly for a second in deep thought. There weren't any words to express her regret for Lydia's experience that she didn't sound like she pitied her.

Instead, she said, "You are a remarkably strong woman.

You took a situation that by all rights should have destroyed you and persevered in spite of it. You made the conscious decision to not let your past define you. It's admirable."

"Thank you. I know I was lucky to have been saved by my drama teacher and the outlet acting gave me to escape. Without that, I have no doubt that I'd be living just like my parents and so many other broken foster kids dumped out onto the streets at eighteen without any preparation for the real world."

Kat was thoughtful again. "But why the need for the insinuated relationship between y'all, then?"

"It started when Lydia asked me to be discreet," Ian answered. "It allows her to appear to be involved with someone while she is able to continue to heal from the damage of her upbringing. It serves me just fine as well because I'm actually a pretty private person and I had gotten to the point where I didn't want to concentrate on much of anything but advancing my career. As I told you the other day, it's really hard to date in Hollywood, and I had gotten tired of trying to decipher who was interested in me, the person versus me, the meal ticket. This scenario allowed me to do that without having to worry about wasting time on people who were trying to find out if I was single, just wanted to date an actor for their own selfish reasons, or deal with speculation about my sexual orientation."

"I asked Ian to please allow me the protection that a perceived relationship would give me so that people would be less apt to dig around in my business, past and present. It gives them something else to focus on."

Kat nodded her understanding.

"I'm extremely distrustful and damaged," Lydia continued. "I expect to be hurt and have a hard time letting people get close to me. Ian was the first person in a long time I felt understood why I'm the way I am. I felt safe with him and knew I could count on him to help protect me, even after we split up."

"So, y'all were together, then?" Kat asked.

"We were, for a short while," Ian confirmed.

"What happened?" Kat looked at both of them.

"We met on set three years ago and became very close friends. With our chemistry, seemed like the next natural progression to become a couple. But we were very discrete because we both felt something was a bit… off.

"Meanwhile, our popularity was growing, and we noticed that it gave us more publicity when people were interested in what they thought was a burgeoning romance between us. We recognized fairly quickly that continuing to be noncommittal about our relationship status worked to our advantage by keeping the focus off of our backgrounds and onto us together in the here and now."

Ian broke in at that point. "Not very long after we got together we discovered that while we love each other deeply, it's a different kind of love, more like siblings. We didn't make a good couple. Meanwhile, though, the interest in our undisclosed relationship status was good for ratings and better secured our continuing run here. The producer liked the buzz we were generating, and it provided us both what we needed, so we have kept it up."

"Honestly, I've noticed that y'all have a very distinct relationship. Y'all are very careful to keep people wondering and do share great chemistry on screen, but also seem fiercely protective of each other, especially Ian toward you, Lydia."

"That's because he is," Lydia stated plainly. "He takes his role as my most trusted friend and protector very seriously. I'm very grateful to have someone who respects me enough to care for me as he does. His friendship has helped me immensely in learning to trust and open up to people. Not through a persona, but as myself. It's like peeling away the layers of an onion. I make slow progress removing one layer, but then a new layer is exposed, leaving me extremely raw for a while. But the shell of layers is getting smaller and smaller."

"Okay, I understand, I guess. But how do I fit into all of this?" Kat wondered.

"You're the first person that Ian has really expressed an interest in since all of this started. Though he's an actor, he truly is a shy and focused person and doesn't like the frivolity and artificiality that Hollywood life promotes, so he does his best to avoid being caught up in it. After some bad experiences, he wanted to focus on his career and would rather be alone than have a person lacking in substance by his side," Lydia answered.

"He has shared that with me. So why this meeting?"

"Because," Ian answered, "we have agreed that to become involved with someone, the other one has to approve. There's so much riding on our discretion, both personally and professionally, that we need to make sure whomever either of us chooses to get involved with is respectful of our situation and willing to play along."

"So, basically what y'all are saying is that if it's okay by Lydia, you and I, Ian, can pursue a romantic relationship, but only as long as I'm okay with it being hidden, because all the while there will still be this guise that y'all are in this nebulous relationship?"

"Yes, basically that's it," Lydia told her. "I'm not romantically interest in Ian at all, but I do have a very vested interested in maintaining the status quo."

"I'm not sure how I feel about that," Kat replied honestly.

"It's your decision, Kat," Ian told her. "I just wanted to make sure that you heard from Lydia directly that she isn't at all romantically interested in me and is perfectly fine if we want to pursue a relationship, as long as we are able to keep up the illusion publicly that she and I are more than likely together."

"So, what would that mean for me, exactly?"

"We would have to be careful about being seen in public together. Any awards show or public appearances, Lydia would still be the one on my arm. We'd have to be discrete about our physical relationship and not have intimate interactions where others could see us, even other cast and crew members. We're a very close family up here, but that won't mean that sometimes someone won't let stuff slip. We'd have to do things together as the three of us sometimes, and you with Lydia alone, to make it look like we're all good friends, so questions can't be raised when we are seen going into my trailer, or for walks or rides together… that sort of thing."

"Sounds as though I would be like a mistress, then? Hidden in the shadows, having to sneak around so others don't find out? Ouch. To be honest, this is hitting a little too close to home after what I'm going through."

"I understand, Kat, and that's one of the reasons I was so insistent the other night that we not go any further physically. It wasn't only about you getting divorced first, but I couldn't tell you about this then without first talking to Lydia, and I didn't want you to feel like a mistress or an adulteress. I wanted to make sure you heard the story from both me and Lydia together so that you knew you were not doing anything inappropriate in terms of our relationship and didn't feel like you had sunk to the same level your husband did. I'm hoping that you think me worth the amount of discretion we would have to use to protect Lydia and her past. Since I have met you, my personal need for this symbiotic arrangement is now only about what the perceived relationship means for our publicity and the future of show, but Lydia's personal situation will not change."

Kat looked intently at them both for a long time. As her eyes scanned back and forth over their faces, she saw Lydia's anxious expression and Ian's hopeful look. She thought about what they had both said to her and pondered if it would really bother her that much. In the here and now, she'd have a relationship with Ian, which would be exciting and surreal. But if things progressed, would she be all right with continuing the charade of him pretending that Lydia was the most important person in his life?

"I have to think about it. I don't really know what to say. I guess being discrete would be good for me, too, at least until my divorce is finalized, even though you have made it clear that we wouldn't do anything inappropriate anyway, Ian, until that happens. But until then, I do need to maintain the image that I was the only one who was wronged.

"However, I also have to consider how I'll feel if at some

point things progress between us, but I'd still have to sneak around with you, Ian. I feel for you, Lydia, I really do. But after the hurt I've experienced, I don't know if I'm emotionally willing to accept feeling like I am less worthy than someone else again, even if it's for a good reason."

Lydia reached out and grabbed Kat's hand. "I understand completely. This is an unusual situation, I know. I think that you're an amazing person and that Ian would be very happy with you. You've got that exact quality of substance, a realness if you will, that he never shuts up about." She elbowed him gently in the ribs. "But I do know that having to be invisible is difficult and emotionally draining. It's hard to stay in the shadows and off of people's radar."

Kat stood up and looked down at both of them. Try as she might, she couldn't shake the feeling that she was leaving a job interview for the position of consort.

"I have to go now so I can get enough sleep to help Melinda and Gerard with the breakfast prep in the morning. I do appreciate y'all's candor with me, though, and have given me a lot to think about."

Lydia smiled at her and Ian stood up and kissed her cheek. He moved over to the door and opened it for her, holding it while she climbed down the stairs.

"I'll talk with you later," he said softly to her.

"Goodnight," she answered distractedly as she stepped outside.

Chapter Twenty-Two

Yet again, Kat had lots on her mind as she worked the following day. On one hand, the scenario Ian and Lydia presented felt exciting: she would be part of a secret that no one else knew. It would also certainly help in terms of her divorce. She wasn't sure how it would look if she was divorcing James for adultery and then turned around and technically committed it herself, in public view, no less. In the rest of the country, it probably wouldn't even be considered an affair, since she was already separated from her husband and living on her own: the intent to divorce was there. But the South was not like the rest of the country. People there held their morals in very high regard and to have it be known that she had started seeing someone else before her and James' divorce was finalized could potentially leave her at a legal disadvantage in terms of the settlement.

But on the other hand, being with Ian was like a dream come true. She would be nuts if she wasn't excited about the news that he, a totally gorgeous actor who was the focus of many women's fantasies, was into *her*.

It was surreal. Every time she looked at him, she found herself having to look away because it filled her with such desire she couldn't think straight. His quick smile, dimples, body, and even hair; it all made her melt and heart beat faster every time she thought of him. It was almost too painful to look at him, like looking at the sun. It had started with that first episode on the morning of her birthday—it felt like years ago now— and had only strengthened since she met him and spent time with him. The difference was that now she knew what she would be missing if she backed away. It was very different to fantasize about someone whom she would never meet from actually having the opportunity to choose whether or not she would be with him in person. It was a scenario she had never dared to imagine.

On the other hand, even though she knew the reasons behind

the need for him and Lydia to continue the pretense about their possible relationship status and that they did not have romantic feelings for each other, she still couldn't shake the feeling that she was doing something sneaky and wrong. Did she really want to be forced to act like "the other woman" by staying hidden in the shadows, not allowed to come out to bask in the glow of her new-found relationship? In all honesty, it made her feel dirty and like a second-class citizen, reminiscent of how she felt when she discovered James' infidelity. Even though Ian had been very clear it would all be for show, the feeling that she would be the second choice, the reserve, surprised her. She had been so frustrated when Ian had stopped them from going any further the other night, but now, in her flurry of emotions, she was grateful.

Kat was also nervous about what it would mean to be Ian's girlfriend. She wondered what it would be like to be with him in every sense of the word. Never one to have a plethora of boyfriends, James had been the only person with whom she had ever had sex, and given her good Southern Christian upbringing, their first time had been on their wedding night. Surely, Ian had been with many different women throughout his life. How might she measure up? Did she know what she was doing, really?

James had certainly seemed to enjoy the intimacy throughout their marriage as far as she could tell, but he didn't have a lot to compare with either, at least until he had engaged in an affair with a much younger and significantly more experienced woman. The idea of being compared to the gorgeous, young, fit girls whom Ian had most likely experienced made her stomach churn. Sure, Ian had said that he didn't mind that her body showed all the signs of her age and having borne children, but he hadn't yet seen her naked, either. She kept replaying a horrific scenario in her head where they would finally be ready to be together and he would take one look at her naked form and run away screaming. *Clothing really does hide a multitude of flaws*, Kat mused.

She continued to keep to herself the next day, ruminating over and over in her mind how to proceed. Her body and her heart were more than willing to accept whatever Ian was offering her, but her mind kept nagging her, asking if she maybe deserved more. In the end, she knew she would ultimately just have to pick something and see how it went. After much soul searching, she decided that being with Ian was just too big of a chance to miss out on. She tried to calm her fears and rationalize that she could always get out, and that she would probably have a few different relationships before, if ever, finding someone with whom to start again. For now, though, it felt like there was nothing wrong with indulging in a little fun! She determined that she could just think of this as testing the waters, as Jen had suggested.

But the one thing she did know for sure was that she didn't want to stay married to James anymore. She knew that she didn't love him any longer and that she would never be able to fully trust him again. Making up her mind to call her attorney and have him file the papers, she glanced at the clock, but saw it was now after three o'clock, meaning back home, it was already after five. She resolved that she would call first thing the next day.

Still, she felt a nagging doubt about her choice regarding Ian and wondered if she was not thinking clearly.

***

After the dinner rush had cleared out, Ian came back and sat on a stool, keeping Kat company while she cleaned up and prepared for the next day. He seemed so hopeful she would choose him that he reminded her of a child waiting for a cookie. His hair, which had been slicked back for the shoot, had started to fall back across his forehead, making him seem all the younger. He also seemed to be walking on eggshells, not wanting to do anything that would negatively influence her decision.

Leaning forward on his elbows on the counter, he stifled a yawn as the hour got later.

"Sleepy?" Kat asked him.

"A little," he admitted. "The shoot today was very physical. Lots of riding, fighting, wrestling on the ground, that sort of thing. It was intense. Days like this make me realize that I'm no longer a young man and I'm happy when it's time to go to bed."

"I understand," she said. "This job keeps me on my feet so much, I'm always excited when I can get into bed."

"Wanna get excited in my bed?" he teased with a wink, letting his guard down for a second.

Kat gazed back at him for a moment. If only he knew how tempted she was to say yes. "I would like to," she finally confessed, "But I'm still pondering what I want to do about our situation. I don't want my judgment clouded."

By this point, Gerard and Melinda had finished their work and gone, and it was just Ian and Kat together in the kitchen. He got up and walked around until he was directly behind her and leaned against her back. "I would welcome the opportunity to cloud your judgment," he whispered in her ear.

Kat turned around and looked into his eyes. She felt her resolve to think objectively melt away as he leaned in slowly for a kiss. Gentle at first, it became more demanding as he felt her respond to his touch. She put her hand on his cheek and he moaned softly. Suddenly, he reached his hands around her hips and lifted her onto the counter.

"Ian, you aren't making this any easier for me to decide," she complained between kisses.

"Good!" he answered huskily. "I want to sway you in my favor."

They began to kiss again, and Kat felt the last of her reservations about the situation quickly melting away. She knew this was not the time or place to think irrationally, but she didn't care. Ian's kisses became more passionate, and she met him with the same intensity. Before she knew what was happening, she had wrapped her arms and legs around him as he stood with his feet planted firmly on the floor.

His hands were on her rear, pressing her further into him. As their breathing rates steadily increased, so did their soft sounds of total relinquishment, of being lost in each other.

Ian was the one to finally break away. "We can't keep doing

this," he said.

Kat began to panic. "What do you mean?"

"I mean I have to step away now or I won't want to."

"Oh!" Kat understood. He was trying to slow things down, cool off a bit.

She sat on the counter, facing him. "I guess I understand that," she said, her chest still rapidly rising and falling. "But I don't want you to step away or to stop. Ian, I respect the fact that you are trying to protect my honor, but honestly, when I'm near you, I can't think of anything else but being with you."

"I know!" he moaned. "This is so hard! All I want to do is to take you back to my trailer and make love to you. I know it's going to be incredible. But I will not allow myself to be the reason you feel guilty or pressured."

"You're certainly making my decision a lot harder. I have, however, made up my mind about one thing: I'm calling my lawyer in the morning and having him file the papers. I still don't know how I feel about this whole situation, but it has made me realize that I'm sure I no longer love James and don't want to go back to him."

"Good. Glad to hear it," he murmured against her neck.

"So, is filing enough for you to not have to worry about making me an adulteress?"

He stepped back a bit to look into her eyes. "I want it to. So much!"

"So, say yes!"

"I don't know, Kat. You still won't be technically divorced."

Kat hung her head. It felt like he was trying to find a reason why he should not be with her. He looked at her and put his finger under her chin and lifted it up.

"Hey!" he said. "Don't do that. Don't think that I don't want to and am trying to make excuses. You can't have any idea how much I want you right now. But I want it to be perfect."

"All right. It's getting late and we should be getting to bed, I guess."

"Mine or yours?" he asked with a grin.

"At this point, Ian, I honestly wouldn't care. A table or a stall in the barn would suffice."

He chuckled and gave her his hand. She hopped gracefully down off the countertop and gently bounced onto the floor on the balls of her feet. Ian wrapped his arms around her.

"Goodnight, Kat. Sweet dreams. I know I'll be having them."

They left the building, and he walked her back toward her trailer. Kat felt the electricity flowing between them, and she knew if she didn't do something fast, she wouldn't be able to stop herself, but there were still people milling about. She leaned in and kissed him quickly on the cheek, thinking that was appropriate between friends and would keep tongues from wagging.

"Thanks, Ian, for the nice night. I enjoyed talking with you." With that, she winked at him and turned on her heel to go into the trailer.

As Kat got into bed, she felt like she was floating on air. She could not believe what Ian was able to do to her. All her rationale and logic flew out the window any time he came near. She took several deep breaths and tried to think about what to do. Dying to call or text Jen, she knew that would be impossible, because she couldn't explain the situation without outing Lydia and Ian's secret. Kat looked up at the ceiling of the trailer in frustration and listened to the wind howling down off the mountains. That was one thing she had yet to get used to up there: the wind seemed to always be blowing. At home, even a slight breeze was rare, unless there was a storm coming. Here, it was a welcome distraction.

She forced herself instead to think about how she would tell James about the divorce. He had texted her several times over the past few weeks, begging her to reconsider, telling her that he missed her, and making sure that she was okay. She kept her responses short and to the point: *I'm still thinking. Thank you. Yes, I'm fine.* She knew, though, that soon enough, he would have to find out that she was going to divorce him. What she didn't know was how to communicate it. She didn't know if that was a conversation she needed to have in person, over the phone, or best yet, just by having him served with the papers. The last option seemed to be the easiest for her, but deep in her heart, she couldn't help feeling that it would be cruel. She tried to remember that she had once loved this man, that he had been her whole world, and that because of that, he deserved better. At the same time, however, she knew it wasn't going to go over well and didn't want to deal with the immediate fallout.

She then began to worry, too, about her kids. How were they going to take the news? She tried to reason with herself that it wouldn't really affect them as they were old enough to be caught up in their own lives. But being a good Southern family, she also knew that the idea of everyone bringing over the kids to Grandma and Grandpa's house for Sunday dinner was something that ran deep.

Olivia will take it the hardest, she supposed. Then, thoughts of Drew popped into her mind.

Always her most sensitive child, she wondered if he would be scarred by this. She knew he was leaving for college sometime in August and that would help him ease through the transition, but she couldn't help feeling nervous about his reaction, nonetheless.

Kat tossed and turned until two a.m., when she finally fell into a fitful sleep. Her dreams were full of crying babies, James' devastated face, and lawyers yelling at each other in a courtroom, hurling papers back and forth between them. When her alarm jolted her awake, she wryly thought that she should have stayed with Ian—there, she'd had her best sleep in a very long time in his arms.

***

After Kat had closed the door, Ian stared after her, willing her to come back out. He had wanted to kiss her so badly before she went into her trailer but hadn't dared with everyone around. He didn't actually care what people thought anymore; his agreement with Lydia was the only thing keeping him from knocking on the door, picking her up, and carrying her back to his bed. He sighed and shook his head in frustration as he began to walk back to his trailer. He didn't know how long American divorces took, but he certainly hoped it wasn't long because his being a gentleman and wanting to do the right thing was getting harder and harder.

Chapter Twenty-Three

Four a.m. came much too quickly for Kat as she struggled to drag her body out of her nice, warm bed. She rued the fact that she hadn't been able to turn her brain off the night before and that she always had to overanalyze everything. Exhausted and annoyed, she wondered why, when for the first time in her adult life she was free to do basically whatever she wanted without having to answer to anyone, she still held on to her practical self. She had just been given an opportunity to throw away everything she had ever known and start over on a new adventure.

Then again, she ruminated, *if I proceeded with Ian under the stipulations that he and Lydia gave me, I would still not be completely unrestricted.*

Kat dressed slowly and bundled up against the cold Canadian morning. "When does this blessed country start to have spring?" she mumbled to herself grumpily.

She was walking along through the dark when suddenly someone reached out from behind a trailer and grabbed her. She started to scream when she felt a hand go gently over her mouth and felt their breath on her ear.

"Shhhh… Kat! It's me. Don't worry," Ian whispered

He let her go and she spun around to look at him. "What are you doing?" she hissed at him.

He took her hand and led her into the woods further away from the trailer he'd been waiting by.

"I couldn't sleep, so I figured I would come out here and wait for you. It wasn't my intention to scare you. I just wanted to see you and couldn't wait until we were surrounded by everyone. I wanted to do this." He leaned over and placed his warm lips on hers. "In fact, I could think of nothing else all night.

"Mmmmm…" Kat exhaled. "I think I can forgive you for almost giving me a heart attack. But I'm an old woman, Ian. You shouldn't do that to me; my heart might not be able take it."

"My heart can't take not being around you. I'm trying to

give you your space, but it's hard. I just want to yell 'Pick me! Pick me!', consequences be damned."

"I know, Ian. I'm just really wrestling with the idea of having to be in the shadows. Right now, I know that it's new and exciting and honestly, I will take you any way I can get you. I mean, I was ready to sleep with you days ago, even if it was just going to be a one-night stand. But will that be enough over time? Will it be like this forever? It almost makes me feel like you are a polygamist, and I would be a sister wife. At what point do you and Lydia come clean? Will you eventually have to marry her at some point? Then I really would feel like a sister wife!"

"Whoa! Kat slow down! What's all of this talk about polygamy and sister wives? No one has said that I'm going to marry Lydia or that this would be forever. But that's a good point, actually. Lydia and I never really did discuss a time limit or where we would go from here. The arrangement felt comfortable to us as it was. I honestly don't think that either of us have thought about a plan on how to get out of it. I certainly didn't plan on meeting you up here and basically having all of my career focus go out the window in an instant."

"I'm glad that you say you understand, Ian. But truly, how would you feel if I told you that I was going to stay married to James, even though I don't love him, and I would be with you except for all of the important occasions in my life, like holidays, when I would be with him, acting like everything was fine?"

"Ouch. I never thought of that like that. That wouldn't make me happy."

"Exactly. I like you, Ian, and I like spending time with you. But I need to know if I like myself more. Which is more important? My happiness or my self-respect?"

"Tough choices. I wish you didn't feel this conflicted. Couldn't we just give this a try and see where it goes without having to overanalyze everything to death?"

"I guess we could, Ian, but welcome to being Kat. I'm dealing with a huge blow to my self-esteem right now with what happened in my marriage, so I have to question whether or not I would agree to the terms of this situation if my self-worth hadn't been decimated by James' betrayal. And truthfully, I was never overly confident when it came to relationships. I was a late bloomer and felt invisible all through high school. Jen was gorgeous and had all of the boys after her, and I looked like I was still twelve at seventeen."

Ian sighed. "Kat, I really wish you wouldn't take this personally. I would ask this of anyone because of my respect for Lydia. But that doesn't mean I'm taking advantage of you because I don't respect you. In fact, if you chose to do this, I'd actually think you are incredibly strong and confident."

Kat had started to stomp her feet and rub her hands together. She had her coat on but had not bundled up for anything more than a quick walk to the kitchen from her trailer.

"You're getting cold, aren't you?" Ian asked.

Kat only nodded. He looked into her eyes with concern and silently opened his coat and motioned to her. She closed the gap between them and put her arms around his waist so he could wrap its edges around her. He tipped his head down and placed a kiss on the top of her head.

"Better?" he asked. She nodded again, this time into his chest.

They stood together like that for several minutes, not talking. Kat listened to the rhythmic beat of his heart through his soft flannel shirt, until she finally looked up at him and told him she had to go help Melinda and Gerard with breakfast for everyone. He studied at her for a long time and then slowly nodded, as he reluctantly opened his arms and let her slide out from his jacket.

"Kat?"

"Yes?"

"Please, tonight, can you help me run lines again?"

"Sure. Wait… why? Is Lydia's voice bad again?"

His eyes twinkled at her as he smiled demurely. "She's fine. I'd just rather do it with you. Means more somehow."

And with that, he took her face in his hands, and gave her a scorching kiss. His cold fingers on her cheeks gave her the chills, and when he finally let her go, she took a few steps backward in an attempt to stay upright.

"'Til tonight," he said as he leaned his forehead onto hers.

"'Til tonight," she whispered back to him. He placed a sweet kiss on the tip of her nose.

"That nose is getting awfully cold. You'd better get inside before you get frostbite."

When she walked for a way, then turned back and took him in, standing between the trees in the murky beginnings of dawn. He had been waiting, watching her walk back toward the road to the kitchen. Smiling, he gave her his salute before starting the trek toward his trailer.

When she got inside, Melinda and Gerard were elbows deep in biscuit dough. The turkey sausage had all been fried and was waiting for Kat to come finish the gravy. Gerard and Melinda each looked up at her and merely nodded their heads in acknowledgement while Kat grabbed an apron and threw it over her head.

"Sorry!" she exclaimed breathlessly. "I must have overslept."

The rest of the breakfast prep went smoothly. Kat still marveled how well they worked together, that they all knew what the others were going to do, even without verbal communication. They rarely had to exchange words, as they had each other's rhythms down to a science. Jen had repeatedly told her that Melinda and Gerard were invaluable, and they continued to prove her right.

When everyone began to file in for their morning meal, Kat was surprised by Ian's noticeable absence, especially since she had just seen him about an hour and a half earlier. It didn't take long to realize everyone else was surprised, too.

"Where is that boy?" George asked loudly, cutting through her thoughts.

"I don't know, sir," said his assistant. "Should I go look for him?"

"You'd better, son. It ain't like him to miss a meal," George replied.

Lydia glanced up at Kat, and Kat just shrugged her shoulders in response. The actress gave the smallest hint of a nod back to indicate she had understood. Kat began to worry and then admonished herself that she was foolish to do so. Ian had only gone back to his trailer, she was sure of it. He said he hadn't slept well, either, and had to have been tired, too. She forced herself to turn her attention back to cleaning up the breakfast remnants and starting on lunch.

Kat worked for quite a bit longer when someone from the crew popped their head back inside the door to the dining hall.

"Still no Ian?" he called.

"Nope," Gerard answered.

"Okay. Thanks."

By this time, Kat began to truly worry. *What's going on? Where is he? It's not like him to miss a shoot, and if he has been asleep in his trailer, someone would have certainly found him by now, right?*

She began to deliberate more about all the possibilities of what could have happened to him. When she finally couldn't take not knowing anymore, she took off her white jacket, hung it on the hook, and walked out the door without a word, leaving Melinda and Gerard to simply look at each other with raised eyebrows and keep on working.

As she walked toward set, Kat wondered what she was hoping to see. Surely if Ian had showed up there, others would have noticed him already. Continuing to walk, she passed the stable and heard some men talking inside about how Ian's horse was gone. Suddenly, Kat got a sick feeling in her stomach. She immediately asked the men if she could tack Lydia's horse to go and look for him. They agreed and helped her, and soon she was on her way. For some reason, she felt in her heart that he had gone to their special place by the lake up the trail. Urging Lydia's horse to hurry, she felt her heart skip a beat when she arrived in the meadow and found it deserted.

Just when she was about ready to turn around, however, she saw movement out of the corner of her eye. It was Ian's horse, standing just at the far edge of the trees.

She carefully steered Lydia's mare toward him as she frantically looked around for Ian but saw nothing. Calling his name, she thought maybe he had gone into the trees, but when he didn't answer, she wondered if he had fallen off somewhere. She tied Ian's horse to a tree and then began to walk Lydia's horse around the lake. That's when she saw him, lying face up in the grass like he was looking at the sky. Moving closer, he appeared to be sleeping, but he didn't stir as Kat jumped off the horse and ran toward him. She was frantically calling his name when he finally sat up a little, groaned, and held his head in his left hand before then sinking back down to the ground.

"Are you all right?" Kat yelled she approached him.

"I'm okay. I just hurt a little. That damned horse must have thrown me. A flock of birds took off from the lake and I guess they spooked him. Next thing I know, I'm on the ground here with you running up to me like I'm dead."

Kat put her hands on her hips. "Well, you sure looked dead, lying there in the grass. Are you sure you're okay? Can you get up?"

Ian sat up for a second, attempted to stand, but then sank back down. "Nope! Not yet. I think I'll just sit here for a wee bit longer."

Kat sat down beside him, and he leaned over to put his head on her shoulder. "My head hurts," he told her miserably.

"I'm sure it does!" she exclaimed.

He moved his head lower until it was in her lap, stretching out his legs. They sat there in that position for a long time before she asked if he was ready to try and stand again. He agreed and this time he did make it to a standing position. Feeling around on his head, he exclaimed, "No wonder my head hurts!"

Kat reached her hand up to feel and had to admit the large goose egg he had found was quite impressive. "Anything else hurt?" she asked.

"Just my pride," he answered with a rueful smile.

"What were you doing up here, anyway? Everyone has been going crazy looking for you."

"I couldn't sleep any longer, and I knew you had to work, but I also knew that I couldn't stay away from you, so I figured I had to get out of there or I would barge in and do something inappropriate. I decided then it'd be best to tack up old Buster here and come up to watch the sunrise to think."

Kat just looked at him, her eyes big. "What?" he finally asked her.

"That's so sweet, Ian. I'm so sorry you got hurt, but to hear that you had to come up here to avoid me because you wanted to be with me is about the sweetest thing I've ever heard. Crazy, but sweet."

"I've been thinking all night about what we talked about, about how I would feel if the situation were reversed, and I had to be in the shadows of your and James' relationship. I wouldn't like it at all!"

"I know, Ian. I don't think anyone would like it— that's my point. Well, except for my husband's mistress; she liked to be in the shadows. 'Got off on it,' is what she said. But don't worry. I've made my decision to give this a try. I certainly don't need anything serious right now after what happened with James, and I don't need to hop from one long term relationship to another. Let's just see where this goes. It may be that once we are off this mountain, things change. No use getting everyone all worked up about pretty much nothing right now, anyway."

Ian smiled happily at her. "That sounds good," he told her.

"Can you ride?" she asked him.

"I think so, if that mangy animal doesn't decide to toss me again," he said in disgust.

"Why don't I take him, and you ride Lydia's mare. She's much more predictable."

"Can you handle him, though?" Ian asked nervously.

"Ian, you never asked me if I'm any good at riding horses. You just assumed that I wasn't. I spent time every summer with my grandparents on their horse ranch from when I was five to seventeen. I rode, broke, and cared for them all. I hadn't been riding since, but once I got back up in that saddle, it all came flooding right back."

She stood beside him as he heaved himself into the saddle and then reached over and handed him the reigns. Mounting Buster, together they set off back toward the set. After a few minutes, Kat noticed that Ian was wincing in pain.

"Ian, what's wrong?" she asked.

"My ribs hurt," he responded through his clenched jaw.

"Oh, no! Did you break them?" she asked, her face full of concern. "Can you ride?"

"I can. Just the bouncing bothers them quite a bit."

They slowly made it back down the rest of the trail. By the time they had made it to the stable, Ian was the color of a sheet. Kat quickly dismounted and handed her reigns to someone standing nearby. She ran over to the mare and helped guide Ian down. Everyone around them murmured as he weakly melted into her, and she led him toward his trailer. She yelled at the small crowd assembling to have someone send a medic.

She got Ian into his trailer and began to help him remove his coat. He sat down wearily, and Kat bent down to take off his boots. Telling her that he wanted to put on his sweats and where she could find them in his room so she could run to grab them, she quickly came back to him on the couch. He slowly stood up in front of her and unbuttoned his jeans. Courteously Kat averted her eyes as he tried to push them over his hips and onto the floor, but he let out a gasp of pain as he bent forward and told her breathlessly, "I can't do this. I need your help."

Kat walked closer to him, telling herself to stay unattached and focus only on the task at hand, to treat him like she would any other person who was hurt: clinically and disengaged.

As she slipped her hands onto the waistband of his jeans and pulled them down, however, she couldn't keep her mind from wandering. She leaned lower down and was soon eye level with his crotch. Trying unsuccessfully not to notice and keep on going, she could feel her cheeks burning, and what's more, she knew the heat didn't come only from her.

She got his pants past his knees and asked him to sit. When he did, she pulled the legs over his feet, freeing him from them. She asked him if he needed help with getting the other pants on and he just nodded in response, as talking seemed to take too much effort. Starting again, this time in reverse, she pulled each leg over his feet and then slowly pulling the pants up. Once again, she was facing his crotch, trying not to notice what was in front of her, and feeling like she was going to faint. Now she had hard proof, literally, of what she was missing.

Breathe! When she looked up, her cheeks burning red, he laughed softly at her.

"You all right down there?" he inquired, a little cheekily. She couldn't respond for a few more seconds.

"Well, then! That was awkward," she told him.

"I guess. We Europeans tend to be a lot less prudish than you Americans, though."

"Yes, and average Americans are way less proper than Southerners, I think."

"I didn't make you too uncomfortable did I, love?"

"You did. But not for the reasons you're thinking. Let's just say it's good that you are hurt."

"Thanks?" he smiled quizzically at her.

"Seriously, Ian. I swear that was about the most sensual thing I've ever experienced."

"Glad to be of service." He grinned at her. Just then came a knock at the door.

Chapter Twenty-Four

Kat opened the door, allowing one of the shoot's medics to walk in. The cute and perky young woman quickly examined Ian's head, checked his pupils, and felt around his ribs. Kat felt a slight tinge of jealously at that, but then chided herself for being so crazy.

This woman is here to assess him and help him to feel better! She was surprised that she had even reacted.

The medic told Ian she thought he had a mild concussion from hitting the ground and that he had most likely cracked a rib or two. She then chastised him, saying he was lucky he hadn't done worse to himself. Advising him that he could go down to a hospital in Calgary, she reported that there wasn't really much they could do for either condition other than prescribe rest and bind his chest, which she could do for him right there.

She turned to collect her bag from the table and said over her shoulder, "Your shirt needs to come off. Can you do it or should she help you?" She glanced over at Kat.

"I think I'm going to need the help," Ian gasped weakly. "This is really starting to hurt."

"The shock is wearing off," she told him simply. "It's going to get worse before it's better. You're going to have to rest for a while and take some anti-inflammatories. We don't really have anything stronger up here, but if you want a prescription, you can go to the doctor we use down the hill or to the hospital; they can fix that."

"I'll be all right," Ian answered. "I hate medicine. I'll just take the anti-inflammatories and rest. This isn't the first time I've had a concussion or broken a few ribs. I am Irish, after all—I spent way too much time in pubs in my youth."

Meanwhile, Kat worried about how to pull Ian's undershirt over his head. It had been easy to pull off the button-down flannel he had still been wearing since she first saw him that morning, but it wasn't his only layer. She knew that it had to be done, but that it was also really going to hurt. She had broken a few ribs herself at fourteen when one of her grandparents' horses had thrown her. Getting dressed—having to bend over and stretch—had made her nearly pass out.

"Okay, Ian. Let's do this. Stay seated and try to put your hands above your head," Kat told him. "I'll then try to get this off without jarring you too much."

He nodded in agreement and grimaced as he reached upward. Kat maneuvered herself so that she was right in front of him. She then bent down and grabbed the hem of his shirt. Glancing up to check if he was ready, she noticed that his eyes were fixed on her neckline, her V- neck T-shirt gaping to allow him a nice view down the valley between her breasts, and he was unconsciously smiling. Shaking her head at the one-tracked mindedness of men, she squared herself and prepared to pull off the shirt, thinking that she just needed to do it quickly, like pulling off a Band-Aid.

She took a deep breath to strengthen her resolve and counted aloud to three. As smoothly as she could in one movement, she got his shirt over his head and onto the couch. They had both gasped while she was doing it, him in pain, and her at the shock of seeing him half naked before her. She had seen his chest the other night, but to see him completely without a shirt made her swoon. His arms were strong, his back and stomach muscular. She knew that somewhere on set there was a gym of sorts set up and it showed that he used it. The show always had everyone fully clothed, as was customary for the period, and even in the more physical scenes, such as when his character Joe was chopping wood or building something, he still had a shirt on. Though it clung nicely to him, it was nothing compared to how he looked without one.

"You okay?" she asked him once she got her wits back about her.

"Yeah," he said breathlessly. "Just glad that's over!"

The medic walked back to where Ian was standing and ordered him to stand up so she could wrap his ribs. She asked

Kat to please stand on his other side so they could pass the wrapping back and forth to avoid accidentally bumping him when reaching around and potentially causing him more pain. The bandaging finished, Kat found the flannel shirt he had been wearing early in the morning and held it out for him, since the medic had pointed out he shouldn't be putting anything over his head for a while, and it would have been too difficult, anyway. He held his arms out as she gently slipped it on, and she moved around to his front so she could button it. Her job now done, the medic gathered her stuff and told Ian again that he needed to rest and should head to bed to do so. She then looked pointedly at Kat while explaining that someone needed to be with Ian twenty-four/seven for the next few days because of the concussion and in case he needed something. She shut the door tightly behind her when she left.

"So…" said Ian.

"Yeah…"

"This is a fine turn of events. I wonder how George will take this." As Ian said it, there was a loud knock at the door and George burst in.

"Probably not well," Kat remarked when she saw the expression on his face.

"Ian! What the hell, boy? I just get back to a normal schedule after Lydia's illness and now you go and maim yourself! What were you thinkin'?"

"I just needed to get away and clear my head."

"Son, you forget that I saw you on a horse that first season. Sweet Jesus, it was all we could do to pray that you wouldn't fall off and break your neck. I would have expected this then, not now."

"I'm so sorry," Ian told him.

"I'm not sure what is goin' on with you lately, but you've gotta get your head back in the game, son. This is costin' us money! Big money!"

"Well, can't you just shoot the scenes that just have Lydia in them for now, like you did with Ian when she was sick?"

George turned to look at Kat as she spoke.

"I reckon that's exactly what we are goin' to have to do," he said. He turned back to Ian. "You do whatever you can do to make sure that you heal quickly, you hear?"

"All right," Ian responded.

"The medic says that he'll need someone here twenty-four /seven for the next few days to make sure he's okay," Kat interjected.

"Well, now, that's another problem. There ain't nobody who can spare that kind of time, except maybe your assistant, Ian. But he's now sick with whatever crap Lydia had, so I don't want him in here a whole helluva lot. That's all I need is for you to get sick and cause further delays."

"I could take a shift," Kat heard herself volunteer.

"You? The caterer? How are we goin' to eat, then, sugar?"

"That's the beauty of this," she rushed on. "I have two assistants who are even more capable than me. Nowhere else do you have extra people like that to spare."

"That's true enough," he answered thoughtfully.

"How you feel about that, son?"

"At least I won't starve," Ian replied, with his crooked grin.

"Then it's settled. Caterer, you talk to those assistants of yours and let them know what is goin' on. I'll have his assistant stop by once in a while to give you a break. That way, you can still supervise that everythin' is goin' okay in the kitchen. If the meals start to be a problem, though, we'll have to do somethin' else."

"Sounds good," Ian quickly agreed.

George bid his farewell and exited the trailer. He had been gone just a few minutes when there was another knock at the door, this one much more timid.

"Come in!" Kat called and Lydia poked her head around.

"Everything okay?" she asked.

"Everything is fine, love. Just took a nasty spill and will be out of commission for a while. It'll be all right."

"What are they going to do with you?" she asked him.

"I have to rest for a few days and see how it goes. Kat has agreed to stay with me most of the time, and Jacob will help out, too, so she can keep an eye on things in the kitchen."

"Ian, do you really think that is a good idea? What will people say?" Lydia sounded almost panicked.

"Lydia, they'll say what George did. There isn't anyone else who can be spared for that long around here when Jacob isn't available. Kat has assistants that can handle the work."

Lydia looked thoughtful for a few seconds. "All right. I guess we don't have much of a choice. Just be careful, please, you two. I'm not ready for this to blow up in our faces."

"We will be," Kat assured her.

Lydia leaned over and kissed Ian on the cheek. "Heal quickly," she told him. With that, she headed back to the set.

"So…" said Kat.

"Yep," said Ian.

"You heard the medic. Let's get you into bed. You'll be more comfortable laying down."

"Only if you promise to lay there with me."

"Ian, I don't think that is a good idea. The way people just burst in here—I don't think I could get up fast enough and locking the door would make it look even worse."

"Then just sit on the bed with me," he pleaded.

He stood up and started to slowly take the short walk to his bedroom. Kat pulled back the covers and he slipped in between the sheets. He smiled at her.

"This reminds me of being sick when I was little and my mother would sit with me," he told her happily. "That's probably why I don't like to be alone when I'm sick or hurt," he added as an afterthought.

Kat sat down on the edge of the bed and sighed. "Can I get you anything?" she asked him.

"No, thanks, I'm good. I'm just really tired. In fact, I think I'll take a nap for a while. Just please stay in here with me."

She got up and placed a kiss on his forehead. "Okay. I'll be right here."

He quickly fell asleep, and Kat pulled out her phone. She decided that she had better text Jen and let her know what the deal was: *Hey*

Jen: *Hey*

Kat: *So… we have a problem…*

Jen: *Oh, no! What? Food poisoning? Norovirus?*

Kat: *Nope. Nothing like that. I'm just having to take some time off for a few days.*

Jen: *Time off? Girl, what are you talking about?*

Kat: *Ian fell of his horse today and got a concussion and broke some ribs. He needs someone to stay with him, but there really was no one else to do it. His assistant is sick. There are three of us in catering and you said yourself that Melinda and Gerard could practically do this gig themselves.*

Jen: *Kat, do you really think this is a good idea?*

Kat: *As good as any other. He has to heal and there are enough of us to take care of business. Everyone else is needed for production.*

Jen: *Okay, I guess.*

Kat: *George is completely onboard.*

Jen: *That's good, at least.*

Ian shifted in his sleep and moaned softly. Kat looked at him and reached over to push the hair off his forehead. She felt helpless watching him so obviously in pain, even while sleeping.

Kat started to feel groggy herself. She leaned against the headboard and rested her head back. Next thing she knew, Lydia was standing in the doorway.

"How's he doing?" she quietly asked Kat.

"All right. He's hurting. He moans in his sleep every time he moves."

"Poor guy!" Lydia said.

"Yeah, he did a number on himself. But it could have been so much worse."

Ian opened his eyes to see both women watching him.

"What?" he asked.

"Nothing, Ian. We were just talking about how lucky you

are that this wasn't worse, and I was about to tell Kat that I'm so glad she knew where you were and found you as soon as she did. None of the rest of us even knew that place existed."

"How's filming?" he asked her.

"Fine, I guess. George is in a mood, though."

"When isn't he in a mood?" Ian laughed and then groaned. "Note to self: don't laugh for a few days."

Ian's assistant, Jacob, with his cold-reddened eyes and nose, came by about four o'clock to let Kat get out and check on things in the kitchen. When she walked in, she saw Gerard and Melinda hard at work with dinner prep. For the second time since they arrived, Melinda called her lucky.

"How come all of the stuff with Ian seems to happen when you are around? You're either incredibly lucky, or you're a total stalker!"

"Nope, not a stalker. Did Jen talk to y'all? Have you got this handled for a few days?"

"Sure," said Gerard. "Without Ian, there's no show. Without a show, there's no paycheck. Go take care of that guy. We're good here."

"All right," said Kat. "You know where to find me if there's a problem."

Kat grabbed some food for herself and Ian and headed back to his trailer.

Jacob had been sitting on the edge of Ian's bed, going over his itinerary for his trip back to Los Angeles over the spring holiday break. Kat and Ian hadn't discussed what he was going to do during the filming hiatus over those ten days. She'd overheard him saying that he had to get back to Los Angeles to get things ready for his mother's upcoming move from Ireland to the house he purchased, but that was all. After Jen insisted that she come back down there over the break, Kat still hadn't given too much more thought to where she was going either, but now that she knew Ian was going back, she thought the idea sounded a whole lot better than her original plan of staying up at the set pretty much alone.

A few minutes later, Jacob stood up and noticed Kat standing in the kitchen area. "Next," he drawled somewhat nastily as he walked past her. Kat smiled sweetly and told him goodbye, then grabbed the food and brought it in to Ian.

"Can you sit up?"

"I think so." Ian tried to push himself up but gasped in pain instead. "Actually, I think I have to go about this differently," he said.

He rolled onto his side and swung his legs over the edge of the bed, using the momentum to help raise his upper body. He then stood, moved to the side, and sat down with much closer to the headboard than before. Kat put down the food and rushed over to help him get his pillow situated, while he pulled his legs back up onto the mattress. Once he was settled, Kat brought him his food.

"Fried chicken," she told him. "I know you like it."

"I do. But I'm not too terribly hungry, though," he replied.

They sat in silence, each focusing on eating their meals. True to his word, Ian ate very little, still seeming groggy and a bit disoriented. By the time Kat had returned from taking the remains of their food back to the kitchen, he was fast asleep.

Kat didn't know where she was going to sleep. There were other options for beds in his trailer, but she didn't have any bedding and it was still cold enough at night that she would need blankets. Already having stayed before with Ian for a night in his bed, she reasoned that this shouldn't be any different when she knew he might need her before morning. She had nothing to sleep in, though, so she took off her clothes and rummaged through his drawers and closet until she found a cool, crisp cotton button down in a soft green. Putting it on, she walked over to the mirror and shook her hair out a bit, noticing how the shirt accentuated the green in her eyes. Making a split-second decision to lock the trailer for the night, she then returned to the bedroom and lifted the covers opposite from Ian before climbing in. It felt both awkward and exciting to be sleeping so close to him and wondered if she would be able to get any rest at all that night. Though she had shared her bed with James just about every night before his cheating had come out, it still felt different now to be next to a man in bed. Even in the short amount of time since she had left James, she had gotten used to sleeping by herself. She listened to Ian's soft, rhythmic breathing, though, and soon she closed her eyes, having been lulled to sleep.

***

At some point in the night, Kat woke up. She lay in the darkness and realized that Ian had turned in his sleep and was facing her. Having flung his arm over her hip, he was also pulling her to him.

"You okay?" she asked.

"I am," he answered gruffly. "Just lonely and a bit cold. Then I woke up and discovered that I had a beautiful woman in my bed who also works to warm me up."

"I stole one of your shirts to sleep in," she whispered. "I hope you don't mind."

He rubbed the palm of his hand up and down just below the hem of the shirt where her legs were visible. His hand lingered on the soft skin of her outer thigh, rubbing it softly with his thumb.

"Not at all," he replied. "I'm sure it looks way better on you than it ever did on me."

"I doubt that," she scoffed. "How's your pain?"

"It seems to be doing a bit better. I'm not sure if I'm healing, the medicine is working, or if I'm just too distracted by having you here beside me to feel it."

"I'm glad you woke me, actually," she looked over at him. Moonlight was dimly coming through the blinds over his window, and she could just make out his incredible features. "I need to set an alarm to go unlock the door. I locked it earlier because I thought it wouldn't look so good if people started bursting in here first thing in the morning to find me lying half naked in your bed with you. Though I think most people with any brain in their head would realize you're in no shape to do anything physical, it would still look bad."

"Mmmm…" he agreed with her. "That's true. But I was kind of hoping that we *could* do something physical. I don't think I can lay here not touching you, knowing you are right here beside me, and go back to sleep."

Kat gently rolled him onto his back, leaning over him, and let her lips linger mere millimeters from his.

"I think that could be arranged," she informed him.

Slowly, she lowered her face to his and began to gently kiss him. He responded in kind and soon their kisses moved away from sweet to growing in need. Kat pushed herself up higher, wanting to be closer to him, eliciting a pained groan.

"Oh my gosh! I'm so sorry! Are you okay? I didn't mean to hurt you!"

"I know," he reassured her breathlessly. "Just a little too much pressure on the old rib cage right then was all."

Kat felt awful as she pushed herself up and looked at him. "I think that might be enough of the physical for one night."

Ian's face fell, though, like a forlorn child, and Kat couldn't help herself. She pressed her lips to his again while she worked her hand under his shirt and began rubbing it up and down his torso. He moaned and grabbed her cold hand, placing it over his damaged ribs. "That feels so good!" he gasped.

"Payback from this morning when you put your hands on my face. You gave me the chills!"

"I was merely making sure you were awake and ready to start your day," he quipped.

"Well, that was accomplished when you grabbed me from out of nowhere. It scared me to death!"

"Sorry about that. I didn't know how else to get your attention without calling attention to myself."

"You could have texted me!" she replied hotly.

"I would have, but I don't have your number," he retorted.

That's when it hit her how fast they were moving. She had gone from meeting him to sleeping in his bed in a little over a month, the first week of which was spent trying to avoid him.

The thought subdued her.

"Now, don't get upset," Ian admonished. "This is exactly why I said we needed to wait to go any further. I knew you would be shocked when you realized how fast we were going."

"I can't believe it. I know we just met, but I feel like we've known each other our entire lives," she exclaimed.

"I feel the same way. That's why one of us has to be the responsible adult." He grinned.

She playfully smacked his chest. As he flinched, she gasped, "Oh! I'm so sorry!"

"It's okay. 'No harm, no foul,' isn't that what you say over here?" he assured her breathlessly.

Kat turned and lay gently back beside Ian. He reached his hand down between them and took hers. Soon they were both back asleep, their fingers still intertwined.

Chapter Twenty-Five

Kat had set the alarm on her phone for half past four. She figured that would give her time to get redressed and out onto the couch in the front of Ian's trailer before anyone came in. When it rang, she left Ian sleeping under the covers, shutting the door behind her, and was seated and reading her email when a knock came not even five minutes later.

The door was then immediately thrown open, and Jacob burst inside with his phone in hand, asking Kat how Ian was holding up. She reported that he had slept for most of the night and seemed to be doing well, then explained that he was still sleeping, and she didn't want to disturb him. Jacob merely blinked at her for a few seconds before saying that he had found a few different possibilities for Ian's flight to Los Angeles for the following week that he needed to look over, and that everything was in order for the closing on his house while he was there. There would be a final walk through beforehand, and then Ian would get the keys. He then stated hotly that he had sent the schedule to Ian's email.

"Please tell him when he wakes up," Jacob demanded. After confirming she would, Jacob turned and left without another word.

Twenty minutes later, there came another knock on the door, much gentler than the first. Lydia popped her head in, and when she saw Kat, she opened the door wider and stepped inside.

"Good morning!" she greeted Kat.

"Good morning."

"How's our patient doing today? Did he get any sleep? Did you?"

"Yes, we both did, thanks. He's still asleep. I stayed with him in there but set my alarm so that I could get out here before anyone came over. It was a good thing, too. You just missed Jacob," Kat told her.

"That *is* a good thing!" Lydia said. "I'm not entirely sure we can really trust that man. He's nice enough, but he tends to gossip with a lot of the crew. My gut instinct tells me to be wary around him."

"Okay, thanks. I'll keep that in mind."

"Kat, I really hope you aren't too weirded out by my relationship with Ian, and I hope you won't hold it against him that he is choosing to honor our agreement. I don't think I've ever seen him so happy. He keeps telling me about how great it is that you treat him like a normal person. Truthfully, he's generally very shy and really hates it when fans fawn all over him. He can't get away fast enough from people when they act star struck. He says that he's nothing special: just the son of a cop and a nurse who was physically blessed with the best of both of their genes."

"Have you ever met his sister?" Kat asked her.

"Yes, a few times. We went to Ireland together and made the trip down to London to see her. She came to L.A. once, too. Nice girl, looks nothing like him."

"Really?"

"Yes, really. She has blonde hair and much lighter blue eyes. She's also very tiny. She looks a lot like his mom, while he took after his dad. His father had darker hair and was tall and broad. Black Irish is what I think it's called. Still had blue eyes, though, just not as bright as Ian's mom."

"How is his mom?" Kat asked her nervously.

"Ah! Getting scared to meet her, are we?" Lydia teased.

"Actually, we haven't even discussed that. I was just curious what type of person she is. He's so kind and loving, I figured that must have been her influence."

"She is kind, and she loves them both very much. But it was hard on her after their father was killed. She worked incredibly long hours. It was his paternal grandparents, who lived just down the street, who took care of them both while their mom was working. His grandma was the epitome of what everyone thinks a grandma is: warm and squishy, baked all of the time, and was gentle and kind. I think that's where a lot of his personality comes from.

"But his father was also very caring and nice. He became a constable because he wanted to help people. Who would have thought helping someone would end with him losing his life? Ian's mom told me that he was just trying to make sure the man got home safely. He was so drunk he could hardly walk and was apparently delusional. He said later that he thought Ian's father was trying to rob him.

"According to the paramedics, his last words were, 'Tell the kids and my wife I love them and I'm sorry.' It was pretty brutal for the next few years. I think without the influence of his grandparents, Ian would have turned out very differently. He still had quite a rough patch for a while as a teenager and into his very early twenties. He got drunk a lot, got into fights in pubs, even had a pregnancy scare with one of his girlfriends."

"What turned him around?" Kat asked.

"I believe it was his grandfather sitting him down and talking to him about how proud his father had been of him and how many dreams he'd had for his future. I think it made Ian aware of his father as a real person and not just some construct of nebulous memories from his childhood. Being seven when he died, he probably just felt that he was missing something major in his life and wanted to find something, anything, to fill the void.

"It was hard for him, harder than it was for his sister. She had their mom, but he was left without a role model. His grandfathers were there for him, but it wasn't the same thing as having a father show him how to grow into a man."

"That's so sad. And being the mother of two boys, I can honestly see how that could be a real issue."

"Wait… What? You've got two boys?"

"Yes, and a daughter, too."

"How old are they? Where are they?" Lydia asked incredulously.

"My older two are at university, and my youngest graduates from high school this year."

"How old are you?"

"I just turned forty-three."

"Oh, wow. You must have been really young when they were born."

"Yes, ma'am. I was twenty-one when I had my first, and was twenty-six when my youngest was born."

"Does Ian know how old you are?"

"I'm not sure. I might not have told him. He knows that I have kids in college, and he knows I was married at twenty, though, so it isn't like I'm withholding information from him or anything," Kat said suspiciously.

"Do you want any more kids?" Lydia pressed.

"I don't know. I don't think so. I don't know if it would even be possible. I'm getting up there to have babies, and honestly, I'm not sure I'd want to start all the way over, anyway. I was kind of expecting grandchildren next, not babies."

"Do you think that is fair to Ian? I mean, I know he has said he wants to have kids, eventually, when he met the right woman. I like you, Kat, but I don't want to see him compromise on something like that."

Kat stared at Lydia feeling angry, hurt, and confused. Why were they even talking about this? Ian and she were just getting to know each other. Why and how were children suddenly coming into this discussion?

"I don't know what to say, Lydia. I guess that will have to be his decision. I can't do anything about my age. It is what it is. I've had my kids already, and truthfully have never even thought about starting over before. I never analyzed it because I never thought I'd have the opportunity to have more."

Lydia smiled at her. "Like I said, Kat, I like you. I can see why Ian likes you, too. You've got a maturity that most women don't have. I'm not talking about age, but rather emotional maturity. And I certainly don't want to make up Ian's mind for him, but I do love him, in my own way, and I don't want to see him hurt. I don't know if he has even really put two and two together about your relationship, if it progresses, with your age and ability to have kids. I don't want him to regret anything, so I would just ask you to please talk to him about this sooner rather than later. I hope you understand."

"I know you care deeply for him, Lydia. I'd never do anything to intentionally hurt him, or anyone else for that matter. That's not how I roll at all," she added as afterthought.

"I know."

Just then, the bedroom door opened, and Ian stepped out. "Are you two talking about me?" he asked, a small, sly grin creeping over his lips.

"Maybe," Kat teased. "How are you feeling?"

"A bit better. Still pretty sore. My head feels better, though. The headache is pretty much gone. Now the bump only hurts when I touch it. The ribs still hurt and make it a bit tough to move around. I don't remember it hurting this much before. I guess my age is catching up with me—I don't bounce back like I did when I was a lad."

Lydia walked over and kissed him on the cheek. "Glad to hear you're on the mend, Ian. As for the age thing, I think we can all agree there." Ian just smiled at her in response.

"I'd better get going to makeup. I have a lot of scenes to work on since I was sick. In a way, Ian, it's good this happened, because it gives me time to get caught up without having to rush. Have a good day!"

With that, Lydia opened the door and walked out.

Ian turned to Kat. "What were you two talking about? It sounded pretty intense."

"You could hear us?" she asked him.

"Not really. More just the intonation of your voices. It sounded like you were discussing something serious. Has something happened?"

"No!" Kat told him firmly. "Just discussing something I hadn't thought about before."

Kat really didn't want to elaborate further. If marriage was a subject that made men run for the hills, how did one bring up the sensitive topic of children with someone they had basically just met and started a relationship with? That seemed to be a recipe to make men run from the planet.

"Are you ready for some breakfast? Since you're up and about, I could go grab you something."

"That'd be superb. What I really want is a cuppa. I've been dying for tea since yesterday."

"Why didn't you tell me that? I could have managed that for you!"

"I know. I guess I just didn't want to trouble you anymore than I already had."

Kat left Ian sitting on the couch and ventured out to the dining hall. As she gathered food for herself and Ian, making Ian's tea just the way he liked it, she made sure to discuss the day's menu and how things were going with Melinda and Gerard. They assured her that everything was moving along fine and reiterated again how her primary goal should still be taking care of the star of the show so that they all still had jobs.

They reiterated that other than a few small hiccoughs now and then, the catering continued to be going incredibly smoothly. Most everything Southern that they hadn't been able to bring with them, Jen had been able to have shipped in. For anything local, like produce and meats, Melinda and Gerard would take turns going to an organic market in Calgary a few times a week that had been willing to arrange for larger wholesale shipments of fresh goods to keep up with the demand of their large group in exchange for a mention in the credits.

Feeling settled that things were still going well, Kat hurried back to the trailer in the drizzle that had begun to fall. She didn't envy the cast or crew when this happened. With the dirt streets, mud seemed to be everywhere on set. The actresses' dresses dragged on the ground getting saturated and filthy, while wagons and horses flung mud up onto everyone's costumes when they went by, keeping wardrobe hectic with trying to keep everyone presentable. The crew, meanwhile, had to contend with wires and cables dragging through the mud, as well as trying to maintain their balance on the slippery soil while holding heavy equipment.

At least the weather was warming up and the flurries seemed to have come to an end. The days were growing noticeably longer now and there were other small signs of spring, as well. Kat had overheard that the spring came with the probability of more thunderstorms, but so far, the Canadian weather had proven fairly hospitable.

When Kat got back to the trailer, Ian was sitting exactly where she had left him. She somehow managed to fling open the door with both hands full and make it inside without dropping anything. She put everything down on the table and then opened his container to put it on his lap.

"Here's your corn oatmeal, biscuits and gravy, and eggs. I am *so* sorry, but they were completely out of okra," she said with a wink.

"Oh, no! Whatever will I do without okra?" he quipped in mock distress. "You know, this corn oatmeal has kind of grown on me. But don't tell the caterer; I don't want her to get a big head or anything."

"See, Ian? You are proof positive that with enough exposure, one can get used to just about anything! It's like toddlers who have to try each new food ten times before they can say they like it. Took you longer than that."

"Hmmph!"

They ate in silence and watched the rain pouring down. The drizzle had turned into full blown drops, and lots of them.

"It's a good thing you didn't go out riding in this," Kat told him. "You would have drowned with your nose pointing up in the air like it was."

"Did you really just insinuate that my nose is so big, rain would come in and drown me?" Ian queried, feigning insult.

"Nope, not at all. Anyone with their nose in the air during a rainstorm is vulnerable. Or, you could have gotten hypothermia and died."

"You're always so bright and cheery!"

They spent the rest of the morning together, Ian lying on his bed and Kat sitting beside him. They started out playing Go Fish, moved on to Twenty-One, and finally were attempting to play poker, but neither of them really knew how, so frequent searches on their phones for what to do often yielded hilarity during which Ian would moan and beg Kat, "Don't make me laugh!"

At lunch, Lydia stopped by, wanting to check on Ian, but also to keep up the façade that they were perhaps a couple. She stayed for about an hour while they all ate, and then headed back to the set. When she left, she bent down and kissed them both on their cheeks.

Chapter Twenty-Six

Over the next few days, Ian continued to heal. His pain was lessening, and he could move around more easily. He still struggled, however, with laughing and coughing after managing to catch the cold Lydia had the week before. Every time he had to cough, he grimaced in pain and looked like he was about to faint. Kat felt helpless watching him struggle but couldn't do much of anything other than comfort him in the form of blankets, soup, fever reducers, and cough medicine.

"I guess you didn't expect to have to take care of me to this degree," he said feebly, as she rubbed Vicks onto his smooth chest.

"It's okay," she replied. "I just want to make sure you get better."

"Speaking of that, what are you doing next week when we are on break?"

"I'm going back down to Los Angeles, to Jen's."

"Oh, good. When are you going?"

"I actually haven't bought my ticket yet," she told him. "I was planning to, and then this happened. I'd better get on that."

"Let me get your ticket. Then you can come on my flight and help me, if you would?"

"Oh, I see... I'm nothing more than your own personal bellboy. Or girl... Seems I'm becoming more of your assistant than your assistant is."

Ian laughed at her. "No, not at all. You're just much better looking and more fun than he is! More like it's another thinly veiled excuse to be with you. I want to spend time with you when we are there, too. I don't think I could go a whole week without seeing you now that you have been with me every day like this. I would go through withdrawal."

"That shouldn't be a problem," Kat affirmed. "As long as I get to go to the beach. I need to get some more vitamin D and warm up my bones at bit. This 'mild Canadian spring' has felt more like a hard Southern winter."

"I'm sure that can be arranged during your trip."

"Would you want to come with me?" Kat asked him.

"I would. I don't know if I can."

"How do you mean?"

"We have to be careful down there. It isn't private like it is up here."

Kat looked at him and said sulkily, "Oh, yeah. I forgot that part where I'm going to have to be invisible."

Ian looked at her and shook his head slowly. "Honestly, I'm not happy about it either, but there will be opportunities for us to be together. I will make sure of it."

"It's all right, Ian. I know what I agreed to. What's Lydia going to do?"

"She's going to Paris with a friend. She's been planning it for a while. Personally, it isn't my favorite place, but she seems to like it."

"I've never been, so I wouldn't know," Kat told him.

"Then that's something we will have to remedy at some point. It might make me like it there more… Well, maybe," he added doubtfully.

"Are you excited to close on your house and get settled? It must be hard to fly back and forth all of the time between here and Ireland."

"It gets old. I'll be happy when my ma is here on this side of the pond, so I won't feel obligated to spend every break I have between projects there with her. I'll be able to pursue more opportunities and not feel guilty that she is by herself."

"I can understand that. I've got to make a decision about what I'm going to do when we are done here. I can't believe we're already almost halfway through."

"What *are* you going to do, Kat?"

"I don't know. I hadn't really thought that much about it until now. I ran away from home, literally. It's been a great, fun adventure, but I hadn't anticipated it ending. I mean, I knew it would come to an end, but it seemed so far away then. Now it is looming, and I'll have to make some tough choices."

"Any chance you would stay in L.A. with Jen?"

"I honestly don't know. I'm not sure if Jen would want me to. I don't really have any marketable skills, except maybe cooking, though. And it's very expensive to live there, so without extra income I don't think my alimony would go far enough to provide me a place to live and the money to pursue some sort of education so that I can get a decent job.

"I sometimes think about going home, but then I realize I won't have any home to go back to. The kids will all be going in different directions, James and I have to sell our house, and at my age, I really don't see myself moving back in with my parents." Kat laughed. "For the first time since I can remember, I can go and do whatever I want and not have to answer for it. It's liberating, but incredibly scary."

"I hope that you choose to stay in Los Angeles with Jen. Personal feelings about you aside, I think that you should pursue the dream you gave up so many years ago. We all deserve to do what we love."

"It would be ironic, wouldn't it? To go through this much living just to come full circle back to the path I didn't take? Not too many people get to experience both their options once they make a decision in life. I'm grateful for what I had with James: my children and our life together. But it feels like it has come to a natural breaking point and a new story for my life is just waiting to be written. I'm not angry or bitter anymore; now it feels like it was just another adventure. It's like Jen took the direct route while I took the scenic one, but ultimately we still ended up in the same place."

Ian smiled at her. "That's a good way to look at it."

They had both been leaning against the head of his bed as they talked, their legs out in front of them. Kat thought about how he was so close, how she could just reach out and touch him. As if he read her mind, he stretched out his arm and took her hand in his. Every time he touched her, it was as though a white-hot flame shot through her body. While they had spent an immense amount of time together over the past few days, they really hadn't had much physical contact, mostly because they felt like they were under a microscope, given that anyone could burst in any time they felt like it.

Meanwhile, Kat was grateful for the fact that it was forcing them to become more intimate on an emotional level. Even though they had just met a short time before, she now felt like she had known him as long as she could remember. She couldn't recall a time in her life where she had been so wholly accepted for who she was. She was telling Ian things that she hadn't even told Jen. There wasn't any game playing or expectation. For the first time in her existence, she could truly be herself and not worry about impressing others. As a good, traditional Southern girl, that sort of freedom was almost unobtainable—to not have to be something to everyone else, even if it meant losing yourself in the process.

That night, Ian seemed almost back to normal. It was still obviously painful if he moved suddenly or coughed and sneezed, but he was better overall. His cold had also dissipated, and though he still moved slowly and deliberately, he felt he was ready to go back to filming in the morning. The medic had come and given him clearance to do non-physical scenes as long as he had shortened hours, as well. As nice as their time together had been, Kat could tell he was ready to get back to doing his job; being idle did not suit him well.

They both also knew that this was the final night Kat would be staying with him, and their recent forays into a deeper emotional connection had led to an overabundance of need to speak to each other physically, as well.

When they were sure that everyone was settled in for the night and no one else would disturb them, Ian stood up from the couch, locked the door, and motioned for Kat to join him. As she rose, he took her hand and led her to his bedroom. She grabbed the shirt in which she had been sleeping and slipped into the bathroom to change. When she came out, his face lit up as he patted the empty space in the bed beside him. She glided over, lifted the covers, and slipped in next to him. Knowing that his ribs still hurt, she scooted carefully over to him and placed her head on his arm which was lying by his side. He turned his face toward her, and she stretched up to meet him in a kiss. As the connection they had shared over the past few days grew more passionate, so had the desire they felt for each other, and now it came spilling out. As their caresses deepened and intensified, it became clear that they were each trying to get their fill of the other to last through their impending separation.

It was the last time they could count on being uninterrupted together, at least until they got to Los Angeles, and Ian closed on his house. His apartment was too public to risk her spending the night there with him. Now was the last time, at least for a while, they could be completely uninhibited in each other's company without fear of being disturbed.

As their kisses continued to fuel their desires, Kat felt the need to get nearer to him. Since she couldn't snuggle in against his chest, she threw her leg over his, attempting to get as close as she could. The heat from her bare inner thigh radiated onto his leg and that was all it took. A moan of yearning escaped his lips and her body responded by pulling her up over him until she was straddling his pelvis between her silky legs.

"Oh God, Kat. This is a bad idea," he exhaled.

"Why?" She blinked coyly at him.

"You know why," he rumbled, his voice deep and husky.

"Am I hurting you?"

"You are, but not in the way you're thinking. Not in a way that makes me want you to stop. In fact, it pains me that I can't let you continue."

Kat chuckled. "Well, it seems like you aren't in any position to shove me off, so I think I will just have to take advantage of your weakened state."

He growled at her. "That is so unfair."

He reached up and began to fumble with the buttons on her shirt. Having succeeded in opening several of them, he reached up and cupped her breasts with his large, warm, masculine hands. She leaned forward instinctually to give him better access, careful to keep her fingers resting lightly on his shoulders and away from his chest. Moving down further, she let her lips find his neck and kissed him in a line from his ear to his collar bone. He shivered at the touch of her moist, hot lips on his skin and rolled his head to the side, giving all the enticement she needed to continue.

"Ugh. Why do I have to be injured?" he moaned.

Kat murmured in agreement as she backed away and began to descend over his chest, his taut stomach, and lower, marking her path with her lips and tongue. She couldn't believe how aggressive she had become in her pursuit to get what she craved.

"Kat?" Ian called softly when her mouth reached the edge of his boxer briefs.

"Yeah?" She raised her eyes to meet his, while her lips continued their ministrations.

"Kat, we have to stop. I'm getting to the point where I'm going to lose control. As much as I don't want to, we have to stop before we do anything that we'll regret."

Kat stopped, and rose slightly to look deep into his eyes, where a look of genuine concern and caring resided. She understood that it had nothing to do with her, or rather that it had nothing to do with his desire for her and everything to do with him trying to respect her and maintain her honor. She sat up fully and slowly slipped off his lap and back onto the bed, trying to maintain as much contact as possible for as long as she could.

"Whoa! That almost made me throw all my resolve out the window."

She lay down beside him and turned onto her side again so that she was spooning against his length and enveloped his leg in hers. She wrapped her hands around the upper part of his arm and told him that she was sorry.

"Whatever for?" he asked her, surprised.

"Because I can't help myself. Ian, I've never been as physically attracted to anyone as I am to you. It feels like we are magnets, pulled together by some powerful invisible force. I

234

can't seem to get enough of touching you."

"I can't get enough of touching you, either. Kat, this is about the hardest thing I've done in my life. Trust me when I say I feel like it's killing me to not fully show you how much I care and want to connect with you. But that's also how I know what I'm feeling is genuine. If it wasn't, I know from experience that I would be putting my wants ahead of your needs."

"I keep telling you, Ian, this being a gentleman thing is nice and all, but really, I don't care. Don't do it for my sake. When I'm with you, I don't even think about still being married to someone else. In fact, for the last few weeks, I've hardly remembered that I had a life before coming up here.

"You have awakened a part of me I didn't even know existed. I mean, sure, sex was nice enough with James, but it was something he initiated, so I did it more for him than for me. I'm already way past the level of desire I ever got with him just anticipating being with you, and I've never been this physically aggressive in my life. With you, I can't get enough and can't think of anything else when I'm around you. There's a chemistry here that is undeniable."

"You can say that again," he murmured. "I've never experienced anything like this, either. But Kat, truthfully, I'm scared. I don't want to screw this up. For the first time in my existence, I feel that connection everyone always talks about; that electricity, that zing. I've been too wary to open up around women and too self-involved to care much about connecting on a deeper level. That first time I saw you, though, I felt it. I knew it.

"Like I said before, that's why I was such a *stook* to you. I was suddenly back in primary six, confused about liking a girl and not having a clue what to do with that information. I reverted back to that boy in the schoolyard who throws rocks at the girl he likes because he can't think properly about the appropriate way to get her attention, except I hurled insults, rather than projectiles. I'm so used to getting what I want, I'd forgotten what it was like to have a woman be a challenge. All I feel now is that

I don't want this to change, so I had better do everything right."

"I don't want you to be scared, Ian," Kat whispered.

"No, I want to be scared!" he said emphatically. "It means that I feel something, something deep that I have not allowed myself to feel very often since my father died.

"Feeling that much hurts, Kat. It makes me literally ache in my chest to think about losing someone else who makes me feel like that ever again. I revert back to that seven-year-old boy who knew the place his father left would never be filled by anyone else. To feel that much, it takes chunks out of your heart and soul that can never be recovered. It isn't easy to be vulnerable to such relationships when you know what it is to lose them, so I just didn't let myself even open up to the possibility. Until I met you."

The more Ian talked about his memories of his father, the more she could see exactly what he meant. It was painfully evident that his father's passing had shattered his world and had shaped his personality into one that tried to love everyone equally without really letting them in.

When that hadn't worked, he got angry and drank and fought. After that too failed, he had tried to find a relationship to fill the gap. Finally, he had given up trying. He realized that nothing or no one could fill in the crater in his heart, so he resolved to meet his needs for affection in the moment and seek his fulfillment elsewhere in the one thing he could control: his career.

Ian also spoke of while he loved Lydia, he had understood that she was even more wounded than he was, and they had realized right away they would never make good life partners because they were both too wrecked and unable to love totally or give completely. A relationship together would have created a cycle of need that would have fed on itself until it had ravaged them both. By instead caring for each other as brother and sister, they were free to love one another without the burden of feeling they had to be responsible for the other's happiness, something that neither of them could have taken on in their broken states.

Kat and Ian spent the remainder of their last night together alternating between sleeping, talking, and exploring each other more intimately. Kat wasn't sure about Ian, but when she awoke in the wee hours of the morning, she was determined to do everything in her power to not let this man slip away.

She sneaked out from underneath the covers and checked the clock on her phone: 5:30 a.m. Moving from the bedroom, she sat in the front room, watching the sky slowly lighten as night gave way to day.

At exactly 8:01 a.m. EDT, a telephone rang on the desk of a Southern law office, and Kat told the person who answered that she was ready to move on.

Chapter Twenty-Seven

Three days later, Kat and Ian were on a plane heading back to Los Angeles. Ian was still moving slowly thanks to his broken ribs, but he was doing much better, and Kat got to experience for the first time what being involved with an actor was truly like. Even though *Western Skies* was a still a relatively small show on a cable network, there were many people who recognized Ian from either his role as Sheriff Joe or his interviews on network T.V. The craziness began during boarding, when one woman saw him as she was walking down the aisle to their seats.

"Oh my God! You're Sheriff Joe!"

Ian just politely nodded and confirmed he was indeed the actor who played Joe. The woman then turned to the three other women she was traveling with. "Look! It's Sheriff Joe! You know, Ian Gregory from that show *Western Skies*? He's the main character! Oh my gosh, I can't believe that I'm meeting you! You're even more handsome in person!"

In the next instant, there was a flurry of activity around them as the women all closed in and began gushing about how much they loved the show, how gorgeous he was, and hassling him about when was he going to propose to Lydia and just be done with it?

The cellphones came out and the women were leaning down next to his seat and snapping selfies. This scenario happened a few more times as the plane was loading, and the flight attendants had to intervene to move people along on more than one occasion. When yet another group of middle-aged women was asked to continue on to their seats, Kat heard one of them ask the other, "Who is that woman sitting next to him?"

One of the others glanced quickly at her and answered, "Probably just a nobody whose seat assignment was there."

Yet another woman in the group exclaimed, "Wow! How lucky is she?"

"He and Lydia are together. Everyone says so. They make

the most perfect couple," replied the first woman.

When the chaos his presence caused finally came to an end and everyone was in their seats, Ian finally looked over at Kat.

"Sorry," he muttered quietly.

"It's okay. I guess it's kind of par for the course."

"I know. But it doesn't mean that I'm not still sorry it happened." He leaned forward like he was getting something out of his bag, inconspicuously motioning her to do the same, and when she bent forward as well, he murmured to her, "Mostly, I'm sorry about what they said, about how you were just a nobody, and that Lydia and I are the perfect couple. I wanted to stand up and declare that you are very much a somebody: you are *my* somebody, and I don't want it any other way."

Kat sat up straight again and looked out the window for a second. She felt a smile come to her lips as she processed what he had said. She turned back around, and he leaned over like he was going to kiss her. Catching himself at the last second, he quickly looked around to see who might have seen them, but luckily everyone seemed too busy doing other things to get ready for takeoff to notice them.

The engines began to rev up and Kat instinctually sat back, and since she had no one's hand to hold, grabbed onto the armrests for dear life. Ian looked over, clearly wanting desperately to do something to help her, but unable to. Finally, just as the plane left the ground he couldn't take it anymore and reached out, patting the top of her hand that was between them and giving her a reassuring smile.

Kat heard a woman in the one of the seats behind them whisper to her seatmate, "Wow! Did you see that? Ian Gregory just reached over to pat the hand of the woman he's sitting next to who's frightened. He's the nicest guy ever!"

Kat glanced at him, and he gave her just a hint of a small smile, letting her know he was trying not to laugh.

The rest of the flight was pretty much hell for both of them. Having spent so much time together over the last week had made them very comfortable with each other, and so spontaneous physical contact was becoming commonplace. To sit next to each other for several hours and act like they were strangers, or at least not officially together in any capacity, was torture. So many times, one would turn to the other and nearly lean in for a kiss or their hands would twitch as they held back from reaching out to grab the other's. They tried to keep their conversation distant, what would be considered proper between strangers or acquaintances, but even that was extremely difficult. At some point, Ian took a pen out of his bag and wrote on his napkin: *This is horrible!* He stealthily passed it over to the side of his tray so that Kat could read it. She nodded subtly in agreement. She pulled a pen out of her purse and wrote on her own napkin: *I know. All I want to do is kiss you right now.*

They messaged each other that way for quite a while before Ian asked the flight attendant for more napkins. When the woman left, Ian furiously scribbled: *Want to join the mile-high club?*

Kat looked intently at him for a second—she was more than willing but his willingness surprised her.

Sure!

Me, too. But we can't. Kat glanced up to see the look of disappointment playing on his features.

Kat leaned back in her seat and closed her eyes in abject frustration. When she turned back to face him, he gave her a small grimace in sympathy.

The rest of the flight passed quickly as they doodled and wrote messages back and forth. Before they knew it, they were approaching LAX, and both knew what that meant: they would be truly separated for the first time since they had gotten to know each other. Quickly, before she had to put up her tray table, she wrote her cell number on a clean napkin and handed it to him. He looked at it and nodded that he understood. He then did the same for her and wrote under it: *I* will *see you soon!*

As the plane pulled up to the gate, Kat felt sick to her stomach. She knew logically it was only ten days and that they would most likely get together at least once during that time. But as they deplaned and she saw his back a few feet ahead of her, she had to fight her urge to quicken her step to catch up with him. Exiting the international terminal, she noticed several people with cameras, some of which were pointed at him. She continued on as she heard one of them ask, "Coming home from filming the new season of *Western Skies*?"

Ian stopped for a second and smiled politely. "I am," he confirmed amicably. Then came more questions and more pictures.

"Where's Lydia?"

"What's happening with the show this season?"

"Are you and Lydia a couple?"

"When are you going to propose to Lydia?"

Of course, all of the excitement he was generating began to catch the attention of more passersby and they too started vying for Ian's attention. All Kat could do was walk on by toward the pick-up lane where Jen would collect her. She couldn't help herself, though, and took one more look back at him over her shoulder. His eyes met hers from across the room and she could see the misery he was in, sure it mirrored her own.

When Jen pulled up, Kat threw her bag into the back seat and settled into the passenger side of the car. Jen then expertly slid into the freeway traffic heading back to her house. As they drove, Kat's phone chimed, and she picked it up: *I miss you already!*

She smiled and pulled her phone close to her chest for a second before quickly texting back: *Me, too. Seems so lonely without you, even though I'm with Jen.*

Ian: *We'll get together soon. Have a good evening. I'll text you later.*

Kat smiled again and put her phone back into her purse.

"Okay. Who was that? What's going on, Kat?" "Nothing. Why would you think something is going on?"

"I know your 'I think I'm in love' face. I had to look at it every day for a year before you married James. Oh, God. It isn't James, is it? Please tell me it isn't James…"

"No! It's nothing. Really! Ian just texted to thank me for helping him get down here because of his recent injury. He's a nice guy. A good friend."

"Kat, the look on your face says he's much more than a good friend. Honestly, what's going on?"

"Nothing. Please, can we just drop it? He was just saying thanks. Nothing else."

"Okay. Speaking of James, where do y'all stand on that?" Jen changed the topic. She knew Kat's warning voice, and she knew if she kept pressing her, she would blow up.

"Well, I actually called the attorney about a week ago and asked him to please file the papers. I'm ready."

"Congratulations, Kat! Welcome to your soon to be new-found freedom. It's really quite awesome, you'll see. I am definitely a fan. Have you told James yet?"

"No!" Kat reacted fiercely. "And I'm not going to, either. I'll just wait for him to be served."

"Whoa, Kat! Isn't that a bit harsh? I mean he's not my favorite person, but maybe he deserves a little heads-up?"

"Nope! No way. He blindsided me with Sam, and now it's my turn. It might not be the most mature way to handle it, but I don't care," she said simply.

"Have you told the kids?"

"No one but you. You're the first. Well, Ian I guess was the first."

Jen looked over at Kat and she raised her eyebrows. "Why would he be the first to know?" she asked suspiciously.

"Oh, you know. I was there taking care of him in a trailer. He could hear me on the phone with them."

Kat knew in that exact moment that this situation was going to be way harder to navigate than she ever imagined it would be. All she wanted to do was gush about Ian to Jen. She desperately wanted to tell someone about how handsome his smile was, how sweet and conscientious he was, how perfect he looked in the morning while he was still sleeping beside her, his face relaxed, looking so youthful, while the rest of him was definitely all man.

She wanted to tell her about his amazing abs and how every time she saw him, it made her heart skip a beat. She would love to share how sweet his kisses were, but that he could turn her on in mere seconds, making her body quake with desire. Thinking about it became too much and she let out a small groan.

"What?"

"Nothing!" Kat quickly recovered.

They drove in silence for quite a while as Jen tried to navigate the rush hour traffic. "You can tell that Ian has a driver," she muttered to herself.

"What's that?" Kat asked.

"Ian must have a driver or something because anyone who has to drive in this crap would never book a flight that comes in at this time of day."

"Sorry. His assistant arranged the flight, so since I agreed to help Ian, he set the time," Kat told her. "How's Lucy?"

"Better, thanks. We're getting the hang of all this stuff. It's really stressful, though. I think if David and I weren't already divorced we would be by now. It's really hard to split the responsibilities between the two households. There's a lot of medicine and paraphernalia, too. One of us always inevitably forgets something with each switch off. I'm so sorry, Kat. I never meant for you to be up there alone this long."

Kat smiled. "No problem! It hasn't been a burden at all. I've had the best time of my life!

"Really? The best time of your life? In the middle of the forest, miles from anywhere, while working your ass off for sixteen hours a day?"

"Yes. I've met some amazing people," Kat told her emphatically. *One in particular*, she internally gushed.

"So, tell me. I'm dying to know! What's Ian like? And Lydia? Are they together or are they not? The more the buzz from that show takes off, the more and more rumors I'm hearing."

"What kind of rumors?" Kat asked suspiciously.

"Oh, you know. Everything from they're engaged to that

he's sleeping around with someone on set behind Lydia's back. Come to think of it, that one is probably because of you!"

Kat had been taking a sip of her water and choked, spraying it in front of her onto the dashboard.

"Sorry!" she sputtered as soon as she could speak again, wiping up the water spots with her sleeve. "I couldn't say. They're very private."

There. They are very private. I haven't spilled the beans.

"So, no more trysts with him, then?" Jen asked, glancing sideways at her friend, gauging her reaction.

"No…"

"Well, do they share a trailer? Does he sneak out to her, or she to him? Do they disappear together? Or have you noticed him doing something with anyone else besides what happened with you?"

Kat sighed. "Honestly, Jen. I don't know exactly where their relationship stands."

Well, it's mostly true. They don't know what they're going to do next, she reconciled with herself.

"Here I thought since you were taking care of him you'd have the inside track about what was going on with them," Jen complained disappointedly.

"Well, Lydia did come every day and talk to him. Us, actually. She talked to us. But they were still very proper with each other in front of me."

This is getting harder and harder. If Jen keeps asking questions, I'm going to have to start lying for real, Kat worried.

In just a few more minutes, they were turning onto Jen's street. Her cute little three-room bungalow was her most prized possession. She pulled into the driveway and stopped the car.

"You ready?" she asked Kat.

They got out and Kat grabbed her bag. When Jen unlocked her door, Kat struggled down the hall to the guest bedroom with her stuff, then walked back out to the living room where Jen had already poured them each a glass of wine and was sitting on the couch.

"So…" Jen started in. "There's something different about you."

"What? No, there's not! What are you talking about?"

"You! You seem so relaxed, so happy. You're practically glowing. I don't think I've ever seen you like this. What's going on?"

"Nothing, really, Jen. I guess I'm just enjoying the fresh mountain air." She quickly took a sip of her wine.

Jen studied Kat for a long moment, but then gave a slight shrug of her shoulders. She reached to put her wine glass on the coffee table in front of her, gracefully leaning over her folded-in leg.

"Tell me what's going on with the business then," she ordered Kat.

They talked for the next two hours about what was working and what was not in their current situation, such as some slight supply issues if the Canadian customs officials kept their shipments too long. For the most part, though, things were going smoothly, and people seemed to really enjoy the food and the shabby chic Southern design that accented the business.

By the time they had finished discussing Kat's work experience, it had gotten dark. They ordered in pizza and sat on the floor eating and talking, reminding Kat of her carefree days with Jen in high school and the days just after. When Kat began to yawn, Jen told her to go to bed, that she would clean up. Kat wandered to her bedroom and grabbed her phone, seeing that she had received five texts. She unlocked it and couldn't help but laugh as she read Ian's messages:

Kat? Are you there?

Kat… Where are you?

Kat… I miss you!

I can't stop thinking about you!

Kat, I want you!

Kat gasped, wondering if that meant what she thought it meant. She took a deep breath and texted back to him: *I'm here.*

A few seconds later, her phone chimed with his response:

Good. I miss you! I'm just sitting here alone in my empty flat, which seems huge after my trailer.

Kat: *I miss you, too. The airport today sucked.*

Ian: *Tell me about it. It was killing me.*

Kat: *I knew you were popular and getting more so, but I didn't think you would be photographed and hounded like that.*

Ian: *It's happening more and more as the show gains in popularity. Then, of course, there's all of the relationship question stuff which piques people's interest.*

Kat: *Oh. Right.*

A few minutes passed before Ian wrote again: *What are you wearing?*

Kat: *A pair of pajama bottoms and a tank top.*

Ian: *Not my shirt?*

Kat: *Nope. Sorry.*

Ian: *Damn, that's too bad. That's how I'm picturing you right now with your long, bare legs peeking out just below the hem.*

Kat: *I left it up at the location. I didn't know it was on permanent loan to me.*

Ian: *As far as I am concerned, it's yours. Have to stop imagining now.*

Kat smiled to herself as she sent back: *Why?*

Ian: *Because I'm here all alone in this flat and all I want to do is drive over to pick you up and bring you back here with me. Then, I would kiss you and caress you and...*

Kat: *Ian, are you trying to have text sex? Is that even a thing?*

Ian: *LOL! If it isn't, it should be. And no, I don't want to have "text sex." I want to make love to you.*

Kat: *Whoa! What?! Where is this coming from?*

Ian: *From being lonely. From wanting to touch you so badly on the plane that my body ached. It's easier to control myself when I'm with you because I see you in front of me: the whole person. In my imagination, though, I remember only how you make me feel and I like it, which then makes me want you even more.*

Jen stopped by Kat's door and stuck her head in, causing Kat to instinctively shove her phone under her leg.

"Whatcha doing, Kat?" Jen eyed her suspiciously.

Kat looked up and guiltily met her friend's eyes. She could see a mix of confusion, concern, and even a little bit of amusement in them.

"Nothing. Just checking my phone before I go to sleep."

Ding! Kat's phone chimed again. Jen just looked at her and shook her head.

"Tell Ian I said goodnight!" she snorted as she headed out the door and down the hall. Kat chuckled to herself as she realized she was acting like her kids when she caught them doing something naughty. She picked up the phone.

Ian: Are *you there still?*

Kat: *Yes. Jen just came by. Hey… you didn't tell me what you were wearing.*

Ian: *Nothing but my boxer briefs. It's hot down here compared to Canada!*

She exhaled sharply at the thought of him like that. She closed her eyes and recalled the image of him in his bed and shuddered. He was too perfect.

Kat: *No fair!*

Ian: *Why?*

Kat: *Because that's something I would like to see.*

Ian: *And how I would like to be seen…*

Kat: *So… What's on your agenda for tomorrow?*

Ian: *The final walk through of the house. The signing is the day after tomorrow.*

Kat: *Ah! Good! Congratulations!*

Ian: *Thanks. It's only a little place, but it will work well for my ma and me and maybe…. whomever.*

Kat's breath caught in her throat. He wasn't really hinting that he wanted them to live together already, was he? While the quick timing of everything made her a bit woozy, the idea of sharing his life and home made her feel all warm inside.

They continued to text back and forth until after midnight when Kat finally had to concede that she was exhausted and needed to sign off.

Ian's last text said simply: *Sleep now.*

Chapter Twenty-Eight

Kat awoke to the beautiful California sunshine. As she lay in her bed, she went through everything that had happened to her in the past seven weeks. To go from thinking she was in love and happy to finding what seemed like true happiness seemed surreal.

Ian kept insisting that he liked her because she was one of the only people who treated him normally. Her mind wandered to the scenes on the airplane and at the airport the day before. She thought she had acted like an idiot when she first met him, but now that she had seen how most fans react, she was beginning to understand why he felt so strongly that she was different. At least she hadn't run around to him and taken a selfie. She even pushed back quite a bit when he gave her attitude. Smiling to herself, she thought that having been the mother of teenagers did have a few benefits.

She got out of bed and padded down the hall to the living room. Jen was sitting at the table in the dining room, drinking coffee and working on her laptop.

"Good morning, sleepy head!" she told Kat.

"What time is it?" Kat asked.

"Past ten. What do you want to do today?"

"Past ten? Seriously? How did that happen?"

"Given the fact that I heard you furiously typing away still at almost one, it isn't too much of a stretch to understand why you slept to ten. Now, what do you want to do today?"

"Hmmmm… I don't really know. I'm always up for the beach. And that giant farmer's market is always cool. Heck, even Disneyland could be fun."

"Let's do it!" Jen exclaimed eagerly.

"What?"

"Go to Disneyland!"

"Um… okay. Are you sure? Isn't it a bit of a drive?"

"Sure! Why not? We're young and free! Everything in Los

Angeles is a bit of a drive. Don't worry, it's late enough now that the traffic won't be too bad, and then if we stay until the park closes, it will be that way again coming back home."

"Well, okay, then!" Kat was getting excited.

They scrambled to get ready, each vying for space in the one tiny bathroom Jen's house had. Kat eventually conceded and just leaned against the doorjamb as Jen put the finishing touches on her make up.

As she was waiting, Kat blurted out, "California always surprises me. At home, I have a huge house: over three thousand square feet, a decent yard, four bathrooms, and it's still worth half the price of this place in its twelve hundred square feet of grandeur."

"Hey!" Jen exclaimed. "I like my house!"

"I do, too. But it's pretty crazy that you paid over $600,000 for it."

"It's all about location, location, location, baby."

Kat grabbed her phone from the tiny bathroom counter to get it out of Jen's way and saw a message from Ian: *Good morning, Kat! Hope you have a good day!*

You, too, she wrote back.

A few minutes later, another message came in:

What are you doing today?

Kat: *Disneyland!*

Ian: *Really? How cool! I've never been.*

Kat: *You should come with us!*

Ian: *I'd love to, but the final walk through is today, remember? Tomorrow though, after the closing, want to come furniture shopping with me? If it were up to me, I would have a camping chair in front of the T.V. and a folding table in my dining room.*

Kat: *I could do that.*

Ian: *Great! I'll come and get you around two tomorrow, then.*

Kat: *Are you sure you want to drive all the way over here to pick me up?*

Ian: *My new house isn't too far from Jen's. I'm just in North Hollywood, not far from Burbank. Up in the hills just a little bit. Nothing fancy.*

Kat: *Okay. See you then!* She sent him Jen's address.

Ian: *Have fun!*

Kat and Jen drove down to Anaheim laughing hard the whole way. Kat was actually worried that Jen would get into an accident the way her tears were falling. They spent the remainder of the morning on the rides, had lunch, and then moved over to California Adventure. As they were riding the giant Mickey Ferris wheel, Jen asked her how she was holding up. Kat knew that a proper response would be something that sounded like she was at least remorseful that her marriage of almost a quarter century had come to an end, but to her, it actually felt like a weight she didn't even know she carried had been lifted off of her shoulders.

"Honestly, Jen, I guess I should be sad, but I can't be. I'm able to think about me and my well-being only for the first time in over two decades. I loved the life I had then, with my family and the kids. I have no regrets. But I feel like that chapter has closed and I am completely okay with that."

"Wow! Really?"

"Yes, Ma'am. My job there was done. My kids are grown; they're doing okay. James didn't want me anymore. So, what would my purpose be? It felt like the chapters in my life book weren't going to contain anything of interest anymore."

"Have you heard from James?" Jen asked.

"Yes, a little. He texts me almost every day, asking how I am and when I'm coming home. I usually just respond that I'm fine and I don't know. He tried to call in the beginning, but I never picked up, so he gave up."

"How do you think he will take being served the divorce paperwork?"

"I don't really care. For the first time in my adult life, I'm having fun and doing whatever I want to do. I don't have to answer to anyone. I didn't realize what I was missing until I had it. I really don't care how he feels because he gave up the privilege of my concern when he started screwing someone else."

Jen just gaped at Kat. Her behavior was so out of character for her usually sweet and demure friend.

"Congratulations, Kat. Bravo! You have finally found your worth. You're right. He's a pig, and it wasn't okay what he did to you!"

They finished up their evening with a late dinner at the Blue Bayou and the fireworks right before they called it a night. They were tired but felt great after a day of fun and fresh air.

"I haven't been to Disneyland since I first moved here!" Jen said as the two women headed back north toward Jen's house in the Valley.

"I haven't ever! We went to Disney World once when the kids were little, but there's something better about coming and seeing where it all started."

When they arrived home, Kat saw that Ian had messaged her about the time they had been eating dinner and had turned off their cells. She unlocked it and began to read.

Hey, Kat. Just finished the walk through. I was thinking about tomorrow, wanted to make sure you could still come with me to pick out some furniture and stuff for the house.

Kat smiled as she wrote, *Sure.*

His response was immediate. Had he just been holding the phone in preparation for her eventual response?

Good! Because if I do it, it will look like a hotel room or a college student's flat. With my ma coming soon, it will need a woman's touch, I think. Still good to come and pick you up at about 2:00?

Perfect. I'll see you then.

Later that evening, Kat went to bed, but couldn't sleep for a long time. She was too wound up from the fun of the day and the idea of getting to spend time with Ian the following afternoon. Laying on her back, she stared up at the ceiling which was slightly illuminated by the glow of the streetlights just outside.

After tossing and turning for several hours, kicking her legs in and out of her blankets and fluffing her pillows for the millionth time, she gave up and grabbed her phone. The time read 1:22 a.m., but she couldn't help herself. She opened her and Ian's earlier conversations and sent *Can't sleep*. It was a few minutes before she got a reply.

Ian: *I'm sorry. I could, and I was having the nicest dream.*

Kat: *Sorry I woke you, then!*

Ian: *I'm not. Hearing from you just makes my dream feel more real.*

Kat: *I'm so looking forward to tomorrow. I know it has been only one day since I have seen you, but it feels like more.*

Ian: *I know. Me, too! I'm counting the hours. I feel like a teenager at school again, longing to see you after class.*

Kat: *LOL! This is not what high school felt like for me! It was more that I would have watched you from afar, trying to send you telepathic messages to look in my direction, but you wouldn't. If you grew up here, you would have been the most popular boy in school.*

Ian: *You aren't like that anymore then, Kat, because I can feel you in the room before I can see you.*

Kat: *What are you needing to buy tomorrow?*

Ian: *I want stuff for my ma's room. A bed, wardrobe, curtains, that sort of thing.*

Kat: *Okay. I can handle that. I hope she likes my taste, though. I'm still Southern, after all. Shabby chic and French-inspired furniture are my preferences.*

Ian: *That's exactly why I need you. I didn't recognise anything you said in that sentence other than "French" and "furniture".*

Kat: *Okay. I get your point. I'd better get to sleep.*

Ian: *Good night, Love.*

Putting down her phone, she tried not to read too much into it, as he tended to call a lot of women, "Love," but her heart soared, thinking that for her, in this instance, it might mean something more than that to him.

In the morning, when Kat went into the kitchen to get her coffee, she told Jen that she and Ian were going to shop for things for his new house. Jen looked up over the edge of the paper she was reading with her eyebrows lifted. "Oh?" she said, her expression and tone of voice conveying it all.

"What?" Kat demanded.

"Y'all haven't even been here forty-eight hours, and are already meeting up? Kat, is this getting serious?"

"He just needs help! And since Lydia is in Paris with friends and his assistant is a guy, he wanted a woman's help with furnishing his mother's room for when she comes to live with him here."

Jen just tipped her head slightly to one side and sighed. "Girl, I swear. I *know* something is going on between y'all!"

"Honestly, Jen, I promise it's not. We just enjoy hanging out together. How can there be anything serious between us? I'm still married!"

"Soon to be divorced, Kat. Just be careful, that's all."

Kat took a shower and prepared for her time with Ian. Having been in Alberta's cooler weather for so long, she wanted to bask in the sunshine and enjoy her California vacation, so she picked out a short, swinging, white eyelet sundress with spaghetti straps, a denim vest, and the cowboy boots she had purchased in Calgary on a whim the time she accompanied Melinda to the market. Her hair looked bouncy and shiny, the slight wave accentuated by the moist, warm California air. She had painted her toe nails the night before, realizing now that it was a bit silly, as she was wearing boots. Still, it had made her feel beautifully alluring.

She sat on the couch, trying to find something to watch on T.V. as she had about an hour to kill before Ian showed up, but she couldn't concentrate. Her stomach was filled with butterflies and flip-flopped every time she thought of him.

At ten minutes to two, Ian's Audi R8 pulled into Jen's driveway. He started to open the door but after looking at his watch, settled back down. He managed to wait only a few seconds before shrugging his shoulders, stepping out, and coming up the walk.

Kat hadn't felt like that excited since she was in college, going on dates with James. Her palms were sweating, so she rubbed them on her skirt right before she reached for the doorknob, just as he was poised to ring the bell. He looked up at her standing in the door for a second, his face expressing surprise and then clear admiration.

"Wow! Kat! You look amazing!"

"Thanks! I've been told I clean up all right. So do you!"

He was wearing a pair of well-worn jeans and a T-shirt that hugged his body closely. His hair fell across his forehead and best of all, he wore a gigantic smile. It was all she could do to keep herself from jumping into his arms.

"Do you want to come in?"

"No, let's just go. I think if I came in, I wouldn't leave again," he joked.

"Okay. Just let me grab my stuff."

They drove in silence while Ian navigated to their first stop of the day. Eventually, he turned to glance at her and said, "Remember how I told you that I struggled driving on the right side of the road up there because I wanted to slip into the proper side for me to drive? Well, I lied. I struggle down here, too. Everything just still feels awkward and wrong."

"Don't worry about it, Ian. I'm sure I'd be a perfect disaster driving in Ireland."

"The hardest thing to get used to is the gear shift being on the wrong side. I still instinctually move my left hand out of habit, instead of my right."

They continued to talk about the differences between the U.S. and Ireland until Ian pulled up to a high- end shopping development. He parked in front of a furniture store and ran to open her door. She thought it was sweet that he always did that, wondering if this was a normal thing for him to do, or if he was just doing it to impress her. James certainly hadn't done anything similar since before they were married.

They walked inside and Kat was overtaken by the beauty of the pieces in the store. Everything was handcrafted and unique. She moved over to a wooden dining chair and discretely looked at the price. Her eyes widened in shock: it was nearly $2,000 for one!

They walked around and discussed the various options and weighed them against what Ian described as his mother's tastes. Telling her that while she had sacrificed her whole life to give him and his sister everything they needed, her room and clothes had been practical and devoid of any ornamentation. Therefore, he really wanted to spoil her for the first time since his father had died, and he was finally in the financial position to do so.

Eventually they settled on a gorgeous Old French- inspired bedroom set for her, so familiar to Kat having grown up studying the latest copy of *Southern Living* that always lay alongside the family Bible on her parents' coffee table. The off-white color of the suite would brighten the room and would not be overpowering in a small space. For his room, Ian picked out a simple squared four poster bed and accompanying pieces— simple, yet masculine.

They also found a nice desk and a daybed with trundle under it, on which other guests could sleep, for his office/guest room. After every piece Kat picked, having discussed the options with their salesperson, she would look at Ian expectantly. He would just nod his head in agreement. He loved her taste, he told her, and was grateful that he didn't have to make any decisions, as hers were perfect.

Together, they chose a farmhouse style table for the dining room with five chairs and a long bench to seat three more people, and for the living room a deep, dark, weathered-looking leather sectional sofa with brass tacks and other furniture, such as a T.V. consul, that held with the old European library style they had settled on.

By the time they were finished, Kat could not believe how much money he had just spent on furnishing his house. She knew that the house itself was fairly modest, but even a modest house up in the foothills did not come cheaply. Now he had dropped close to $30,000 on furnishings, and still wanted to remodel the kitchen.

Ian asked Kat if she would also be willing to go with him to a kitchen design showroom to explain to him what the best outfitted kitchen for a true chef would entail. She agreed, so they got in the car and drove again to a store that only carried top-of-the-line appliances and fixtures.

They wandered endlessly around the SubZero refrigerators and Viking and Wolfe brand stoves and hoods. She helped him design a kitchen with two sinks, one out of copper for food prep; the other, a deep, white farmer sink for large dishes with a faucet that pulled out for easier access to clean large pots and pans. The countertops would be poured stained concrete with a subway tile background, and the cabinets, a deep cherry wood. They were also incredibly tall, with shelves on the bottom that slid in and out to avoid standing on one's head to retrieve something. After Kat mentioned it had always been her dream to have a faucet plumbed in on the wall behind the stove for the easy filling of pots, Ian even asked the sales rep and designer to make it happen.

When he had spent tens of thousands of dollars more, Kat couldn't hold her tongue any longer. Pulling him aside, she asked pointedly, "Ian, just for whom exactly are you building this incredible kitchen? Do you suddenly cook?"

He laughed at her. "Hardly, love!"

"Then for whom?"

"Well, it increases the value of the home. Also, my ma likes to cook. And," he dropped his voice so she had to lean in to hear, "I'm hoping that someone who knows what they are doing might be convinced to come and give me lessons."

She smirked at him. "I'm sure that Melinda, Gerard, or Jen would be happy to do that for you."

"I'm sort of hoping for more of a live-in. At least at some point." He shrugged and gave her his infamous cocky grin. She blushed furiously and dropped her gaze to the ground.

Having finalized things for the remodel, they walked down past the other stores to a coffee shop. As they were exiting, Ian turned and leaned down toward Kat, whispering that he was missing her beignets with his coffee and that she was converting him to this Southern comfort food thing. She looked up at him, her eyes sparkling. "Glad to be of service," she replied with a laugh.

With that, he leaned over and gave her a kiss on the cheek and grabbed her free hand for a just split second until they both realized what they had done. In looking around, they thought they had dodged a bullet—no one was really paying them any attention. What they failed to notice was the camera shooting frames of them between the trees surrounding the parking lot.

Chapter Twenty-Nine

Two days later, Ian had the keys to his new house in hand. He had asked if Kat wanted to be there when the items he'd purchased were delivered, and she, not wanting to give up an opportunity to spend time with him, had eagerly agreed.

When he came to pick her up, he informed her that he needed to make a trip to a hardware store to buy some screwdrivers, a hammer and nails, and other such supplies. It seemed an innocent enough outing, but they were still oblivious that they were being followed by a photographer.

***

The unrelenting paparazzo who had been following Ian Gregory and the mystery woman who was not Lydia Swan couldn't believe his luck to be getting this kind of dirt ahead of anyone else. He was now patiently biding his time, stalking his target wherever he went, waiting for any further opportunity to substantiate the tip he'd received.

Though the actor was not a mega star, he was becoming well enough known that interest in his private life was growing. The photographer had followed the couple to the actor's new address but parked a few houses down to be as inconspicuous as possible. Walking up the street, past the house, he discretely snapped a few photos before returning to his car, determinedly waiting for his subject and the woman to exit the dwelling once again. His tenacity soon paid off, as he wasn't waiting long until a large delivery truck from the store he'd seen them at two days earlier pulled up in front of the house and the pair emerged.

They were standing close together on the lawn, looking at each item before directing where it should go.

The shutter on the camera snapped rapidly, capturing images of the scene. It was quite obvious that the woman was certainly someone who was more intimate with Ian than a stranger or interior designer would be. What the photographer couldn't figure out was if they were close friends, siblings, or if they were lovers, and Ian was indeed cheating on Lydia.

Whatever the story, it hardly mattered; the paparazzo only needed the money shots to make it look like there was something going on between the actor and his mystery guest, regardless of reality.

***

Ian and Kat spent the rest of the day arranging furniture. Once they had set up what little they could without the contractors' work being finished on the update, they went around and admired their choices in each room before turning their attention to unpacking the boxes he needed for his stay over the next few days. Kat's choices for Ian's mother's room fit perfectly and the lighter colors helped to not overwhelm the space. The master was the largest of the three bedrooms and had been recently renovated in an edgy masculine style, with sleek lines and varying tones of black and grey, but Kat's touches had softened the room just enough to make it more inviting.

The living room, meanwhile, was a nice blend between an old-world study and parlor. Kat had been a bit perplexed by his design requests until she helped him unpack box after box of books, many leather-bound and old. As night started to settle on the Valley, they finished up the last few boxes.

"Good thing I didn't have much stuff before!" Ian remarked. He went on, explaining he'd only furnished his L.A. flat with the bare essentials as he'd considered Ireland his true home before now, so there wasn't much to get through. The kitchen remodel fixtures were tucked safely into the garage for the contractor to work with once they were back in Canada.

"So, all of those books are just 'bare essentials', then?" Kat teased. "Now I understand the need for your living room to look like a library."

"Well, what else does an introvert do with his time?" he quipped back, breaking down the last of the boxes. "Want to go grab a bite now?"

She nodded.

"Great! I know a great little Italian place just down the canyon a short way."

They got back into his car and headed downhill a few miles. He pulled up in front of a tiny restaurant and once again, hurried to open her door. As they made their way inside, he also held open the door to the building and when they were at their table, held out Kat's chair for her. Kat just shook her head.

"What?" he asked.

"Do you always do this kind of stuff, like pulling out chairs and opening doors, or are you trying to impress me?"

"No, I do! Like I told you before, I'm just a nice Catholic boy who was raised by my grandparents and mother. I was taught young how to be a respectful gentleman to women."

"It's nice. The South is sort of the last hold out for that here, and even there it's going away."

They stayed talking in the restaurant until they were the last patrons by far. The staff were clearly starting to get annoyed because they wanted to finish up for the night and go home when Ian finally looked up from their conversation and took notice of the line of them just waiting along the back wall displaying various expressions of boredom.

"Sorry," he told them sheepishly, as he signed his credit card slip. He then got up, helped Kat out of her chair, and they walked out the door to his car.

A camera shutter fluttered once again in the distance.

Ian drove Kat home, but it was very clear that neither of them wanted to say goodnight, so Kat invited him into the house for a little while. They walked through the door to find Jen sitting on the couch watching a documentary on the Himalayas as she sorted through invoices. She glanced up when they came in and then did a double take.

"Oh!" she exclaimed.

"Hi, Jen. Sorry to startle you. This is Ian Gregory."

"I know!" she responded lamely.

Kat turned to Ian, "And this is my Jen."

He took a step forward and offered his hand with a polite, "Nice to meet you."

"That accent!" Jen exclaimed dreamily and then looked frantically at Kat to see if she had truly just spoken out loud. After so many years in the business, Kat knew Jen didn't react like that very often anymore, but it seemed there was something about the very handsome Ian Gregory standing in her house that made her lose herself for a moment.

"I could say the same for you!" He smiled graciously at her.

Jen jumped up from the couch, grabbing the papers from the coffee table and moving them to the dining room, before she went into the kitchen and grabbed three glasses, along with a nice bottle of cabernet.

The conversation was a bit strained at first as Jen was still a bit shocked and star-struck at having this man sitting in her living room, but it wasn't long before Ian had them rolling on the floor recounting tales from his youth.

In turn, Kat and Jen talked about the South, interrupting each other as they told him stories about themselves growing up.

"There was this one time when Kat was tired of being flat chested in eighth grade. I had gotten boobs way before her. So, she sneaked one of my bras and filled it up with toilet paper. It looked great…"

Kat jumped in, "Yeah, great until after P.E. when we had to shower and change, and there were tiny bits of toilet paper stuck all over my chest because it was September in the South at ninety degrees and about one million percent humidity, and I had sweated so much outside. Thank goodness Jen saw it in time and threw her towel at me. I was able to wrap it around me and rub off most of it off by the time we hit the showers."

"Poor Kat!" Ian sympathized, putting an arm around her shoulders, and giving her a friendly squeeze. "One time, this big fellow was heading straight at me. I had been talking to his girl while he went to the toilet. One look at him and I knew he was pissed. Both mad and drunk," he paused and looked over at Kat, giving her a wink, "I let him run at me and at the very last second,

I darted to the left and he ran into the wall behind me, knocking himself out cold. For the rest of the night, anytime anyone needed something from that side of the pub they had to walk over the big, unconscious drunk guy." They all laughed at the image.

"It sounds like you had a bit of a rough adolescence, Ian," Jen remarked.

He quickly looked in Kat's direction and she gave him the slightest shake of her head, letting him know she had said nothing.

"It was okay," he told her, shrugging. "Lots of Irish boys get into scrapes. Heavy drinking and youth generally don't go well together."

They continued on like that, sitting and talking until one a.m., when they finally decided to call it a night but had agreed to go to the beach together the next day. Kat walked Ian to his car and when they were at his door, he pulled her in close to him. He held her for a second and then leaned down to kiss the top of her head. His lips lingered there as he inhaled the fragrance of her shampoo mixed with her own personal scent. He let her go and she stepped back up onto the curb.

"Until we meet again!" he told her softly.

"Until we meet again," she replied.

When Kat went back inside the door, Jen was cleaning up the empty wine glasses and bottles, along with plates of cheese, fruit, and cookies. She stopped and glanced at Kat before smiling and looking down again as she walked away.

"What?" Kat asked her, following her into the kitchen.

"Just thinking."

"About?"

"Ian."

"Oh."

"He is an incredibly nice guy, Kat. Like really nice. Not affected at all. I don't think I've ever met an actor who is more down to earth."

"Yes, he's pretty unique."

"So, how long have you been sleeping with him?" Jen dropped a bomb.

"What?" Kat indignantly replied. "No! No, Jen! We aren't sleeping together. Where in the world did that come from?"

"Kat, I've known you forever. I know when you're hiding something. Y'all are way too intimate with each other to not be sleeping together."

"Jen, we are not sleeping together!" "Sure!"

"We aren't!"

"Okay…" Jen replied incredulously.

"Jen, listen to me. We are *not* having sex! We just got to know each other very well during those days that I stayed with him when he got the concussion. We are like brother and sister!"

"Based on what I saw tonight, I wouldn't want to be a part of that family if that's how y'all act toward a sibling."

"Jen, honestly. We are *not* sleeping together." "Okay, then. So, tell me about his and Lydia's relationship, then?"

"There's not much to tell," Kat lied. "They care about each other. That much is clear. Can we drop it please? I'm tired."

"Sure," Jen replied, conceding that Kat was not going to break. "What time do you want to head to the beach tomorrow?"

"I don't know. We told Ian to get there about noon, so maybe we should get there at around eleven-fifteen, so it looks like an accident we bumped into each other."

"Right."

"Have a good night!" Kat called to Jen as she started back to her room.

"Oh, I would, if I were sleeping with that man," Jen muttered to herself.

***

The next morning, Kat and Jen headed off to Malibu Beach, sunscreen, snacks, and towels in hand. Kat couldn't wait to get a little color back onto her body and was so excited to get to see Ian again that she could hardly stand it.

A little after noon, he walked up to them and put his chair

down a few feet from theirs. A few minutes later, he leaned over the side of his chair and asked if he could borrow their sunscreen, stating that he had forgotten his. It seemed innocent enough, like it was the best way to meet someone at the beach, until Kat handed it to him, and he reached everywhere but his back.

"Would you?" he asked.

"Sure," Kat replied. She squirted out a generous amount as he took off his shirt and she began to rub it on his body. She tried to be smooth so that anyone around them wouldn't know how incredibly much she was enjoying his sun-warmed skin and his scent that somehow smelled almost like fresh-baked bread. Her hands lingered a little longer than would be appropriate for a stranger, though, so he slowly turned to her and asked, "Almost done there?"

Kat realized what she had done. She had dawdled too long, been too intimate, giving the impression that this was more than just a chance meeting. Confirming she was finished right then, she wiped the excess cream on her towel.

After that, it was easy to tell that Ian was an actor. Besides her faux pas in the beginning when she was rubbing the sun screen up and down his back, he played the part of getting to know them perfectly.

At first, he was just chatting from his chair. Then, a while later, Jen asked him if he wanted some snacks. He quickly jumped up and settled on their beach blanket to sit down between them.

They all ate and laughed together, alternating between running down to the waves and lying on the blanket, all propped up on their elbows, talking. Quite frequently, people would look over at them, wondering if perhaps they had seen Ian before—he looked vaguely familiar—but thanks to the bright sun, his wearing a ball cap and aviator sunglasses, and the fact that he was usually dressed in period clothing when fans saw him on screen, no one recognized him well enough to place from where exactly they had seen him.

In the late afternoon, the three packed up, climbed the hill together to the parking lot, and said goodbye as they walked to their respective cars. Ian had already told Kat earlier in the day that he would text her that night and see her the next day.

Kat and Jen arrived at the house both bushed but happy. They showered off the beach sand and dressed in their PJs, settling in for a night of Chinese delivery and a bottle of wine. Jen reached over and flipped on the T.V., switching through channels until she came upon an episode of *Western Skies*.

"You know I've never seen this show?" Jen asked Kat.

"No! Really?" Kat asked incredulously.

"Yes, really. I meant to before we were supposed to go up there, but then you came and Lucy got sick and, well, I just never got around to it."

They watched the episode and Jen watched Kat closely as she tucked her legs under her on the couch and leaned forward, staring intently while biting the end of one of her pinkies. *God, he is beautiful*, Kat thought with admiration.

When the show was over, they said their goodnights and headed to bed. Kat picked up her phone and saw that Ian had texted her: *Goodnight.*

She responded, but he did not, so she figured that he had already fallen asleep.

***

There was obviously something going on, Jen knew. What that something was, though, was what she was unsure of. Ian and Lydia had never come out and confirmed or denied their involvement with each other, so she just couldn't figure out the need for all the secrecy? If they were together, then obviously, he would be cheating on her. But, if they weren't together, why would it matter if he was seeing Kat, unless Kat wanted to keep it quiet until her divorce was finalized?

Jen tried to wrap her mind around the different possible scenarios and thought about how much Kat had changed in the last two months. Gone was a woman so filled with a sense of responsibility and propriety, it was unhealthy. For the first time since they had gone their separate ways, Jen thought, Kat seemed completely happy. She certainly looked about ten years younger, and her laugh was quicker, not to mention that her eyes sparkled. It wasn't that Kat was being immature or irresponsible, but that she had loosened up and started to understand it was okay for her to still enjoy her life. It was the first time in a long time that Kat had only focused on what she wanted to do, and Jen could tell that her old friend was back.

Chapter Thirty

Early the next morning, Kat awoke to Jen storming into her room. She was holding something in her hand and looked perplexed and angry all at once.

"Look at this, Kat! This is bad!" she said, shoving something in her face.

"What? What is that? I can't even focus yet."

"I went to the market this morning to pick up a few things and I just happened to look over at the tabloid rag section by the checkout stands and saw *this*!" She threw a few different newspapers onto the bed. Kat sat up and grabbed one.

"Oh, no! No, no, no! We were so careful. How could this have happened?" she moaned as she combed through pages, seeing pictures of her and Ian at the coffee place, at his new house, the restaurant, and when he embraced her as he was leaving Jen's place the other night. There were even pictures of them at the beach together when she was rubbing the sunscreen onto his back. Each shot had been perfectly timed to catch all of the small, intimately physical moments between them.

Then she read the headlines.

Is Ian Gregory Cheating on Lydia?

If the Cat's Away, the Mouse Will Play

Ian Gregory: New House and New Girlfriend?

"Oh, God!" Kat let out a sob.

"I knew it!" Jen exclaimed angrily. "I knew that y'all were sleeping together and you lied to me!"

"Not really, Jen. We are not sleeping together."

"You really expect me to believe that? Kat, what the hell is going on? You tell me everything!"

"Yes! You have to believe it. There are very good reasons to believe it and a history I can't get into. Please, Jen, don't be angry. I wasn't hiding anything from you that I wasn't hiding from anyone else. The true story lies only between Ian, Lydia, and me, and I am not at liberty to divulge any more than my part in this, which is that I agreed to keep it quiet because it doesn't look so good for my divorce, either."

Jen simply glared at her for a second, but then Kat saw that her resolve was beginning to weaken, before Jen finally sighed and said, "Okay. Fine. I believe you."

With that, Kat grabbed her phone and wrote Ian: *We have a problem!*

Ian: *I know! My manager just called, as did my publicity team. There's nothing they can do. I've never been tabloid fodder before. This got past them, and it's everywhere!*

Kat: *What are we going to do?*

Ian: *I don't know. Just get over here.*

Kat jumped up out of bed and ran past Jen. She grabbed her purse and asked Jen for the keys to her car.

"Kat, stop! You can't go out like that! You're wearing your pajamas!"

With an exasperated sigh, Kat threw everything down and ran back into her room. She grabbed a pair of jeans, threw a T-shirt over her head, and grabbed her hair, slapping it into a messy ponytail. She ran to the bathroom and rubbed on some deodorant and quickly brushed her teeth. She ran back out, past Jen and grabbed her keys. Jen held out her hand to stop her.

"Kat, you can't take my car. This is L.A., remember? I need it today to get around. Let me throw something on and I'll drive you there. Ian can bring you home."

Kat sat impatiently as Jen rushed around getting herself ready. Kat kept looking at the clock on the wall, wishing Jen would go faster. When she came out into the living room, Kat was already at the door and stepping outside.

"Geez!" Jen called, running to catch up. "Wait a second."

Jen typed Ian's address into her GPS, and they drove silently along. All of a sudden Kat burst out laughing.

"What's so funny, Kat?" Jen prompted her. "Nothing. Except for the fact that we both forgot my car is sitting in your garage. You know? The same one I drove 3,000 miles in to get to you?"

Jen chuckled too. "Oh, yeah! Duh."

"Thank you for driving me, though. I don't think I'm in any shape to be operating machinery right now!"

"Yeah, probably not."

They drove along in silence again, and Kat found herself pushing her feet against the floorboard in an attempt to get there faster. Every light seemed to take forever, and traffic was at a standstill. Eventually, they made it off the freeway and onto the surface streets to Ian's new house.

Before Jen had even stopped the car completely, Kat had opened the door and jumped out. "I'll call you later!" was all she said as she ran up to the front door. She rang the bell and waited in torment for what seemed an eternity for it to open, worrying about who could be lurking in the bushes, trying to get a picture of this, too.

When Ian finally opened the door, he stood with his phone to his ear. He nodded and raised his eyebrows at her in a greeting before stepping aside to let her through while continuing his conversation as he shut the door. It didn't take Kat long to figure out it was his agent, and they were working on damage control. She could hear snippets of conversation from his side, though she tried hard not to listen. Ian sounded angry, sad, and exasperated. He kept asking "How did they find out?", "How did they find me?", and "Why do they care?"

A few minutes later, he ended his call and walked over to Kat. He looked done in and weary of the whole situation already, and it had just come out that morning. He just stood there, wearing plaid pajama bottoms and a faded T-shirt, his hair flopping onto his forehead and his expression that of a forlorn little boy.

"Hey," he greeted her meekly.

"Hey."

They stood locked in place for a second, just staring at each other, neither one knowing what to say or do.

Finally, Kat took a few tentative steps toward him, and he opened his arms to her. She stepped into them instantly and wrapped her arms around his body, holding him tightly while he absentmindedly ran his hands up and down her back. Eventually, she tipped her head up and he leaned down to give her a gentle kiss on her lips.

He broke their embrace and ran his hand through his hair. "Well, this is a fine mess, isn't it?"

Kat couldn't contain her emotions anymore. She began to cry softly, scared of what this would mean for him, for her, and for Lydia. He stepped forward and wiped the tears from her cheeks and told her not to worry; it would all work out.

"Has Lydia found out yet?" Kat asked him. He admitted he hadn't heard from her yet, but he was sure he would.

"Ian, how did this happen? We were so careful! The moments that photographer captured made us look way more intimate than we really are, except when we are alone. We could only be friends as far as anyone else knows, but the photos make it seem so much more than it was."

"That's the game they play," he said with disgust. "It's what sells those rags."

His phone rang again, and he picked up the call. Kat could hear the yelling on the other end from five feet away from him. It didn't take long to figure out that it was George on the phone, and that he was beyond miffed at the situation.

"What the hell?" Kat heard George holler, "What in God's name is goin' on? I'm gettin' bombarded by calls from Lydia's people and the network execs. What the hell have y'all done? Advertisers are threatenin' to walk! All of the marketin' that this relationship status of yours and Lydia's does is worth millions, son. You know that! You cannot just go out and start screwin' some nobody because you're lonely there and not expect it to get out! Y'all have royally messed things up and everyone is fit to be tied."

Ian squared his shoulders as he glanced at Kat. "She is *not* a nobody!"

"Well, she sure as hell ain't Lydia, though, is she?"

"No, she is not. But I don't care. I agreed to do this for

Lydia, to protect her. It was not supposed to be a marketing tool for you or the network. This is my life, George! You can't dictate to me who I can and can't love off screen!"

"What the hell do you mean, you did it to protect Lydia? From what? We all just figured y'all were screwin' each other and tryin' to keep it on the down low. But it started to become and continues to be a major promotional tool. Everyone is talkin' about y'all, which means people are talkin' about the show. It's a hook, boy. You and Lydia generated y'all's own publicity better than just about anyone else could have."

"George, I don't want to be a 'hook'. I want a life. The arrangement worked fine for a while, but now I want to own my life again," Ian answered defiantly.

The two men went back and forth for a few more minutes. Ian finally disconnected the call and gave an exasperated sigh. He walked into the living room and sat down on the couch, placing his head in his hands. Kat, not knowing what to do, slipped in next to him and began to rub his back.

"This was never supposed to be permanent. Lydia and I never agreed that this would be permanent," he mumbled.

"I know," Kat told him soothingly.

"How can they try to dictate what I do off screen? How can my love life be for purchase? The network and production company want to add this to my contract. Seriously? Who adds a relationship clause to a contract? Can they even do that?"

"Wait… What? What are you taking about, Ian?"

"They are talking about making this nebulous relationship status of Lydia's and mine part of our contracts. It's generating a buzz that brings in viewers and makes them money."

"Can they do that?" Kat was amazed.

"Apparently. But I need to call my agent and double check with her. I don't think this is right."

Kat sat back on the sofa and tipped her head back. She couldn't believe it. How could a job have that much power over someone's personal life? She put her hand over her mouth and sighed.

Before she thought about it, she blurted out, "I guess we should have just slept together anyway, since everyone already thinks we are. At least we would know what we're missing."

Ian lolled his head over to the side to face her and slowly smiled. He leaned back next to her and grabbed her hand. They sat in that same position, staring at the ceiling together for a long time, neither of them saying anything, just thinking about their situation. Here, they felt safe. They were together, joined at the hand, protected from prying eyes and cameras. Each was contemplating what this now meant for their budding relationship and how they would ever make it work. Now that people had seen her, any activity they engaged in publicly could be potentially captured. That meant that all of their interactions would have to take place in secret. Kat began to feel once again like a mistress in a loveless marriage.

How strange the world can be that I'm now inadvertently, if only theoretically, on the other side of what happened to me with James? The irony was too much, and she started laughing.

"What's funny?" Ian asked.

"This… This whole situation. I went from being the wronged wife when my husband was having a secret affair to being the secret mistress in a non-existent, but realistic looking and well-marketed relationship."

As they sat there and let her words run through their heads, Ian's phone rang out again, startling them both from their quiet reveries.

"It's Lydia," he said, after looking at the phone. "This isn't going to be good." He sighed before swiping his finger across the screen.

"Hello?" he said cautiously. All he heard on the other side of the phone were sobs. "Lyds. Lydia! You've got to calm down. It's okay. It isn't the end of the world." Lydia just continued to bawl into the phone.

Ian put the phone on speaker and told her that Kat was with him, and they were both on the line. All of a sudden, Lydia went into hysterics. "What did you two do? I'm over here in Paris with friends, and when I get back from dinner, I have a billion messages from everyone."

"Nothing, Lyds!" Ian replied. "Some paparazzo got some shots of Kat and me out and about. There was nothing inappropriate, I promise. They just chose the photos that made us look the most intimate. We haven't even held hands in public. Relax. This will go away!"

"Ian, they are talking about adding this to our contracts; that we have to keep this up in order to keep our jobs. Can they do that?"

"I'm not sure," he responded. "I was just about to call my agent when you called."

"What are we going to do?"

"I don't know."

"Why were you two so careless?" Lydia asked accusingly.

"We weren't, Lydia! It's just that for the first time since we've been more recognizable, you were not there, so it attracted attention. We can't keep this charade up forever, you know. We both want to have a life!"

"I know, Ian. But now they're talking about making it part of our contracts. I never meant for it to get this far."

"Me, either, Lyds. I think that was fine for when things were status quo, but we really need to sit down and talk, the three of us, when we get back to the location and decide what we want to do and how we get out of this."

"I agree," Lydia said quietly.

"You do?" Ian sounded incredulous. He looked up at Kat with a quizzical expression, raising his eyebrows in surprise.

"Yes. Ian, I've met someone."

"You have? Oh, Lydia, that's great!"

"We're just getting to know one another, but I really like him. He's French, also an actor, and he's a friend of one of the girls I came here with. So, honestly, I can't get too mad at you, when the exact same thing could have happened with me. I just don't want them to put this into our contracts. Kat, are you there? Are you okay?"

"Yes, Lydia, I'm here, and I'm okay. I'm just shocked. I knew that the paparazzi were ruthless, but I had no idea how they could turn something so innocent into something that looks so scandalous. They used the shots taken just at the right times."

"I know. That's what they do," Lydia told her, echoing Ian's earlier statement. "I'm going to sign off now. I'm meeting André for a drink in a little while. Ian, please tell me what your agent says. I'll put in a call to mine, as well. Let's see if they are both in agreement. Love you!"

In that moment, Kat seemed to be a thousand miles away and looked utterly shell-shocked by the time Ian ended the call. Despite her eyes on him, she wasn't really seeing him. Ian looked down at her phone at what had caused her deer in headlights demeanor. A text from James read, *How could you? How could you serve me with divorce papers without telling me first? And how can you be screwing someone else already? Kat, just remember that you are still my wife, so you are no better than I am.*

Kat silently began to cry. "Hey! Hey!" Ian lifted her chin with his finger so that he could look her in the eye. "You *are* better than him. You haven't slept with anyone but your husband. You know it, and I know it. This is exactly why I was so insistent that we wait. It doesn't matter what the rest of the world thinks, we know the truth. You have nothing to apologize for or be ashamed of."

"I know," she whispered almost inaudibly. "It's just that I wasn't expecting my two worlds to clash so forcefully within the span of five hours. I should have told James, I guess, but I was too caught up in my desire to stick it to him for once."

"Are you going to answer him?" Ian asked her.

"Yes," she said as she began to type: *James, I am so sorry. I should have handled this better. I apologize.*

She sat back and waited. Her phone chimed in just a few seconds: *How could you, Kat? How could you just abandon me and find someone new?*

By this point, Kat was already way past the breaking point

for her emotions. She couldn't help herself as she furiously typed: *Isn't that the pot calling the kettle black, James? As I recall, you started this when you started screwing Sam behind my back.*

She waited a few more seconds, while Ian watched helplessly beside her. A message came immediately back from him, but it wasn't what she expected: *Kat, I love you. I made a mistake. I don't want to fight. I don't want to lose you. Please, can we just talk this out, in person, before we sign the documents?*

Kat didn't know how to answer. Finally, she wrote that she would have to think about it. Then she added: *Please stop contacting me for a while. I need time to think.* With that her arm went limp, her phone dangling precariously in her hand, her body slackened like a ragdoll.

Ian took Kat's phone to keep it from dropping and saw her final message. Turning and looking her straight in the face, he asked, panicked, "What in the hell did you mean that you need to think about it?"

"Because I do," she said simply.

"You're thinking about going back to him? Please don't!" Ian implored her, his voice anguished, the emotions of the day affecting him, too.

"No! No, I meant I need to think about if I'm willing to meet with him in person before we sign the documents. I don't want to, but it might provide the closure we both need. I'm just not sure right now."

Ian breathed a deep sigh of relief and let the issue go for the moment. They spent the rest of the afternoon each doing their own form of damage control. Kat was being hounded by phone calls from her mother, father, and brothers, and texts from Jen, and even Holly and Ashley. Apparently, news of an actor's love life spread faster than the speed of light. Her mother was the worst by far, trying to guilt Kat into staying married to James by declaring over and over that hers would be the first divorce on either side of their family and that she couldn't bring that kind of shame upon them. She begged her to reconsider, saying, "What will people think?"

Kat finally had enough, though. "They can think whatever they'd like to, Mama. I am done living my life just to please others. I don't love James! I love Ian!"

"How can you love someone you just met two months ago, sugar?"

"I don't know, Mama. But I do! I do love Ian. He makes me feel like, for the first time in my life, I'm perfect the way I am."

Kat had moved into Ian's bedroom to speak to her entourage, so Ian could speak to his uninterrupted, but now she felt someone watching her. She turned around and saw Ian, leaning against the doorjamb, his call clearly over. She panicked. *How long has he been standing there? Did he just hear me tell my mother that I love him? How mortifying!* She felt like she'd die of embarrassment.

Her eyes met his, and he mouthed, "I love you, too!"

"Mama, I have to go." She abruptly ended her call and ran into Ian's open arms. All of their pent-up feelings from the day came pouring out as their embrace intensified. There was nothing sweet about this encounter; it was strictly about fulfilling desire.

Ian picked her up and carried her to the bed, where he lay her down gently before ripping his shirt off over his head and climbing up next to her. His hand went under her shirt and over her abdomen until it came to rest under her bra, caressing her breast while he kissed her. She sat up and he pulled her shirt over her head, throwing it on the floor.

He tried to undo the clasp on her bra, too, mumbling about how hard these things were, "like chastity belts for breasts…" When he finally popped the fastener, her breasts spilled out as her bra slipped down her arms. He lay her back down and began caressing her lips with his, before starting down her neck, across her collar bone and down, his roughened, masculine hand running up and down the satiny curves of her torso, eliciting sweet moans of pleasure from her in the process. Her responsiveness was driving him crazy, his desire overtaking him. To her great delight, he continued tracing his soft, warm tongue down her stomach until he reached the waist of her jeans which he slowly unbuttoned. She could only focus on how much she had to have him; she had never felt such lust before.

Lifting her hips slightly, he pulled her pants down over her legs until they dropped to the floor. Then the spell was broken, and she suddenly felt self-conscious laying in only her underwear as Ian stood frozen above, gazing down at her.

"What is it?" she asked nervously, trying to cover herself up with her arms while terrified this would be when he realized that she was a forty-three-year-old mother of three and would run away screaming. But instead, he simply grabbed her wrists and gently pried them away so he could continue to admire her.

"Nothing. You're just so beautiful."

That was not what she was expecting to hear and once she processed it, she sat up and reached for him. He needed no more coaxing to lay back down beside her, and they picked up where they had left off.

They spent what seemed like hours exploring each other with their eyes, hands, mouths, and tongues. Finally, when she couldn't take it anymore, Kat implored, "Please, Ian. Love me!"

"I do love you," he mumbled, his searing mouth running down her neck.

"That's not what I mean. I want you. Now!"

He pulled himself up and looked down at her. "We can't."

"Why not?" she was begging. Again.

"You know why."

"Ian, I don't care! He has been served the divorce papers. He already knows about us. It's been over since the day I left to come here. Please!"

Holding himself above her on his arms, he stared into her eyes for several seconds. Her pleas and writhing beneath him with wanton abandon must have broken his resolve because finally he asked, "Are you sure?"

"Yes, I'm sure!" she panted breathlessly. "I've never been

more sure of anything in my life!"

He sighed as he relented. "Okay."

She scrambled to help him pull down his pants and then he slowly, teasingly, slid her underwear down. In a tangle of arms and legs, they were so close now. As she felt him move over her to settle between her thighs, Kat closed her eyes and held her breath in anticipation… until the ringing of his phone jerked them both out of the moment. He looked over at it on his bedside table and heaved a large sigh, shaking his head. "Kat, love, I'm so sorry, but it's my agent. I have to take it."

Kat nodded and lay back on the bed, groaning quietly in frustration, her body still humming from the endorphins of her arousal. They had come so close. All she wanted was to be together fully, to express all of her feelings for him physically. She watched as he pulled his pants back on and sat down on the end of his bed, and then got up and went to his closet, pulled out a button down, and slipped it over her naked body. He glanced up and gave her an approving look as he continued his conversation.

Chapter Thirty-One

A few hours later, after the flurry of phone calls and texts seemed to have slowed down for the time being, Ian and Kat decided that they needed to eat. They ordered Indian food for delivery and sat on the floor of his living room, talking about what would happen next in between sharing curry flavored kisses.

Ian's agent told him she had spoken with an attorney and verified that though what they were trying to do was highly unorthodox, ultimately the network and production company could decide what they would and would not allow from their actors, at least the relatively new or unknown ones who had little to no bargaining power. With fame the game changed, but in the beginning the attitude was that there were always thousands of others who would kill to get a part if the original actors didn't want to acquiesce to their demands. She had also regretfully confirmed that if they made it a part of his contract for the next season and he signed it, he would have to adhere to the clause regarding his and Lydia's perceived relationship. Since it was not in their contracts now, however, they were technically not obligated to keep up the charade, but then they both risked not being asked back for the next season if they did not. Given they were the stars of the show, his agent doubted that would happen, but she still couldn't guarantee that one or both of them wouldn't be fired. Ian was incredibly angry and dejected, and Kat just sat helplessly by while he debated what he wanted to do, whispering to himself, talking out his options.

"I could do this, or I could refuse to do this and walk away. But how can I walk away when I just bought this house? Oh my God, how did this turn into such a mess?"

By the time the food had come, they had talked, and Kat told him that she didn't care if she had to hide in the shadows, as long as she could be with him. She told him that she cared for him entirely too much by this point to give up now. As she spoke, he cringed, knowing it was far from ideal.

They talked long into the evening about how they could both pretend Ian was possibly involved with Lydia while maintaining their own relationship. Eventually Kat looked up at that clock and saw that it was nearly midnight. She asked him to please drive her back to Jen's now that it was dark and hopefully no one would see them.

"Stay," he said simply.

"What do you mean, 'stay'?"

"Stay. Here. With me. Tonight," he implored.

"Ian, how would I get out of here tomorrow without being seen?"

"I don't know. I don't care. I don't want you to leave. Please stay with me."

"I don't know if that's such a good idea," she responded. "Someone is probably watching the house now, just looking for any opportunity to take more pictures. They would have seen me go in and not come back out. I would rather go back to Jen's when it's dark."

"Okay, then. I'll take you back tomorrow night. Please, just stay. I don't want to be alone with this tonight. If you go back, you will have Jen and I'll be here by myself, ruminating about this over and over inside my head. I feel like everything is crashing down around me and I've let everyone down. Please, Kat, I need you."

Kat studied Ian's face and decided he was right, he needed her to stay. He was obviously deeply distressed about the situation, worried about his career, Lydia, and her. "All right," she relented.

They headed down the hall to his bedroom and both collapsed on his bed. The emotions and passion that had driven them to this place hours ago combined with the following stress and turmoil had now exhausted and drained them both. Ian reached for her hand and as he rubbed his thumb across the top of it, he apologized again, telling her that she deserved so much more than this. They both fell into restless sleep, each rerunning the scenes from the day over and over in their nightmares.

First thing in the morning, Kat's phone sounded off. She grabbed for it and fumbled with it before answering, "Hello?"

"Hi. Kat, are you okay? You didn't come back here last night."

"Yes, I'm fine. Ian had just asked me to stay."

"You still going to tell me that y'all aren't sleeping together?" Jen inquired.

The memories of how close they had come the previous afternoon came flooding back to Kat and she sighed. "No. Still aren't," she said, obviously exasperated.

"Y'all are just crazy then!"

"Probably," Kat agreed.

"Have you seen the papers today?" "No. Why? Have you?"

"Yes." Silence.

"And…"

"And you aren't going to like it."

"Okay, Jen. Enough games! I'm too tired to do this. What did the papers say today?"

"Did you check your texts yet this morning?"

"No. Not yet. You actually woke me up when you called."

"Just check your texts, Kat. I sent you a few pictures."

"Hold on." Kat exhaled, annoyed.

She opened her messages and pictures of several tabloid magazines stared back at her, all plastered with the most unflattering photos of her. The headlines made her sick.

Kat Anderson: Ian's 'Southern Comfort.'

"Ian, how could you?" Lydia implores.

Kat Anderson Files for Divorce to Become Ian Gregory's Mistress! Lydia Is Devastated.

Of course, someone had managed to find a picture of Lydia, looking beautiful with tears brimming and shinning in her eyes.

But the worst read: *Who Is Kat Anderson: Her Best Friend Spills All.*

"Oh, God!" Kat exhaled.

"Yeah. You want me to tell you what it says on the inside?"

"I don't know. Do I?"

"Well, here's a little gem of a quote. 'Kat was always a bit of a loose cannon. She has done her own thing as long as I've known her. It doesn't surprise me at all that this happened. In fact, I know that she thought Ian was gorgeous and left specifically to go and find him. She left behind her poor husband and their high school-aged son, plus two more in college. It's a tragedy. I would gather it was a midlife crisis.' Three guesses who said that."

"Ashley."

"Bingo. Sure as hell wasn't me."

"Oh my God! Now what?"

"Well, the 'Kat' is out of the bag, so to speak, so I would suggest you get ready for an onslaught of photographers and requests for interviews. Oh, and you'll probably want to change your cell number."

"Oh Lord, help me!" Kat cried out. The full force of what was happening hit her hard and fast. She had gone from an invisible housewife to public enemy number one in he eyes of all of the *Western Skies* viewers. She would be single-handedly blamed for the breakup of Ian and Lydia's "relationship." She groaned. "What am I going to do?"

"What's done is done. Y'all will only be down here two more days, then will be mostly secluded again up at the set for the next month or so. Just lie low there, and hopefully this will all blow over as soon as the next star decides to do something stupid."

"You think Ian falling in love with me was stupid?" Kat whispered.

"No, of course not! That's not what I meant. But trust me, in a few days someone will get busted for a DUI or yet another divorce will be announced."

Kat felt Ian's arm go around her waist as she stood in the living room, shaking with fury. She crumpled into him as the impact of what was being said about her sunk in. When she was safely in Ian's arms, she began to cry. Jen heard her and told her to go, that she would talk to her later.

When the call ended, she turned completely to face Ian and threw herself into his arms, collapsing onto him. He half-led, half-carried her to the sofa while she sobbed. He asked her what was wrong, and she simply handed her phone to him on which the tabloid cover pictures glared garishly.

"Kat, I am so sorry. I'm just so incredibly sorry. I cannot believe what a mess this is. If I could do anything in the world to stop it, I would."

Kat couldn't answer, she was crying so hard.

"Ian, I can't do this," she finally managed to squeak out. "My kids and my parents will see this. What have I done?"

Ian just held her, at a loss on how else to help her, as she sobbed into his chest. Finally, he said, "Kat, I love you. You love me. That's all that matters, and we will get through this. I promise."

She so badly wanted to believe him, but at the same time, it didn't seem possible.

They spent most of the day on the couch, Kat curled up against Ian as closely as possible. They hardly spoke, just comforted each other with their presence.

Later, Ian got up and went to take a shower and Kat continued to sit on the couch in the living room for a while until she couldn't take being alone anymore. She walked down the hall, into the ensuite bathroom and sat on the closed toilet lid while he washed, her knees pulled up like a small child. When he opened the steamy shower door, he was surprised to see her there but smiled as she said forlornly, "I didn't want to be alone."

"That's okay, love. I don't mind. You could've joined me."

"I'm sure I need a shower," she murmured. It dawned on Kat that she hadn't showered since the evening before the news had broken.

"Let me get a towel and we'll get you cleaned up," he told her.

He opened the linen closet and pulled out a new, fluffy towel, one of the ones they had recently picked out together, then walked over to the shower and started it again. He adjusted the temperature until it felt right and then he went to Kat to pull her up by her hands. He led her over to the shower, removed her clothing, and helped her in before dropping his towel to the floor and joining her. He stood behind her as she let the water run down her face, her tears mingling in the trails. She ran her hands through her hair to saturate it as Ian picked up a shampoo bottle and put some in his hands. As he lathered up her hair, she simply stood in place, letting him. He helped her rinse it out and then repeated the process with conditioner.

Taking his bath puff, he then soaped up her entire body. He knew his job at that moment was to take care of her, as she was obviously in no state for him to do anything but. Carefully getting out, he wrapped his towel around his middle before reaching over and turning off the water, then took her hand to lead her out of the shower. She stood dripping on the bathmat as he wrapped the bath sheet around her and rubbed his hands all over to remove the excess water.

When he'd finished, he grabbed his comb and began to run it through her hair, straightening and untangling it.

When they were done in the bathroom, Ian led Kat back to his bedroom, where he got out another of his shirts which he helped pull up her arms and over her shoulders as he moved around to button the front. Once she was dressed again, he turned down the covers of the bed and tucked her inside of them, then bent down and placed a soft kiss on her forehead before leaving the room.

Kat lay in his bed, staring at the wall. She felt like she was in a trance. How was she ever going to get out of this mess? It had never been her intention to start something serious with anyone. She thought she had been too raw from her separation to even look at a man again. Then, Ian had been such a jerk when she first met him that she could hardly believe she was lying in his bed now, after taking a shower with his help, in his house, even as his life and career were crumbling around him. Jen was right: Ian was about as genuine as a person could be, despite his increasing fame.

But Kat's doubts kept creeping in. What would happen if the contracts for Lydia and Ian said that they had to maintain this fictitious rouse they had going on? Where would that leave her? Where was she going to go after filming was done? Should she plan on staying here with Jen and still try to make a go of her relationship with Ian, or would it be pointless if they could never be seen together, and if they were, it could make him lose his job? She thought about going home, but after the divorce and the house sold, there would be no home to go back to. What happened if Ian's fame continued to grow? Would he get tired of her and want someone younger? Her mind kept spinning from one question to another, and she felt like her head was going to explode. She knew that she should sleep; that she would feel much better once she did, but she just couldn't make her mind shut off.

In about an hour, Ian came in to check on her. He found her still staring at the wall exactly as he had left her. Kneeling down in front of her, his face was filled with apprehension as he ran his hand over her forehead, pushing her hair back before leaning in further to give her a kiss. "Kat, it's okay. This will pass, I promise. Like I told Lydia, this isn't the end of the world."

Kat looked away from the wall and met his eyes. His look of genuine concern stole her heart. She slowly reached up and he leaned into her, allowing her to wrap her arms around his body. He stayed like that until he couldn't stand not to move, then got up and walked around to the other side of the bed and crawled up behind her. He wrapped his arms around her and held her until she fell asleep.

***

As Ian lay there with Kat in his arms, he wondered what he was going to do. Would he just walk away if they tried to add any sort of clause about his relationship status to his contract? Would Lydia? They certainly wouldn't fire them both, would they? One lead star could be written off of a show, but both seemed impossible. It would be the kiss of death for the program, he was sure. But, if they did fire him, would he really be willing to give up everything he had worked so hard to accomplish for a woman he had known two months?

But what an amazing two months it has been, he thought. *It feels like years.*

Kat's earlier declaration that she would stay with him even if she had to hide had been exactly what he had selfishly hoped she would say, but when she had actually said it aloud, it broke his heart.

If I truly love her, how could anything about such a situation be okay? And I do love her…

Ian was convinced that he had met his soul mate, but how far would that take them? Would it be enough? He had never really thought about what he would do for a living if he wasn't an actor. Acting was the only thing that he had wanted to do since he was old enough to know what an actor was. To a young boy, being an adult and getting to dress up in costumes every day and play pretend seemed like a dream come true. He had struggled to get to where he was, but it was finally paying off. Would he be able to walk away if that was the only way to keep Kat? He found he couldn't answer that.

He, too, eventually drifted off to sleep.

Chapter Thirty-Two

While Kat sat and watched, like a child listening to their parents having an intense conversation that wasn't understood, Ian spent the whole next day working with Jen, preparing for he and Kat to head back to Canada. Jen had graciously agreed to pack up Kat's things and bring them to her, so she and Ian didn't have to be seen together. They also arranged for her to pick up Kat the next day so that they wouldn't go to the airport at the same time. There wasn't much they could do about her sitting next to him on the plane, but they thought once everyone else was seated that there shouldn't be any issues. Jen and Ian worked well together to plan everything out in order to ensure that Kat's mental health stayed intact.

Once everything was finally packed and ready and Jen had left, Ian and Kat went to bed. Both of them were entirely too spent to do anything more than hold each other throughout the night.

When the morning came, however, Kat watched as Ian lay sleeping beside her, his body facing hers. His relaxed breathing held her attention for a long time, until he slowly opened one eye and then the other.

"Hey! Good morning! Were you just watching me sleep?"

Kat nodded.

"How are you today?" he asked solicitously.

She looked at him and croaked out the first words she had said in close to thirty-six hours. "I'm okay."

"You ready to fly back up north? Jen will be here soon to take you. I won't be coming until later, but we'll still sit together on the plane, okay?"

Kat merely nodded again, and he rose up on his elbow, attempting to give her a kiss on the cheek. Turning her head at the last second, he instead ended up kissing her lips, and that was all it took.

They were hungry for each other, both determined to move

further than they had before. As their kisses became more passionate, it was clear neither one was going to even pause this time. Kat watched, transfixed, as Ian's fingers nimbly unbuttoned and pulled apart her shirt, exposing her torso. Unlike their first encounter, when he had told Kat to slow down, things were moving fast and furiously, and this time he was the one who was frantic, thrilling Kat. They rolled around naked in the sheets, skin on skin, until he was on top of her. Kat's hands were on his back pulling him toward her with incredible force. She wasn't cognizant of when her body arched up to meet his, but he closed his eyes for a second, as if he had finally accepted he could let go and lose himself in her. Her silky warmth beckoned to him, stealing any last remnants of his self-control. She felt his body tremble with the need to give into his desire. Gazing up at him, she was willing him to join with her when the doorbell rang.

"Ignore it!" Kat pleaded, involuntarily digging her nails into his back, trying to hold him in place.

He wanted to, but the mood was broken. Sighing, he sat up and then picked up his pajama pants off the floor and grabbed an old T-shirt out of his dresser drawer. The bell rang again, and he rushed out to answer it. Soon, Kat heard Jen's voice echoing down the hall. "Sorry I'm so early. I guess I overestimated the traffic to get here."

Kat heard Ian's reply, her frustration rising as she realized that the spell was once again broken. "No worries," he said, "It's okay. We were just getting up, anyway. I'm going to go get showered and changed and make sure Kat does the same. Feel free to make some coffee or tea or anything you'd like in the kitchen."

***

Ian padded back down the hall, wondering why every time he and Kat got so close, something disturbed them.

Was it a bad omen, a sign that they weren't supposed to be together? Doubts began to creep in again. In one month, the season would wrap, and they wouldn't be in Canada anymore.

Was George right that he just fell in love with Kat because she was there? Would he have fallen in love with her if he had met her in L.A.?

When he walked into his room and saw her sitting up in bed, with her hair and the sheets all tousled around her, he knew. He absolutely, without a doubt, would have loved this woman anywhere, anytime, and he was all the more determined to find a way to make this work.

"Jen's here," he told her.

Kat nodded at him. "I heard the two of you talking when she came in."

"You're all ready to go as soon as you are showered and dressed. Don't worry about anything. I'll see you on the plane."

Kat blinked at him a few times. "All right. Thank you, Ian, for everything."

"You mean thank you for destroying your life and making you look like the biggest harlot in America?" he asked with a rueful smile.

"No," she said, shaking her head at him. "Thank you for being there for me after I found out I was the biggest harlot in America. I really appreciate how you took care of me. I'm sorry I freaked out."

"It's okay, Kat. We're all allowed to freak out every now and then."

***

Kat got ready and headed toward the kitchen where Jen and Ian were excitedly discussing the ins and outs of being a Hollywood caterer. She smiled when she saw her best friend and her *Whatever he is*, she thought, together and getting along as she pulled out a bar stool at the island. It was an incredibly stark contrast to how Jen had been around James, both of them barely tolerating each other only for her sake.

Ian got up and poured Kat a cup of coffee, setting it in front of her. Jen pushed a plate of cheese, crackers, and fruit toward her. They then talked easily together about the set in Alberta and if Jen was going to be able to make it up there to see it before the season was done. Ian enthusiastically encouraged her, and she said that she would try.

Looking at her watch Jen said, "Okay, Kat. It's time to go."

Kat stood up and looked miserably to Ian. Even though she knew she would see him in just a few hours, he was her rock through this whole ordeal, and being separated from him would feel like being a child without her security blanket. Jen would be able to walk into the airport with her, but once she got through security she was on her own until the plane was ready to board— alone with her thoughts and quite possibly public scrutiny. She walked over to Ian and wrapped her arms around him. He bent down and gave her a kiss, telling her reassuringly that he would see her soon.

By the time the women were headed to the airport, the morning rush hour traffic had dissipated somewhat, and they were able to make good time. Jen pulled into the parking lot.

"You ready?" she asked.

Kat took a deep breath and nodded. The whole reason they had devised this plan was so that Kat could get through the airport undetected. Even though her face was plastered onto every celebrity rag and magazine in the country by this point, Ian and Jen had hoped that if she was alone, she wouldn't be recognized. Jen helped her carry her bags and stayed while she got checked in. When it was time to head to the security line, Kat leaned over to Jen and gave her a big hug.

"You are the best friend a girl could ever ask for. Please come up there soon. I'll miss you."

Jen handed Kat her carry on and assured her that she would come up, even if it was just for a day or two, before the last month of filming was done. Kat turned and walked toward the long line of people waiting to be screened before boarding their planes.

She made it through security and found her gate without issue, got herself a bottle of water, and sat down to stare out at the planes taking off and landing. They looked so graceful and well-orchestrated that Kat really didn't understand why she had such an irrational fear of flying. Knowing that Ian had promised he would be there beside her later, though, helped to calm her nerves.

As the time of departure got closer and closer, however, Kat began anxiously looked around for any sign of him. The flight attendant began to call for the first-class passengers to board, so Kat grabbed her things and walked alone down the gangway toward the plane. She quickly found her seat, stowed her stuff, and waited. And waited. And waited. She began to panic as the plane's engines began to rev up and Ian was still nowhere onboard. Then suddenly, as the crew was getting ready to shut the door, he came rushing in and slid into his seat next to Kat. He was wearing sunglasses, with a baseball cap pulled down very low, and he kept his head down as he stowed his things, before turning to her and smiling sweetly.

"I told you I would be here," he whispered to her.

Their plan appeared to have worked. No one seemed to recognize either of them. Ian was even able to hold Kat's hand on the take-off and landing. As soon as the plane was settled at the gate, Ian jumped up and grabbed his stuff and ran. Kat had a feeling of dread as she remembered how James had done the same thing to her in Las Vegas a few months earlier, but this time she knew why. Ian wanted to get far ahead of her so that if anyone was waiting for them, she wouldn't get caught in his vicinity.

Meanwhile, Kat couldn't decide if she felt like a mistress or a stalker. She waited until just about everyone was off the plane before she disembarked and walked into the building. After clearing customs, she looked up and saw Melinda waving to her and she didn't see Ian anywhere.

Their plan must have worked. Melinda helped her grab her bags and they headed out toward the parking garage, where Gerard was already waiting in the car with Ian. Ian watched Kat visibly relax as she slid in next to him, knowing that the worst was over for the next few weeks while they were filming up there. She couldn't bring herself to think about what would happen after that.

As they pulled out of the airport, Kat and Ian both sighed in relief. Kat had not realized how much tension she'd been carrying with her from this whole adventure until she realized that with every mile they drove further into the trees and away from prying eyes she could breathe that much easier.

When Gerard pulled up in front of the caterers' trailer, Ian jumped up and grabbed the doors for Kat and Melinda. Melinda turned to look at Kat with a surprised expression that quickly turned into the "You lucky bitch" face that was now so familiar. Kat just smiled slightly and shrugged her shoulders as Ian carried her bags into the trailer for her and took her hand in his to say goodbye. He turned to go back toward the car, when he suddenly flipped back around and mouthed, "I love you!" and gave her his infamous salute.

Production would not start up until the next day to give everyone a chance to make it back up to the set. Lydia was due to come in on her flight from Paris via Montreal later that night. Melinda and Gerard had prepared foods that would stay hot for hours without spoiling—soups and chili—so that people could wander in to eat whenever they got back and were hungry. As soon as she was unpacked, Kat headed toward the kitchen, her mind set on finding something else to do other than pine over Ian.

The location had been essentially deserted while they were all gone, but the few stable hands who had stayed to take care of the animals had used the kitchen to cook and had made a mess. While Gerard and Melinda continued cooking and keeping the serving trays full, Kat rolled up her sleeves and got to work. She scrubbed the wall behind the stove where splatters of someone's soup or spaghetti sauce, she couldn't tell which, were everywhere. She mopped the floors and reorganized the refrigerators, and finally scrubbed down Jen's pots and pans. They were clean, but obviously the people who stayed here did not understand or appreciate the importance of them to the success of Jen's business. She removed all of the blackened and brown stains on the sides from spilled over food that had baked on. Just as she was finishing, she looked up and saw Ian standing in front of her in the dining area. She felt her stomach flip-flop and she smiled at him. He returned her smile with his lopsided grin and moved to grab some food.

The crew was not quite as friendly and open with Ian as they had been before, Kat noticed. She wasn't sure if it was because they had all been separated for a time, if they were tired, or if they had heard about Kat and Ian being photographed together and were thinking he was two-timing Lydia. Kat hoped that it was one of the first two reasons and not the third, but she thought she also noticed extra stares and looks as people had passed by her to get their food.

After dinner, Kat stayed and cleaned up for the night. She knew that Melinda and Gerard had been up very early to get the food ready so that they could go down and pick up Ian and Kat as a favor to Jen, so she sent them back to the trailer with reassurances that she could get it all done herself. In fact, she told them, she welcomed the distraction.

About ten minutes after they left, Ian came in and gave Kat a fright when she saw him, as he had come in through the back door. She let out a little yelp and he laughed at her, telling her he really didn't mean to keep scaring her.

"I just wanted to come and tell you good night," he said as he bent down to kiss her softly on the lips. "I don't think I'm going to like sleeping alone after having you beside me the past few nights."

"I know. I'm dreading it myself, though I won't miss the snoring," she said, as she playfully elbowed him in the stomach.

"Hey! I don't snore!" he protested.

"Oh yes, you do. You can really saw that lumber."

"Are you sure it wasn't you?" he asked incredulously, his head cocked to the side.

"Positive," she said, as she crinkled her nose at him.

Ian walked up to Kat and took her in his arms. He leaned

down to give her a kiss that started out sweet, but as it deepened, grew in excitement. Their tongues tangled, and their lips danced perfectly together as they nipped and nibbled at each other. They were getting carried away as Ian pushed Kat up against the counter and lifted her onto it again like he had just a few weeks ago. Things between them then quickly heated up to the point that they forgot where they were and that they could be easily seen.

Kat wrapped her legs around his Ian's hips and worked his shirt out of the waistband of his jeans, before slipping her cool, soft hands down and kneading her fingers into the muscles of his rear as his mouth left a trail of small, molten kisses down her neck. Suddenly, the door opened bringing both Ian and Kat abruptly back to reality as they sprang apart. Lydia was standing in the doorway, backlit from the lights behind her. She peered into the kitchen and saw Kat with Ian standing beside her and proceeded to walk toward them. Kat still sat on the counter, rubbing her fingers subconsciously across her swollen lips. She watched as Ian closed the last few steps between them and gave her a hug and a kiss on the cheek. "Welcome back!" he told her.

"Thanks. What were you two doing in here?" she asked. Then, she looked at Kat and it became very apparent to her that she had interrupted something.

"Oh! I'm so sorry! I didn't mean to intrude. I couldn't see anything when I came in here," she stuttered. "I'm hungry and was hoping I could find a snack before bed. It's almost breakfast time in Paris… That isn't very hygienic, you two!"

"You're fine," Kat told her. "You're not disturbing us. We really shouldn't be doing this in here anyway, given that anyone can walk through that door any time, just like you did. Not to mention that you are right: making out on the counter of a commercial kitchen is definitely not up to health code! What can I make you? I can heat up some leftovers or I can make you a sandwich."

"A sandwich sounds great!" Lydia said appreciatively.

While Kat got to work, she listened as Ian and Lydia caught

each other up on what happened. Kat kept hearing her name in little snippets of the conversation but was trying to hide her eavesdropping as she finished making Lydia's food.

"Can they really do that, Ian?" Lydia asked him disbelievingly.

Kat couldn't hear Ian's reply. She had learned that when he got upset, he became surreally calm and quiet, but she did see him nod his head in affirmation.

"How can they dictate our private lives like that?"

Kat walked up and gave Lydia her plate and then turned to walk away. Ian jumped up and pulled out a chair for her and told her to sit. "This involves you too, Kat." Ian turned back to Lydia. "According to my agent, who double- checked with an attorney, we are their employees, and they technically have the right to ask for anything legal to be in our contracts because we have to sign it in agreement. If we don't, then we don't work. It's ultimately our choice, as messed up as it is.

"You know how we aren't allowed to change our hair style or color during filming without prior approval, so that the season all looks consistent? Because sometimes, they pull clips from earlier episodes that they didn't use as filler for others, and sometimes we film out of order? It's sort of like that."

"Okay Ian, I get that. I know I can't go and shave my head. But how can they dictate what I do with my life for the other eight months of the year?"

"I don't know, Lyds. That's just what my agent told me. According to her, although she has never dealt with this particular stipulation before, production companies and studios do sometimes write in some pretty outlandish things in Morality Clauses. Apparently, way back in the day, Will H. Hays started using them for actors, allowing studios to then control their lives beyond their work. She gave me several examples of how actors had to get permission to marry, which wasn't always granted. That's what happened to Jean Harlow. She wasn't able to marry because the studio thought that once she was a wife she would no longer be considered a 'bombshell.' And God forbid if an actress got pregnant. They had no choice but to have the abortions the Studios arranged, or they would lose their jobs.

"Nowadays, these clauses are still common, but more in terms of saying how actors must conduct themselves in public in order to not cause embarrassment. Apparently, it's just like anything else they can control, like our appearance. Regardless, they have us over a barrel. We either do what they ask, or we are off the show.

"She did say, however, that we could both just out ourselves now before the new contract. Since there isn't a clause in our current contracts, we won't be breaching it and there is nothing they can do other than not offer us contracts for next season, and she doubts very much they would cut both of us from the show, since the whole story pretty much revolves around our characters, which we have developed. We can come clean, Lydia, and get this out in the open so we can all move on with our lives."

"I'm not ready, Ian," she whispered, her eyes filling with tears. "I'm scared."

Ian reached out and covered her hand with his. "Come on, Lyds. I know we never talked about this ending, but I think we both knew it couldn't last forever. Where would we have stopped? When we pretended to be married? When we had a baby? At what point were we going to say enough is enough?"

"I don't know, Ian. I guess I never thought about it. It was working, so why would I think about changing it? Look, I know you two want to explore your relationship and that it will be hard with our arrangement, but I just cannot do it right now. I'm not that popular and recognizable enough yet that even if my past gets out, I would still be able to get another contract. My life isn't exactly going to stand up to the squeaky-clean image the network is trying to promote and cash in on."

Kat felt like she was watching a tennis match, bobbing her head back and forth as they spoke to each other, and she could tell that Ian was getting frustrated. He let out a deep sigh and said, "Lydia, I know! But I'm almost thirty-eight years old. I want to settle down and have a family. You know I love you, but only as a brother. What I want for my life now isn't possible with our current arrangement. When are you going to let us move on?"

Lydia looked up at Kat and their gazes locked.

Lydia eyes asked her a question and Kat slowly shook her head no. Of course, she hadn't had the conversation that Lydia had asked her to have with Ian when they were spending all of their time trying to put out this fire. Lydia looked pained for a second and then turned back to Ian.

"I apologize, Kat, but Ian, where do you see this relationship with Kat going? She's still married. You're five and a half years younger than she is. She was in kindergarten when you were born, for God's sake. She has three grown children. I think if you want to pursue a relationship with her you need to weigh what you want with what you are going to be able to get. Are you willing to give up everything at this point for something that might not check all of the boxes in your future?"

Ian shoved back his chair and covered his eyes with his right hand, rubbing his forehead. "Lydia," he said. "That's not fair. There isn't one perfect person. Relationships are a give and take. At this point, I don't know what will happen. Forgive me, Kat, but we are still in early days here. Who knows what will happen when we get done and get back to the 'real world?' But regardless, right now what I do know is that I don't want some network or production company feeling they have the right to dictate what I do in my private life!"

Kat felt like she had been simultaneously slapped in the face and punched in the gut. How could she have been so stupid? She felt like an old, useless burden; washed up and dried out. Her heart was breaking as she slowly stood up and told them both, "Well, how about this? I'll make it much easier on both y'all. I'm out of here." With that, she turned on her heel and walked out the door.

She managed to hold it together until she made it to her bedroom in the R.V. before she broke down quietly sobbing.

What had she been thinking? Funny how when they were in Los Angeles together, he was talking about the future and telling her he loved her and wouldn't let her go, and now, back up here with Lydia, his tune had suddenly changed, and it was "early days," as he put it.

The reality of her situation hit her like a ton of bricks. She was crazy to think that this escape from her reality was permanent. She had a life to go back to, responsibilities to take care of.

Knowing she didn't want to go back to James, however, she still decided that she needed to get out of there to wallow in her self-pity in peace. She texted Jen and told her, *I'm sorry, but I can't do this anymore. You will have to find a way to come up here and take over.* Then she promptly cried herself to sleep.

Around two a.m., Kat awoke, listening again for the strange sound that had pulled her out of her deep sleep. She was completely still and waited in the darkness for it to repeat. A few seconds later, she heard a sort of scratching, knocking sound and she got up to investigate. She moved back the blind and saw Ian standing outside of her trailer.

He motioned her to open the window, so she did. He came close and whispered to her, "Kat, love, listen! I'm sorry. That didn't come out the way either of us meant it. I do love you and I do see you in my future."

"Save it!" Kat hissed back at him as she shut the window and the blind, then crawled back into bed.

This navigating relationship stuff was for the birds, she thought. At least when married, she hadn't worried about it. Now, it was like being thrown into a freezing lake. She wasn't ready for the shock of it all, the roller coaster.

Having spent the past two decades secure in where she was and what she was supposed to be doing, this was all new territory. Her last thought before falling back into a restless sleep was, *At least I didn't sleep with him!*

Funny how the thought that he had been right all along could make her cry so much.

Chapter Thirty-Three

A few hours later, Kat was up with Gerard and Melinda as they trudged to the kitchen. Though her face was swollen, her eyes red from crying, and she was unusually quiet, at least Kat didn't have to answer any questions from her coworkers. They just shared a look between themselves and carried on with what they were doing. Kat kept herself busy as far back in the kitchen as possible and refused to make eye contact with either Ian or Lydia. Ian stood still and studied her for a long time before he gave up and went to sit down. He left a short time later to get ready to be on set and Kat breathed a sigh of relief. Now, if only she could keep that up three times a day for the next four weeks, she would be fine.

A little while later, when Melinda and Gerard had gone back to the trailer between the breakfast and lunch rush, Kat was still in the kitchen, finding things to organize and clean in order to occupy her time. The door opened, and Lydia stepped in, looking gorgeous in her period costume and makeup, her hair curled and put up. She walked over to Kat and stopped in front of her.

"I'm sorry I did that last night, Kat. I shouldn't have worded it that way," she began. Then, as an afterthought, she added, "But I'm not sorry I said it. You and Ian have some major discussing to do."

"Is this supposed to be some kind of apology, Lydia? Did Ian send you in here to try and fix this?"

Lydia wouldn't meet her eyes.

"I will take that as a yes," she huffed, turning away.

"Kat, come on. Talk to him. He's really taking this hard. He feels like he has destroyed your life. You can't just cut him out. Let him apologize."

Against her better judgment, she looked up at Lydia and mumbled, "I'll think about it." She then marched away to the freezer, taking her time moving things around under the guise of searching for something.

When she came out a short time later, Lydia had let herself out and she was once again alone with her thoughts. How would she react if he came to apologize again?

Wanting to be strong and stick to her guns, Kat also knew that one look at him, and all of her resistance would come tumbling down in an instant. She would be pulled back to him like he was magnetic. She tried hard to think of what she wanted to say to him to express her anger when the inevitable came, but every time she did, the tears came back.

The front door opened again while Kat was crouching down on the floor, organizing the pots and pans. She hadn't noticed before when she was so consumed with Ian, but the kitchen was a disorganized nightmare. Hearing the sound, she started to say, "I don't want to talk anymore! Please leave me alo…!" but was interrupted by a familiar voice.

"Kat?"

Kat sat back on her haunches and told herself she was hallucinating. It just wasn't possible. She stood up, needing to look over the counter to confirm her suspicion. Standing in front of her was James. She gasped. "What are you doing here?"

"I came to see you. To talk."

"James, this isn't a good idea. This is my job. I have work to do. I'm coming back in four weeks for the boys' graduations. Can't we just talk then?"

"Kat, I've asked you and asked you to talk to me, but you are ignoring me. We were together twenty-three years. Don't you think I deserve a few hours of your time to talk this through?"

Kat only glared back at him. Finally, as he continued to hold her gaze, her features softened a bit, and she took a deep breath.

"I guess you're right. We need to come up with how we are going to divide our assets. It will save money if we can do it ourselves without having to use our attorneys."

When she looked up into his face, she saw his crestfallen expression. She knew she should be furious with him for the turmoil he had produced in her life, but when she saw his familiar features, she thought about their being together for all those years and decided that he did deserve better than her ignoring him.

She took off her apron and hung it on her hook. Grabbing a glass of water, she asked James if he wanted one, too.

"It's straight out of the Canadian Rockies," she told him. "You wouldn't get anything like this anywhere close to home."

He shrugged and said, "Okay, I guess. Thanks." They sat down together at a table.

"So…" Kat said.

"So…"

"How'd you get up here? How did you find me? I mean the set?"

He looked down at the ground. "I kept calling Jen and begging her. I told her I wouldn't stop until she told me where you were. I finally called her from a phone at the airport in Calgary and she answered. Figured it was you, I guess. She told me where you were since I was already up here."

"You flew up here not even knowing where I was?" Kat asked him, surprised.

"Yes."

"How did you even know I was near Calgary?" she sounded suspicious.

"You told me when I called you that morning in L.A. and you thought I was Jen, right before you were going to fly out. And then I saw it in all of those entertainment rags. I read them all," he sounded disgusted. "They said that you had met that guy on the set of his show in Canada, near Calgary, Alberta."

"Wow, James, great detective work. I'm not surprised, however, as you were so good at hiding your almost year-long affair from me. Perhaps you should change careers to a private detective."

"Kat, don't start. Please," he begged her.

"Don't start? Really, James? I didn't start it. You did! You did the minute you started pursuing another woman."

James hung his head and reached out to grab her hand. Suddenly, the door opened, and Ian stepped in. He saw Kat sitting at a table, holding hands with a man he had never seen before. Confused, he looked over at her, his eyes asking her a question.

"Oh, God," she muttered under her breath. She had thought her two worlds had collided before, but that was nothing compared to this mess.

"Hi, Ian. I would like you to meet my husb… I mean James Anderson."

Ian's eyes met hers. His opened wide with shock before he looked down at the table where James was still holding on to Kat's hand after having been interrupted mid- conversation, and back up to meet her eyes. Kat just smiled weakly at him in response.

Ian, ever the actor, recovered quickly and stepped forward to shake James' hand, saying halfheartedly, "Nice to meet you," mostly because it would cause James to remove his hand from over Kat's.

James stood up and shook Ian's hand. "Nice knowing you, Ian. You're Irish?"

"Yeah, I get that a lot," Ian responded dryly.

"I've read so much about you," James said pointedly, "I figured I would have known that."

"Yeah, well, born and bred Irishman right here."

The men stood close to each other, and were saying all of the right things, but Kat could feel the undercurrent of tension between them. She felt she needed to diffuse the situation as quickly as possible before something bad happened, so she stepped forward and asked Ian if he needed anything. The tone of her voice made it clear that she was in no mood to deal with either of them, so he simply said, "I just wanted to come in and check on you. Lydia said she had a conversation with you earlier."

"I'm fine, Ian, thank you. I'll catch up with you later." Her eyes told him in no uncertain terms that she would not be challenged right now. In fact, she looked downright terrifying. He took a few steps back and said, "All right. That's fine. I'll see you later."

"That's what you think," Kat heard James mutter under his breath. Both Kat and Ian turned to look at him.

"What?" she asked him.

He puffed up his chest and squared his shoulders and said, "That's what you think!" much louder this time.

"Excuse me?" Kat stared at him. Ian was clenching his fists, the muscles twitching in his set jaw. This was escalating way out of control, but she couldn't hold back. "James, you have no right to say that!"

"I do, Kat! I do. I've come up here to take you, my wife, home so we can sort this mess out and continue on with our lives. Your little adventure into the woods to find yourself needs to come to an end so you can get back to what really matters."

"'My little adventure?' Is that what you just called this?"

"Yes! You came up here and played all independent, and then you started sleeping with this clown to get back at me. Well, it worked, and I feel awful. We're even. Let's go home."

Kat saw Ian start toward James and jumped in front of him. "Ian, I think it's best that you go," she told him firmly.

He looked at her for a second and then returned his focus to James. "We did not sleep together, because I would not let her reduce herself to your level. I actually possess some self-control."

"Like I'd believe you?" James snidely commented, raising his voice.

"Ask her!" Ian yelled back.

They both looked expectantly at Kat. Now they had really put her in the middle. Technically, she and Ian had not had sex yet, so she looked James in the eye and told him, "I can, without a doubt, tell you that we have not had sex. Ian is a gentleman who wanted to wait until I am fully available to protect me from hating myself as much as I hate you!"

With that, she gently gave Ian a push toward the door.

"Thanks for stopping by," she told him as she shut the door in his face.

***

Ian stood in front of the closed door for several minutes in shock. *What the hell had just happened in there? That was James?*

He hadn't expected him to be that good looking. He had imagined a balding, bland accountant stereotype, not a six-foot, two inch fairly fit middle-aged guy with a fabulous head of hair.

Who the hell did he think he was, though, ordering Kat around like that? Ian was livid about the whole situation. But then he did have to wryly smile at how well Kat had handled herself. She had expertly managed to dismiss him and kick him out before he had even realized she had done it.

He walked back toward the set. Lydia saw him and asked, "How'd it go?"

"Not well," he said curtly.

"What happened?" Lydia grabbed his arm and stopped him. His eyes were stormy, and his jaw was clenched. Lydia didn't think she had ever seen him look so angry, not when something wasn't going well on set, not even when all of this news broke.

"I don't want to talk about it," he mumbled.

"Ian, you are clearly upset. What happened? What did she say to you?"

He stopped abruptly and looked at her, his anguish apparent. "Her husband showed up here, okay? I walked in on them sitting at the table, holding hands. He told her he had come to take his wife home and that if she had slept with me to get even, it had worked."

"Wow!"

"I know! And the worst part is everyone keeps saying that we are sleeping together, and we haven't. Not once. We have gotten close a few times, but we have not actually done it."

"Ian, do you really expect me to believe that?" she asked him incredulously.

305

"*Of course*!" he hollered at her. "Why would I lie about that? Especially to you? Kat's not just another notch on my bedpost, Lyds. I think I might actually love her. No, wait. I know without a shadow of a doubt that I love her! I can't explain it, but I've never met anyone like her before. She is The One."

"But, Ian, what about your dreams of having a family? I hate to say it, but I don't think it has even dawned on you that she's no spring chicken. Her kids are grown. Are you willing to give all of that up for her?"

He stood in place, his chest heaving as what Lydia had just said sunk in. His eyes narrowed and his jaw twitched before he said, "Have you discussed this topic with her before last night?"

"Sort of," Lydia responded nervously. "I asked her to talk with you on the subject so you would know if you were on the same page. That's it, I swear, Ian."

"*Lydia*! Whatever gave you the right to think you could do that? How dare you? Lyds, I love you, but I could strangle you right now! *Why* would you ask her to do that?" he exclaimed at her.

"Because I care about you, Ian, and I don't want you ending up married to someone ten years from now and feel like you missed out on something."

Ian took in a ragged breath, trying desperately to control his temper. He didn't lose it often, but when he did, it was far from pretty. "That isn't your decision to make, Lydia," he said quietly, in a tone she knew meant he wasn't far from blowing up, "It's mine. Mine and Kat's. You, more than anyone, should know that creating a child doesn't make you a parent."

He took a deep breath and his shoulders drooped. Looking up at her, he muttered, "I've got to get to work," and he walked away, leaving her standing in a side street of the set, alone.

***

Meanwhile, Melinda and Gerard had come back to help finish preparing lunch, and Kat had made it clear that James was not to disturb them. He sat at a table in the far back corner and watched her move around the kitchen, thinking to himself, *God, she is beautiful and kind, gentle, and generous. What the hell was I thinking, going after Sam? Look at her in here. She's in her element. She never looks as beautiful as she does in the kitchen.*

He immediately admonished himself for thinking that because it made him feel like a 1950s husband. But it was true, he knew. She enjoyed her job and it showed, with her cheeks growing rosy from the heat and her eyes dancing. He knew he shouldn't be surprised, as she had always thoroughly enjoyed preparing food for their family; it was how she expressed her love. What did surprise him was how he could have been so stupid to take her for granted. He sat and contemplated on how he was going to get her back.

After the crew and actors had finished lunch, he had eaten with Melinda, Gerard, and Kat, an uncomfortable silence surrounding them. The conversation mostly consisted of asking someone to pass the salt and pepper.

James dug into his plate of food, and he smiled with appreciation. As he broke into his square of cornbread, he looked at Kat and exclaimed, "God, I've missed your cooking!"

Kat gave him a tight smile and replied tersely, "Thanks."

He took the hint and ate the rest of his meal in silence, sneaking glances in Kat's direction, but she refused to look at him. For the first time, he really began to worry that he had actually lost her. This was so out of character for her; she was so docile, accommodating, and unassuming at home. Here, she was like a completely different person, sure of herself and stubborn, like no one could force her to do anything she didn't want to do.

If she had just been like this at home, he thought miserably, *then maybe I wouldn't have gotten involved with Sam.* There was something incredibly sexy about her new- found independence and confidence. If this is what their separation had done for her, then he thoroughly approved and couldn't wait to get her back home with him.

***

Kat, Melinda, and Gerard cleaned up and started to do the dinner prep. Kat smiled to herself as she realized that they were having catfish again, remembering her conversation with Ian so many weeks ago. Then, she remembered how he had treated her the previous night and her smile quickly faded. She was in a real predicament.

James' showing up had really thrown her for a loop.

When did he become so proactive? she wondered.

Of course, it had to be while she was struggling to find her footing in her relationship with Ian, too. Part of her just wanted to pack up and go home with James and pretend the last two and a half months had never happened. Maybe she had gotten Ian out of her system, she contemplated, and she could be happy again going back to being James' wife.

But then she really started to think about what that would entail, having to step back into her old life and be the person everyone expected her to be, not the person she truly was. She saw endless days of doing nothing at home, only going to the gym or shopping to get out while James worked, Saturdays with the T.V. blaring college football games while she stood in the kitchen preparing snacks for everyone else, Sundays at church, and holidays with the family. The kids would all be gone doing their own thing. They didn't need her anymore. She would be isolated in James' world where he controlled everything, including her. That's when she knew for sure that she was over him. Nothing about her old life sounded remotely appealing.

Kat watched as James sat patiently through dinner while people on set came and went, and while she and the others cleaned up.

When they were finished, Melinda and Gerard looked at her expectantly as they started to leave, but she told them that she would be there shortly and bid them good night.

She had to hand it to James and his tenacity to sit there all day long, driven by his determination to speak with her. Moving to the table where he was sitting and pulling out a chair to sit down, she noted how he had never bothered to pull out a chair for her like Ian did, but then she admonished herself for letting thoughts of Ian invade her head. She knew what she had to do didn't have anything to do with him; she wanted out of her marriage whether Ian was in her life or not. She took a deep breath and said, "James, we need to talk."

"I know. Kat, I'm so sorry that this ever happened. I don't know what came over me. I was stupid and selfish and thoughtless. You are the one I love. You are the one I have a history with. Sam was new and exciting, but she's shallow and petty. I want you back. You're not a little girl, but a woman. I miss your company."

"I know how that feels," she said simply. "I felt that way in the beginning, too."

"And now?"

"Now, I feel nothing. I'm sorry, James. You will always be my ex-husband and the father of my children, but I do not love you anymore. The idea of going home with you and trying again feels like a lifetime prison sentence."

"What are you saying?" James looked stricken by her words.

"I'm not coming home with you, James."

"But why?" he whined. "We have twenty-four years of history together. You're going to just throw it away for one indiscretion?"

And there it was once again. Whatever lingering uncertainty Kat may have had disappeared again the instant he uttered that word.

"James, we have been through this before. It was not once, and it wasn't an indiscretion. It was flat out lying and betrayal for almost a year. You're completely clueless about how lucky you are that you didn't pick up some disease from her that you could have brought home to me. Thank God Jen was smart enough to make sure I got tested for everything under the sun when I got to her. I'm clean, praise Jesus, but it was no thanks to you. Or maybe it was... Maybe the fact that you hardly touched me for a year protected me."

"You aren't any better!" James was losing his patience. "You took off across the country without letting anyone know where you were going, came up here to gallivant in the mountains with a bunch of Hollywood people, and started sleeping with the star of the show within eight weeks of leaving me. You need to get off your high horse, Kat, before you fall off."

"Wow, James. I don't even know how to begin to respond to that one."

Now James began to get downright nasty. "Who's going to support your little adventure now, Kat? If you think I'm going to continue to pay for some other man to screw my wife, you've got another thing coming."

"James, in case you haven't noticed, I have a job. I haven't touched the money in the account since I got to Los Angeles. But, please, do whatever you have to do. I'm sure the judge will come up with a more than fair alimony settlement, given the circumstances."

James went pale for a second and then regrouped. "Not when I get through explaining what you did, running off and getting involved with someone else. I was willing to work this out, and you ran away!"

"James, do you not remember that you only wanted to reconcile after Sam dumped you? Speaking of which, how did that happen?"

James looked down at the table. "She said I was too needy," he told her.

"Interesting," Kat replied thoughtfully.

"Kat, I was used to you. I was used to how you cared for me and the kids. How you cooked, did laundry, took care of everything. Sam wasn't interested. She only wanted sex, not a relationship. These younger girls don't understand that a man needs to be taken care of!"

She just gaped at him. Did he really just basically say that Sam dumped him because he wanted her to be the maid, cook, and the nanny? What about partner, friend, and lover? Weren't those important? She knew they were, her mind wandering back to Ian and how he made her feel exactly like that. She thought about how happy she was when they were together and that they truly enjoyed each other on every level.

"James, I'm sorry. I know you won't like to hear this, but I don't think I ever loved you. I loved the idea of you and the family we would build together, but now that I've been seeing Ian, I can tell that he and I have a friendship, a companionship, that I never felt with you."

"You never loved me?" He looked devastated.

"I thought I did. In a strange way, I actually did too, I guess," she told him honestly. "But looking back on it, we had nothing in common. We were just playing a part.

Funny how the time I've spent with an actor is when I have felt the most natural. There's an odd sort of irony in that, isn't there?" Her last sentence was for her benefit, not his, as the realization hit.

"Ouch, Kat. That hurt."

"I'm sorry, James. Looking back on it, I never should have married you. I was too young and too impressionable. I molded into the person everyone expected me to be and buried my own wants and desires in a place deep inside of me. Now, I've found my passion for life. For all parts of my life…" She trailed off, deciding to leave it at that.

James sat quietly as he let the full meaning of her words wash over him. He eventually looked up and she saw that his eyes were glistening.

"So, this is it?"

"I think so."

"Is there anything I can do or say to make you come home?" he begged her.

"No. I'm sorry, James. You will always have a special place in my heart, but I'm not in love with you."

"So, what are you going to do now?" he asked with a shuddering breath.

"I'm not sure. That's the beauty in this. For the first time in my life, I'm in total control over what happens to me. Jen has said I can stay in Los Angeles and work with her. Maybe I'll come back home to the South. I don't know, and what's more, I don't need to know right now. It's a fabulous feeling!"

"What about Ian?"

"What about him?"

"Are you still going to be with him?"

"I don't know. He's a fantastic guy, but I'm not sure I want to be with anyone right now, at least long term. But, maybe, yes, we will stay together and try to make a go of it," she replied with a shrug.

"What will you do when he realizes that he can have any woman in Hollywood, and he's stuck with you?" Nasty James was beginning to resurface.

"James, he could already have any woman in Hollywood, and right now, he's choosing me. If it will stay that way remains to be seen, but you have to understand, I'm not doing this for Ian, I'm doing it for me. He's just along for the ride."

James slowly stood up, realizing it was a lost cause. "I'd better start heading back to Calgary, then. I'm scheduled to fly out tomorrow. If you want to use your ticket to come home for the boys' graduations, you can use it then. No sense in having it go to waste," he said sorrowfully.

"James, I really am sorry that it all ended up this way. I thought we would be the ones to make it."

"I'm sorry, too, Kat. Really sorry. I wish I had realized how good I had it when you were with me. I will always love you. You can always come home."

Kat opened her arms and James fell into them. They held each other for a few minutes, each taking the time to say their own private goodbyes. When he began to pull away, he leaned over and kissed her cheek.

"Thanks for being my everything," he whispered before he turned and walked out the door.

She got up and followed him through the open door and watched as his car drove out of sight. She closed the door and promptly went to a table on which she put her head on her arms and sobbed with a mixture of grief and relief.

Chapter Thirty-Four

After a good long cry and the realization that she had shed more tears in three months than in the last twenty years combined, Kat decided she should head back to the trailer and try to get some sleep. She walked as quietly as she could over the gravely path, trying to not wake anyone. Looking up at the sky, she saw the now familiar beauty of millions of stars glittering on what appeared to be black velvet. Taking a deep breath, she felt the world lift off her shoulders.

She slinked unobtrusively past Melinda and Gerard's bunks to her room and closed the door. As she started to undress, she pulled her phone out of her pocket. In all the events of the day, she hadn't looked at it since turning off her alarm at four-thirty that morning. The first thing she saw was a text from Jen, saying: *Heads- up. James is up there and coming to you. Sorry, doll. He weaseled it out of me.*

Kat just shook her head.

I figured that out when he was standing in the dining hall, she replied.

It was late in L.A., too, and Jen might already be asleep, but Kat waited briefly for a reply anyway.

Sure enough, her phone vibrated, and she looked down to a response: *So sorry! He blindsided me, too. I got a call from a Calgary area code and figured there was an issue with something up there.*

Kat: *It's okay. I forgive you.*

Jen: *BTW, I'm coming up there the day after tomorrow.*

Kat: *Why?*

Jen: *Because you said I needed to?*

Oh, yeah, Kat thought and then sighed.

Kat: *You really don't have to. I don't know where I would even go. I was just upset.*

Jen: *So, I gathered. Well, regardless, I'm coming. I haven't been up there yet and as the owner of the company, I should probably make an appearance.*

Kat: *I guess.*

Jen: *Melinda said she or Gerard will pick me up in Calgary, as they have to do a supply run then, anyway.*

Kat: *Okay.*

Jen: *Good night, Kat.*

Kat: *Good night.*

Kat lay in her bed and wondered what she should do now. She had calmed down a lot since the other night, when she had stormed out of Lydia and Ian's discussion. At the time she sent Jen the text, all she wanted to do was get out of there to avoid facing her embarrassment over what had transpired. She was just still so raw from James' dismissal via betrayal, she couldn't face taking anymore rejection and had overreacted. But now, after her talk with James, she remembered she wasn't there for Ian. He wasn't what brought her to this place; it was her need to find herself and to feel useful again, and it had worked. She felt that she had purpose again and that she would be able to stand on her own two feet, if maybe with a little support from friends every now and then. She was proud that she had managed to come and make everything run smoothly so that Jen could concentrate on her daughter and get her well. Of course, she knew that Melinda and Gerard had a lot to do with the success of the operation, too, but she was the one ultimately responsible and she hadn't gotten them fired. But now that Jen was coming, she didn't have any excuse to stay longer.

The next day, Kat spent a great deal of time reorganizing what had already been reorganized twice before. She was nervous about Jen's arrival and wanted everything to be perfect, but also couldn't think of anything else to do in her down time, and it kept her thoughts occupied and away from Ian. After lunch and before dinner prep, though, she decided she really couldn't do anything else in that room, so she decided to grab her sneakers and head out for a run.

The air was warm but the breeze off the mountains was crisp. The leaves had come out and there were flowers blooming in the meadows between them. Kat struggled at the start of her run, having been off her foot for so long when she sprained it and then not doing much physical during the weeks she was taking care of Ian and in Los Angeles. But, after a mile or so, she found her groove. Her legs felt lighter, and her breath came more evenly. Each step up and down the hills, around the turns of the path, brought her more peace.

When she found herself standing in the beautiful meadow she and Ian had discovered next to the lake, she stopped. She hadn't realized she'd come so far. Turning around, she started back down the mountain, but not before looking back over her shoulder at the special place they shared and thinking back to sitting on the shore, talking, and getting to know each other. It was there she had truly gotten to know the real Ian Gregory—Ian McGregor—and found herself in the process.

She descended the trail and emerged from the woods on the corner of the set. Standing still for a second, her eyes scanned the sight before her. They were evidently filming some sort of scene on Main St., but Kat's eyes wandered to the right, off a little way from the main street to the schoolhouse. She squinted a little at the flurry of activity there and she stepped out to get a closer look.

Ian was kicking around a soccer ball with the kids from the show and they were all laughing, obviously having fun. Since children, with the exception of the boy who played Sarah's son, weren't an integral part of the storyline, they weren't always present on set. Instead, the kids were extras who would come up for a day of shooting and then go back home again until the next time they were needed for specific scenes. The production tried to hire as many local kids as possible, most of them coming from Calgary and the surrounding area, though some came from as far away as Vancouver.

As Kat looked on, one of the smaller boys—he was probably only about seven—fell down and Ian bent to lift him up. She watched as he knelt down to brush the dirt and grass off the boy's clothes and then patted him on the shoulder before the child ran off again. A few minutes later, one of the bigger boys managed to steal the ball out from between Ian's feet, bolting away as Ian took off running after him. The kid took his shot at the makeshift goal, the ball sailing easily past the child playing keeper, and threw his arms up in victory. Turning around, the boy said something to Ian with a smirk, who responded by pulling his head into a soft headlock and giving him a gentle knuckle rub, ruffling his hair as they laughed.

Watching Ian interact with the kids and seeing the sheer joy on his face as he ran around with them and kept them occupied between calls brought home to Kat just how much Ian loved children. She thought back to her life when her kids were around these same ages and her memories of doing things like this with them herself. Knowing she would always treasure those times, when she thought about it, she concluded that no one should have to be without that experience if they didn't want to be.

She stood still, watching for a long time, her arms crossed, making up her mind then and there that Lydia had been right: Ian would regret not having children one day. Standing in place a few minutes more as the implications of the situation sunk in, she then noticed that Ian had looked up in her direction. He had his hands under the arms of one of the kids, lifting her up and down off of the ground, the child's legs tucked under her as she laughed, refusing to put her feet down. Holding Kat's gaze for a second, he then smiled and nodded at her in greeting. Kat couldn't take the heartbreak anymore, so she simply turned and left.

She spent the rest of the evening trying to focus on her work. Even though Jen was not her boss per se, she still felt a responsibility to her to show that things had run well in her absence. She hadn't even thought about Ian since returning to the kitchen and she was happy about that fact when it dawned on her. Closing up the place for the night, she headed back toward the R.V., where she quickly fell into a fatigued sleep.

Morning dawned cloudy, with a low, wet fog hanging over the set, certainly matching Kat's mood. She had made up her mind about what she was going to do. As she had told James, her new-found independence didn't come from Ian, so now for his sake, she was going to prove that she really meant it. She decided to ignore him as much as possible until she found the strength to tell him that it had been fun, but it was over now, and that there would be no further obstacles to his career or future plans because of her. It would make everyone else's problems disappear, and as she had already nursed one broken heart, she knew she could handle a second. It was a win/win for everyone, except her, but in true Kat fashion she believed that everyone else's needs were more important. Old habits die hard.

She figured she would be better able to stick to her plans once Jen arrived as she wouldn't have to be in the kitchen during mealtimes, saving her from having to see Ian or Lydia. Jen would also keep her occupied, so she wouldn't feel lonely until after she decided where she was going when she left. By the time breakfast had rolled around and people started filing in to eat, she had everything wrapped up nicely in her head.

Then, Ian walked in, and it was like all the air was sucked from the room at once. Kat was hit full force with what seeing him always did to her. She took in a deep breath as she looked for an escape to the back of the kitchen. He had come in earlier than usual, so she had been out front, helping to make sure that everything was set out properly, and not hiding in the back, cleaning. She was trapped. Looking into her face, he solemnly said, "Good morning, Kat." His expression, typically so happy, was unusually dejected.

Being caught off guard, she wasn't sure how to react. *How could this be so hard? I've known this man eight weeks. We had a fling. It was fun. A total rebound relationship. So why am I more upset about this ending than about leaving James?*

Kat cleared her throat and looked up into his eyes. It was a big mistake. She felt all of her anger, frustration, and, worst of all, determination, melt away. *No!* she told herself firmly. *If I love this man, then I have to do this. It isn't fair to him. I can't give him what he deserves.*

318

She looked down again and mumbled, "Good morning," and then turned and walked away. She could feel him still standing there, boring holes into the back of her as he watched her retreat. Someone behind him said something, knocking him out of his stupor, and Kat saw from the corner of her eye that he had moved to go find a table.

There! she told herself. *It wasn't so bad to talk to him. Now if I can only keep this up until the show is over, we will go our separate ways and can forget this ever happened.*

It all sounded so easy, so why did her heart feel like it was breaking in two? She decided that the first time would be the hardest, and after that she should be able to talk to him more easily as time went on; maybe they would even end up friends in the end.

Melinda headed down the mountain to buy more supplies and to pick up Jen from the airport soon after lunch. Kat had little to clean up, as she had gotten so far ahead of the meal prep after breakfast and had finished earlier than normal, so she wondered what she should do to occupy her time. Remembering how her run yesterday had cleared her head, she decided that she would do it again and relished her escape from her troubles into the fresh mountain air.

As her feet pounded the ground, she told herself that she was over Ian and that it had all been great fun. But then she would think back to the times when they were together, and she would remember how they would talk, and how he would hold, kiss, and stroke her, so she would shake her head in an attempt to clear the images from her mind and pick up her pace.

The flashbacks kept coming though, regardless of what she did. The night she helped him run lines when they had ended up in his bed. The time they spent in Los Angeles together, twice almost making love. She recalled her frustration when they had been interrupted both times after getting so close. Kat groaned aloud, remembering her excitement and anticipation, and began to run even faster. She felt like she was trying to run away from the memories and self-doubt but just couldn't go fast enough.

Finally, when she felt she couldn't run another step, she bent over and put her hands on her knees, trying to catch her breath. She began walking in tight circles with her hands on the back of her hips and her head turned skyward. After she cooled down a little, she found a downed tree and sat on it. She had to sort through how to proceed.

As she sat, she took stock of her life. Forty-three years on the planet, and she felt like she had nothing to show for it, other than her three kids. Knowing her time on location was quickly coming to a close, and with that a return to reality, she needed to make some decisions about what came next. She had already determined that she did not want to go back home. Whenever she thought about her time there, it seemed like a whole other lifetime ago. She didn't know much, but she knew she was not the same person she had been before she had driven across the country.

Kat eventually resolved she would focus on her friendship with Jen and that she would most likely go back to Los Angeles with her if she would be okay with that. She might even work with Jen for a little while if the offer was still open. Unwavering about needing to get some self- confidence, she recognized the best way to do that would be to surround herself with people who loved her the way she was and didn't try to change her or have certain preconceived notions about her. *People like Jen*, she thought. *Or Ian.*

She groaned again, realizing that she had come all the way around to where she had started, namely thinking about how good Ian allowed her to feel about herself. So, she went back to trying to determine the best way to navigate her interactions with him for the next few weeks until she could get away without further breaking her heart.

Kat mulled over the idea that she could stay up there for a few days until Jen got settled into the routine and then she would go back to Los Angeles for the last three weeks of filming. That time would give her the opportunity to focus on the divorce and getting her financial and emotional houses in order. Satisfied, she thought she had it all worked out. Feeling hopeful again that she could get out of this situation and focus on who she was and what she wanted next out of her life, she decided to share her plans with Jen as soon as she could. What she didn't count on was that Jen had plans of her own.

Chapter Thirty-Five

Jen arrived in the late afternoon. Kat and Gerard had been handling the dinner prep and so she arrived to a kitchen engulfed in wonderful smells, with steam rising from pots. It was a gorgeous presentation, and Jen nodded her approval as she walked into the room and looked around.

"This looks great, y'all!" she exclaimed happily.

Kat was shifting her weight between one foot and the other, itching to talk to Jen about her plans, but she knew it wasn't the right time. She did, however, want to mention to her that she needed to escape before everyone else came in for dinner. Her eyes followed Jen around as Melinda and Gerard explained the operations and showed her how her business had been run over the last nine weeks. Meanwhile, Kat stayed quiet, not adding anything to the lively discussion, but after a few minutes Jen noticed that she was mute. She thanked Gerard and Melinda for their hard work and walked over to Kat, who was standing at the back of the kitchen by the refrigerators and freezer.

Coming up beside her and putting her arm around her, she asked, "How you doing, Kat?"

Kat could barely speak. All the emotions of the last few weeks were nearly brimming over. She hiccoughed and Jen told her, "Hey, look, we've got this handled. Go back to the trailer and we will talk later, okay?"

Kat could only nod in response and walked out the back door, grateful she was able to get away. Jen always knew what she needed and having her arrive and take over was just the release that Kat needed. She made it back to the bedroom of the R.V. as her sobs began. The most frustrating thing though was that she wasn't even really sure why she was crying.

It was as if with Jen's arrival, she felt safe to finally let loose of the frustration, loss, pain, and confusion, not only about the one incident, but rather the whole experience of the last three months. She was mourning the loss of the life she'd had, the one she thought she was satisfied with until all hell broke loose. She cried in anger and sadness because the situation with James led her to discover a life she could have had all along: anger because now she had seen how fulfilling it could be to live for herself a little and her own desires, and sadness that she hadn't figured it out much sooner, that so much of her life had passed without her realizing and actualizing her true self. Then came the guilt over wondering why she hadn't been fulfilled by her old life. Many women had lives just like hers had been, with a husband and children, and they didn't run off when things got tough, or they felt like something was missing.

Ironically, it was also incredibly distressing knowing that if James had not cheated on her, she would still be living her old life, never knowing what she was missing. She was fascinated by how she could grieve so much for her old life when she knew now it had not been her best life.

Next came the issues with Ian. She began to feel a bit sorry for herself, wondering why it wasn't until she was forty-three that she met a man like him who was able to accept her just as she was, even encourage it, rather than requiring her to mold to his expectations. Beginning to laugh, though, she realized it was because if she had met him when she was twenty, he would have only been fourteen. The ridiculousness of the age difference in that context hit her hard and made her think about how illogical she had been to assume that a relationship with him was even possible, which then started again the whole mental cycle about how she felt old and how much life had passed her by without knowing what exactly she needed to be fulfilled.

By the time Melinda, Gerard, and Jen came back to the trailer, Kat was completely cried out. Though she didn't have any solutions to her issues, acknowledging them had been extremely cathartic. Her burdens hadn't lessened because of her personal introspection, but the process allowed her to feel a little more grounded where she stood. After all was said and done, the one thing she knew she had gained from the whole experience was that she now felt empowered to find solutions that would best fit her needs.

Jen came into the room, took one look at Kat's swollen face and red eyes, and cried, "Aw, honey!"

Kat glanced up at her and mumbled, "Don't be nice to me! I just stopped! I don't want you to be nice to me, because then I'll start to cry all over again."

Jen sat down on the bed beside Kat and told her that it was perfectly okay to cry, and that in fact she didn't think healing could properly begin until there had been a good cry. Kat smiled at her and claimed she had cried enough to heal an army then but would be better in the morning.

"Thank you for giving me the break tonight. I just can't face seeing Ian or Lydia with all that has gone on."

"I figured," Jen told her. "By the way, Ian looked really shocked to see me up here. He didn't know I was coming, he said."

"He's right," Kat said. "I haven't spoken to him in days. It's easier to just make it a clean break and get on with my life."

"Kat," Jen cautiously continued, "he didn't look too happy when you weren't there. The whole time he was talking to me, he was looking around for you. When I called him on it, he said that he had been trying to talk with you for a few days now and that you kept avoiding him, so he couldn't."

"He's right, Jen."

"Why?"

"Because I have nothing to say to him," Kat replied in a matter-of-fact tone.

"Did it ever occur to you, though, that he might have something to say to you?" countered Jen.

"What could he possibly say that would change anything? He's still going to put Lydia's needs above mine and I'm still going to be almost six years older than him. I was ridiculous to think that this would ever work. I had no business jumping into something so soon after James. I've decided that it's just easier if I avoid them until I'm ready to get out of here in a few days."

"Whoa, what?" Jen exclaimed. "What do you mean that you

want to get out of here in a few days? Kat, the show still has at least three more weeks of shooting, and I'm only up here for four days. That's all I could get David to agree to as he's still so freaked out about how to care for Lucy on his own. In fact, we are even beginning to discuss living under the same roof again; that it might be best for us, at least until we get this whole thing figured out."

Now it was Kat's turn to be surprised. "But you got my text about how I couldn't be up here anymore!"

"Yes, Kat, I did, but I figured that you were upset and maybe needed a break, and I needed to come up here anyway to show my face to the producer at least once to make it look like I give a crap about my business. And that's the issue: we have a business to run, regardless of personal feelings. I'm actually doing some catering for a small indie film and have to get back to that, so I am counting on you to get us through the last of this one."

"Can't Gerard or Melinda handle it?" Kat whined.

"Probably. But they aren't the ones who need the boost of self-esteem. Kat, if you can handle this, you can handle anything. You have had a helluva year. Heck, you have had a helluva three months. You have to learn to stand on your own two feet and how to deal with life without avoiding the unpleasant.

"I think that is how this whole mess started, actually. I remember you were having doubts about marrying James, but rather than causing a problem by breaking it off, you went along with it and figured it would be good enough.

"You have learned to cushion yourself from your own desires and needs, and while it may seem like it works, it also robs you of passion. It makes it almost impossible to feed and nourish your soul. You need to stay here and do this so that you can show yourself you can conquer anything, even when it's uncomfortable or hard. There's no taking the easy way out of life, Kat. With the good, comes the bad, the difficult. You're getting on the path to good by allowing yourself to feel and experience, but there will be hiccoughs and upsets along the way, and you have to deal with those, too. Being settled is a boring place to be. Those who are settled have given up on making their lives any better than they are. There's a huge difference between contentment in one's life and being settled and stagnant."

"Jen, I can't stay here for several more weeks and face him every day!"

"Kat, can't you look at it as a good thing that this happened? Instead of focusing on what didn't work, focus on what did! You were free with him, who you are supposed to be. How you are with me, but you were that way with everyone. You wore your heart on your sleeve. What you had with Ian wasn't a failure, it was an awakening."

"How so?" Kat asked incredulously.

"Because it happened. You let go of all of the expectations and traditions and baggage and just went for it. For once, you were gratified because you weren't being what you thought everyone else needed. I'm sure that even the sex was more pleasurable for you because it was about desire, not duty or obligation."

"Jen, we never had sex! How many times do I have to tell you that?"

"Sure, Kat. I saw his facial expression and messy hair, not to mention the fact that his pants were inside out, on that morning when I rang on the doorbell to take you to the airport. He was obviously roused from something he wasn't very happy to have had to stop. You can't deny it."

"Well, actually, I kind of can," Kat told Jen with a sheepish smile. "When you rang the doorbell, we were just about to… you know. Like literally *just* about to. I had finally convinced him that I was okay with it, and he'd just decided that if I was, he was. I've never wanted to kill you as much as I did in that instance!"

"Sorry!" Jen laughed. "My timing was impeccable, I know. I knew as soon as he opened the door that my being there early was not a welcome thing. You could smell the sex on him. But when I tried to slink away and come back later, he told me to come on in."

"I know," Kat said flatly. "I was there. In bed. Naked. Totally left wanting him and not getting him because of you!"

"That's what I mean, Kat. You were so uninhibited! I saw how y'all interacted that night at my house and also at the beach. There was an intimacy there that you never had with James. You were comfortable with him, and he was comfortable with you."

"Oh, God, Jen. Did you have to bring all of this up? I was so close!"

"I did. Because I don't think this is done yet. You have to talk to him, Kat, not avoid him, even if it's just for closure."

"I'll think about it." Kat responded, doubtfully. Then, she registered something that Jen had said earlier.

"Did you say that you and David are thinking about moving in together?"

"Yes. It would make taking care of Lucy that much easier. We'd both be there to help each other help her."

"And it would make you a family again," Kat added. Jen just looked at her.

"Jen, are you and David getting involved again?"

"I can't explain it, Kat, but this whole thing with Luce has made me see what an incredible man he is. He's patient, kind, giving, and loving. I don't know if it was me who has changed or him, but one day, it just clicked. He's the man with whom I'm supposed to be. Oh, and the sex is incredible!"

Kat laughed. "Well, I wouldn't know what that's like, but enjoy! Honestly, though, Jen, he *is* a good man. I've always liked him. He has loved you and accepted you all along."

"I know. I think I just finally realized that being tied down isn't necessarily a bad thing if you don't feel like you are. I watched my parents and you and James, and I was terrified that what had happened to my mother and to you would happen to me. I saw you slowly lose yourselves to become someone else's ideal and I didn't want to become that. It dawned on me, though, that David has never expected me to change. Not once."

"So, are you getting remarried?"

"Kat, we never really divorced. We separated, but we just never bothered with the legal side of things. I called him my ex, but really, I was just too lazy to make it happen. Well, not lazy… focused on other things."

"Are you kidding me? You never told me that!"

"Sorry, Kat. It just never seemed like something that I needed to discuss. You know me: laws and rules are merely suggestions. I didn't need to get a piece of paper that showed we were no longer together. We figured it wouldn't matter until the day came that one of us found someone else to marry, and neither of us were looking for that."

Kat glanced at the clock and saw that it was now almost midnight. As good as it was to be talking face to face with Jen again, she knew that 4:30 a.m. would come very quickly, so they both rolled over and fell asleep, just as they had done so many times before as teenagers having sleepovers, after sharing their inner most feelings and secrets.

Chapter Thirty-Six

Kat awoke to Jen getting up off of the bed. Years of being a caterer in Hollywood had made her an early riser, usually waking up before her alarm. Kat, on the other hand, had always been a night owl, so these early mornings were not her friend. While Jen was always peppy and happy in the mornings, wanting to carry on conversations with people, Kat required half a pot of coffee before her brain would fully engage.

Jen jabbered all the way from the R.V. and into the kitchen. She talked while they prepped chicken and waffles, grits, and biscuits and gravy. She spoke to everyone who came in to get their food and had everyone smiling, if not laughing. Kat had always admired how free- spirited and open Jen was. She could talk to anyone with an easy familiarity that made them feel relaxed, like she had been their best friend for years. Most of the good gossip she heard was revealed to her by the stars themselves because they felt so comfortable being around her. Of course, it hadn't hurt that she never told anyone what she had heard, except for Kat, who never had anyone else to tell who cared enough for her to even be tempted to break Jen's confidences.

After the first wave of crew, the rest of the set came in to eat. It didn't take long for Jen to find Ian and give him a big hug. Kat tried to ignore him, but she couldn't miss how he looked over Jen's shoulder and locked his eyes on hers. A look of sadness clouded his face until he pulled back from Jen, then Kat could hear that they were catching up and laughing. Jen was introduced to Lydia, and they spoke together for a few minutes, talking about the food.

George came up to them, and Jen charmed him in a matter of seconds, as well.

"Well, young lady," he drawled, "this is about the best darned operation I've ever had on set. The food is amazin'! Just like my meemaw made when I was a boy, without all of that stuff that makes it bad for us. Not only that," George patted Ian on the back, "this boy even got some one-on-one nursin' from one of your employees."

Jen graciously smiled and said, "Thanks. I appreciate that, sir. As for one of my employees, Kat is actually co-owner with me. Come on over here, Kat." Kat gave her a look that could have killed but then recovered quickly as she came forward, all smiles and Southern manners.

George took her hand and said, "Y'all have been fabulous and I'm goin' to make sure y'all are up here again next year, God willin' this show gets re-upped for another season."

He looked pointedly at Ian who threw his hands up and cried, "Hey, don't look at me! Besides that slimy veg, it has kind of grown on me." He looked directly at Kat, running his eyes up and down her, and said, "All of it," with meaning. Kat looked down at the floor, trying to will her cheeks to stop blushing.

"Thanks, sir. It has been our pleasure," she mumbled.

With that, Kat excused herself back into the depths of the kitchen, while Jen mingled and socialized.

When everyone had cleared out, the four of them got to cleaning and prepping for the next meal. Melinda, Gerard, and Jen all laughed about past jobs and experiences that had been less than ideal and how wonderful it had been this time to work with such down to earth, real people. Jen looked pointedly at Kat and said, "Kat's been spoiled, y'all. She hasn't had to deal with the divas we've had to placate, has she?"

They all agreed that as a first assignment, this one had been incredibly forgiving and fun, but they all warned her that she should not expect it to be the norm, especially back in Los Angeles. Jen had said that the virtual isolation of being on location broke down barriers between people, so they became more relaxed and friendly with each other, almost like a family, and Kat could only confirm it was true.

In the mid-afternoon, Kat grabbed her running shoes and headed out. She asked if Jen wanted to come with her, but her friend had acted strangely, being especially vague about her afternoon plans. Knowing that Jen hated to exercise, Kat merely shrugged and hit the trail.

Meanwhile, Jen had agreed to meet Ian to discuss "The Kat Situation," as he had dubbed it. As soon as Kat took off, Jen marched over to his trailer and knocked on the door. He opened it and looked around before letting her in.

"So…" said Jen when she sat down on the couch.

"Thank you for coming, Jen. I'm at a loss."

"What do you mean?"

"I mean that I don't know why Kat is ignoring me." His expression was miserable. "Ever since a discussion between me and Lydia and her, she has cut me out. Then James showed up, and I walked in on them."

"Wait… what? You walked in on them?" Jen asked, surprised.

"I did. Wait… Not like that. But they were in the dining room alone and when I walked in, he was holding her hand and they were having an intense conversation. Jen, she's going back to him, isn't she?"

Jen couldn't stand it. She generally would have told him that she didn't want to get involved, but he looked so hopeless and dejected, she couldn't find it in her heart to say that. "No, Ian. She and James are not getting back together. I'm not sure what you saw, but she is not interested in returning to her old life. He blindsided her by coming up here unannounced. He blindsided me, too, actually. When I saw a Calgary area code, I never would have guessed who it was. The fact that it was James and he had flown in and was trying to find out where she was really shocked me.

"Anyway, Kat sent me a text that night, the night of your and Lydia's big discussion with her, saying that she couldn't stay up here anymore. Her ignoring you has nothing to do with her wanting James, of that I can assure you."

"Then why?" he looked pained.

"Ian, that's not up to me to answer. You'll have to talk to her yourself."

"Jen, I've tried. But every time I come near her, she finds some way to get out of it. Will you please help me set something up? I don't want her to get the chance to blow me off again."

"I don't know, Ian. That could end badly for both of us. You haven't felt the full wrath of Kat's Irish temper."

He simply stared at her for a second before speaking. "Seriously? You're warning an Irishman about an Irish woman's temper? My dear Jen, she has nothing on the lasses I've dealt with at home. She's a pussy cat! All I need is for you to help me set up a meeting that looks like it was just by chance. Could you help me with that much? Please? I promise I'll make it look random. I *am* an actor, after all," he said with a wink.

"Why, Ian Gregory, are you trying to charm me into doing what you want me to do?"

He flashed her a dimpled grin. "I don't know. Is it working?"

When Jen got back to the trailer that evening, she thought that she would try to approach Kat sensibly. She didn't quite feel right about trying to set a meeting between her and Ian when she knew that Kat had been so adamantly against it. Jen figured it was already a hard-won victory that she had convinced Kat she was needed up here for the rest of the shoot and had gotten Kat to concede that she maybe would speak with Ian at some point if only for the sake of closure.

In actuality, Jen could have stayed up there and Kat could have handled the very small indie job all on her own. David was feeling much more comfortable with Lucy than Jen had let on, but she selfishly wanted to get home to her own little family.

"Kat?" she asked as she walked into the small bedroom.

"Yeah?"

"Can we talk?"

"Okay. Look, Jen, if this is about how I keep bowing out at every meal, please just know that I won't do it once you leave again. I just need to get a little distance to make this easier on me, so I'm taking it while I can."

"No, it isn't about that at all. I just want to know how long you are planning on ignoring Ian? I talked to him today, and Kat, he feels really badly."

"I don't know why? This solves all of his problems. He doesn't have to worry about pissing George off, or the executives, fans, or even Lydia. He's also free to find someone with whom he could have a million kids if he wants. It's a win/win for him!"

"Except, Kat, he won't have you, which I think is the one thing he wants most of all," Jen said quietly.

"I'm just not going to let that happen, Jen. Now, please. You're here for just three more days. I don't want to argue about this anymore. I promise that I will eventually talk to him before the season wraps up, okay?"

Jen stared hard at her friend, squinting a little. Finally, she conceded. "Okay," she relented, sighing in frustration.

It was abundantly clear to Jen that she was going to have to go along with Ian's suggestion to set up a "chance" meeting. But how would she do it? It wasn't like they could go to a bar or restaurant and just have him "randomly" show up there while in the middle of nowhere. As she and Kat settled down for the night, Jen wracked her brain, trying to think of something that sounded legit. Finally, right when she was about to fall to sleep, it hit her: exactly what she needed to do.

The following day, Kat again managed to sneak away from the kitchen before anyone came in to eat. Ian glanced up questioningly at Jen in the morning at breakfast and she only held up a finger, signaling him to wait. Lunch came, and his expression was all the more inquisitive. Jen simply glared at him, her look telling him to back off. Just when he was standing up to leave, she walked over to him and said, "Come into the kitchen on your way out." He smiled at her, relief apparent in his face.

"Okay," she said when they had moved to the back of the kitchen, away from any prying eyes. "She really doesn't want to see you, Ian. I tried…"

Ian interrupted her. "Please, Jen, don't tell me that she said she won't and you're just going to drop it. I know she is your best friend, and you have no loyalty to me, but you have to know, I really, really want to be with Kat."

"Ian, if you hadn't interrupted me, I would have told you that against my better judgment, I've decided that the only way we will get through that tenacious, stubborn head of hers is to go along with your plan."

Ian's eyes lit up. He grabbed Jen's hands and said excitedly, "Thank you! Thank you! Thank you!"

"Not so fast, lover boy," Jen scolded. "All I can do is facilitate this 'chance' meeting. I have no ability to make her actually stay and talk to you."

"I know. But you will get me closer than I've been in days."

"So, here's the deal, my friend. The only thing I can think to do is to go running with her in a little while. If she believes it, that in of itself will be a miracle. Exercise and I have a hate/hate relationship, and as soon as I ask her to run with me, she will most likely catch on that something is up. But there isn't any other place I can think of up here. In the middle of nowhere, the opportunities for chance meetings are extremely limited."

"I understand. How shall we go about it, then?"

"Is there a specific place she likes to go or a trail she likes to take?" Jen pushed.

"There is! There's a meadow by the lake. We've been up there quite a few times together."

"Great! That'll work. Now, how do I plan to get her up there without asking her about it directly?"

"I think if you just asked her if she had a favorite place to run here, that's where she would go."

"What happens if she doesn't?"

"That's just a chance we will have to take."

They spent the next few minutes planning that Ian would soon take off running ahead and continue up the trail past the meadow a little bit. He would start to run back down at three o'clock, which should give Kat and Jen time to almost get to the meadow. Ian leaned over and kissed her cheek.

"Thanks, Jen. You're a doll!"

"I hope this works, Ian. Otherwise, I may be needing to sleep in your trailer tonight!"

He grinned at her. "Something tells me Kat wouldn't really go for that."

"Nor would the rest of the world," Jen muttered under her breath.

When Kat came back after the lunch crowd had returned to the set, Jen told her casually that she wanted to go on a run with her when they were done. Kat gaped at her, one of her eyebrows up in question.

"What did you say?" she asked Jen incredulously.

"I said I want to go for a run with you in a little while."

"Jen, are you sick? You never want to go for a run with me. You have told me since I first met you that you are allergic to exercise."

"Yeah, well, things change. Ever since Lucy got sick, I took a play from you and have been running to ease the stress, okay?"

"All right," Kat replied suspiciously.

"Great. Let's go get changed and head out. I'll talk to Gerard and Melinda and make sure that they have everything under control, and then let's hit that trail!" She was trying really hard to sound way more enthusiastic than she was feeling. In fact, she felt she would rather have a root canal than endure the next two hours.

Thirty minutes later, they started out. After about ten steps, Jen's legs and lungs began burning, and she was cursing the fact that she had ever let Ian talk her into this. When Kat looked over at her, however, she immediately changed her expression from anguish to a bright smile. When Kat turned back, Jen's face quickly went back to expressing the pain and suffering she was currently enduring.

"You aren't the only actor, Ian Gregory. This had better be worth it!" she mumbled under her breath.

Kat turned toward her and asked, "What did you say?"

"Oh! I said, 'This is an even better workout!'"

"It is tough. The elevation here is a lot higher than either of us is used to. But the scenery makes up for it, right?"

"Sure," Jen wheezed out between pants.

Kat kept up her dialog about the beauty of the place and regaled Jen with stories of the various flora and fauna she had encountered since being up there. She seemed to truly be in her element and apparently didn't notice that Jen was not responding. In fact, Jen was simply trying hard to not fall over dead on the side of the trail. She wondered to herself what people would say at her funeral. *Jen always said that exercise would be the death of her!* she could hear her family and friends saying. She smiled in spite of herself. Ian so owed her, and she was going to make sure she collected.

"Maybe an all-expense paid trip to Ireland is in order!" she muttered to herself.

Finally, she couldn't go any further. "Kat!" she cried with her last gasp of air. Kat turned around and saw Jen was weaving as she was struggling to put one foot in front of the other. She patiently waited for a second while Jen walked over to the side of the trail, and with her hands resting on her knees, proceeded to gag and cough. Kat couldn't help smiling to herself. Jen would never be a great athlete, that was for sure.

"Okay," Jen said, after a few minutes. "Let's keep going!"

"Are you sure, Jen?"

"Yes. Yes! I can keep going, though maybe we should just stick to walking for a while. It's so pretty up here. I don't want to turn around quite yet."

"Just wait, then. There is the most incredible meadow about half a mile up the way. It's so lush and green, and has a small lake there, too."

Jen saw her chance. "Sounds nice! How'd you find it?"

Kat suddenly drew her lips together in a thin line.

After a second of hesitation, she simply replied, "Ian."

"Oh! We don't have to go there if you don't want, Kat."

Kat took a deep breath and sighed. "No, it's fine. I can't let what happened with him ruin everything about my experience up here. This place is so beautiful. It's just painful because Ian and

I had some of our best times together up here."

Jen felt very guilty. She hadn't wanted to hurt her friend and silently prayed that Ian's plan would work so that this meeting wouldn't permanently ruin Kat's affection for the beautiful spot.

They started up the trail once more and were almost there when Jen checked her watch—3:01 p.m., it read—and just like clockwork, she saw a figure come up the next rise in front of them. She tried not to react, but she involuntarily gave a big sigh. Kat turned to her.

"Are you all right?"

"I'm fine, Kat. I just wasn't expecting to see someone else up here. It scared me!" she said.

There. Totally saved that one! She thought proudly to herself.

Kat squinted at the figure coming nearer. A few steps closer and Jen heard her suck in her own deep breath.

"Oh, crap!" she exclaimed. "It's Ian!"

Chapter Thirty-Seven

Ian slowed his pace to a walk as he approached them.

"Good afternoon, ladies."

"Good afternoon!" Jen replied. "Out for a run?"

"I am."

They both looked over at Kat, who stood silently seething. She glared intently at Ian.

"You planned this, didn't you?" she accused him and then she spun to turn on Jen. "And you went along with it!"

She was so mad, she actually stomped her foot, making Ian and Jen burst out laughing at her display.

"We did, Kat." Ian admitted, clearly having a hard time keeping his affection for her out of his voice.

"Well then, enjoy the rest of your run together!" she exclaimed as she turned on her heel to start back down the mountain. Ian and Jen shared a worried look between them before Ian took off jogging after her. He ran just past her and then turned around, running backward, and trying to talk to her. Kat ignored him until he tripped and landed hard on his backside.

"Oh my gosh, are you okay?" Despite her anger, she was now trying hard not to laugh.

"I am," he replied with an embarrassed grin. "But now that I've mortally wounded my arse in an attempt to speak with you, will you please agree to talk to me?"

Kat tipped her head to the side, contemplating his proposal. As much as she knew she didn't want to get sucked back by his pull, she couldn't help herself. "I guess," she finally relented.

"Great! Let's go to our spot."

Jen ran past them. "I'm going to head down to help Melinda and Gerard with dinner prep. Enjoy!" she sang out to them.

"I am going to kill her!" Kat exclaimed.

"Don't do that, Kat. She was trying to help. I put her on the spot, and she agreed to do it. She cares about you and wants to make sure that you aren't just being stubborn."

Kat's eyes flashed at him. "Stubborn? Is that what she said? I'm stubborn?"

"No, actually," he replied with a quick grin. "I'm the one who says you're stubborn! As a mule, too!"

Kat stared at him, annoyance and exasperation clearly written all over her face. "How, pray tell, am I stubborn, Ian?'

"For one, you won't let me get a word in edgewise," was his clipped response.

She inhaled deeply. "Okay. Fair enough."

They continued walking toward their meadow, neither of them saying anything more along the way. They made it to the lake and sat down by the shore. Ian waited until she was situated on the grass before he dropped down in front of her.

"Kat?" he asked sadly, as he took one of her hands in his. "What happened?"

"What do you mean?

"I mean what happened to us?"

"I think we are just at totally different places in our lives and we both want different things," she replied honestly.

"Kat, do you even know what I want?" he asked her, obviously annoyed.

"You made it pretty clear, Ian, that you wanted your cake and to eat it, too." Her eyes flashed back at him, and he noticed they were especially green when she was mad.

"What are you talking about?"

"You! You and Lydia. Y'all had a discussion right in front of me like I wasn't even there! Y'all were both making decisions about my life with no regard for my feelings about the situation."

"I know, Kat, and I'm sorry. I've been replaying what I said that night over and over in my mind since that day. I want to apologize. By trying to make Lydia understand that I wouldn't accept being told what I can or can't do in my private life by some entertainment conglomerate, I made it sound like you were irrelevant to both me and the situation.

"I never meant for that to happen, to make it sound like I

was just having a fling up here with you when I said it was early days. What I meant was that even though we hadn't been together that long—but even if we had—I have a big problem with stipulations controlling my private life being written into a contract like I'm a commodity to be owned. This is my life, and I want to live it as I see fit, not based on what will get the best ratings for a T.V. show."

"I understand, Ian. But that's not all." Kat bit her lip, trying to keep her emotions in check.

"Oh, no! Are you going back to James?" he asked abruptly, sounding crushed as he stood up and walked away a few steps, running his hand through is hair nervously.

"No! It isn't that at all!"

"Then, what, Kat?"

"Ian, I can't be with you," she wailed.

"Why ever not?" he inquired., confused.

"Because Lydia is right. I'm old. I have grown kids. You aren't even forty yet!"

"So? Age is just a number, right?"

"It is if you are a man!" she retorted hotly.

"What's that supposed to mean?" He looked genuinely confused and then concerned when she didn't respond. He walked over to her and stooped down, wrapping his hands around her upper arms, and gently squeezing.

"Come on, Kat. Talk to me!" he implored gently.

Despite her best efforts, she could not keep her emotions under control. She took in a ragged breath. Finally, she responded, "Because age isn't just a number for women, Ian."

He looked at her with total confusion. "What are you talking about?"

"Ian, I'm over forty! Do you know what happens to women when they reach their forties?"

"They hit their sexual peak?" he said, sounding hopeful.

She couldn't help but smile at that. "Yes, Ian, there's that. But do you know what else?"

"No…"

"Women start to go through menopause. And before that, it starts to get really hard to get pregnant. And then, even if you do, there are all these risks that go along with advanced maternal age. Not to mention the risk of birth defects goes way up!"

Now Ian looked utterly lost. "Kat? I don't follow you!"

She straightened up and took another deep breath. Knowing she was just going to have to say it, she blurted, "Ian, Lydia was right! You shouldn't waste your time on me! You need to find someone with whom you can have children!"

He shook his head in disbelief. "Where is this coming from?" he begged her.

"Ian, I've seen you on the set with the kids. You're a natural. They love you, and it's clear you love them, too. If you and I got together, then that might not be a reality for you. In fact, it more likely wouldn't than would! You say you don't care, but you could very well change your mind one day, and I couldn't handle any more rejection over something out of my control. I love being a parent and I can't deny someone else that opportunity."

He was quiet for a few minutes, letting her words sink in. Finally, he looked down at her and asked, "Is that what this has all been about? You thinking that you weren't good enough for me because you might not be able to have any more children?"

"In a nutshell, yes… among other things."

"What other things?"

"I'm not comfortable being hidden in the shadows. I want someone who's willing to fight for me and to do everything in their power to keep us together, and not have the relationship watched over and calculated by someone else. I know you love Lydia, but I would want you to show me that my needs are more important to you than hers if I was to be with you."

"Wow!" he exclaimed. "I don't even know what to say about all of this…."

Kat stood up and began to turn around to walk away from him. She knew she had blown it. Talking about kids, telling him he needed to choose her needs over Lydia's? What in the hell was she doing?

On the other hand, though, she was proud of herself for vocalizing her feelings, instead of swallowing them like usual. She realized that Jen was right. If nothing else, this discussion would bring her closure.

When she had taken a few more steps away from him, she felt him gently tug her elbow, pulling her back. He stepped to her side so that they were facing each other and put his mouth on hers. Wrapping his arms around her back, he proceeded to kiss her with such feeling that her knees began to buckle. After a few seconds of shock, Kat began to respond. She kissed him back with fervor and felt her heart start to soften, and she began to let out small sounds of contentment the more intense their kiss became.

Finally, when they came up for air, he held her at arm's length and bent his knees slightly so that they were roughly the same height. Looking into her eyes, he told her, "Silly Kat! What am I going to do with you?"

"Huh?" She was confused.

"You have had way too much swirling around in that head of yours!"

"What do you mean by that?"

"I mean, do you always psychoanalyze everything like this? If so, it must be exhausting!"

"I'm not psychoanalyzing anything! It's just the way it is. These are things that could be real issues for us, and I don't think you fully realize all of the ramifications!"

"Of what, Kat?"

"Of what could happen to us if we continued to have a relationship."

"Let's start back at the beginning of what you said, shall we?"

She only could nod her head. Her earlier elation at expressing herself was gone and she was now feeling completely mortified. He motioned to the ground for her to sit and he settled in beside her.

"Kat, I know how old you are," he said simply. "And even though I'm an actor, I did go to school and, amazingly enough, was actually quite good at it. I have some idea about biology. I also have a sister, a ma, and two grandmothers. Believe me, once my father died, I was surrounded by a lot of estrogen!"

Kat only stared blankly at him. "Your point?" she asked dryly.

"My point, Kat, is that I'm not ignorant. I know that after forty, having kids can be an issue for women, a much bigger one than when they are younger."

"And?" Kat just wanted him to just spit it out, certain that he was going to tell her that being a parent was an experience he didn't want to forego.

"Do you really think that I'm that shallow that I'd only assess a potential love interest in terms of what she can give me versus what she can't? Possibly can't? Did it ever occur to you that if having my own biological kids was truly my top priority that I would have picked up whoever was willing and able along the way?

"You know that having kids is hard. So do I. It's something I would never take lightly. As much as I'd like to have children someday, I'd want to make sure it was with someone whom I loved and enjoyed first and foremost, because, as you well know, it takes a big toll." He took a big breath and sighed before continuing.

"I don't have many memories of my father, but what I do recall is that he and my mother were very much in love. I remember them dancing together in the kitchen on Saturday mornings. I remember her kissing him goodbye at the beginning of every shift and the worried look that came over her face as the door shut, wondering if it would be the last time she saw him.

"And then that fateful day came, and she grieved for a very long time. I think she hasn't stopped grieving, honestly. She never remarried or even expressed interest in anyone else. My father was the only man for her.

"When you grow up with a love like that as your model,

Kat, it makes everything else seem pretty insignificant. I know that my sister and I were products of their love for each other, not the foundation of it, if that makes sense. I think they would have been just as happy if we had never come along. Not that they didn't enjoy us, but we really only enhanced what they had. We were not their main focus or goal." He stopped again and was quiet for a few seconds, seeming to think about what he wanted to say next.

"That's why, I think, since reaching adulthood, I've never been quick to jump into a relationship just for the sake of being with someone. Of course, when I was younger, I had my wild oats to sow and all that, but honestly, I've been looking for a true life partner for a long time; a real connection with someone is not something that I can get from just anyone. I want what my parents had." Ian paused wistfully before continuing.

"Sex is great, kids are nice, but when push comes to shove, it's going to be me and my beloved, long after those other things are gone. We all get old, our bodies don't work like they used to, and kids grow up and move away, as you well know. When I commit to someone, it will be because of all the things I want to share with them, not because of what they can give me."

Kat sat and pondered his words for a long time. She looked out over the water and tried to process what he had said. Finally, she said simply, "It seems your parents' relationship was extraordinary."

"It was. There's never been a comparison between what they shared and anything I've experienced… until now. When I was a youth, I asked my ma why she was still pining away for my father. My girlfriend and I had just had a pregnancy scare and my ma was trying to tell me that I needed to be more careful: that having children was not to be taken lightly, and that without a good, steady, and loving relationship, they would be more apt to tear apart a union than to add to it. She was trying to explain that a good foundation is what's needed in a family.

"I will never forget her answer. 'Ian,' she said, 'I had heaven on earth with your father. So, now I'll wait patiently to be in

344

heaven with him rather than settle for less on earth, simply because I'm lonely.'

"It really impacted me. I had been jumping from girl to girl and bed to bed trying to find something that was illusive at best. But lust and gratification are not love, Kat. Sacrifice and selflessness are, and I've never met anyone before you for whom I'd be willing to sacrifice my own happiness for theirs. I'm not going to get involved with a woman if I don't feel that, especially just to bring a child into the mix."

Kat again was silent. He had given her much to think about. She had no idea that he was so introspective and that he had put so much thought into what he wanted out of his life and a partner. She had never heard a man speak so candidly about love being a partnership where both people complimented each other and everything else was a bonus. She didn't know what to say.

"So, what I'm trying to tell you," he continued, "is that I would rather have you than have children with some random person just because you might not be able to. I'm not Henry VIII: I do not need an heir, and I am not going to cut off our relationship by the proverbial neck if I can't have a biological child with you. What I want is to be happy and fulfilled and to do that for you, as well. If kids become a part of that, so be it, but that has never been my ultimate goal in any relationship. They would be a bonus."

"But Lydia's right, Ian," Kat finally spoke up. "You are man, still a young one at that. You could potentially have children up into your eighties, like Charlie Chaplin did."

He chuckled. "Oh, God. While I pray that the function is still there and that I would get a lot of practice, the idea of becoming a father at eighty is less than appealing. My much younger wife would potentially be changing two sets of diapers." He shook his head. "Just because I could, Kat, doesn't mean I would.

"As for Lydia, because of her experience, she should know better than thinking that genetics make a family. There are tons of kids like her all over the world; kids whose biological parents are less than adequate. Those kids need loving homes, too. We both know what happened to Lydia when she didn't get that. And hers was a success story. Think of all of the girls who never make it out of that hell to go on and do other things in their lives. They follow the same patterns and examples, and the cycle continues.

"That is why I'm so careful to protect her. She was victimized and exploited her whole life. She deserves to be where she is today and not dragged down because of it."

"She's very lucky to have you, Ian."

"Why? Just because I'm a nice guy who won't use her for my own purpose and then abandon her for my own gain? Kat, that isn't luck. It's called being a decent human being. She hasn't gotten to experience that from many people in her life."

"Are you sure you aren't in love with her?"

"I'm sure. I love her, but I'm not in love with her. I feel for her as I would a sibling, and she obviously does for me, too, which accounts for her putting her nose where it does not belong! She's lovely, but to be brutally honest, she is too damaged to be what I'm looking for in a relationship. I'm not faulting her; she had to become that way, to look out for herself above all others, because of her experiences. But I want someone with whom I can love and be loved equally."

"That all may be well and good, but that doesn't change the fact that we can't be together publicly because if we are, we are risking Lydia's anonymity. I know it's petty and selfish, but that still feels a bit like you would be choosing her over me."

"I've thought long and hard about that. She and I never came up with a formal agreement. As I've said before, I was okay with it because it didn't leave me at any disadvantage. In fact, until now, it helped my career. I can't fault her for not wanting our agreement to end, because we never discussed that it would, and I know what it could mean for her. In all actuality, though, she was as shocked by what has transpired as I was. We were both happily existing in this nebulous status quo before I came up here this time and met you. I'd never even thought on that there may come a time when this wouldn't work for one or both of us any longer, and I'm sure she hadn't, either.

"Give me a chance to talk with her. Let me reason with her and come up with a plan that works for both of us before you decide. Not only that, but there's also still that looming question of if we will have something put in our contracts. So, in other words, I'm asking you to please be patient- just a little longer. Know that this will come to an end, but it might not be right away. What you have to do now, my dear Kat, is decide if you are okay with the situation for a while until it all gets sorted out."

Kat nodded at him.

"Good, then. Are you ready to head back?"

"Yes."

He held out his hand to her and gently pulled her up. Keeping hold of it for a few more seconds, he then used it to pull her in closer to him to give her a kiss on the top of her head.

"You know where I stand, love. It's up to you to decide what works for you," he told her as they started back down the mountain.

Chapter Thirty-Eight

Ian walked Kat to her R.V. where a Fed Ex envelope addressed to her was waiting on the step. As he picked it up and handed it to her, he said, "I know you have a lot to think about swirling around in that beautiful head of yours. Consider it carefully, Kat, and let me know what you come up with. I'll be waiting." With that he gave her a kiss on the cheek, his salute, and walked off toward his trailer.

He was absolutely correct. She had a whole tornado of thoughts whirling through her brain. Never had she known a man to be that in tune with his emotions, let alone have such empathy and compassion. He was unique in that while he was able to eloquently express his inner most thoughts, he also still had that gift most men seemed to possess: the ability to take a step back and look at a whole situation, unbiased by their own emotional investment. In contrast, in her experience, women generally weren't capable of being as objective in matters of the heart. While Kat felt like she was in a jumble of puzzle pieces and had to find where she fit in; meanwhile, Ian already seemed to see the whole picture long before it was finished.

She tried hard to do what he had asked: to think objectively about what he had said and how it would impact her. The one thought that kept coming back to her over and over again was how much she respected him. He was incredibly kind and conscientious and so in tune with what he was looking for. In actuality, she had to admit, his emotional age was much more advanced than his thirty- seven years. He seemed far beyond her level of maturity and understanding, that she knew for sure.

All through the dinner hours, she sat and analyzed everything he had told her, trying hard to distinguish exactly what her own personal impasse had been with the whole situation. Then it hit her like a ton of bricks.

The underlying emotion behind all of her issues was fear, more specifically the fear of further humiliation. She had been humiliated by James' blatant rejection of her when he cheated and then again when it became a scandal. She was then humiliated when she was targeted as the "other woman" in Ian and Lydia's pretend relationship, not at all helped by the media's plethora of unflattering photos and stories about her plastered in publications across the country. Then, to add insult to injury, it happened yet again when Lydia pointed out that Kat was old-perhaps too old to have any more kids. Somehow it had all converged until she believed that she was past her prime and therefore no longer worthy of love or happiness.

It was only then, after realizing all of the very public ways she had been told she wasn't good enough had taken their toll, that she admitted to herself she had been reluctant all along to make a decision regarding Ian out of fear of further shame.

The fact that Ian wanted to keep their relationship under wraps hadn't helped her feelings of worthlessness, either, because she felt rebuffed. No matter what he said his motives were, she couldn't help but feel that the real reason he was choosing to maintain the status quo with Lydia was that he was afraid of the ridicule he would suffer if he was seen in public with plain, old, undesirable Kat instead of his youthful, talented, and gorgeous co-star.

She saw for the first time how her own deep-seated insecurities about her age and feelings of inadequacy had unified until they had left her already poor self-esteem hanging by a thread, and therefore unable to accept that Ian truly wanted her. It was only then Kat finally understood that she had been highlighting all her faults, trying to beat Ian to the punch, when she had started to care too much for him in a subconscious attempt at self-preservation. When she was honest with herself, she knew she had never truly believed that she was good enough for him and had consequently convinced herself that he was simply enthralled with the excitement of a new and clandestine relationship and not her. Her fear was that once his infatuation wore off, he would find her just as valueless as James had, ultimately hurting her even more because she was ill-equipped to handle any more pain.

Instantly, she felt like a fog was lifting as clarity came rushing in. Fear had been what had inhibited her for most of her life. It had resulted in her being constantly anxious, afraid of dismissal and rejection, of letting people down, of what others thought, and of being insufficient. Jen had been spot on when she said that Kat avoided unpleasant situations; only then did she realize she did it because she hated being told she was a disappointment.

She then thought of what set Jen apart from her and came to the conclusion that Jen did not let fear inhibit her. Jen leapt first and worried about the consequences later.

Kat on the other hand never did anything without carefully examining the risks vs. benefits because she didn't want to be scorned for doing something wrong. Her whole life before now, starting with the relationship with her mother, had been spent trying to win other's approval and love. To prove that she was worthy of love. She sat on the bed in a stupor, shocked at what she had discovered about herself.

Kat understood now that what she needed to decide was whether or not she was ready to take a leap of faith with Ian and trust that everything would all be all right, regardless of how it might turn out, even if it meant risking more feelings of pain and rejection. Could she finally believe in herself enough to not let those around her dictate her self-worth? Did she have the confidence to chalk up any failures to learning experiences, rather than personal attacks? If she and Ian failed, would it actually be better to have loved and lost, than to have never tried?

She was still ruminating on all of this when Jen, Melinda, and Gerard came back to the trailer. Hearing their footsteps and conversation, peppered with soft laughter as they climbed up the steps and came in through the front, she was still sitting in place as Jen opened the bedroom door and turned on the light. Turning around, Jen gave tiny yelp when she saw Kat's tearstained face looking up at her from the bed.

"Kat, holy crap! You scared the bejeesus out of me! What are you doing in here in the dark?"

"Thinking."

"And doing it in the dark makes that better how?"

"I was just too spent to get up and turn on the light."

"I was hoping that you were with Ian. He didn't come in for dinner tonight, so I figured that maybe the two of you got some issues out of the way. But by looking at you, I can see that it was wishful thinking," Jen said sadly.

"No, Jen. It wasn't. We did talk and cleared up a lot of things."

"So why are you in here crying and not with him, then?"

"Because he asked me to please think about what he had said and then decide what I wanted to do."

"Said about what?"

"About me, about him, about us... he wanted me to hear how he feels and then decide if I could accept it."

Jen looked concerned. "Accept what? What did he say?"

"He told me that he had never found anyone else like me before and that the age difference didn't matter; that age is just a number. He also said he wouldn't care if we couldn't have kids together, that he was more interested in being a partner than a parent. Then he told me if kids came into the picture, they would enhance what we would have, but it would never be why he would or wouldn't choose to be with me, or anybody else for that matter."

"Wow! Kat, that's amazing!"

"He also asked me to be patient while he worked with Lydia to come up with a plan about when they can end this illusion they have created and let them decide on an ending point which would give Lydia a chance to properly handle any damage control, hopefully before the powers that be could slip a clause about any of this into their contracts."

"Wow! What are you going to do?"

"I don't know."

"What do you mean you don't know? Kat, this guy is a one

in a million. You would be stupid to give him up! Why would you be stupid?" she implored, completely exasperated.

Kat glanced up at Jen. "Because I'm scared."

"Scared of what, exactly? This man has poured his heart out to you!"

"Scared of being humiliated and hurt again."

"By whom? Certainly not by Ian?"

"Jen, I don't know!" she cried. "All of my life I've been trying so hard to please everyone. I don't know what to do with someone who genuinely likes me for me, just the way I am. I'm scared to open myself up just to be rejected once again. How can I be good enough just being myself when I wasn't good enough when I was trying to be perfect?"

Jen sat quietly for a few seconds before she responded. "Perhaps it's all about perspective."

"What does that mean?" Kat demanded.

"It means that perhaps it wouldn't matter how perfect you tried to be for the wrong person; they were still the wrong person. To balance that, perhaps your imperfections are exactly what make you the perfect person for someone else."

Kat mulled over that for a while. "How could I have made it so far in this life without finding someone like him before?"

"Honestly? Because I don't think that you would have been ready for it. Though, on second thought, you actually have, Kat, just not romantically. You have me, you have Holly. Both of us are happy to love you just the way you are. Your brothers, too, come to think of it. And how about your father? There are many people in your life who love you without your trying to earn their approval and acceptance; many of us who wouldn't change a thing about you. You just couldn't see it until you were able to step away from the preconceived notions you had about what your life was supposed to be. You've spent entirely too much time trying to fit into life instead of having life fit you."

"Ugh, Jen. That hurt!"

"Good! It should hurt! You've been torturing yourself for far too long, trying to be someone you aren't. Believe Ian when he tells you that you are exactly what he wants. Don't try to convince him he's wrong, or he might just start to believe it, like James and your mother. If you walk around thinking you aren't good enough, everyone starts to believe it, doll!"

"Do you think I was crazy to start all of this?"

"Yes. But, Kat, there are good kinds of crazy, too. There are kinds that pull you out of your comfort zone and push you to be better than you ever imagined you could be."

Kat sat on the edge of the bed in silence for a long time, leaving Jen unable to tell if she was angry, hurting, or sad. When she finally spoke, it was simply to say, "You're right."

"Excuse me?" Jen inquired. "Did you just tell me that I am right?"

"Yes, Jen, you're right. For too long I've let others convince me that I'm not good enough based on their ideas about how I should live my life. I owe it to myself to not have to work so hard. I'll try this with Ian and see if he means what he says. Let's see if he still thinks I'm as perfect for him as he thinks I am."

"Good girl! At worst, it's a learning experience, but at best, it's the chance to be truly happy."

Kat took several minutes to think before she answered, "Okay, then. For once, I'll just take the leap of faith and jump in. I guess the fear of losing out has finally overtaken my fear of losing control. I'll tell Ian tomorrow."

"You sure you don't want to tell him tonight?"

"Yes, I'm sure. I'm too tired. I just want to go to bed. Thanks, Jen, for being my oldest and truest friend. Thank you for pushing me when I won't push myself."

"My pleasure. I don't know where this journey will end for you but enjoy the ride!" Jen looked down at the bed and found the Fed Ex envelope where Kat had thrown it when she came in. "Hey! What's this?" she asked.

"Oh! I forgot about that. I don't know."

Silently, Jen handed it to her and looked on expectantly as Kat opened it. As she pulled out the contents, she began to laugh.

"What?" Jen demanded.

"It's my divorce paperwork!"

"What?"

"Look, Jen. It's the final divorce decree. All I have to do is sign this and Fed Ex it back and I'm free! Quick, find me a pen. I can't wait to have this over with!" Jen pawed through her purse and pulled out a pen. Kat ceremoniously pulled off the cap and signed her name with a flourish.

"How did that happen so quickly?" Jen was shocked.

"When James came here, we reached an agreement. He finally accepted it was over. When he went home, we began to text back and forth about the assets so that we could save money on attorneys. He was actually quite generous. We're selling the house with a closing date at the end of August, so Drew can get off to school first. I get half the house, and half the investments and retirement savings. Obviously, there's no child support needed. He's buying out the rest of my car loan with his proceeds from the house and he will pay the difference in his raise into the account he opened for himself for five years, or until I remarry, as alimony."

"Wow, Kat. He did good! I'm glad that he was reasonable and accommodating."

"Me, too, Jen. In the end, we remembered that we were friends above all else. I wish him no ill will and he wishes me none, either. We realized it would be best for the kids if we split amicably. In fact, he even offered to let me stay there when I go back for the boys' graduations in a few weeks, but I said I'd just stay with my parents or get a hotel. Seems like it would be a little too awkward otherwise."

"You think?" Jen asked, sardonically.

"Now all I have to do is put these in the enclosed package and somehow get them down to Calgary in the morning to send back overnight."

"There's always someone going to Calgary. In fact, if you wait until the day after tomorrow, I can do it when I leave."

Having settled all that, Kat and Jen soon fell asleep.

Kat woke up not long after, though, when a gust of wind

dropped a pinecone on top of the R.V. with a large thump. Laying in bed, she wondered how she was ever going to get back to sleep. She was so keyed up about meeting Ian the next day and telling him that she was willing to let go of her fears and truly give them a shot, she didn't know how she could ever make it to morning. Then it dawned on her. She didn't have to.

Chapter Thirty-Nine

Kat quietly slipped off the bed, pulled on her coat and shoes, and left the R.V. as silently as she could, willing every little squeak and click to go undetected. As she walked as softly as possible across the gravel and branches littering the ground, she thanked God for the strong breeze that was blowing briskly off the mountains, camouflaging any sound she did make from anyone who might hear.

When she got to Ian's trailer, she reached up and tentatively knocked on the door. She stood waiting for a few minutes and then tried again, a little louder this time. She listened carefully, until it sounded like there was movement inside. The door slowly cracked open and there he was, in nothing but a pair of pajama bottoms slung low on his hips. When he saw it was her, a slow, sleepy smile played across his lips, as he wordlessly opened the door wider and took her hand as she stepped up.

"Kat," he exhaled softly as he shut the door and walked toward her.

"Hi, Ian. Sorry to wake you."

He ran his hand through his rumpled hair. "It's never a problem, Kat. Any time."

"We need to talk."

"Okay."

"Is this a good time?" she asked him, it suddenly dawning on her that he might not be keen on being woken in the middle of the night when he had to be filmed in a few hours.

He chuckled. "Well, I'm awake now," he said.

"I don't want you to look tired on camera tomorrow."

"Kat, that's what coffee and makeup artists are for. What's up?"

"Okay, Ian," she said quietly.

He was quiet for a moment, obviously expecting her to elaborate a bit more. When she didn't, he prompted, "Okay what, Kat?"

"Okay. Let's try this."

"Try what? Give this a go?"

"Yes. I'm willing to try to let go of my fears and trust you have my best interest at heart and that you love me like you say you do, with no expectations."

"Kat, love, are you certain?"

"Yes!" she exclaimed. "I am sure. I'm going to do something crazy for once. Doing what I want to do, and not just go with the flow."

"Even though you know that we may very well have to be hidden for a little while? Are you sure you are okay with that? I don't like that you think you don't mean as much to me as Lydia," he said, his voice thick with emotion.

"Did you talk to Lydia about that?" she asked him, suddenly remembering he had said he was going to do that.

"I did, tonight after running lines. She and I have agreed to keep this up for six more months. That gives her time to get her PR team prepared to handle any fallout she will get. It also gives us time to figure this out. If it doesn't work out, we will reevaluate. That part was all her words, not mine," he quickly added. "I don't doubt this is going to work." He flashed his overconfident grin, letting his dimples shine through.

She nodded slowly as she thought about what he had said. "That sounds reasonable. I like your optimism."

"But, Kat, that might be all null and void if they add any clauses to our contracts. Then it might mean at least a year. Would you be okay with that?"

Her shoulders slumped. She took a deep breath and told him, "I won't like it, but I'll do it if I have to. Just as long as I get to see you..."

"Here's the thing, Kat. I will have my house in Los Angeles. We can do whatever we want there, as long as we are careful. I might have smaller projects sometimes, but they will most likely not be on location like this. This show is only a twelve-to-fourteen-week shoot. I can fly home to you, you can fly to Calgary, and I can stay there with you in a hotel, or I can, I don't know, hire you as my personal chef. This *will* work out!

"Then, after next year, Lydia and I agreed that if the show is re-upped again, we would stand tall together in telling the executives that we will not have any more clauses like this written into our contracts. Hopefully by that time, the show will be popular enough that we'll have that kind of leverage. If the show is canceled, then it'll all be moot, anyway. Agreed?"

"That sounds like a good plan."

They stood facing each other in the semi-darkness, neither of them sure how exactly to proceed. Then, drawn like two magnets, they found each other and wrapped themselves into a tangled embrace. As he hugged her, Ian breathed, "Oh, God, how I've missed this. Kat, all I wanted was to touch you this entire last week. My body craved being near yours."

He walked them over to the couch and gently pushed her to sit. Sitting down beside her, he began to caress her hair, her face, and her shoulders before leaning back and admiring her for a minute. As he then bent forward to place his forehead on hers, she slowly reached her right hand up and placed it on his cheek before she stretched up to kiss him squarely on his lips. She moved her head to the side and murmured breathily into his ear, "I think we have some unfinished business to attend to. What do you think?"

Ian didn't need to be asked twice. Scooping her into his arms as he stood, he then walked carefully down to his room. He gently placed her on the bed, and lay down beside her, enjoying her curves. His hand crept under the thin strap of her shirt and pushed it over her shoulder, exposing the warm, silky skin of her neck and collarbone in order to lavish small, sweet kisses down from just under her ear. Kat's arms went around his neck and his lips began searching hers. Gentle at first, the passion between them grew until their kisses were deep and intense. Ian's excitement building, he slipped his hand under her shirt, gently stroking his thumb back and forth over the nub on her breast, wanting to feel his effect on her. One look in his eyes told Kat that this time he was determined to surrender to his desire.

She could tell that his body was more than ready, and while still kissing him, she began to fumble with the tied strings of his pants. Abruptly, he sat up and, pulling her with him, frantically drew her shirt up over her body and threw it aside, his eyes lighting up in delight with the realization she was naked under her pajamas, giving him unencumbered access to her breasts. He gently guided her back down until he was hovering over her, and she arched into the molten heat of his mouth, feeling like she was about to combust. His skin against hers was warm and soft and taut across his muscular physique. Kat knitted her fingers into the silky hair at the back of his head as he changed his focus, kissing and gently nibbling from her neck all the way down to the waistband of her pants. Kat's sharp inhale gave way to a small squeal as his hand worked its way under the elastic and moved lower down her abdomen, until he was gently caressing the sensitive crease between the inside of her thigh and torso, inadvertently tickling her. Eliciting a disappointed whimper, Ian pulled his hand back, and slid his way back up her body with his tongue, stopping to give her most sensitive spots extra attention.

When he came up beside her, there wasn't any denying that he was as ready as she was. Feeling a distinct hardness against her leg, she gently pushed him over onto his back and began to kiss him, pulling at his bottom lip with a soft nibble. He gasped and moaned as she worked her way over to his ear and ran her tongue lightly along the outside edge. As she slowly slid one of her legs over his thigh, his eyes closed in ecstasy until she gracefully pulled herself up and over to straddle him. He took a deep breath and tried to sit up slightly, reaching for her, but she nudged him back down and began to move over his body as he had hers. Beginning with his mouth, she languidly kissed him, past the deep v in his neck, to his chest and down, until she finally reached masculine trail of dark hair that began just below his navel and disappeared beneath the waist of his pajama pants, a sharp contrast to his hairless chest. Her fingers traced the line and slipped below his waistband as her mouth began to meander her way back up again. He gasped sharply as her hand found what it was seeking, and as she began to stroke up and down, he let out a low, primal moan. He tried to reach down to pull his pants down over his hips, but borrowing from his playbook, she grabbed his wrists and admonished him with a wicked grin, "Slow down. What's your hurry?"

He looked into her eyes and groaned. "Kat, you are killing me. I can't take much more of this! God, I want you!"

She moved her torso down past his hips, kissing him lower and lower, pulling his pants down in front with one finger. Her mouth nearly caressing something other than his abdomen, her hot, moist breath on him was so tantalizing it was driving him to the brink of insanity. He wanted her to venture further in her endeavor, but to his extreme disappointment, she worked her way back up his body, until she was lying flush against him. He let out a heavily pained sigh and began moving beneath her, willing her with his body to go back down, words having failed him. When he couldn't get her to budge from working her mouth over his neck, he began to move his large, masculine hands up and down her smooth bare skin, further inflaming their hunger. Kat continued teasing his lips with soft, feather-light kisses, resisting his attempts to pull her into a deeper clinch, and was loving the effect she was having on him until finally, when it felt like he might lose all conscious thought, he flipped her over onto her back in a last-ditch effort to reclaim the upper hand. He knew that he had to slow them down or he wouldn't make it much longer. So many weeks of anticipation and longing were making him much more hot-blooded, and he had waited too long for this to succumb to spending himself prematurely.

With Kat beneath him, he was more in control of the situation, and he was determined to use it to his advantage to ensure she wanted it as badly as he did. Her desire grew exponentially as he let his mouth explore her torso, working his way lower and lower while locking his eyes on hers. When he again arrived at the waist of her bottoms, he began to once again to stroke the soft, sensitive flesh that waited below. As his fingers began to explore further, she eagerly rose her hips up to meet him and he knew then that it was time. Lovingly holding her gaze with his, he slowly pulled down her pants, consciously prolonging her sweet agony for as long as possible, before casting them onto the floor, then quickly followed suit with his own. The anticipation making her ache with longing, Kat realized that she had never before in her life felt such need. She agonized that he would once again stop in an attempt to save her honor, but the pent-up emotion of the last few weeks was overtaking him, as well. Even so, he still didn't forget what he had promised her.

"Kat?"

"Yeah?" she sighed.

"As much as I want to do this, I need to make sure you're okay with it. I know I told I could wait until you're divorced, and I'm still willing to, but if we go much further, I don't think I'll want to stop."

Kat began to laugh softly. "Funny you should mention that," she told him, as she raised her hand to caress his cheek. "Remember the envelope you handed me this afternoon that was sitting on the steps of my trailer?"

"I do."

"That was my divorce decree, and now it's all signed, sealed, and ready to be delivered on Jen's way back to Los Angeles. So, for all intents and purposes, I am divorced."

His heart skipped a beat as he processed what she said. "Are you serious?"

"Never more!"

The yearning he had been suppressing hit him full bore. However, as he settled between her thighs, just when he was about to let go and let instinct take over, Kat spoke again.

"Ian?"

"Mmm?"

"I'm nervous."

"About?" He continued to languidly kiss her along her jaw.

"I've only ever been with James. I don't know if I know what to do or if I'm any good at it. I never had anyone to compare with or tell me differently.”

He buried his face in her neck to hide his smile. “Kat,” he mumbled into her shoulder, “it isn’t rocket science. I promise you if you had three kids, you know what you are doing.”

“So then why did James go somewhere else, then?”

“Because he was stupid?” Ian was beginning to feel frustrated.

Of all of the times for her to be psychoanalyzing! he thought, rolling his eyes, and sighing softly as he slid off to her side.

“I haven’t any idea why he did that.” he said, while continuing to expertly explore every sensitive crease and whorl with skilled fingers. “I’m not sorry he did, though. If he hadn’t, we wouldn’t be together right now. I haven’t any doubts that we’ll be compatible. I know from tonight and our past experiences that you certainly know what you’re doing—you make me crazy with wanting you! But if you’re too conflicted, we can wait. I told you that I’m not in any hurry and I want to make sure you feel comfortable.”

She adverted her eyes as the tears came. “I’m sorry I’m so vulnerable about this. After all that happened, it’s hard not to think it was because I wasn’t good or exciting enough.”

Realizing that this was not going to be a conversation that would be quickly concluded, Ian reached over and pulled her shirt off its perch on his lamp and his pants up off the floor. Placing the former in his lap, he silently handed the shirt to Kat, as he contemplated what to say.

“Kat, I can’t imagine why James did the things he did. Hell, I don’t even know why *I* do half the things I do. But I can tell you that he was crazy. You are beautiful, kind, and gentle. Even if you’re the worst lover in the world, those skills can be learned. What’s inherent about you cannot be. He was an *eejit* as far as I can see, and you are much too good for him. And I can promise you, my dear Kat, that if nothing else, I’m man enough to tell you if I’m dissatisfied with something rather than go sneaking behind your back to address it. You deserve better.”

She studied him but he couldn’t read her expression.

362

Mentally, he was fully prepared to be thwarted yet again in his physical attempts to show her just how much he desired her. Her long-term comfort and security meant more to him than a few minutes of pleasure.

After a several moments, however, she nodded her head. "Okay," she whispered, "I'm ready."

"Are you sure?" He looked deep into her eyes, trying to see if this was what she wanted or if it was only fear of disappointing him that drove her change of heart. He saw a light of determination glowing back at him.

"Yes, I'm sure! I promised myself that I wouldn't let my life be dictated by fear any longer."

And with that, they picked up where they had left off. When the moment finally came when he gently pressed forward and they were at last joined together intimately as one, it was as if the world stopped and everything else disappeared, surrendering to the desire they had been denying.

"All right?" he whispered in her ear.

All she could do was nod into his chest. Any hope of coherent speech had left her as he moved adeptly above her.

It didn't take long until the love they felt for each other culminated in an overwhelming explosion of emotion and ecstasy rolled into one.

As their breathing steadied, they pulled apart and he rolled over onto his back. "Kat, your worries were completely unfounded. That was exquisite!"

In her own warm and pleasant stupor, she responded, "I think I might have had the wrong partner before." She still couldn't comprehend that her body was able to feel like that.

He grinned boyishly at her. "Oh, yeah? Why is that?" he asked.

"Because it is like nothing ever existed before you."

"Good enough for me!" he exclaimed happily.

After a few seconds of silence, he reached down and took her hand in his, and told her, "You know, I was nervous, too."

"Really?"

"I was," he confirmed.

"Why?"

He turned onto his side and gently brushed the hair back off of her forehead with his free hand before landing a gentle kiss. "Same reason as you were: it's intimidating for anyone to be compared to someone else," he said.

"Believe me, Ian. There is no comparison. At all. I didn't know that I was capable of feeling so good! What you did to me... *wow*! Is it even legal for it to feel that incredible?"

He laughed softly. "That's the way it's supposed to be, I think."

"You think?"

"Yeah, Kat. That was a pretty earth-moving experience for me, too. Nothing like I've ever experienced, anyway."

He rolled over onto his back, taking her with him.

His arm wrapped protectively around her as she curled tightly around him. He took his free hand and captured hers, which was gently stroking his chest, intertwining their fingers as he lifted their hands to his lips to place a gentle kiss on the back of hers.

"Thank you," he told her simply.

"For what?"

"For this. For taking a chance and letting go. For trusting me. I hope that you never find that to do so was unfounded or unwise. I hold you in the highest regard."

She didn't know how to respond. But he felt her tears trickle off of her nose onto his chest and he leaned down and kissed the top of her head, smiling. They held each other as they fell asleep, sated, and fulfilled.

A few hours later, Kat woke up hearing another strong gust of wind. The air in the trailer had grown significantly cooler. She inched her naked body closer to Ian's, covering herself with more of the blanket, rousing him slightly from his slumber in the process. He stretched out his leg and gave a deep sigh as his arms went around her. She took the opportunity to pull herself up to his ear, whispering, "Wanna go again?" His eyes flew open, and she relished the fact there was no faster way to wake a man than with a proposition of intimacy.

This time their movements were slower, less frenzied, as they took their time, savoring and enjoying each other. As they reached their pinnacle, Ian grasped Kat's hands and held them above her head, gazing intently into her eyes before sending her tumbling over the edge into bliss.

Chapter Forty

W hen Kat awoke the next morning, Ian was already gone. She panicked, thinking that he had sneaked out and left her after their night together, but then laughed when she realized how ridiculously paranoid she was being. She was waking up in his trailer! Rolling over to grab her phone, she saw that it was well after 8:00 a.m. By now there was no way to sneak away undetected, as the whole production team would have been awake and moving around for several hours. Kat worried about what she should do—she would most certainly garner attention if she just waltzed out of Ian's trailer in her pajamas.

Where are my pajamas? she panicked.

She found them folded in a pile on the side of the bed and put them on. As she turned back around, she saw a note lying on his pillow. She picked it up and smiled as she read:

Good morning, Kat. I'm leaving you a note so that you don't worry that I've run off. I have to go to work, so I decided to let you sleep but I'll text Jen and ask her to bring you some clothes after breakfast. Thanks for last night and I'll see you later. Love, Ian.

He knew her so well, guessing exactly where her mind would go when she woke up and he was gone. She reflected on the night before and how happy she was that she had thrown caution to the wind and took a chance, completely contrary to her nature. As she lay in bed, the intoxicating scent of Ian embedded in his sheets enveloping her, she tried to recall a time in her life when she had ever felt as much pleasure as she had the night before. She came up with nothing. While sex with James had been fine, or so she had thought, anyway, making love to Ian was perfection. It was as if they were made for each other. They fit together perfectly, like a lock and key, and were already exactly in tune with each other's movements and responses. She couldn't help but wonder if it had been beginner's luck or if this would continue, but she was definitely looking forward to finding out.

After dozing for little while longer, she was suddenly aware that there was someone outside the trailer. Thinking it was Jen, she got out of bed and was about to walk out and open the door, when she saw through the slits in the window blind that it was Jacob, Ian's assistant. There was something about him that always bugged her, but she couldn't quite pinpoint what it was.

She heard the door open, and she stood behind the door to Ian's room, trying not to be seen. Hearing him rustle papers around, she wondered what he was looking for, and why Ian would send him there when he knew she was most likely still in the trailer? She held her breath and willed that he would quickly find whatever he was seeking and leave. When it had quieted down and she thought he might be leaving, she let herself exhale a bit. His hand was almost on the door handle and, from what she could see through the crack in the door, he was empty handed. She was wondering what he could possibly have been doing there when her cellphone pinged, alerting her to a text message. Jacob turned and looked around suspiciously. Kat couldn't make it to her phone without letting him know she was in there, so she instead prayed that whoever had sent the text wouldn't send her any more. She then watched helplessly as Jacob picked up Ian's cellphone from table, looked at the screen, and then smiled as he put it down before turning and exiting the trailer.

Kat let out a huge sigh of relief. When she was sure Jacob had walked far enough away, she went to check Ian's phone herself. On his lock screen, she could see that Jen had messaged him: *On my way with her clothes now*. She gasped. Jacob had to have realized she'd spent the night with Ian. She began to panic as Jen walked up to the trailer and opened the door.

"Kat?" she asked softly.

"Back here!"

"Oh, good. I brought your clothes. Pretty funny that I get to do your walk of shame for you. Don't tell me I never did anything for you!"

"Thanks, Jen. I'm so glad it's you; Ian's assistant just left!"

"Did he see you?" Jen asked nervously.

"I don't think so… But I think he may have seen your text."

"Well, hopefully, since he didn't see you, he won't know what it was about!"

Once Jen left the bedroom, Kat checked her phone for her own missed message, saw that it was a text from Drew asking when she would be home for his graduation, then she quickly changed and got ready to leave with Jen. As they exited the trailer, she looked up and saw Jacob looking in their direction. It was obvious he saw her, but he didn't react. Instead, he looked back toward the scene being filmed. Still, Kat got an uneasy feeling in her stomach that something was not right.

As they walked back toward the dining hall to prepare lunch, Jen asked, "So, you sneaked off in the middle of the night last night? How was it? Was it everything you thought it would be?"

"Yes, and *much* more. It was *amazing*."

"Glad to hear it! Now I don't have to play match maker anymore!" Jen said, sounding relieved. "And I'm glad you finally admit to sleeping with him!" she continued jokingly.

Kat shot her a look of mock annoyance before answering with a laugh. "Believe me, if I could, I would shout it from the rooftops!"

When the set broke for lunch, Ian walked in to get food with Lydia, laughing at something she had said. He looked at Kat, though, and gave her a subtle nod of his head and a quick wink, sending her stomach somersaulting. She tried to keep busy and not just stare at him, but it was incredibly difficult. Still basking in the afterglow of last night, she was trying to wrap her head around how she had ended up being the one in his arms. She had to look up at one point, though, when she felt like she was being watched, and saw Jacob was once again staring at her. Even worse, he held her gaze defiantly when their eyes met. Kat turned away first, now concerned with trying to look engaged with something, and not like she was just staring out at Ian.

During the afternoon lull in the kitchen, she made up her

mind that she wanted to take a walk down to the set and see what Ian was filming for the day. The scene was theoretically an action sequence involving him riding his horse at breakneck speed and then jumping off, tackling a criminal he was supposed to be pursuing. Kat knew she shouldn't, but she couldn't help herself from being drawn in by both the excitement and fear of watching it all unfold. She grabbed Jen and told her that she should see the filming of the show before she left the next day. Jen knew exactly what Kat's motives were, however, and after having been on countless sets over her years in the business, she could have very easily done without, but she went with Kat anyway for moral support.

As they got closer, they saw Ian deep in conversation with George and the other actor from the scene. It was obvious that George was giving them last minute instructions to make it look better and more realistic. Ian glanced up in their direction as they approached the boundaries behind the crew. He looked exhausted and Kat felt a pang of guilt knowing why he was so tired. He must have felt her watching him still, however, as he quickly looked up and gave her a small smile, easing her mind slightly.

She held her breath as the scene played out before her and was thrilled when it went off without a hitch. Even though Ian had lied about his experience on a horse, he had since become a very skilled rider and he and his horse worked together seamlessly. The animal anticipated his every direction and accommodated him easily. George walked over to Ian and slapped him on the back, obviously pleased the scene had come together so perfectly. Ian was then dismissed and, as he walked past them without breaking character, tipped his hat slightly, saying "Ma'ams," in his American accent. Kat felt her knees go weak and her heart start to race, making her suddenly feel flushed.

She turned to Jen and said, "That is about the sexiest thing that I've ever seen! Why don't men still do that? We would all swoon. Wow!"

Jen laughed and said, "I don't know. The downside to equal rights, I guess. We sacrificed chivalrous men."

"Well, they need to be that way again! It works! I'd be putty in his hands right now."

The rest of the afternoon and evening was bustling with food preparation and clean up. Just as they were about to head back to the trailer, Kat got a text from Ian: *Wait there for me. I'll be there soon. Fancy a moonlit walk?*

She discretely showed Jen her phone and Jen nodded. "Hey, Kat, could you please stay and check the menu for the next couple of days against the supply list and make sure there is nothing we need to add before we go down to Calgary tomorrow? I don't want us to forget anything. Sometimes I feel like I threw y'all off your groove when I showed up in the middle of a smooth- running operation."

"Sure thing," Kat replied. "I'll see y'all later."

It wasn't more than five minutes later before Ian walked through the door. He closed the steps between them with long confident strides and immediately took her into his arms. "Hi,' he greeted her, before leaning down to kiss her.

"Hi!" she responded when he let up.

"Did you enjoy watching us film this afternoon?" he asked her, his eyes twinkling at her.

"I did."

"I could tell."

"More than anything, though, I wanted to jump into your arms right then and there when you walked past us and tipped your hat, calling us ma'ams. That was so incredibly hot!"

"I could tell that, too. Your eyes were burning a hole through me. Ready for our walk?"

"Absolutely."

They exited through the back and began to walk up into the woods. As soon as the night and surrounding trees had swallowed them up, Ian reached down and took her hand. There was just enough moonlight to wind their way up the trail.

"So," he said, swinging their hands playfully as they walked, "how was your night last night?" he asked her.

"Fabulous. Amazing! How was yours?"

"I'm a little tired," he admitted. When she was about to tell him she was sorry, he grinned and teased, "Because someone kept stealing the covers!"

"Me? Excuse me, but I was the one who woke up because I was cold, not you!"

"I think we more than warmed you up after that, though, didn't we?" he answered seductively, making her shiver at the memory.

"All right. I will give you that."

They walked along the trail in silence for a while until she asked, "So, what's our game plan?"

"How do you mean?" he asked her.

"I know we have to be discrete, but how do we do that and still find time to be together without one or both of us dying from exhaustion? It isn't exactly like I can just waltz into your trailer when everyone is still awake and having to wake up at four or four-thirty, I can't be waiting up until midnight every night until everyone else has gone to bed."

"I know," he said. "I've been thinking about that, too. Makeup told me today that I looked knackered. That's fine for a day of action scenes but may come back to bite me in the arse for closer shots."

"So, what do we do?"

"I'd say we bide our time. Enjoy being together like this, small walks, runs, rides. Take every opportunity we can to sneak off together when we are able and have you come to me at night now and then. It's still risky though, so we'll have to be cautious. Like this morning. Looking back on it, I should have asked Jen to bring your clothes to Lydia and then asked Lydia to bring them to you. Everyone knows you and Jen work together and it doesn't look any better—in fact it probably looks worse—to have her come to my trailer. It could look like I've moved on to my next conquest."

"Oh, yeah. I didn't think about that…"

"It's probably fine for today, but we will have to be more careful in the future. Maybe you should get some extra things from your trailer and give them to Lydia to put in mine so that we don't have to worry about that happening again."

"That sounds like a good idea," Kat responded, secretly thrilled with the prospect it would be happening again.

"I know this is less than ideal, but we only have about three more weeks up here, anyway. Hopefully, if we continue being careful, the executives will forget about adding any morality clauses to our contracts, and once they are signed, and we are done filming and back in Los Angeles, a lot of these issues will disappear. There are many more celebrities who are much more famous and interesting than Lydia and me, and the focus will shift even further away from us once it isn't all over social media that we are up here filming the next season. In fact, we'll probably be forgotten about in the time between wrapping up here and maybe a talk or awards show where she and I will have to be seen together again. Then, it will be calm again until the season we are just finishing airs. By that time, almost six months will have gone by, and Lydia and I can work out the final details from there."

"I understand. It's still less than my ideal, but I know I've accepted it."

"Mine, either, love. I promise we will be together as much as possible, though. You can always come to me with Lydia in the evenings and while it won't be so romantic, we can all still hang out. Some P.D.A. is okay, too," he said with a wink, "as it isn't a secret to her what's going on."

They stopped along the trail and Ian followed Kat's gaze to the stars and full moon above them. "Look at that!" he exclaimed.

"I know. I feel about these stars the way you talked about the mountains when we were first getting to know each other. It's almost as if you can see eternity."

"I haven't really seen a moon like this in a long time either. Probably since I was a lad on camping trips."

"You mean with the Irish Boy Scouts?" she teased.

"I do, indeed!"

"I never knew the heavens could look like this until I came up here. I had no idea these colors and milky appearance even existed. It's like God's masterpiece."

"You're religious, then, Kat?" he asked her.

"I am—I guess about as much as any Southern girl. How about you?"

"I grew up like just about every Irish child: Catholic. I'm not particularly devout or even that religious, but it has definitely left a mark on my immortal soul, I guess. It helped a lot when my father died. I was able to envision him among the angels in a place far better than here."

"That's so sweetly sad," Kat told him.

"How so?"

"It's sad that you had to think about that at such a young age. Even my grandparents were all still alive until just a few years ago. By then, they were older and had lived a good life, so while I was sad, I didn't feel that they were cheated. It must have felt like you and your father were cheated."

"It did. I was sad when I was younger. By the time I was a teenager, I'd become sullen and really angry. I loved my mother and my sister, and my grandparents were helpful too, but I had so many questions about my place in the world, girls, and what I wanted to do with my life, and I felt like I was alone. I needed my father. That's when my grandfather sat me down and really talked to me, and it helped straighten me back out."

"I can't even imagine how hard that must have been."

"It's certainly something I never hope to do to my loved ones," he responded evenly.

"But that scene today... Do you ever get worried that you will fall and get hurt doing a stunt like that?"

"Sure!"

"Then why do you still do it?"

"Because I can," he answered simply.

"How do you mean?"

"I mean that I like that I can do the physical stuff; it makes me feel like I'm not as old as I am. It satisfies my need for an adrenaline kick and makes me feel alive. 'Boys will be boys', and all that rubbish."

"You really are quite the horseman now," she told him.

"Thank you! I've gotten a lot better than I was, that's for certain."

They continued to talk as they walked back toward the set. Kat was glad he felt comfortable discussing his father with her in more depth, as it gave her a greater understanding into what made him tick. With all he had been through, she could easily see why he was so different from anyone else she'd ever met. He was ruggedly masculine, but it was mixed with a compassion that could only come from experiencing a great loss. Growing up surrounded by mostly women likely contributed, too. He had clearly learned to be the man of the house, tough and strong, but because of his loss and pain—and that of his family's—he also had great empathy and understanding. It was obvious he had engaged in years of introspection.

When they reached the edge of the trees, he held her back from stepping into the clearing around the set and bent down to gently kiss her on the lips. Kat was melting into him as his hands held her face and his lips danced on hers, the intensity between them growing the longer they embraced. When they finally pulled apart he implored, "Stay with me!"

"You have no idea how much I want to! But I don't think it would be a good idea."

He placed his forehead on hers as he ran his hands up and down her arms. "I know," he said sadly. "I just want to have you beside me so much. I know that six months is not a long time, really, but I don't want to be without you at night, especially now that I know what I'm missing." He groaned as he leaned down and kissed her deeply again.

"Oh God, Ian. Don't do that. I'm trying to be responsible and strong."

"You're making it very hard," he responded, and she could

physically feel his double entendre.

"Believe me, I know," she whispered.

After a few more kisses, they let go of each other and he watched as she walked away. When she'd gotten about halfway to her trailer, though, he sprinted up to her and grabbed her hand.

"Come on," he said in a low voice in her ear. He took her and led her to his trailer, looking around to make sure no one was around. Once the door shut behind them, he took her into his arms and kissed her with as much intensity as she had ever experienced.

"I… can't… yet… say… goodnight!" he told her in between kisses.

"Ian, are you sure? We're taking a big chance."

"I don't care," he said into her neck. "I'm a grown man. There isn't a person alive who should be able to tell me who to love."

"What about Lydia?" she asked breathlessly "I don't want to… get you… fired!"

"I really don't care at this point, honestly."

She really couldn't and didn't want to argue with him. Her reasons for being careful were irrelevant now that her divorce was about to be finalized. His and Lydia's need for anonymity and the potential impact on their career still mattered, however, and she didn't want to have this be something he would later regret if consequences of their rashness came crashing down.

"I'll stay with you until you fall asleep and then I'll leave," she told him.

"What I really want is to have you with me. Under me, more specifically," he replied with a roguish smirk.

"I know. I want that, too. But I don't want to be the reason you lose your job."

Without another word, he led her back to his bed.

He kicked his door shut behind him and she stretched up to meet his kiss. Brushing her hair to the side, he lightly kissed her neck from just under her ear to the top of her shoulder. She moaned and shivered beneath his touch. He ripped her shirt over her head, and she tried not to gasp as the back of his finger slipped between the lace of her bra and her skin. He caressed her breasts for a few seconds, before reaching behind and swiftly unhooking the clasp.

"You're getting better at that," she teased.

"Just more determined," he murmured against her lips. His scorching mouth moved lower and as his tongue danced around her breasts, while sighs and moans of desire escaped from Kat's lips. His every touch went straight to her heart. After a few seconds, her hands went instinctively to pull his shirt from his jeans. She clawed at it, her fingers searching desperately for the warmth of his skin beneath.

Slipping her index fingers under the sides of the waistband, she ran them around to the front, where she started working on the button. Already straining against the pressure building there, Ian groaned when Kat's ministrations released him from the confines of his pants. He rolled his head forward and put his forehead on hers. As she bent down to remove his pants, she paused to give him small, teasing kisses all around his most sensitive areas.

Ian was more than ready and even though he knew he should take more time with her, he hadn't been exaggerating when he said it would be difficult to hold back now that he knew what it was to make love to her. His need was building and knowing that being alone with Kat would be a rare event, his hunger for her was tinged with an air of desperation.

There was a flurry of clothing and blankets as they lay back on the bed, their limbs wrapped around each other. After several kisses, he rolled over the top of her. Once he started, it was only seconds before he released. Trying to catch his breath, he immediately apologized to Kat. "That hasn't happened in years! I'm so sorry!" he panted.

Kat tried hard not to giggle at the horrified expression on his face.

"It's okay!"

"No, really, it's not! I'm just so exceedingly attracted to

you, and then the anticipation makes it even worse when I don't know when we'll be able to do this again. I'm so incredibly sorry. Give me a bit, and I promise I'll make it up to you!"

"It's nice to know you are human," she reassured him. "It wasn't like I didn't enjoy it! It was incredibly erotic to see you so excited. I've never before experienced someone that enthusiastic to be with me."

"Like I said, it was because now I know what I've been missing," he mumbled into his pillow as he slapped it in frustration.

"Honestly, Ian, it's fine. In fact, it was very endearing."

"You haven't got any idea! This was all I was thinking about all day. Let's just say it was a good thing I didn't fall off my horse face first while filming, because I wouldn't have hit the ground all at once, if you catch my meaning. It certainly made riding an experience!"

Kat laughed. "Well, I'm truly glad you enjoy me so much that it happened."

He still looked embarrassed even after all of her reassurances. Meanwhile, she couldn't get over how incredibly alluring it made her feel to have a grown man perform like a teenager because of her. Never before had she felt so beautiful or enticing as she did at that moment, and true to his word, after a small respite, he did make it up to her, turning all of his attention and devotion to Kat's gratification. She hadn't ever experienced such incredible pleasure as he elicited, making every effort to ensure she was compensated for his previous early finish. He began by tenderly pressing kisses on her temple before lavishing them along her jawline. Pausing near her ear just long enough to whisper how much he adored her, he continued to work his way all the way down to her belly button and below. She gasped as he expertly maneuvered his mouth and tongue, making sure she was completely satisfied.

True to Ian's promise, it wasn't long before he was ready once again. This time, he moved unhurriedly, both of them savoring every sensation. He gazed into Kat's eyes as he thrust tantalizingly slowly above her, wrapping his arms around her, murmuring how much he loved her. When she felt she could no longer hold back, she succumbed to his expertise, yielding to her body's release. As the waves of pleasure rippled through her, his passion increased, obviously fueled by her response. Just as Ian was coming to his own satisfying completion she felt herself respond a second time to his concluding strokes. Her eyes popped open in shock, to see him gazing down and smiling at her.

As they lay exhausted and spent, still breathing hard, she shook her head.

"What?" Ian asked.

"Wow!" was all she could manage.

They snuggled into each other as their breathing slowed and he bent down and kissed the tip of her nose. "So did I make it up to you, then?" he asked with a grin, his eyes shining at her.

"I didn't know that was even possible. I thought to have that happen twice in a row was like finding the lost city of El Dorado: everyone always talks about it, but no one ever seems to get there."

"So, that's never happened before?" He was obviously quite pleased with his prowess after hearing of her body's accomplishment.

"No! It was very rare I would get there once!"

He laughed, his pride in what he had done evident. "I guess I was just getting warmed up the first time."

After several minutes had passed, Kat rolled over and looked at the clock. It was long past midnight, and she knew that it was now or never that she get up and slink back to her own R.V., though it was the last thing she wanted to do. She extricated herself from Ian's drowsy hold on her and he rolled over, propped up on his elbow, to watch her pull on her clothes.

"Kat, please don't go," he murmured sleepily.

"Ian, you know I have to. If I don't go now, I won't be able to drag myself out of here until morning again."

He nodded slowly and solemnly. "I can't wait until this is

all over and we can do what we want."

She pulled on her shoes while he rose up off the bed and walked around to her. Pulling her into his arms, he grumbled, "I can't wait until we don't have to leave each other."

"Me, either." She captured his lips with hers. "Goodnight, Ian."

He let her walk away from him but held onto her hand for as long as he could before he let it slip from his grasp. "Goodnight, Kat," he whispered.

She walked out the door, closing it gently behind her, and stood in the cool night air for a few seconds, taking deep breaths to try and get control of her feelings which were running at one hundred miles per hour through her heart. Willing herself forward, she had to struggle to put one foot in front of the other, fighting her urge to run back to Ian's arms and bed. When she finally arrived back at her own R.V., she felt as though she had run a marathon. She opened the door and quietly slipped past Melinda and Gerard's sleeping alcoves and into the bedroom she was sharing with Jen. As she fell exhaustedly into bed, she remembered Ian's endearing look of complete horror when he realized he'd climaxed early. Smiling to herself, her final thought before drifting off to sleep was, *At least I know he's not always perfect.*

Chapter Forty-One

Morning came much too quickly for Kat and as soon as she opened her eyes, her mood matched the gloomy skies as she realized it was the day Jen was heading back to Los Angeles. Knowing that Jen had to get home to Lucy and her recent reunification with David, Kat selfishly wanted her to stay with her. She loved having someone there who knew what was going on with her and Ian.

Soon after breakfast, Melinda grabbed the supply list while Jen retrieved her bag and Kat's divorce papers in preparation for her trip back down the hill to Calgary. As she and Kat stood in front of the car, Jen leaned over and gave her a hug. "Thanks for running everything up here so smoothly, Kat. It has been a huge relief to know that things were going well."

"Honestly, it truly is Gerard and Melinda. I feel a little like you've been paying me to do nothing but fall in love."

"It's not! You've kept things running as they're supposed to. You've done the meal planning, made sure you always have everything you need, and most importantly, kept George satisfied. That isn't easy!"

"Thanks, Jen. For everything! I'm going to miss you these next few weeks."

"My pleasure, Kat. And I would pay good money all over again for you to truly do nothing more than fall in love. I can't remember a time when I've seen you so relaxed and at peace. Ian seems to bring out the Kat I've known and loved for a long time, but no one else ever really got to see."

"I never have been happier. Truly, if nothing else, Ian has taught me what I want out of a relationship, even if it doesn't work out with him."

"Oh, it will work out, Kat. I've seen the way that man looks at you and the lengths he will go to pay you attention. He is a man in love. Frankly, Kat, it wouldn't surprise me if you end up marrying him by the time they come up here to film the next season."

"We'll have to see if there even *is* a next season," Kat responded, rolling her eyes.

Jen just shook her head. "Mark my words, Kat. One year from now, you won't recognize your life, and it will be a good thing."

Kat gave her a final hug before she climbed into the car.

Once they had pulled away, Kat went back to work, focusing on getting food prepared for everyone. She knew that things on the set were really picking up the pace now that there were only about three weeks left of scheduled filming. The schedule could be prolonged if necessary, but no one wanted that, especially those who would have to finance it. Ian had warned her that regardless of how much they tried to adhere to the schedule and how hard everyone worked, when it got close to the end, things would get crazy. She therefore had decided to focus on what she could control, which was to make healthy and accessible food to keep up the cast and crew's strength and morale.

When everyone finally dragged themselves into lunch much later than normal, they were caked in mud and dripping from the rain that had started to fall soon after Jen left. It was clear that it had not been a good day on set, and everyone was on edge. Ian and Lydia trudged in among the last group. He looked utterly done in and George was berating him about how tired he looked and was acting, telling him he needed to get his head on straight, before marching away. Ian noticed Kat watching him and he gave her a rueful smile before heading off with Lydia to spend their break going over the next scene. When they finished they got up and left without so much as a glance in Kat's direction. She tried not to panic but did wonder if he was still embarrassed about what had happened the night before or regretted not getting enough sleep. Seeing George tell him off reminded her that the show was his primary reason for being there and that he had a job to do. It was easy to get caught up in the romance and excitement of their new relationship, but when push came to shove, the reality was that Ian was still being paid to be the lead actor and it was crunch time.

A little after three, Melinda was back with the needed supplies. She, Kat, and Gerard worked together to put everything away and then prepped the evening meal. Kat had not heard from Ian all day and was trying to convince herself that it had nothing to do with her. Finally, at around five, he sent her a text: *So sorry. Rough day. Love you and see you when I can. Don't worry.*

She took a deep breath and continued on with her work. Everyone came in late again for dinner with many grumbles about failed equipment, missed lines, and leaking buildings. Ian and Lydia didn't show up until almost ten after Kat and her team had already cleaned up for the night. She sent Gerard and Melinda to bed while she warmed up some food for the two actors. When she brought over the plates, they both looked up, thanked her, but then immediately went back to their discussion.

Kat felt like a third wheel and didn't know what to do. The kitchen was cleaned, and everything put away, but she had to stay until Ian and Lydia finished. She didn't want to intrude, though, as they seemed to be having a heated discussion about how a scene had gone — Lydia was really angry that Ian had missed some cues and caused multiple takes. She tried hard not to listen, but she couldn't help but hear Lydia tell him, "Ian, I understand that you are excited about you and Kat, but honestly, you have to pull your head out! Like George said, get your head back in the game! I've never seen you this out of it or unprofessional before. George is getting pissed. What time did you go to sleep last night?" He merely glared at her in response.

"Ian, seriously. What time did you go to bed last night?"

He finally conceded, admitting, "Late."

"You've got to stop that!"

"I know, Lyds. I really do. But I just wanted to spend some time with Kat."

"It's only a few more weeks, Ian. That's all we have left, and we still have a third of the season left to shoot. I'm sorry, but Kat is just going to have to understand that it'll be all work without play. It will be long days and nights."

"Lydia, it isn't her. It's me. I begged her to stay with me last night. She actually left sometime around two."

They both got up and Kat rushed over to take their plates. "I'll take those," she said. After hearing what Lydia had said about her having to understand, she felt compelled to be overly accommodating.

Ian leaned over and gave her a kiss on the cheek. "It's going to be a long one. Now that it's finally warming up, the night shoots are starting, and they're brutal. I'll see you when I can."

"It's all right. Y'all go do what you need to do."

Lydia and Ian went back outside, and Kat finished the last of their dishes and went to bed. At 3:00 a.m., she got a text that said: *We just finished. Up and out again by 8. So tired. Love you and I'll see you ASAP.*

Kat smiled to herself and drifted back to sleep.

The next week was more of the same. Everyone was weary and no one seemed well-rested. They wandered in at all hours, requiring more of the craft services side than proper catering, demanding coffee, tea, and sweets to keep their energy going. Kat joked with Gerard and Melinda that the network should also film a show about zombies, as they had a whole set of people to use as extras and could save money shooting the two shows at once.

Ian texted her every night between two and three, telling her he was sorry and that he loved her. She rarely saw him outside mealtimes, and then he was unable to speak with her with so many other people were around. But he had warned her, so she was prepared. She missed him, but she knew that in just a few weeks, the craziness would all be over.

The following Friday morning, when they had been on set for hours the night before, Kat got the idea to bring breakfast to Lydia and Ian. She brought Lydia's to her first and then headed over to Ian's trailer. Completely worn out and disheveled, he looked amazing. He had opened the door and run his hand through his hair and then across the stubbly beginnings of a beard he hadn't shaved yet. Telling her to come in, she could see that he still had to get ready, so she didn't want to get in his way. She instead gave him a quick kiss on the cheek and told him she would see him later. She then turned around and almost ran smack into Jacob.

"Good morning," he said, sounding suspicious, his eyes questioning why she was there.

"Good morning! Just bringing Ian and Lydia some breakfast so they didn't have to take the time to come in this morning," she sang out to him over her shoulder. There still was something about him that made her skin crawl.

As things continued on this frenzied schedule, Kat and Ian rarely communicated in person beyond clandestine glances. Their relationship now consisted of a few texts back and forth, usually revolving around apologies from Ian for how everything was going.

The next Wednesday night, however, he sent her a text that said he was done early for the night and wanted to see her. He walked over to the kitchen around ten and they took a walk up into the woods. The night was dark, and they couldn't see very well, but as soon as they were up past the tree line, he began kissing her with unparalleled ferocity, apologizing in the brief moments between each embrace as she tried to assure him it was okay.

"This is all I've been thinking about. It's all that has kept me going," he told her. Given his intensity, Kat believed him.

After several minutes, they were able to calm down and take some deep breaths. "God, I want you so badly right now, but there are too many people around with everyone's crazy schedules."

"I know," Kat replied. "It's okay. It's just for a little bit longer."

"It's always tough by this point, but I've never looked forward to the end of a shoot as much as I am this one."

He once again set his lips on hers, conveying all he wanted to say but was too exhausted to put into words. His arms were around her waist, pulling her tightly into him as he shuddered slightly. Losing track of all space and time, Kat ran her fingertips up and down Ian's back deepening the passion between them. After a few minutes, he pulled back and took a deep breath. "We've got to stop," he sighed, resting his forehead on hers.

"I know," Kat said wearily.

"It's the last thing I want to do, but I have to get to bed. Tomorrow's going to be a long and grueling day and then Lydia and I have to run lines. I don't know when I'll get to see you next, and I can't stand it!"

"Really, Ian, I understand. Just take care of yourself. We'll have plenty of time later."

"That reminds me, Kat. What's going to happen when we are done up here?"

"How do you mean?"

"I mean, where are you going?"

"Well, in two more weeks, I have to go back for my boys' graduations."

"So, you've decided you're going home?" he asked, sounding slightly dejected.

"No. It's not home anymore. I'm going to go to my sons' graduations. Just like you're busy right now with your job, I'll be busy then with mine: being their mom."

"Then where will you go after?"

"I don't know, honestly. I was going to go back to live with Jen, but now that she and her husband are back together, I probably shouldn't stay there for more than a few weeks... I haven't really thought about it. I will have to think about getting my own place, I guess. Jen says I can keep working for her, so at least I have a job."

"Move in with me!" Ian blurted in a moment of desperation, feeling as though she was slipping away.

"What?"

"Move in with me!"

"What about having to stay under the radar? That will be virtually impossible if I live with you."

"I know. But I love you; I'm willing to take the risk. I just can't stand the thought of not seeing you every day."

"But what about your promise to Lydia?"

"Honestly, I'm finding it harder and harder to care about that."

"Ian, I won't let our relationship be the reason you break a promise to a good friend. Part of why I love you is your compassion and loyalty. You committed to helping her and I know why, but more importantly, I admire you for it. I promised you that I'm not going anywhere for as long as you want me, and I'll wait for however long it takes."

"But I don't want it to take long. That's my point. I want to be selfish and put my wants above everyone else's expectations. Compassion and loyalty are so much easier when I have no competing emotions, nothing to sacrifice. Kat, I want what I want, and more than anything, I want you."

"But, Ian, isn't your mother getting here soon? She needs to get settled and you need to find your groove with her before you bring anyone else into the mix."

"She is. She's actually coming a few weeks after you head home."

"Well, get her settled and let's see how things progress and we'll go from there, okay?"

"I guess," he responded, sounding dejected.

"Ian, I think you're so exhausted that you're not thinking this through clearly. You have a rare opportunity to go to bed relatively early tonight. Take advantage of it and sleep well."

"I don't want to. I'm exhausted, but I finally have some time to be with you. I hate that with everyone wandering around, we can't risk more than this." He kissed her forehead gently. "I'm so sorry. I know this is less than ideal."

"This is temporary. I knew it was coming. It was a bit of a shock, yes, but I'm over it now. Just hang in there—we're in the home stretch!" She reached up to lightly touch her lips to his one final time before they headed back to the set. "I promise I'm okay. You just focus on what you need to do."

"I love you, Kat," he told her emphatically.

"I love you, too. Sleep well."

***

The next morning dawned chilly and gray. Everyone was again grumbling about the weather, hoping it would hold because more rain would put them even further behind schedule, and there was talk about setting up extra lighting since the sky was so dark. Kat could tell everyone was stressed and desperate to wrap and go back to their regular lives. People were also sick of one another, and tempers were flaring.

The next time Kat saw Ian and Lydia, they were clearly involved in a very tense conversation. Kat couldn't hear what was being said but wished she could, given that they both kept glancing in her direction. When they were finished eating, Ian got up and walked out without even acknowledging her. Lydia, however, began to walk toward her and Kat's stomach started churning.

Here it comes, she thought, despite being clueless about what "it" was. Being the type of person she was, though, she automatically jumped to the worst-case scenario.

"Kat, I have to talk to you about something. Can you come back into the kitchen with me? I have some special dietary issues that will require a bit of extra work for you, I'm afraid."

"Um… Sure?" Kat could tell by her expression that Lydia was using this as an excuse to talk to her privately.

As soon as they reached the back of the kitchen, Lydia explained, "I've got to talk fast; I'm expected on set. Ian asked me to tell you that we are having a meeting with George tonight about our contracts for next season and that he won't be able to see you tonight, but that he loves you. You know he has to leave his phone in his trailer while on set, but he'll text you when he goes to bed."

Kat nodded. "Tell him that's fine. This crazy schedule is also requiring us to be here longer than usual, so I'm really busy, as well. Tell him I'm all right and I love him, too, please."

"Will do," Lydia confirmed as she turned away.

Kat finally returned to her trailer that night at eleven. Gerard had agreed to take the late shift, and Kat had never been more relieved to get off her feet. She had taken off her shoes and was just about ready to change when her phone chimed with a message: "Kat, get over here quick!"

She put her shoes back on and told Melinda as she headed out the door that Ian had texted her and she was going over to see what he needed. As she walked across the set, she wondered what was going on. There were too many people out milling around for him to risk her being seen coming into his trailer alone.

Arriving at the door, Kat knocked and was surprised to see it was Lydia who opened it. She beckoned for her to come in and closed the door behind them. Both she and Ian looked done in, but there was something else, too, written on their faces that Kat couldn't quite discern. Her stomach flip-flopped, even though there was no logical reason for her to be nervous. She opened her mouth and heard the words, "What's going on?" spill out.

Ian just looked at her solemnly, so Lydia began, "We just had our meeting with George."

"Oh?"

"Yeah. It didn't go well."

"It's bollocks!" Ian interjected. He was obviously very angry and trying hard to keep his temper under control.

"What happened? What did he say?"

"Well, it appears that you and Ian haven't been as careful as you should have been..." Lydia began.

"Stop that, Lyds," Ian interjected angrily. "We've been plenty careful. We've hardly seen each other in the last two weeks. Hell, we've hardly even texted."

"Well, someone had to have seen you!" Lydia snapped back.

"What is going on?" Kat cried.

"Our contracts," Ian spat out.

"What about them?" Kat asked glancing back and forth between Ian to Lydia.

"They included the clause," Lydia said in a matter- of-fact tone.

"They added the clause? Are you kidding? What does it say?"

"The morality clause they threatened us with. Ian and I are not allowed to have any sort of detectible public relationship with anyone else for the whole of this next year, through filming next season, or we will be fired.

"Basically, in order to keep our jobs, they're making us maintain the illusion that we're most likely in a relationship with each other for publicity purposes," Lydia explained.

"What?" Kat exclaimed. "Can they really be that specific?"

"I have a call into my agent again, but it seems that they can, because they did." Ian told her glumly. "They have us over a barrel, Kat. They know that we won't say no to another season because we need the work and love what we do, and they're counting on the fact that one of us will not let the other down."

"What are y'all going to do?" Kat asked flatly.

"Whatever we have to," Lydia responded. "We would be fools to give this up."

"That's where we differ, Kat," Ian answered, looking pained. "The problem is from how this clause reads, if I stand up to them myself, not only would I be sacked, but Lydia would be, too—one of us is replaceable, but both are not. They know this and used it to their advantage by making each of us contingent on the other.

"The fact is that technically my character is easily disposed of as the town sheriff, so I could be replaced without it affecting Lydia's part. But it would blow their ratings, so they are making it as difficult for that to happen as they can. We could try to call their bluff by both threatening to walk, but there's no guarantee it would work, and if they cancel the show, there are a lot of other people whose jobs would also be impacted.

"I'm still prepared to take my chances. Lydia's not. And she's trying to convince me to stick it out in case they really would sack both of us and cancel the show."

"For God's sake, Ian!" Lydia burst out. "It's only a year! We already discussed the fact that next year, after the third season has aired and the fourth is being filmed, if the show is still growing in popularity, we'll have more power to negotiate our next contracts."

"A year is a long time, Lyds," Ian said softly, walking over to Kat and taking her hand in his. "I'm not getting any younger. I want to settle down."

Kat looked at both of them. She knew what she had to do to keep Ian from doing something rash, still concerned that he was too exhausted to think rationally. "Ian, you can't give all of this up for me. Who knows if this will really work out? Maybe when we're done up here, we'll find out that it was just a fling. Maybe you're my rebound relationship after my divorce."

"You can't expect me to believe that," he said, the hurt evident in his quiet voice.

"All I am saying is that it's too soon to impact a lot of people's lives just for us; not when it's early days, like you said. A year really isn't that long… It'll work out if it's supposed to." She hoped that by sounding confident she could also convince herself.

"How did anyone even find out we are still seeing each other?" Ian cried out to no one in particular. "We have been so incredibly careful!"

All of a sudden, it hit Kat like a bolt of lightning. "Jacob," she whispered.

"What?" asked both Ian and Lydia at almost the same time.

"Your assistant. I think he's the one who knew! He came in here that morning you let me sleep in while you went to work. I hid between the open bedroom door and the wall. My phone chimed that I got a text, but he saw your phone and thought it was your message, I guess. I could see him through the gap: he picked it up, read something, and then smiled before he put it down and left. Once he was gone, I checked and saw it was the text Jen sent you about bringing me my clothes. All day afterward, he was watching me watching you. It had to have been him! No one else knew but Jen, Melinda, and Gerard, but none of them would have told anybody."

"Really?" Ian asked her. "Why didn't you tell me?"

"Really! I told Jen, but I guess I forgot to tell you with how busy things got."

"There's something about that guy I've never trusted, Ian. He seems a little too calculating," Lydia told him.

"That smarmy son of a bitch!" Ian erupted. "I will most definitely be speaking to him in the morning! I'm going to find out what that little *gobshite* knows!"

The three of them sat together in silence for a few minutes. Finally, Ian stood up and declared that he was tired and needed to go to bed. The women stood as well, and Lydia leaned over to kiss him on the cheek. "Goodnight," she told him.

Kat went over and stood in front of him. He seemed distant and preoccupied but managed to lean down and peck her on the lips. "Don't give up on me, Kat. We'll figure something out," he whispered.

"I know. It's okay, Ian. Like I said, if we are meant to be, everything will come together."

"Well, I'm fully committed to it working out," he stated. "Are you?"

"Yes, of course!" she declared, firmly.

"Good!"

"I'm only up here for a little more than week or so still. Then I go back for the boys' graduations. We can figure it out from there, all right?"

"Okay," he reluctantly agreed and gave her a hug.

As they walked out of his trailer and toward Kat's, Lydia turned to her and said, "I truly am sorry."

"It really is okay, Lydia. Like I said, if we're supposed to be together, I have to believe it will all sort itself out," she replied, trying to sound a lot more self-assured than she felt.

Lydia smiled gently. "Goodnight, Kat."

"Goodnight," she returned, closing the R.V. door softly behind her and wondering what would happen now.

Chapter Forty-Two

The next morning, neither Ian nor Jacob showed up for breakfast. Kat tried to keep busy but kept wondering what was going on. She saw Lydia, but the actress just shrugged her shoulders, letting her know that she didn't have any more information than Kat did. By lunch time, she was anxiously waiting for an update, but none ever came.

The push on the set meant that Kat, Gerard, and Melinda were pretty much in the kitchen non-stop from four-thirty a.m. to one or even three a.m. each night to make sure that everyone was able to eat when they could, even if it wasn't when they wanted. They all took turns stepping out to take small breaks or go and lay down, but no one was getting enough rest. By three p.m., Kat could hardly keep her eyes open, so she told her colleagues she was going back to the trailer to rest. She got settled in her bed and was out as soon as her head hit the pillow, but only an hour later, there was a knock at the door. Kat rose and answered, finding Lydia on the other side.

"Hi, Kat."

"Hi. What's up?"

"Ian's really busy today and very nervous about any more speculation, but he asked me to come by and tell you that you were right; it was Jacob."

"I knew it!" Kat cried.

"Yeah, apparently it was him all along. He picked up on you guys almost before you did and tipped off his cousin, who is a paparazzo, before you had even gotten down to L.A. for the break. The guy was waiting for you when you got there."

"What in the world? What would prompt him to do something like that? What a little weasel!"

"Money! What else?"

Kat just shook her head in amazement. "I still don't get how people think profiting off the lives of others is okay."

"Welcome to my world," Lydia chortled disdainfully.

"There are always people who are willing to make a buck on the backs of others. Now you see why I am so determined to keep private. The press would have a field day with my life story."

"Yeah, I guess they would. I'm sorry, Lydia. It must be terrible to have to always be looking over your shoulder, terrified that someone might figure out your secrets."

"That's the downside of this life. We live in a fishbowl and have to take the good with the bad. It was fine when the show was new, and we were off of their radar. No one cared about us. But as the show has gained popularity, so have we. People expect us to be together in real life simply because they like our chemistry on the show. I'm very worried about what will happen now when we go back home. The whole mess over the holiday break will mean we'll be under a lot more scrutiny.

"Before all of this, people left us alone because there wasn't any real story there. People just wanted so desperately to believe that we were a couple, even without us confirming it, and since it was such sweet thing to speculate about, everyone worked harder to try and prove it more than disprove it, if that makes sense."

"Yeah, I think so. Assuming you and Ian were a couple made people happy."

"Exactly! People wanted it to be true because it was a Hollywood fairy tale. That is until Jacob came along and saw an opportunity to make a profit."

"I don't know what to say, Lydia. I'm just sorry this happened like this."

"Me, too, Kat. To be honest, I'd never seen Ian so happy. I'm sorry that this had to happen just when you two finally got into a groove."

"Well, like you said, it's only for a year..." Kat sighed. "Tell Ian I miss him and that we *will* figure this out. Right now, I should be the least of his worries. Please tell him to focus on his job and that I'll be fine."

Later in the evening, she got a text from Lydia's phone. It said simply: *I'm so sorry. I can't risk sending this from my phone, so I borrowed Lyd's. We'll get this sorted out. I love you.*

Tired and distracted, Kat responded: *Yes, it will all work out. Don't worry.*

The next morning, Lydia approached her in the kitchen. Behind the counter, she handed her a folded piece of paper. When Kat looked at her with a questioning expression, Lydia only smiled and then turned and walked away. Kat put the paper in her pocket and focused on keeping everyone nourished until a lull in the mid- afternoon when she walked out the back door of the kitchen and pulled the piece of paper back out. She smiled softly as she began to read Ian's handwritten words flowing across the page.

My Love,

I can't figure out a way to speak to you privately like I want to. Since I can't seem to find the opportunity to tell you how I'm feeling, I figured I would go old school and write letters to you, which ironically seem more secure, at least until we are done up here. Lydia has graciously agreed to be my postal service.

Before I met you, I thought I was happy with my life. I had my dream job and felt that it was all I needed to be fulfilled. I had people who would tell me what I wanted to hear. I could find companionship with whomever I wanted. But, that first time I met you in the kitchen and you acted so normal, so unimpressed, you brought me up short. I knew that day, in that moment, that you were unique. You were the first person outside of Lydia and my family in a very long time to tell me like it is and not coddle me. I realised then that you were incredibly different from anyone else. I knew I couldn't impress you with my persona and instead had to be myself, and it was a scary realisation, honestly.

The day you fell, and I found you on the trail, I felt I was given an opportunity to show you who I really am.

That time in hospital was the first time in I don't know how long I allowed myself to relax and open up to talk about things that I had told very few people. My soul just surprisingly seemed to know even then that I could trust you enough to be vulnerable. I have not been disappointed.

Please don't give up on me, on us. I'm pleading with you to give me until we are done up here to figure this all out. Promise me that you won't overanalyse. I swear none of this is a reflection of how I feel about you. At this point, I'm just too exhausted to think clearly. I feel that I'm being forced to choose between the love of my job and the love of my life, and to give up either would break my heart and spirit. Please know that if I could do this any other way, I would.

I know what I'm offering is far less than you deserve, but I'm a spiritual man who's praying vehemently that you see the potential in us enough to give us this year until we can have what we both really want and deserve. I know my feelings won't change for you during that time and hope that yours won't, either. I've never felt this way about anyone in my life thus far. It's as if you were made for me but it has taken me a lifetime to find you.

When you get back to L.A., I am determined to find a way to make this work. I promise we will see each other as much as possible. Please don't think that just because I'm going ahead with this ridiculous demand that you are not the most important thing in my life. You're all I think of when I wake in the morning, when I go to sleep at night, and most of the time in between. I see us growing old together. Please, please just give me this year and I promise I will then give you a lifetime worthy of you. I love you.

All my love, Me

The final words became blurry as her eyes filled with tears. She had never received a hand-written love letter before. Never before had anyone made her feel so valued, so special as he had with his tender words. All of her life, she felt that she was constantly disappointing everyone with everything she wasn't.

Now, she felt for the first time as though she was truly loved and adored for everything she was, without even trying. She collected herself and headed back into the kitchen, back to help Gerard and Melinda with the work for the evening.

When Ian and Lydia came in with several others to get their food, it was after nine o'clock and once again, they were engrossed in conversation. But every once in a while, she felt like she was being watched and would glance up to see Ian studying her, his eyes asking her a question. Though there was so much she wanted to say to him, she knew she could only give him a small smile and go back to her tasks. When they left, Kat was extremely frustrated about being so disconnected from him, having him so near, but not being able to talk to or touch him. She wanted nothing more than to fall into his arms but knew that there was nothing she could do to change their situation. *It's only for a little while longer*, she told herself resolutely.

She walked back to her trailer and decided that she needed be able to communicate with him, too, so she found a piece of paper and a pen and began to write. It felt so antiquated to correspond that way and she actually struggled after writing half a page, as her hand began to cramp. She laughed to herself about how spoiled everyone had become with the advent of technology, making writing by hand basically obsolete. At the same time, though, she felt a connection with what had flowed out onto the paper, much more so than when she would type something out in a flurry of activity, not truly planning what she wanted to say in advance. Somehow the physical act, writing by hand in her own belabored words, felt so much more intimate.

Dearest,

Thank you for your beautiful letter. Thank you for taking the time to write to me. Never have I felt so loved and cherished as I did reading the words that you took the time to write out, especially when I know how hard you're working right now and how tired you must be.

As I write this to you in reply, I feel that handwritten letters are a dying art that needs to be rekindled. There's something so romantic, so intimate, in having to really think about what one wants to put down on paper when simply backspacing is not an option, when deletion isn't possible. What we write on these pages has the potential to survive any changes in programs or operating systems.

I'm sitting here thinking about you and how to tell you how deeply I feel for you. First off, I miss you... terribly. I'm honestly wondering how I can feel so lost without someone whom I've only known for such a short amount of time. I'm confused about how strongly I feel about you after only three months and wonder how it can instead feel that I have known you for a lifetime?

Please don't worry about the issue with the contract. We discussed this, and I knew it was a very real possibility. I also thought very long and hard about it before I agreed to pursue our relationship, knowing the risks. My only complaint is that I didn't know how much I would miss talking and interacting with you! I feel like I'm going through withdrawal, and it's made all the harder by knowing we are both here but cannot be together. I fight myself every night not to go to you. I know, though, that it could get you fired, and I cannot risk that for you; I won't. I know this is your dream and I would not do anything to jeopardize it for you.

I'm fine, truly. As I've said before, I know that this is who you are, and I admire your dedication and compassion. I know you're doing this because of a promise to a friend and that kind of loyalty and sacrifice proves how incredible you really are. Those qualities are what made me fall in love with you and I know that you will treat me with the same level of devotion.

Though it feels like forever, two weeks isn't that long. Soon all of this will be over, and we'll see what the next chapter holds. I truly hope that you will continue to be the main character in my continuing life story.

Yours, K-

She folded the paper and resolved to somehow get it to Lydia in the morning. She fell asleep with a smile on her lips, feeling closer to Ian even though he had not been physically near her in several days.

***

The next morning, Kat kept feeling the paper in her pocket, reassuring herself that it hadn't fallen out. She waited until Lydia came in with Ian and she walked over to them to say good morning. She then went to work arranging the corn muffins and biscuits on a tray, standing close to Lydia, while their backs were turned to the tables in the room. She slipped the paper from her pocket and grabbed a plate, holding the letter underneath and handed it all to Lydia. "Here's a plate for you!" she told her cheerfully and then walked away. Lydia looked a little taken aback until it registered what she was holding on the underside of her dish. A look of understanding came across her features as she quickly grabbed a napkin and placed it under her plate, as well. She continued with getting her breakfast and walked with Ian to a table. Kat wasn't sure how or when Lydia would be able to slip the letter to Ian, but she knew she had no other option than to trust that Lydia would.

Over the next few days, their "postal system" continued to work. Ian would write Kat a letter which Lydia would hand her at night, and she would have one to hand back in the morning. Depending on the type of day they had had, the letters were varying in length, but the sentiments were always the same. However, as she read Ian's progressively expressive declarations, Kat began to worry if this was too good to be true. Five days after the first letter, her doubts began to creep in. She tried to push them to the back of her mind, but they lingered in her psyche, playing upon her insecurities.

Dearest,

The next morning, Kat had butterflies in her stomach as she managed to hand off her letter to Lydia. She felt anxious and unfocused all that day and the next, taking deep breaths to calm herself. Two days later, Lydia still had nothing for her. She began to panic until Lydia sent her a text late that evening.

Long days yesterday and today. Be patient.

Even with Lydia's message, Kat began to worry even more that perhaps her letter had struck a chord with Ian, too, and had him also thinking that this perhaps was not reality, but rather like a scene from a movie or play where two people were merely acting their parts.

The following day dragged on. She had not written another letter because she felt that until she heard from him, she really had nothing more to say. All through breakfast and lunch, she tried not to get agitated that he had not yet responded. *He is busy!* she would chastise herself. *I'm not the only thing on his mind right now. He'll get back to me when he can.*

Still, for the rest of the day, there was nothing. She didn't even see either of them that evening because she had taken the earlier shift in the morning; Gerard was handling the late diners and the clean-up alone that night.

In the morning, three days after she had given Lydia the letter, she finally received a response. She was in the middle of breakfast and starting lunch prep, so she shoved the paper she got from Lydia into the pocket of her chef's jacket and tried to focus on her responsibilities until she was able to take a break in the early afternoon. Though exhausted herself, she decided to take a walk up the trail to the beautiful meadow and lake before reading the contents. She made it to her destination, took a deep breath when she had settled herself on the grassy shore, and pulled the paper from her pocket.

My Love,

I apologise for the delay in giving you a response. Your last letter gave me a lot to ponder, and I wanted to mull it over before I answered you, so I could respond with logic rather than emotion.

I can see how you could worry that what we are perhaps feeding a delusion we have created with our hopes and dream for the future. However, I don't feel this way; I am very cognisant that what I'm putting into words on this paper is exactly how I feel about you. Though we haven't known each other long, I know exactly who you are.

I'm concerned that you seem to be under the impression that

I'm falling deeper in love with you only because I'm getting caught up in the romanticism of not being able to see you and, of course, then carrying that through to these subsequent letters. I assure you, though, that I do not see this as a modern-day Romeo and Juliet situation, but rather these letters are merely a means for me to communicate with you when we are apart. While they do make me long for you all the more, I was already infatuated with you on some level from the first day we met, and it has only grown from there.

So, I'm writing not to be some quixotic hero, but because I'm unwilling to let this time go by without telling you how I feel about you. It's killing me that due to our current circumstances I can't see you, so I'm instead forced to write down how much I care for you rather than tell (and show) you in person. I will say that I feel a bit ridiculous to be this distressed, as two weeks is not a long time in the greater scope of things, but I promise you that I've spent this time- too much time, truth be told- thinking about us objectively. I can tell you that I feel a whole piece of me has suddenly gone missing and the need to feel closer to you while we are apart is overwhelming. You are all I think of while I'm awake, and I dream of you at night. The one thing this forced separation has taught me is that I know with certainty after this is over, I don't ever want to be apart from you again.

I meant what I said when I told you that I've never felt this way about anyone before. Now, when I think about my future, I can't imagine you not in it. I implore you to please think seriously about what I asked you that night amongst the trees. I want you to move in with me. I don't know how we would make it work, but I'm determined to find a way. All I know is that I need to fall asleep with you at night, every night, and wake up with you every morning.

So, to address your concerns, no, I do not think that our communicating by letter is idealising anything that wasn't already there. I'm selfishly doing it for me, because while I write, I imagine you here with me, laying with me in bed, and it quells my loneliness.

I have always loved letters not only because texts and emails can be easily hacked or read by others, as we have already discovered, but because they are much more intimate. Believe me, though, when I say that I am not writing you anything that I would not tell you in person or over more modern modes of communication. Please don't doubt how I truly feel for you. Move in with me....

With all my love, Me

Kat reread his letter several times, wondering how to respond. Though while he was saying all of the right things, she still wondered if he was moving too fast. He really seemed to be taking the old adage of absence makes the heart grow fonder to heart. She knew he had asked her to move in with him before all hell had broken loose, but she also knew he was naturally exuberant and spontaneous, and so she hadn't been sure if he had been caught up in the moment and asked before really thinking through the ramifications. While what he was relaying to her was consistent and precisely what she wanted to hear, she still wasn't convinced that he wasn't feeling pressured to move their relationship along at faster pace in response to the looming end of their secluded world in the mountains.

Time was becoming an issue. There were only five scheduled days left of filming for this season. Everyone had moved passed exhaustion to the point of near collapse and Kat was still convinced his lack of sleep was clouding his judgment when she responded.

Dearest,

Your last letter was lovely. The way you write continues to take my breath away. I feel like a heroine straight out of a romance novel.

I've been doing a lot of thinking, too, and I wonder if perhaps we are moving too quickly because we are both feeling

402

the pressure of knowing that this is all coming to an end? I wonder if you are perhaps saying you want me to move in with you because you are worried about what will happen next between us? I can't help but wonder if you would still feel this same way if we had met in Los Angeles?

Having just come out of a twenty-three-year relationship with someone I thought I loved, I want to make sure that momentum, comfort, or ease and/or complicity are not the driving forces behind your haste in pushing our relationship on to the next level.

To be honest, a year of being low-key and moving slowly doesn't sound so bad to me. I want to make sure of my feelings, and yours, as well, before we jump feet first into something that we should not do on a whim.

I do love you and I do want to pursue our relationship, but please do not feel as though you have to rush the natural progression of things for my sake.

I miss you and our talks. If nothing else, I look forward to when we will have the freedom and privacy to communicate with each other whenever and however we would like.

Please thank our postal worker for continuing to be our go-between.

Yours, K-

Kat did not receive an answer back for a long time. Things were so crazy on set that she, Lydia, and Ian were hardly ever in the same place at the same time anymore. Everyone was panicking about wrapping up and making up for lost time due to poor weather, illness, and injury. For Kat, it was fascinating to see how the air around them seemed to hum with the stress and tension in this final push until the minute the cameras started rolling and everyone instantly became a consummate professional.

The few times Kat actually made it out of the kitchen between the almost non-stop food prep that was now required and beginning to pack and clean in preparation for the trip back to L.A., she was surprised to see that Ian and Lydia were just as adept in their roles as they had been at the beginning, when things were more relaxed. One would never know by watching them that it was frantic chaos all around them. She also understood why Ian's letters were not coming as frequently when she saw what they were up against.

The few times they actually got to see each other, they would lock eyes and hold their gazes until the very last possible second. If they were very lucky, and he was walking with someone, they were able to exchange quick pleasantries, each inquiring how the other was doing, but there certainly wasn't any time or possibility for private, in- depth conversation.

The next time Lydia handed her a letter, Kat hadn't seen Ian at all. She asked Lydia if he was all right and was assured that he was just incredibly busy, but Kat's anxiety drove her to want to read his letter immediately. She had a feeling that this letter was one she would want to read carefully and respond to right away. In her anticipation, the walk back to the refuge of the R.V. seemed to take forever. Her hands were shaking by the time she sat down on the bed and opened the folds in the paper to reveal his now familiar handwriting.

My Love,

I must say that I am concerned with the tone of your last letters. It feels as though you are pulling away.

I'm not moving fast because of any other reason than that I love you and now that I have finally found you, I don't want to waste any more time. I know that because I'm an actor you seem to think that I'm being overly passionate or dramatic about our situation. I'll confirm that I am indeed passionate about you; more passionate than I've ever been about anything before in my life, but it is honestly not making me do things in haste.

I am concerned that you seem to be looking for reasons to pull away because you are worried I'm going to hurt you. You asked me in one of your letters if this relationship happened only because we were isolated up here on location, and if I had met you in Los Angeles, would I have ever given you the time of day?

I have been thinking a lot about this and while I assure you that I would notice you anywhere in the world, I can't help but ask you the same thing. Would you have paid me any attention, or taken me seriously, if we had met in Los Angeles?

After much introspection, the only thing I can say for certain is that it would have been different. I don't think it would have happened so quickly or so easily. Having been on sets there, I can tell you that there is a definite separation between the supporting staff and the actors, much more than there is while on location where everyone is thrust together almost all of the time, so it gets intense.

Back there, we all have our own lives and when we go home, work is just that: work. But I still would have questioned you about grits, and you still would have answered, so yes, rest assured that I would have found you in L.A. and fallen for you there, as well, for all that you are and which others are not.

I can't force you, nor can I seem to convince you. All I can think to do is tell you again that I love you. I'm keenly aware that what I am offering is not what you deserve, nor is it what I want. It pains me greatly that you'll be forced into the shadows for the next year. What I really want is to shout out to the entire world that I am in love with you, that I have finally found you. You have changed my focus and opened my eyes.

But I have promised you all the while that we will go as fast or as slow as you want, and that has not changed. You can't know how sorry I am that all I can offer you at the moment is dictated by the people who sign my paycheque. If I hadn't just bought my house or wasn't preparing for my mother to move over here, I would just walk away from all of it to be with you. But acting is all I know, so instead, all I can do is try to assure you that regardless of what the world thinks, you are the one for me and there will never be anyone else. I love you.

Kat felt like she couldn't breathe. She was scheduled to fly out to get back for her sons' graduations in three days. She already knew that despite her earlier epiphany, she had been doing exactly what Ian had suggested she was doing, but she was surprised he was astute enough to notice that she was pulling away, again trying to protect herself from heartbreak and rejection. For what felt like the millionth time in the last three months, Kat reminded herself of the conscious decision she had made to not let the fear of "what ifs" dictate how she would pursue what she wanted, but old habits die hard… She grabbed a piece of paper and wrote her reply.

My Dearest,

You're right. I am pulling away from you once more for fear of being hurt. I'm preparing myself for the very real possibility that once we leave this safe haven and have to deal with the real world that we may feel differently about each other, more specifically, that you will feel differently about me. I want desperately to believe that won't happen, but based on my recent life experiences, I have to say that I am more of a pragmatist than you are.

Real life—paying mortgages and going to work every day— is not romantic and it can be grueling. I know through experience that sometimes love alone is not enough, and sometimes what we think is love is not.

I will always be grateful for what I've received from you in these last few months. You have given me a reason to smile, made me feel beautiful, and showed me that I could open my heart to someone again. I pray that when we get back to reality and the everyday struggles of life that this will continue, but I also know that relationships are hard, and it will only be made harder when we have the added burden of having to be so careful to hide the fact that we are involved. I'm so terrified that you will risk or give up everything only to one day discover I'm not worth it.

I promised you that I will give this a shot. But I can't promise that it will all work out and we will live happily ever after, which is why I can't move in with you and have you jeopardize everything else in your life. All I can guarantee you is one day at a time and pray that you will not be disillusioned.

I'm going back for the boys' graduation in three days. I haven't figured out how long I will stay or when I'll return to L.A., but when I get back, let's see where we are. Let's see if in a few weeks' time, when we are back to the grind, if we feel the same way; if you feel the same way.

I know I do care for you very deeply, probably more than I've cared about anything or anyone before, except for my children. Therefore, my greatest fear is that one day you will wake up and decide that you made a mistake because we acted too recklessly.

I know that you will be busy these last few days. I don't expect a reply. But know that I'll contact you when I'm back in L.A., and I promise we will go from there.

Please take care of yourself and know that you have been instrumental to my journey of personal discovery over the last few months. Whatever happens, I wish you the best and hope that we will always be friends.

Yours, K-

Hurrying back to the kitchen because time had gotten away from her and it was now well past Melinda's scheduled turn to rest, Kat folded the letter and put it in the pocket of her chef's whites. In the craziness of the evening meal and clean up, coupled with her exhaustion, she forgot about the letter and hung her jacket on the wall when she finally left for the evening. It wasn't until noon the next day, when she put her hand into her pocket, that her memory was jogged as soon as she felt the cool, smooth paper beneath her fingers. Not knowing when she would see Lydia again, she decided to take it to her trailer and managed to slip it under the crack at the bottom of the door. She then took a deep breath, squared her shoulders, and walked away.

The next day was filled with last minute preparations for Kat's impending departure. She felt guilty about leaving Melinda and Gerard up there for the remainder of the shoot, though it looked as if everyone's hard work was paying off and that the filming would not extend much past the original date of completion. Her colleagues were fine with her leaving, assuring her that of course she should go back for her kids' graduations and that once everything was finished, they would be fine to pack up and drive back to Los Angeles without her. The fact that she had yet to receive a reply to her last letter played in the back of her mind, but she was too busy and keyed up about what was awaiting her at home to let it be forefront in her thoughts.

The morning of her departure, Gerard put her bag in the car and gave her a hug. Melinda was going to run down the hill for what was hopefully the last time to get supplies after she dropped Kat off at the airport. They climbed into the car and as they drove down the road Kat's tears began to silently fall. Melinda glanced over at her and asked her if she was okay.

Kat smiled and said, "Yes, of course. I'm just having to say goodbye to a very special place. Up here in these mountains is where I found myself when I didn't even know I was lost. I feel like I'm leaving a friend. I don't want to return to reality. These three months up here have been the best time of my life. But, no matter what happens from now on, I know I will be okay."

***

Back on location, Ian finally had a chance to read the letter Lydia had given him the night before. As soon as he could the following morning, he had hurried over to Kat's trailer just a few minutes after Melinda and Kat had pulled away. Finding nobody there, he jogged to the kitchen and found Gerard. He called out to him, "Hey! Have you seen Kat?"

"Yes. You just missed her. She and Melinda left about five

minutes ago."

Ian ran his fingers through his hair and tried to hide his agitation. "Okay. Thanks," he managed to call back as he walked away.

He couldn't believe that he had been so close. He was just minutes too late from being able to tell her that he didn't care about the ramifications; he was choosing her. Feeling his eyes well up, he thought about how stupid he had been to let his ego get in the way of talking to her last night when he had read her last letter. As he lay awake in the early morning hours, he had finally realized that she wasn't telling him goodbye, she was merely giving him the opportunity to do what he loved without feeling pressured by her. Her selflessness was the final nudge he'd needed.

He also realized that he had not given her a lot of reason to believe that he meant it when he had told her she was the most important thing in his life. After repeatedly choosing his career and his promise to Lydia over Kat, and with her damaged self-esteem, he now realized that his words would never mean as much as his actions.

He had one more scene left to film that day and so, as he took the final steps back to Main Street, he shook his head slightly, took a deep, cleansing breath, and told George, "Let's do this so we can go *home*!"

Chapter Forty-Three

As the plane touched down at Hartsfield-Jackson, Kat took a deep breath and blew it out to calm herself before she made her way through customs and out to the arrivals area. After glancing around she saw her mother and father waiting for her, and quickening her pace, closed the gap as she reached out her arms to encircle them both. She placed kisses on their cheeks and held on tight for a few seconds before stepping back and saying, "Hello!"

"Hello, sweet pea! Well, look at you! You look so... healthy! That mountain air certainly has worked its magic on you. Look at you, comin' back all au natural," her mother drawled.

"Thanks, Mama," Kat said, choosing to not let the dig about her natural, unmade-up appearance affect her. Instead, she thought back to what Ian had said early on, that he wanted a woman who could roll out of bed in the morning after a night of loving him and not take three hours to get ready.

"Hello, beautiful!" her father drawled, as he pulled her in for a quick peck on the cheek. "Sure has been lonely round these parts. I'm glad that Canada finally gave me back my sunshine!"

They walked to the parking garage and climbed into her father's car. As they drove out, she looked at the drab, boringly familiar scenery around the airport and felt like she was dreaming. In her heart she was still surrounded by the serene beauty of the expansive prairie sky where it met the towering rocky peaks of the mountains. Unwilling to accept her reality and acclimate to the change in environment, she longed to return to the trees, grass, and flowers that had become so familiar in the last three months and reminded her of precious memories. Closing her eyes, she was instantly transported back to the meadow and lake, which she had dubbed her and Ian's private retreat. Sighing, she quickly realized that it was quite possible she would never see that amazing place again in her lifetime.

"What's the matter, sugar?" her mother asked. "Tired?"

"Yeah, a little," Kat admitted. "These last few weeks have been grueling to say the least. Toward the end there, we were keeping the kitchen running pretty much twenty-four hours a day, each of us taking eight hour shifts on a rolling schedule, to keep up with the crew and actors. They were filming pretty much twenty-four/seven."

"Sounds excitin'! Did you get any good dirt on what will be happenin' next season? You know, I started to watch that show after all that unsavory business with you and that Ian guy came out. I have to admit that I'm hooked!" her mother told her.

Kat laughed, "Yeah, he has that effect on people." She then realized what she had said and that it would now open a discussion she wasn't prepared to have with them yet.

"Who does, sugar?"

"Oh, I meant the show. It kind of sucks you in. I did help Ian run some of his lines, but I had to sign non- disclosure agreements when I got up there stating that I wouldn't talk about anything in the upcoming season. I can tell you it will be great though!"

"Well, that's just too bad, then." Her mother seemed to pout. "Have you spoken to James?"

"Yes, Mama. We have been texting back and forth. Now that the divorce is finalized, we have actually become friends of sorts again. We have been talking about the kids and planning the parties. He asked me to cater them, so I'll be going up to the old house in a few days. Speaking of which, could I borrow your car, Mama? Mine is still in L.A. at Jen's house."

"That'll be fine, darlin'," her dad interjected, before her mother had a chance to respond.

Her mom turned back to look at Kat in the seat behind her. "So, I'm sure that you know two of your brothers are comin', too?"

"Yes, Mama. They both texted me to let me know."

"Oh, good. I wasn't sure if you had contacted them after all of this nonsense."

Kat sighed. This was not going to be easy. *It was true what they say: you can't go home again*, she thought.

"Christopher said that he and Jessica and the girls were coming. I haven't heard more about Thomas' plans though, other than that he's coming."

"Laura is comin' with him too, but they are leavin' the kids at home with her parents. Somethin' about how it was too close to the end of the year. I'm sure that you know Jonathan is travelin' in Europe right now for work, so that's why they won't be comin', though I don't understand why Ellen couldn't have come by herself with the boys…" Kat's mother huffed.

Probably since he's the first born, she will never be good enough for him in your eyes, especially since she's a Yankee! Kat thought as she rolled her eyes heavenward.

"So, tell us about what happened up there," her father asked. He realized what he had just said; how it could prove the perfect opening for his wife to begin to interrogate Kat, so he quickly added, "I mean how was it?" and cleared his throat.

Obviously, neither of her parents knew how to broach the subject of Ian and their purported affair. Kat was kind of enjoying watching her parents squirm and decided to play along, just because she could.

"Oh, you mean what else did I do besides supposedly getting involved in a clandestine affair with a totally amazingly hot man?"

Her parents looked at each other before her mother said simply, "Yes," and quietly coughed into her hand. Kat decided it probably wasn't the time to expound upon how wonderfully intimate she and Ian had been, both in and out of the bedroom.

"It was great! So beautiful! The mountains are breathtaking. I would go for runs, hikes, and horseback rides as often as I could. My friend Ian often times went with me, and it was a great chance to get to know each other better." Even though she knew it would be awkward to talk to her parents about a man other than James, Kat decided that if she was going to be resolute in leading her own life, it would be necessary to make them uncomfortable. Ian had been too much of an integral part of her life for the past three months to just ignore.

"So, I guess a reconciliation with James is definitely out of the question, then," her mother stated sadly.

"Yes, Mama. We're divorced. Even without Ian, I've come to realize that I was not living up to my full potential. I've discovered that there is so much more to me than just being a wife and mother. I have passion!"

Her mother gasped.

"Not like that, Mama!" Kat admonished, though she realized that her mother wasn't far off in that department, either. Somehow, though, she figured that sharing her new- found discovery that she was capable of multiple orgasms was something that would cause both of her parents to have heart attacks and die right there.

"Sweet pea?" her mother inquired in a desperate attempt to change the subject after several seconds of silence.

"Yes, ma'am?"

"What is the plan, then? Where are you goin' to live? What are you goin' to do?"

"First I'm going to get through these next few weeks. Then, I'm flying out to Los Angeles and I'm planning to work with Jen for a while. She and David are reconciling, so I don't think I can stay there with her at the house for too long, but I'll find myself a small place and go from there. It will be the first time in my life that I don't have to answer to anyone, and it feels amazing!"

"Jen's reconcilin' with David?" her mother asked, sorrowfully.

"Yes. Why?'

"I guess I'm just surprised to hear that. I thought it'd be you and James who would reconcile, not Jen. She always seemed like she was a rollin' stone. Now, y'all seem to have flipped roles."

Kat sighed and then took in a sharp breath. "Mama, I'm just going to get this out of the way now. I'm sorry that things didn't work out between James and me, and I'm sorry that mine was the first divorce in the history of either side of our family. But I won't apologize for standing up for myself and not getting walked over. I found my voice, and most of all, I found myself. I don't know what will happen with Ian, but I can tell you that he had no bearing on my decision to end my marriage. He was actually very concerned about me and wouldn't allow us to sleep together while I was still married." Both of her parents choked.

"Kat, you really shouldn't be talkin' about details like this with your parents!" her mother bristled.

"Why not? Ian became important to me. Also, I was married and have three kids. It shouldn't come as a shock to y'all that I have sex. I don't know what will happen now that we are going back to our regular lives, but regardless, I value what he did for me as a person. He became a very close friend and someone I hope will continue to be a big part of my life. But if he can't, or won't, then that's okay too. I'm just grateful for him showing me that I am beautiful and relevant and have a lot more to offer than my ability to cook, keep house, and make a Christmas card look good."

Her father again cleared his throat, looked back in the rearview mirror, and caught Kat's eyes as he said, "Baby girl, that is all any father would ask a man to do for his daughter."

Her mother could only gape at him, too shocked to know what to say. A few seconds later she finally reprimanded him, "But they aren't married!"

"So what?" her father countered. "She was married and look what that got her. It certainly didn't stop James from doin' what he did. I think it's actually quite noble that this Ian has enough respect for our daughter that he was willin' to do what was in her best interest, while the man with whom she was legally wed could not keep his pants zipped!"

A shocked silence fell over the car. Being Southern, Christian, and ruled by social norms that were sometimes behind the rest of the country's, sex was not something that was often discussed, especially between a father and his daughter.

Kat finally broke the silence, "Thanks, Daddy."

The car remained quiet for the rest of the trip as there wasn't much left to be said. Kat was satisfied in the realization that she had, for the first time in her life, not let her mother's opinions of her dictate how she felt about herself or what she said to her.

***

The next few days flew by in a blur. Kat and James had indeed been doing a lot of texting and had decided they should get together over the weekend to start packing up the house in preparation for it to be sold. A little apprehensive, she drove to her old town, through her old neighborhood, and pulled up the driveway. She was really surprised to find it didn't feel like home anymore, even though she had lived there for the better part of two decades. As she looked over the brick façade, the front porch with the matching white rocking chairs under the porch fans, the flowers and the rose bushes planted by her own two hands, she was truly astonished that she felt so little connection to the place. She expected the memories of the life her family had shared together to come flooding back, but instead, she felt disengaged and a little awkward. It was as though she were disturbing something sacred from the past, a sort of museum display of a life belonging to someone else from long ago.

As she continued to the front door she saw her neighbor, Jill, working in the yard next door. She glanced up at Kat and then did a double take before standing up and walking over to her.

"Kat, is that you?" she asked.

"Yes! Hello, Jill! How are you?"

"I'm okay. How are you doing? I'm so sorry to hear about the divorce. I really thought y'all would be two of the ones who would make it."

Kat smiled at her sadly. "Yes, it certainly wasn't in my plans, but sometimes what we think our lives are supposed to be and what they actually are become two very different things."

"But you're doing all right?"

Kat had always enjoyed Jill. She felt like she could be

415

candid with her, as they had shared many of their ups and downs throughout the years they had lived next door to each other. "Jill, actually I'm really good! For the first time that I can remember, I'm truly happy. It hasn't been easy, but it was necessary!"

Jill smiled back at her. "That's good to hear, Kat. I'll be sad to lose y'all as neighbors. Y'all've been great. But I'm glad that you're happy and I wish y'all the very best." She leaned in and gave Kat a hug with one arm, still holding her gardening shears, while her other hand held her sun hat on her head.

"Thank you, Jill. I'll miss you, too."

Jill returned to her yard as Kat went up the front steps and stood outside the door for a second, wondering how she should proceed. This had been her home for almost a quarter of a century, but she didn't know if she should use her key, ring the bell, or walk right in. Even though it was still her house, it was no longer her home, so she decided to ring the bell.

It was a few seconds before she heard James yell out, "Just a minute!", and then his footfalls as he came into the entry way. He opened the door and said, "Hello, Kat."

Kat suddenly felt very self-conscious; "Hi, James. Thanks for letting me come and do this while I'm here."

He stepped to the side and waved her in. "Not a problem. This is still your house, too. We need to pack and get ready for the closing. Also, please don't feel weird about using your key. It's perfectly fine to just come on in."

She looked up at him and smiled. "Thanks, James. Truly. Thanks for being so nice about this."

He looked down at the floor, unwilling to meet her eyes. "I messed up, Kat. I did this. The best thing I can do to make it up to you is finally act like an adult and try to ensure that this goes as smoothly as possible."

They went inside and began to sort through everything they had accumulated during their life together. Over the next few days, they laughed, cried, talked, and even argued about what to do with each thing. Kat was really surprised at how much James fought her for many of the family mementos of their lives together. She had thought that being a man, he wouldn't be so sentimental about things like photo albums of family trips or the items their children had made throughout their school years. In the end, she had to reconcile herself with the fact that he was their father and acknowledged how lucky they all were that in his own way he had as strong an attachment to them as she did. It warmed her heart to know that their journey together had not been for naught and that they really should be proud of the family they'd raised. It was still bittersweet, though, to know that things would never be the same again.

After they had done a majority of the sorting and packing and James had returned to work, Kat began to make the food for Derrick's graduation party on the upcoming Saturday, after his ceremony. There was something very cathartic about standing in the kitchen, preparing food for the first time since her return from Canada. As she chopped, stirred, and baked, the memories of her time on location came flooding back to her. She smiled as she remembered the day Ian had come into the kitchen, helped her peel the potatoes, and finally tried greens.

She hadn't heard anything from him, but she'd kept in contact with Melinda since she'd been home. Her colleague had been texting her that they were finishing up and that Ian looked terrible—all of his sparkle was gone, he was quiet and withdrawn, and he appeared absolutely miserable. But, she also said that it was incredibly demanding and everyone on set looked like death warmed over. Last she'd heard they were definitely going to be done by Friday and she and Gerard were pulling out on Saturday morning to begin the long trip back to Los Angeles. Kat had asked her to please tell Ian hello if she saw him and let him know that she was thinking of him, hoping he was well.

Wednesday night, she had gone back to her parents' house, completely spent and wanting only to fall into bed, when her phone dinged. Thinking it was another text from James, Jen, or one of her kids, she didn't think too much about it when she picked it up and saw it was in fact a text from Melinda. She unlocked it and smiled as she started to read: *Hi, Kat. Didn't get to say a proper goodbye before you left. Dare not use my or Lydia's phone to contact you. Melinda is letting me borrow hers. Once I'm back in L.A., we will catch up.*

A new bubble popped up: *Can't wait to get back to my life. Finally done Friday. Calgary until Saturday, then Lyds and I fly to New York for talk show interview Monday AM, L.A. Tuesday. I promise we'll talk after that. Take care.*

Kat wrote back: *Thanks for the update. Be safe.* There was so much more she wanted to say, but he was being pretty non-committal in his text to her, so she tried not to read too much into his message and kept her response simple. She was pretty sure the fact that he was using a virtual stranger's phone had a lot to do with it, but she also was convinced that she hadn't been wrong about his feelings changing once he was facing his return to reality. Telling herself that time would tell, she was grateful that the events of the next ten days would keep her so busy she wouldn't have time to sit and dwell on it.

Thursday morning began the real rush. Olivia was coming in later in the afternoon, driving home from school after her last final. Derrick was still at his apartment in town where he lived with a couple of his buddies, but he, too, was planning to come home that night. Her brothers were coming in Friday, and Drew had been in and out with finals and friends through it all.

As she continued to clean and prepare for Derrick's party, the kids came in one by one. Olivia, who arrived first and squealed when she saw her mother in the kitchen, ran to give her a hug.

"Hi, sweetheart!"

"Hi, Mama! It's so great to see you! Hey, you look so different. What's different?"

"I don't know, honey. Nothing, really, I guess."

Olivia stepped back and really looked at her mother. "Something sure is. How was Canada? Was it beautiful? How was it working with television stars? Is Ian really as gorgeous in person?"

"Whoa, Olivia!" Kat laughed. "One at a time! Let's start with how Canada was. It was fabulous! Simply breathtaking! I've never seen such beautiful country! I would love for you, me, and the boys to go up there some time. I think you'd be shocked by the utter exquisiteness and solitude up there."

"I looked it up online when you first left. The pictures really did look gorgeous!"

"How about you? How's school?"

"It's good! Really good! Like I texted you back in March, I've settled on doing social work for my degree. I'm really enjoying it and look forward to making a difference."

"That's wonderful!" Kat cried. "What made you finally decide to settle on that?"

"I don't know. Just reading a lot about the foster care system in one of my sociology classes and thinking about how those kids really need an advocate in their lives."

Kat wanted so much to tell her how right she was, about Lydia sharing that it had been just one person, her drama teacher, who had cared and ultimately changed the course of her life. But of course, she couldn't do that, so she simply said, "You're right, sweetie. I know people who have benefited greatly by just having one person give a damn."

Suddenly, something sparkling on Olivia's hand caught her attention. Kat grabbed her hand and brought it up to her face, and then looked up at Olivia.

"What is this?" she demanded.

"That's another thing I need to talk to you about, Mama. Remember Jackson, the guy I started dating back in November? He came over during winter break?"

"Yes."

"Things have gotten very serious since around when you left. He asked me to marry him last night, and I said yes!"

Kat stood in complete shock. She vaguely recalled meeting a guy around Christmastime, but with Olivia that wasn't unusual, so she didn't think much of it then. But now it hit her how much she had missed by leaving home.

"Mama? Aren't you going to say something?" Olivia asked nervously.

"Oh, baby girl! It sure is a beautiful ring. I'm so sorry I wasn't aware that things were getting that serious between y'all. I have to say I am a bit shocked, though. How come you didn't tell me that things were moving in that direction?"

"I don't know…You weren't here, and I knew you were busy up there. I guess I just wanted to wait until I saw you in person to tell you. And to be honest, I didn't think it would happen this fast myself."

"Do you love him, Olivia? I mean really, really love him? Like he takes your breath away when he walks into the room and your heart beats faster any time you think of him? Do your knees go weak when he kisses you?"

"Mama! What kind of questions are those?"

"Trust me, Olivia. They're important ones. Do you really love him?"

"I think so."

"Then, sweetie, if you can't answer that question with a resounding 'Yes!' I will just ask you to go slowly. If you don't know for sure, if when you look into his eyes you can't see forever, or when he's away from you, you don't feel like a piece of you is missing, then please don't marry him just yet."

"Where's all of this coming from?"

"Just trust me. Don't do anything because you get caught up in the inertia and don't want to make waves. You deserve your world getting rocked. How is he physically? Does he make sure you are enjoying it, too? Does he make you melt when he touches you?"

"*Mama*!" Olivia loudly admonished, her cheeks reddening. "Really!"

"Well, does he? Do you feel like he completes you, makes you a better person? Is there no better place than next to him, or better yet, under him?"

"Oh, my gosh, Mama! I can't believe you just asked me that!" Olivia exclaimed, her cheeks blazing.

"It's important, Olivia. *Really* important."

"Is this because of what has happened between you and Daddy?"

"Yes. Partly, at least," Kat answered honestly.

"Well, didn't you have those things with him?"

"To be honest, I don't know, Olivia. Times were different back then. Nice girls didn't get into situations where we would know beforehand how a man would love us. Now, things have changed. You don't have to wait, then settle."

"We haven't done *that*, so things aren't so different! I plan on waiting until we are married!"

"That's your choice, sweetheart. But I will tell you if that's the reason for your haste to get married, it's the wrong one. Sex should be with someone you love. It should be an expression of the emotion and desire y'all have for each other; the ability to say something with your body that you sometimes can't put into words. Even if y'all wait to have sex, if he doesn't make you melt now, especially when y'all aren't, then he won't later when y'all are."

"Is this because of you and Ian?" Suddenly, Olivia opened her eyes wide, a realization hitting her. "Oh my gosh, Mama! Did you sleep with him?" Her voice raised an octave at the end of her question.

"All I'll tell you is that when you have a true level of openness—a genuine intimacy and trust with someone—the physical just sort of falls into place."

"You didn't answer my question!"

"Let's just say that I discovered what I wanted out of my life, every aspect of it, and leave it at that."

"Does Daddy know?"

"Olivia, we are divorced. It's really none of his business now what I do or with whom. Please just really think hard about whether or not you can see yourself with this man for the rest of your life. Search deep in your soul to see if he enhances you or makes you feel stifled and unfulfilled, like you have to always be better than what you are."

"I don't know," Olivia whispered to her mother. "I don't think he does."

"If you don't know right now, then please promise me that you will have a long engagement. In fact, please try to wait until you're done with school, or at least very close to it. You never know what might happen in your life and you need to finish so that you can take care of yourself. If you love him and he loves you, then y'all can wait for each other until you're done doing what you need to do for your own wellbeing. As long as he respects and understands that, then y'all have my blessing. But, please, I'm telling you as your mother to really dig deep and make sure that he compliments who you are and does not make you feel you always have to be perfect or change to please him. All right?"

"All right, Mama."

"Come here!" Kat told her, as she folded her only daughter into her arms. "I love you, kid. A lot."

"I love you, too. It's nice to have you home!"

Kat just smiled in response. It didn't really seem appropriate to bring up that it wasn't really home anymore. She hadn't quite figured out how she was going to tell the kids that she was planning on moving out West to Los Angeles in a few more weeks. It felt like so much was changing right now that she didn't want to turn their worlds even further upside down.

Kat and Olivia began to make dinner together. They talked and laughed as they caught up about the last three months. Though they were having fun, Kat couldn't shake a feeling of sadness that in her quest for her own identity, she'd left her kids to fend for themselves. But she was also proud of how well they were able to cope without her.

The plan was for the family to eat dinner together at the house that night. When Olivia and Kat had just about finished the meal preparation, Drew walked through the door.

"Hey, Mama!" He and Kat had already had a chance to catch up with her being at the house so much in the past week, but he was still happy to see her.

"Hello, baby!" she cried, as she opened her arms and gave him a big hug. "How was school?"

"Great! One more week and I'm outta there!" he declared with glee.

***

Kat, Olivia, and Drew were all laughing and talking in the kitchen when James walked through the door. He stood just on the other side of the island, watching his children and his former wife interacting together. It broke his heart to see what looked like old times unfolding before his eyes, all the while knowing it would never be that way again and that it was his own doing.

When they saw him standing there, they all said hello and asked how his day was. Looking a bit wistful, he responded that it had been okay. He then went upstairs to his room to change his clothes, and looking around, took note once again how empty it looked with only his things in there. Knowing that when Kat came back she would obviously want her belongings, he still hadn't realized how familiar and comfortable he'd been with her presence filling their home, even after she had left. Seeing that everything was packed up and gone, it hit him that it was truly over, and she would never be his again.

When he came back downstairs, the kids had set the table and Derrick had arrived. Everyone joined together in the breakfast nook and bowed their heads together to bless the food. The serving dishes were passed around as they loaded up their plates with fried chicken, mashed potatoes, fried okra, and fried apples. At first, very little was said as they ate. It dawned on everyone that the situation was a bit awkward, as it was the first time they had been together as a family since the news of James' affair had broken and Kat had left. But after several minutes, the kids began talking amongst themselves and then Kat joined in, the conversation turning toward reminiscing about times gone by.

"Remember the time at Disney World when Drew cried for an hour because he dropped his ice cream?" Olivia asked.

"What? I did not!" he exclaimed.

"You sure did!" Derrick answered him. "Even after Mama bought you two more. Everyone in the park was staring at us!"

Kat then began laughing about the time a wave had bowled over Olivia while they had been at the coast. She described how her daughter had been crying when she stood up, obviously shaken and full of sand, but after Kat had cleaned her up, she had happily run right back into the water.

James was fairly quiet, however, just watching his family interact. He had a running dialog in his head wondering how he could have been so stupid to let all of this slip through his fingers. But eventually, even he joined in, remembering the time he taught Derrick how to use the leaf blower and was covered from head to foot with lawn debris when the boy hadn't quite gotten the hang of it yet.

They all sat for hours, laughing and sharing the special memories they had created as a family. When they finally noticed the time was getting late, Kat stood up and declared that she needed to start cleaning up, as she had a long drive back to her parents' and would be coming up again the next day to finish the party preparations and spend more time with the kids. James stated that he had taken the next day off, so he would also be around and then told Kat she didn't have to clean up.

"The kids and I can do it."

She was shocked. "Really?"

"Yes. It's the least we can do after you made this amazing meal. Let me walk you out."

Kat leaned over and gave each of her kids a hug and a kiss, suddenly feeling very sad to leave them. They, too, seemed to cling to her just a little bit longer before releasing her from their grips.

James walked her out on the front porch and onto the driveway. He felt he had to say something; it was now or never.

"Kat?" he began nervously.

"Yes?"

"Thank you," he quietly told her.

"For what?"

"For being you."

"Thanks, I guess, though I don't really know who else I would be anymore."

He took a deep breath and began to speak very fast. "Please, Kat, don't go. I'm so sorry! I am so incredibly sorry I was so stupid and selfish. I don't know what I was thinking. Watching you here today in the house, cooking, interacting with the kids, I felt like I was having an out of body experience. You seemed to be right where you belong, and I can't believe I was such an idiot to let you go. Please, Kat, I still love you! Please come back to me. I need you! I want you!" He gave a half choking sob, leaned toward her, and kissed her on the lips.

Kat was stunned. She stood in front of this man, this man she had been together with for more than half of her life. On one hand, she completely agreed with him. It had felt so comfortable and familiar to be there with her family, in their house, just like old times. She thought about how much easier it would all be if she could just slide back into her old life.

But then she remembered how Ian had made her feel. How his touch was like an electric shock, how his breath on her neck made her go weak, and even how his scent was the most enticing one she had ever experienced. She instantly thought back to their times together, how he had made her feel like she was all he wanted in the world and that she was the only one for him. Recalling the times they had made love, she thought about how kind, gentle, and attentive he had been. Smiling to herself, she recollected his horrified expression when he realized he'd gotten too carried away too quickly and how sweetly he'd made it up to her. She pictured his face as they moved together, like they were a perfectly timed machine, while he gazed into her eyes and whispered that he loved her as they climaxed in unison. Feeling her body involuntarily shudder with desire at the memory, James pulled back from the kiss and looked at her expectantly.

"Kat, I love you. Please!" he begged.

Kat stood quietly, weighing her options in the dark on the

driveway beside her mother's car. For just the briefest of moments, she seriously considered relenting and walking back into the house with him, just pretending that the last four months hadn't happened. Unsure of where she stood with Ian, reconciling with James would mean guaranteed stability and her life would certainly be less complicated. She also hadn't realized just how deeply she missed her children until they were all together again. But then she recalled the talk she'd had only hours before with Olivia about how it was important to not get caught up in the inertia of the situation simply because it was easier. She also remembered telling her that a man should make her feel complete when she was beside him, not lacking.

"James, I'm so sorry. I love you, but not in the way you want me to, not in the way a person should be loved in a relationship. You will always be the father of my children and my first love, but I just can't. I really am so incredibly sad that it had to end this way."

James began to silently cry. It broke her heart to see the pain he was in, as she realized in that moment that she really did still care deeply for him. She silently opened her arms and he fell into them, his face buried between her neck and shoulder as his body shook with grief. She could think to do nothing more than pet his head and murmur to him that she was sorry and that he would be okay.

After a few minutes, he stepped back and looked at her. "Is it because of him? Is it because of Ian?" he spat out.

Kat knew she had to tread carefully. "I do care for him very much, as well, James, I won't lie. And to be honest, I've never felt so loved and cherished as I did with him."

This admission made James tear up again.

"But no. Even if Ian wasn't in the picture anymore, which seems to be the case actually, I can't come back to you."

"Why?" James whined like a pitiful child.

"Because I don't love you like that, James. I want to want you, to desire you. I want it to be like magic when we are together."

"Like it was in Vegas?" he asked her.

She thought cautiously for a few seconds. "Close," she relented, while thinking that what she really wanted to say was, *You mean after you had sex with your mistress a few hours before we did?* She knew it would serve no purpose to rehash it, though. It would make it seem like she still cared about what had happened that night and quite frankly, she really didn't anymore.

"Close?" he sounded hurt and confused.

"James, I don't want to tell you this, but as you were finally completely honest with me about Sam, I need to tell you about Ian. We did sleep together." She heard him groan and saw his hands clench and his shoulders rise in anger, but also that he was trying desperately to control it.

She hurried on, "It was after you had come up there and wasn't until the night that I signed the divorce documents and got them ready to send back to you; he wouldn't let us before that. But, James, I had never wanted anything so much in my life as I did in that moment. I'm sorry and I'm sure it's painful to hear, but it was truly earth-shattering, for both of us."

James hit his forehead with his hand and left it there with his eyes closed. He took a few raged breaths. "Where is he now, then?" he asked her. "If he's such a nice guy and it was so earth-shattering, then why isn't he here?"

Kat didn't have a good answer for that. Knowing that Ian had to finish the current season, she was also painfully aware he had to deal with the contract issues for the next one. She also knew that he was worried to contact her in case somehow the powers that be got wind of it and fired him. However, she had a nagging feeling that she couldn't shake: if he loved her so much, why wouldn't he stand up and fight for her?

"I don't know," she finally admitted to James.

"Until he is here and with you, then, I won't give up hope. You've changed Kat, but so have I. I know now how incredibly lucky I was to share my life and my bed with you and I'm so angry with myself that I took you for granted. As much as it kills me to hear you were with another man, I know I fully deserve it because I'm the one who started all this and drove you to it. I'm willing to forget it ever happened if you are. I want you back, anytime, anyplace."

Kat gave him a small smile. "Thanks, James. Truly, that was the nicest thing you ever said to me. But, for right now, with or without Ian, I still have a lot of self-discovery and growing to do. I appreciate that you still care for me and that you are willing to work with me for the sake of the kids. Let's just leave it at that for now, shall we?"

James nodded as he stepped away from her and opened the car door. She kissed him on the cheek as she slid into the driver's seat, and he closed the door behind her. He stood in the driveway as she backed out and drove away. Kat checked one more time in the review mirror and saw him standing where she had left him with his face in his hands.

Chapter Forty-Four

Friday passed in another blur of preparations and arrivals of family. It was initially very uncomfortable for Kat to see James when she arrived back to their house the following morning, but after she had gotten to work and with having the kids around, things eventually became much less awkward.

There had been some confusion about where Kat's brothers were going stay. It hadn't dawned on anyone until right before they arrived that Kat's house wasn't really a viable option anymore. As uncomfortable as it was for Kat to be around James, James was even more nervous about having one or both of Kat's brothers staying at the house when she wasn't there, even though they had known each other for over twenty years. The situation once again drove home to Kat how the consequences of the divorce spread out far beyond her immediate family, like ripples on the water. It had eventually been arranged so that both brothers and their families could stay at their parents' house, but because Kat was also there, it had proven logistically difficult to get everyone settled into one place.

Kat returned to her parents' home around five p.m. and was immediately greeted by her brothers who enveloped her in a giant bear hug as soon as she walked through the door.

"Hey, guys!" she exclaimed, grinning happily, as she pulled back from the embrace.

"Hi, Kat!" said Christopher. "You look good, baby sis."

Kat blushed and looked down at the floor. "Thanks, Christopher. So do you!"

Thomas had always been the most reserved of the three brothers, but he, too, was obviously excited to see her. "You do look great, Kat! What's different?"

"I don't know. I guess all of that fresh Canadian mountain air?"

As per the norm, after sitting together and talking for a while, the women found themselves in the kitchen, preparing the food, while the guys all stayed out in the living room, talking about sports. The conversation in the kitchen revolved around the lives of Kat's brothers, their wives, and kids. Since they lived so far away, Kat's mother rarely got to see her grandbabies—except for Kat's three— more than once or twice a year.

Christopher and Jessica's girls, Emily and Brooklyn, who had come along with their parents, wandered into the kitchen to get something to drink. They squealed when they saw their Aunt Kat and ran to her for hugs.

"Hello, girls! How are y'all?" she asked them.

Emily, the eldest of the two at thirteen, had grown a ton since Kat had seen her last and was becoming a beautiful young lady. Brooklyn, at nine, was still cute as a bug and her bubbly personality made her incredibly easy to love.

"I'm good!" Emily said.

"Aunt Kat?" Brooklyn asked.

"Yes, sugar?"

"Were you really up in Canada where they're filming that T.V. show?" she asked, her eyes wide.

"Yes, baby girl, I sure was."

Perhaps because she was unaware or because she just didn't think, Emily piped up with, "O-M-G, you are so lucky. I'd just die to get the chance to meet that Ian Gregory guy. He is *so* hot!"

Kat heard a collective gasp around her. Jessica jumped in right away. "Emily! You shouldn't be talking like that!"

"Why not, Mom? He is!" She seemed genuinely confused.

Kat's mother and sisters-in-law glanced around at each other, trying to come up with something to say. Kat had to chuckle and figured she would save everyone from the uncomfortable feeling that was pressing in on the room.

"You know what, Emily? I agree. He *is* super hot!"

There was a collective sigh of relief behind her, and Kat smiled in spite of herself.

"So, what was he like?" Brooklyn asked. "I just love his horse! He's so pretty!" Of course, being only nine, her focus was naturally drawn to the animals and children on the show, not yet noticing the attributes of the adult actors.

"He was really nice! Well, at first he wasn't. He was kind of a jerk. And he asked me what grits were! Can y'all believe that? But his horse is really beautiful. And guess what? I got to ride him!"

Brooklyn squealed and clapped her hands together. "Really?"

"Yes, ma'am," Kat answered her. "I also got to ride Lydia's—the woman who plays Sarah's—horse. She was a sweet little thing."

"How did that happen?" Emily asked her.

"Ian and I went riding quite a few times."

"What? O-M-G! You went riding with Ian Gregory?" Emily excitedly screeched.

"Yes, I did. I also helped him when he fell off his horse. The horse got spooked when some birds flew up off the lake. He had gone out for an early morning ride and hadn't made it back, so I went looking for him and found him at the spot we always rode to. He got pretty hurt."

"Is he okay now?" little Brooklyn piped up.

"Yes, sweet pea. As far as I know, he's fine."

"You can say that again!" Emily stated knowingly.

"All right, girls, time to leave the kitchen. Out with you!" Their mother shooed them out the door onto the screened in porch.

No one in the room knew what to say and they all were looking at the floor. Finally, Kat couldn't take it anymore.

"Okay… I know this is awkward," she said.

The two sisters-in-law glanced up at each other and then looked down at the floor again.

"Let's talk about the elephant in the room, shall we?" Kat just wanted it out in the open. "Yes, James cheated on me. Yes, I left him. We're now divorced. Yes, we are amicable. I did go to Canada, I did ride horses and run and talk with Ian Gregory extensively."

She so badly wanted to add, "Yes, we also made love several

times and it was awesome!" but knew she couldn't and figured that if she did they would die of embarrassment anyway.

Again, it was quiet around her. Finally, Laura broke the silence, "So, I'm just dying to know. Are Ian and Lydia in a relationship?"

Kat glanced at her mother, who said nothing and wouldn't make eye contact with her. "It's complicated," she said.

"Was he as nice as everyone says he is?" Jessica apparently couldn't help herself.

"Yes, eventually. Like I told the girls, he was really a jerk to me at first. But after a while, he was incredibly nice."

"What about that Lydia?" Laura asked her.

"She's nice, too. Pretty quiet, though."

It grew silent once more. Kat could tell that they were also just dying to ask her about the alleged affair and photos from Los Angeles, but neither of them dared to bring it up.

Kat, on the other hand, was desperately wanting someone to talk to about everything. She longed to tell them about how his arms felt around her, how he smelled, how he tasted faintly like peppermint every time they kissed, and how adored and secure she had felt under the weight of him as they made love. She battled with herself to keep quiet when all she really desired was to admit everything they saw about L.A. was essentially true and share that she had never had such amazing sex before in her life. Wanting to be able to gush non-stop about this wonderful man was almost killing her, knowing that she couldn't even dare trust her family members, because if it got out, it would be the end of his role on the show, maybe even his career. In that moment it struck her that if she and Ian decided to maintain a clandestine relationship for the next year, it was going to be very hard to not have someone find out just by her accidentally spilling the beans. She had only considered how they would keep things under wraps from the public, not about how it would be to have to lie to, or at least omit, information from the people closest to them.

When the evening meal was ready, the family came together

432

in the dining room. Thankfully, most of the conversation continued to revolve around her brothers and their respective work. They seemed to want to avoid talking about anything to do with Kat's current situation and she was happy to oblige.

After dinner, Kat grabbed a glass of wine and went to sit out on the screened in porch. She'd always loved the night sounds and the tranquil flickering of the lightning bugs this time of year. She could hear frogs croaking somewhere in the distance, along with crickets and the soft wind blowing through the pines, and saw lightning firing up in a distant cloud on the horizon. After a few minutes, the screen door opened, and her sisters-in-law joined her. They sat together, quietly enjoying the surroundings for a few minutes before Laura broke the silence.

"So, Kat. How are you holding up?"

"I'm doing okay, thanks, Laura."

"You certainly have had a whirlwind of a few months!" Jessica interjected.

"That I have."

"How are the kids handling all of this?" Laura inquired.

"They seem to be doing fine. It certainly helps that they're older. I do feel a bit removed after having been gone for so long, though. Like when Olivia came home the other day, she was wearing an engagement ring. That was a shock!"

"What?" both of them cried.

"Yes, she's now engaged to a guy she brought home for a day over Christmas."

"How do you feel about that?" Jessica asked her.

"It blew me over, honestly. Not that it happened, but that it happened without me having any clue it was going on. But we've talked and I feel like she understands that she needs to finish school, or at least be close, before marrying, and that she needs to make damn sure he's who she thinks she can spend the rest of her life with. I warned her not to rush into anything; to take her time to get to know him and get to know herself, too, then see if he enhances her or drags her down."

"Speaking of that, how's James doing, Kat?" Jessica asked,

finally mentioning the other elephant in the room.

"He's doing all right. This has been hard on him. I don't think he ever thought I would actually leave him."

"How is it to be back here with him?" Laura prodded.

"It has been decent, actually. He and I got the house sorted and my stuff packed. I've spent every day of the last week over there between packing and cooking for tomorrow. We've spent the most time together we have in I don't know how long."

"How's he taking the divorce?" Jessica asked.

"I think it's difficult for him. I don't know if the full reality of what happened has hit him yet. But the divorce itself was very easy. He was generous and kind, probably out of guilt and maybe a little hope, but it was settled really quickly.

"He came up to see me in Canada when the papers were served, but I told him it was over. He tried again last night, telling me he wanted me back and that he was so sorry, but I just don't want to do that."

"Because you're in love with Ian?" Laura asked.

"Yes," Kat answered before she thought. There it was again, proof that it was going to be next to impossible to keep this hidden from everyone. "I mean, no. Not at all."

She tried to cover her tracks. "Ian's a great guy. He has become an amazing friend. I do love him, but not in that way." She prayed silently they wouldn't pick up on her lie. "I love Lydia, too. They're both a lot of fun and very kind people."

Kat then tried to steer the conversation to a safer topic, where she wouldn't have to worry so much about slipping up and making a mistake. She started to ask them about her nieces and nephews, always a safe and detailed conversation between mothers, and the rest of the evening passed without incident.

Saturday morning dawned bright as everyone hurried to get ready and out the door to fight the traffic around the university. At the ceremony, Kat cried tears of pride and joy as she saw her oldest boy walk across the stage and move his tassel from one side to the other. She slipped her arm through James' and squeezed, awed at what they had accomplished together and then she realized what she had done. Seeing him gaze down at her with a surprised, hopeful expression, she quickly removed her arm and patted his. She then pondered how old habits die hard: once a person becomes physically intimate with someone, it's hard to go back to what is considered appropriate for a strictly platonic relationship.

Back at the house, the party went off without a hitch as friends, family, and neighbors all came to congratulate Derrick on his accomplishment. The only truly awkward part of the day came when she was face-to-face with James' parents for the first time since she had left. Though they were very gracious and warm in true polite Southern fashion, she still couldn't help feeling the undercurrent of disappointment and displeasure that she hadn't just forgiven their son and returned to life as everyone had known it.

The whole family pitched in to clean up the house, so there wasn't really a moment when she and James had to interact alone together. He was very pleasant, but she could feel the dejection and sadness seeping out of him and, even after everything he had done, it still broke her heart. When it was time to leave, he grabbed her hand and kissed her cheek. He leaned over and whispered, "We raised a hell of a kid."

Kat felt her heart melt as she smiled back at him. "We sure did, James. He's a good man."

"As long as he's a better man than me," he told her, his meaning evident in his tone of voice and mannerism.

Later that evening, when her parents had gone to bed, Kat sat in the living room, enjoying the silence around her while she processed the events of the day. She turned when Christopher and Thomas walked into the room. They each plunked down on either side of her on the couch and sat there quietly for a few minutes. Finally, Thomas broke the silence.

"How are you really doing, Kat?"

"I'm okay."

"Really?"

"Yes, really."

Christopher piped up. "I know I'm forty-five years old, but man it was hard not to deck James when I saw him today!"

"Honestly, I thought the same thing. It doesn't matter how old we get, you don't mess with our baby sister!" Thomas added.

Kat laughed. "Still my overprotective big brothers. Thanks guys, but that won't be necessary."

"I still can't believe what he did to you!" Christopher declared in disgust.

"I couldn't either at first. But I'm doing fine now."

"So, who's this Ian guy?" Thomas asked.

"He's just the lead actor in the show I was working on. He's a nice guy."

"How nice?" Christopher inquired suspiciously, his eyebrows raised. "Does he know you have three older brothers?"

Kat laughed at him and punched him gently in the upper arm. "He does. I think he's a little intimidated by it, honestly."

"Good!" her brothers said in unison.

Again, Kat chuckled. "Thanks, boys. It's nice to know that y'all still always have my back."

Christopher leaned over and put his arm around her shoulder. "I gotta say, Kat, you look better than I've seen you look in years. I know this has been hard on you, but you really do look happier and more importantly, confident." Thomas murmured his agreement.

Both of her brothers leaned over and kissed her cheeks on their way out to their respective rooms. Kat turned off the lamp and sat in the darkness for a long time, all of the emotions from the last little while coming out as her tears silently ran down her cheeks. She was having a hard time reconciling everything swirling in her mind. Her immense pride in her children and the joy that she and James had shared in raising them blended with the pain that she had endured because of James' infidelity, and even the pain that he was now experiencing as he faced the consequences of his actions.

But most of all, she cried about Ian, wondering what was happening and where they stood. She truly missed his company.

Finally, at one a.m., she crept upstairs to her old bedroom and because of the emotion of the day, fell immediately into an exhausted sleep.

Chapter Forty-Five

Sunday morning ushered in another mad rush as the family all struggled to get out the door in time for church. Once they arrived in the parking lot, it dawned on Kat that things could get very uncomfortable now that she was outside the sanctuary offered by her family and friends. Her realization was quickly confirmed as they walked inside, and she caught the many sideways glances in her direction. She tried to focus on what the pastor was saying, but she kept feeling people were looking at her, even making quiet comments, and then began to worry she was just being paranoid.

When the service was over, she meandered to the back of the church with her family, stopping to shake the pastor's hand. He smiled warmly at her, but Kat felt uncomfortable as he had been the one who'd married her and James. She felt she needed to explain herself to him, even though he had said nothing more than, "Good morning, Kat! It's so good to see you!" Instead, though, she just mumbled that it was nice to see him, too.

Gathering on the front lawn where everyone was congregating to socialize before heading home for their Sunday dinners, Kat still felt the scrutiny of those around her. She wondered how much gossip her mother had endured since the news had broken about Kat's divorce and alleged affair with a not only famous, but from all appearances, involved man.

Suzanne, the daughter of her parents' neighbor walked up to her and said, "Well, hello, Kat Curtis! So good to see you here. Last I heard, you were up playing house in Los Angeles with that dreamy Ian Gregory."

Kat retorted quickly, "That was just a side trip to see my friend Jen. You remember her? Actually, I spent most of my time up in Canada cooking for him and one hundred others on the set."

"I sure do love that show," said Rebecca, another woman Kat had gone to school with. "That Ian guy is so good looking!

I can't believe you got to work with him!"

"Isn't he though?" questioned Suzanne derisively. "And she didn't just work with him, at least as far as those pictures showed. I can't fault you, though, Kat; I would play house with him, too, if he asked!"

The two women giggled while Kat gritted her teeth and looked on. To have her experience with Ian reduced to mere scandal infuriated her. She caught sight of her father and seeing her escape, told them sweetly, "Nice talking with y'all," and hurried off to walk with him as he went to get the car. Sensing how uncomfortable she felt, he simply slipped his arm around her as they headed away from everyone.

Sunday dinner at her parents' home with the family was chaotic, noisy, and fun. Kat's kids had all come down to join them, and the house was alive with conversation and activity. After the meal, while everyone was still seated and conversing with each other, Kat observed her father sitting back in his chair, overseeing it all with a contented smile on his face. Kat got up and walked over to him, putting her arms around his neck. He reached up and patted one of her forearms, and she came around to the side of him, squatting down to his level.

"How are you doing, Daddy?"

"I'm doin' great, baby girl! Just look at all of this! This is our legacy right here. Whoever would have guessed that when your mother and I got married fifty-three years ago, our union would lead to this?"

She smiled softly at him. "You did good, I would say!"

"I would say that, too."

Kat was quiet for a second, looking out over the dining room with him, listening to the raucous conversations and loud laughter. She took a deep breath. "I'm sorry, Daddy. I'm sorry that I let you and Mama down."

"What in the world are you talkin' about, darlin'?" he asked her, turning to study her face.

"I'm sorry that I'm the one who disrupted the perfect family y'all had built by getting a divorce."

Her father sat quietly for a second before answering, "Kat, honey, you didn't really have any other option, at least how I see it. James stepped out on you. To be honest- now don't go tellin' your mama this, 'cause I'll deny it — I would have been disappointed if you had stayed."

"What? Why?"

"Because you deserve better, pumpkin. I can tell you now that I never was that fond of James. He was a little too mealy-mouthed and wishy-washy for my likin'. He lacked passion for just about everythin', except maybe football. Over twenty years of y'all bein' married and he was still unable to relax and carry on a normal conversation around me and your brothers. He didn't do you justice, sweet pea. I like what I'm seein' in you a lot more now. You're relaxed and finally comfortable in your own skin."

Kat placed her hand on top of her father's as it rested on the arm of his chair. "Thanks, Daddy. That means a lot."

"The only good thing you got out of all this are those wonderful kids over there. I'll give James credit there; together y'all raised some pretty amazin' young people."

"Yeah, I'm very proud of them, too. And you're right; James has always been a good father. I would never deny that."

There was a lull in the conversation, and everyone noticed Kat and her father quietly talking together at the head of the table. Kat's mother decided then that it was time for dessert, so the women cleared the table and brought in the peach pies. Kat didn't remember exactly what everyone talked about for the rest of the night, but she couldn't remember a time when she had felt more content to be with her family. She was calm and sated as she saw everyone interacting and felt blessed that for the first time in a very long that she was happy just to be.

Chapter Forty-Six

Kat awoke to a stormy morning, and the gloom affected everyone, resulting in a late start to the day. Kat came downstairs in her pajamas and robe, passing through the living room on her way to the kitchen to get coffee, and saw her dad, brothers, and Laura, all watching a morning news show. She glanced at the clock and was shocked to see that it was 8:55 a.m. Pouring herself some coffee, she joined her mother at the table in the breakfast nook. She was supposed to meet Holly later for lunch, but she had several hours before she had to leave.

"Mama?" she asked.

"Yes, sweet pea?"

"Do you want me to make some breakfast for all y'all?"

"If you wouldn't mind, that'd be wonderful."

"After what I just did in Canada for three months, cooking for this crew will be a piece of cake."

Kat stood up and pulled on an apron. She opened the fridge and pulled out eggs and milk, bacon, and sausage, and was in the middle of making waffle batter when she heard Laura calling her name. She walked out into the living room and asked, "What is it?"

Then she looked at the screen. Sitting in the chairs next to the two co-hosts of the morning show that came on after the news were Ian and Lydia.

"They just came out," Laura told her, "They're talking about how they have been in Canada, filming the third season. I thought maybe you'd want to watch."

Kat slowly walked over and sank down into the couch, oblivious to the looks from everyone around her. She took in a deep breath as she saw him there in front of her.

God, he is magnificent!

"So, Ian and Lydia… you just got back from Canada where you finished filming the third season of *Western Skies*. How was it?" the perky female co-host asked.

Ian looked over to Lydia, so she began. "It was so incredible. It's always so much fun to be up there. We all become so close, like a big family. It's so sad when we have to leave and come back to reality." She stuck her bottom lip out in a bit of a beautiful pout.

"That's okay, though, since you two still have each other, right?" the more stoic male co-host asked.

Ian jumped right in and pretended that the last comment had never been uttered. As he opened his mouth, his glorious accent tumbled out, tugging at Kat's heart strings.

"The scenery up there is amazing. And the stars… you have never seen so many stars in your life! It's like you can see eternity." Kat smiled when she heard that, recalling their night in the woods, looking up at the sky together.

"This little show that seemed to pop up out of nowhere is suddenly not so little anymore! So, everyone is dying to know. Is there going to be a fourth season?" the energetic interviewer asked.

Lydia quickly answered, "We're in the middle of contract negotiations right now, actually, so yes, there should be a fourth season, unless you guys hate the third one, I guess!" Everyone in the audience laughed.

"I don't think that's possible!" said the woman.

The man inquired seriously, "So do we finally get to see some action between the two of you? I mean between Joe and Sarah? Ian?"

"Let's just say that I don't think anyone will be disappointed," Ian replied vaguely.

"Tell me," the woman leaned forward and dropped her voice slightly, as she suddenly turned serious. "What was all that nasty business in California earlier this spring, Ian? Have you and Lydia moved past that, and are you all right now? When are you going to finally come out as a couple and stop all of this speculation?"

Kat's dad's head snapped up and he looked over at her to see her reaction. She smiled weakly back at him.

Lydia unleashed a tinkling laugh, leaning her head over on Ian's shoulder as she said, "I guess we will just have to wait and see."

Ian, however, was staring down at the floor, saying nothing. After a few seconds, his head popped up. He turned slightly and leaned over to Lydia, who had straightened up again, quietly saying, "I'm sorry, Lyds. I can't do this anymore."

Even from the living room couch, Kat caught the look of panic and shock on Lydia's face, but Ian's expression was determined. Lydia quickly recovered and gave him a small nod, replying softly, "I know. It's okay. I understand."

Meanwhile, Kat's family members in the living room were all instinctively leaning forward, waiting for what was coming next.

"What can't you do anymore?" the female co-host asked, confused.

"This. I don't care anymore if I get sacked!" Ian said resolutely. He leaned over and reached for Lydia's hand. "I love Lydia, but not in the way everyone thinks. We have never been a couple, really, and now we never will be, because I'm in love with someone else."

There was a collective murmur from the audience, both in the studio and in the living room. Kat's family all instantly turned toward her to gauge her reaction.

The co-hosts were obviously flustered by what had just transpired on their nationally televised show. It took them a few seconds to recover, but eventually the woman asked him, "What did you say?"

Ian sat up straighter and looked out into the audience. He spoke loudly and definitively. "I love someone else."

"Who?" asked the man.

"You all know who. I'm in love with Kat Anderson."

Again, Kat heard a collective gasp.

"I am *completely, emphatically, desperately* in love with Kat Anderson, the woman from the photographs with me in L.A."

"You mean the caterer?"

"I do," he confirmed.

There was absolute silence in the studio, as nobody really knew what to say next. Ian took a deep breath and continued.

"At this point, I don't care if they sack me and write me off next season. I have to do this. I'm in love with Kat and I've treated her horribly over the last few weeks while I wrestled with myself about signing next season's contract or not. She deserves better. I know now that I need to take a stand and let the whole world know how I feel about her, because I can't force her into the shadows any more just to generate ratings."

"Lydia?" asked the woman. "How do you feel about all of this? Did you know?"

"Yes, I knew," she replied quietly.

"How are you holding up?"

"I'm fine. Like Ian said, we were never a couple... Everyone has just always assumed we were, I guess, because we are such close friends and we do have great chemistry together on screen." She looked up at Ian and smiled. "Once we realized what was going on and what the speculation about us was, it was just easier for many reasons to keep up the rouse. Then, the inertia of the situation just kept pushing it onward."

Ian broke in. "The network and production company liked the media buzz we created for the show, so they made our contracts for next season contingent upon the continuance of our pseudo-relationship in order to force us to keep it up. But I can't do it. I won't..." He sounded choked up.

"So, you haven't signed your contracts yet for season four?" the man asked.

"I have," Lydia responded quickly. "But Ian hasn't. Like he said, he has been wrestling with this for several weeks."

"I can't believe that they would do that to the two of you!" the woman said indignantly.

Lydia gave a rueful smile. "We were told we generated our own marketing and publicity better than anything they could have done."

"So, what happens now?" asked the man.

"I don't know," Ian answered honestly. "They have threatened to terminate both of us and the cancel the show if we don't comply. But I guess the first step for me is to get up and walk out of here. If you will excuse me, I have somewhere else I need to be." And with that, he stood up, gave Lydia a hug and a kiss on the cheek, unhooked his mic from his clothing, and shook the hands of the co-hosts, before walking stoically off the sound stage.

Everyone in the studio was too shocked to react for several seconds. The male co-host recovered first and asked Lydia, "Why would you two agree to do this?"

She sat back in her seat on the couch, took a deep breath, and said, "Let me tell you a little story…"

Kat didn't hear anything more. Her head was spinning, and she felt like her heart was going to beat right out of her chest. She looked up at the shocked faces of her family members all around her and didn't know what to say.

Emily finally broke the stunned silence. "Did Ian Gregory just say that he's in love with Aunt Kat?"

Her mother looked at her and said, "Sure sounded like it."

"Aunt Kat, did you and Ian Gregory fall in love?" Emily asked.

"Yes, we did, sweetheart," Kat managed to reply. "I am head over heels in love with that man!"

Kat had no idea what to do next. She felt glued to her seat but also like she needed to get up and move. The energy coursing through her veins was electric—she felt like she was on fire. So much for keeping this quiet! He had told her he loved her in front of essentially the entire world.

Her phone suddenly dinged. She picked it up and read a message from Holly:

Based on what I just saw, I think you'll be needing a rain check on lunch. I've got a feeling a much more important person will be wanting your attention.

Kat struggled to form a cohesive sentence as she typed: *You saw that?*

Holly: *Honey, the whole East Coast just saw that!*

Her phone dinged again, and she grinned widely as she read: *I love you, Kat. Unequivocally with everything I am. Don't move. I'm coming for you!*

Kat: *I love you, too, and I'll be waiting!* Her fingers flew over the keypad.

Ian: *Wait, Kat. Where am I going exactly?*

She laughed out loud, oblivious to everyone around her.

Kat: *Oh, yeah, that* is *kind of important. Actually, let me come and get you.*

Ian: *NO! Don't do that. I don't want to the first time I see you in this many weeks to be at the airport, in front of everybody. I don't want you to get caught up in any media circus, either.*

Kat: *Okay.*

She proceeded to type out her parents' address and then sprang up and ran to her room to grab her running shoes. She knew she had to get out and get active or the nerves and excitement she felt would consume her. Her feet hit the pavement in the neighborhood until she was able to get to the greenway close to her parents' house, and then she ran along the trails, jumping over tree roots, all the while dodging bicycles, strollers, and other runners, as the rain poured down, but she didn't even notice. Her mind was busy whirling with all of the possibilities that his public announcement would bring.

When she got home, she grabbed her razor, towel, and clothes and ran to the bathroom, jumping immediately into the shower. After the last three weeks, she was actually a bit more *au natural* than she'd ever intended to be.

She finished getting ready, throwing her hair back in a ponytail and putting on some mascara and a little lipstick, and an hour later was downstairs in the breakfast nook with her mother. She needed something to do to pass the time until Ian arrived because she could hardly sit still with anticipation.

Her mother looked her over and coolly said, "If this Ian is on his way here, don't you think you should go get ready, sweet pea?" with her eyebrows raised.

"I'm ready!" she responded.

"Honey, you need to go fix your makeup and hair. This man just declared his love for you on national television! You don't want him to get here and realize he made a mistake, do you?"

Kat just shook her head. "Mama, you aren't ever going to understand, are you? Some men like a woman who isn't a replica of a Barbie doll. Ian's one of them."

"I'm sure he told you that to be nice, sugar, but every man wants a beautiful woman on his arm. Look what happened with you and James, and that was when you were makin' an effort!"

"Oh, Mama!" Kat huffed. "You did *not* just say that… You did *not* just say that James had an affair on me because I didn't take care of my appearance!"

"Sweet pea, she was years younger than you! We have to put in a little more effort the older we get. There will always be beautiful young women out to steal their hearts."

"You are right, Mama. There will always be younger, more beautiful women out there. The difference is that there are men out there who don't care. They love the person inside the package, not wrapping!"

Kat got up and marched into the kitchen to begin cleaning up the abandoned makings of her family breakfast. When that was finished, she went to the refrigerator and began pulled out different contents and got to work.

Nothing passed the time faster than cleaning and preparing food and she was determined to do something other than sit and argue with her mother about the woman's archaic ideas of gender roles in a relationship.

"What are you goin' to make?" her mother called from the adjoining breakfast table.

"Great-grandma's stew and soda bread. Something that will keep me here and busy for a long time," Kat answered shortly, still bothered by their earlier discussion.

She got to work and was completely absorbed in her preparation when her phone dinged. She picked it up to see that Jen had texted her. She began to laugh as she read: *Girl, what the hell is going on? I just saw Ian telling the world that he loves you.*

Kat: *I guess you are three hours behind me!*

Jen: *It's everywhere! It's on every entertainment website and it's the talk of the town! I'm getting alerts from every site to which I'm subscribed. There hasn't been anything like this since Tom Cruise jumped up on Oprah's couch!*

Kat: *Really?*

Jen: *Yes! Check out TMZ if you don't believe me!*

Hang on! Kat sent and then opened TMZ on her phone. Sure enough, there it was, the top story: *Ian Gregory Breaks Lydia Swan's Heart on National T.V.* Directly below that was, *Lydia Spills All About Her Horrendous Childhood!*

Oh my God, you are right! she messaged Jen.

Jen: *I know I'm right. It's everywhere here. So, what's happening next?*

Kat: *I don't know. Ian sent me a text that he was coming here and asked for my parents' address.*

Jen: *Let me know what happens! Also, when you will be back? David and I have to clean out the guest room before you come. We just dumped most of his crap on the bed when he moved back in.*

Kat: *Not sure yet. Definitely not before Drew's graduation on Friday.*

Kat signed off and looked at the clock. Just a little after noon. Her father and the boys had gone golfing, so it was only Kat, her mother, her sisters-in-law, and nieces left in the house. Jessica and Laura seemed to be as keyed up as Kat felt and they kept jumping up to stir the pot on the stove or to wash dishes that had accumulated in the sink.

No one said much, as it was obvious Kat was in her own world, trying desperately to keep busy.

Chapter Forty-Seven

At five past two in the afternoon, the doorbell rang. Kat flew out of the kitchen and flung open the front door. There Ian stood before her, wearing well-worn jeans and a T-shirt, his hair tousled across his forehead after obviously having run his hand through it. Kat couldn't help herself. She squealed, and threw herself into his arms, wrapping her legs around his waist as he had just enough time to drop his bag on the porch before catching her.

Ian set her down and held her cheeks, kissing her repeatedly while they both tried to talk at the same time.

"I can't… believe you did… that…"

"God, I can't… believe how much… I have missed you…"

"I can't… believe you are… here standing on my front porch…."

"I love you, Kat."

After a few minutes, Ian stopped and noticed the women standing behind Kat in the doorway. He cleared his throat and ran his fingers through his hair again before stepping around Kat and extending his hand.

He went first to Kat's mom and said, "I'm Ian McGregor. So pleased to meet you!" Kat's mom's eyes widened as she saw him up close. She seemed to forget what she was doing for a second but recovered quickly and took his hand.

"So nice to meet you, Ian. I love your show."

"Thank you, ma'am," he replied, looking back at Kat and winking. He had obviously done some homework on how to speak to a proper Southern mother. He then looked at Kat's two sisters-in-law and held out his hand to them as well. Laura took it and told him that she was married to Kat's brother, Thomas, but Jessica just stared at him, unable to do anything else. Ian shrugged his shoulders as he lowered his hand, then turned back around to grab his bag before wrapping his other arm around Kat's waist.

"Come on inside!" Kat excitedly told him. "You can put your stuff in my room!"

Kat didn't miss the reproachful look she got from her mother, but she led him up the stairs and down the hall to her room anyway.

As soon as they stepped inside, Kat closed the door behind them, and he pulled her into his arms. She felt faint as he kissed her with the all the passion of the pent-up desire he had struggled to keep hidden for the last month. She met him in his hunger with her own need and was soon matching his enthusiasm. He led her to her bed and her knees buckled as they hit the mattress, spilling the two of them backward over the top of it. Kat knew they were taking a huge risk but couldn't help herself.

As his hand traveled up her shirt and his lips worked their way down from her ear to her neck and down across her right collar bone, she let out a low, sensuous moan that only enticed him further. She tangled her fingers in the hair at the back of his neck and he exhaled sharply.

"You cannot fathom how much I've been dreaming of this!" he whispered. He reached behind her and pulled out her elastic, spilling her hair all around her shoulders. He inhaled sharply at the view before him. "God, Kat… You're beautiful!"

She stretched up and placed her lips on his, effectively silencing him for a few seconds. As it became clear that they were getting carried away, he suddenly pulled back and sat up.

"What?" Kat whimpered.

"Do you forgive me?" he asked her, his hands lightly gripping her upper arms and looking directly in her eyes.

"Forgive you? For what?"

"For being so damned thick and not putting you first. I'm sorry it appeared that I was choosing my career or Lydia over you. I can't believe that I was so incredibly weak and confused that I didn't do this weeks ago. I should have stood up for you from the beginning. The day you left, I was coming to tell you that I didn't care anymore, that all I wanted was you, but you had already gone. Then I got scared, thinking that I had already lost you, but I was so damned exhausted that I couldn't think straight about how to fix it. All I could focus on was finishing up, of surviving until we wrapped, so I could get back to you."

"Shhhh… Ian, it's okay! I know why you did it and I admire you for it," Kat hushed him.

"No, it's not. I didn't only do it to protect Lydia. I did it because I was concerned about losing my job." He hung his head, obviously ashamed. "I should've realized sooner that you're all that really matters, everything else is replaceable. All I could think from Friday night to Monday morning while I was alone in my hotel rooms was what if you had come back home and gone back to James because I was such an *eejit*, but I was too scared to ask. This morning, I couldn't take it anymore and the only solution I could think about was telling everyone how I feel about you."

"I can't believe you did that! On national T.V.!"

"I finally realized that you deserve for the whole world to know that I choose you. I am so sorry that I didn't comprehend that sooner."

Suddenly, there was a knock at the door and Kat and Ian sprang apart. Kat straightened her shirt and ran her fingers through her hair, while he sat up and adjusted himself to try and better hide his physical response to her as she stepped forward to answer. Outside stood her two nieces looking expectantly at her.

"Is he really here, Aunt Kat?" Emily softly asked.

Kat couldn't help but laugh. "Yes, girls, he's really here. Give us a few minutes and we'll come downstairs, okay? Ask Gramma to give the stew a good stir for me in the meantime."

"All right, Aunt Kat," Brooklyn answered, her eyes wide. "Did you tell him that I love his horse?" Kat heard him chuckle behind her.

"Yes, sweetie, he knows that you love his horse." At that moment, Kat looked at Emily and saw the question in her eyes, begging her not to say what she had said about Ian being hot. Kat just smiled reassuringly at her and shook her head, letting her know that she had nothing to worry about. Emily let out a sigh of relief.

"Where were we?" she asked him as soon as she shut the door and returned to him.

"About here, I think," he said as he kissed her deeply. "That feels about right."

"We need to get out of this room! My mother is well-known for her tendency to just burst in," Kat said after a few minutes, while Ian was once again kissing her neck and running his hand up under her shirt and over her curves. He pulled her closer and she released a quiet moan, which he silenced by putting his lips on hers. Her hands wrapped around his low back at the top of his pants, her fingers lightly stroking his skin as he kissed her lips.

"Really, Ian, we need to stop," she told him reluctantly. "I'm so sorry, but if we keep going, I really won't be able to quit, and someone could walk in at any minute. I know you said that you wanted the whole world to know you love me, but you probably don't want them to see it in action."

Her body was screaming to connect with his, but she knew that it was too risky in the middle of the afternoon inside her bedroom of her childhood home.

"It's okay. You're right—I'm not that kind of actor," he laughed as he gently drew her head back in and gave her a soft kiss on her lips. "I *really* want you, but we have all of the time in the world."

"We'd better head downstairs before they send up a Southern Baptist search party." She opened the door and led him down the stairs into the kitchen.

When they stepped into the room, Jessica, Laura, and Kat's mother, who were sitting at the table in the breakfast nook, all turned at the same moment to look at them. Kat smiled knowingly as she noticed the three very different expressions on their faces. Her mother looked suspicious and slightly stern. Laura looked at Ian admiringly. Jessica had that glazed-over, deer-in-headlights look Kat had observed on most other female faces when they saw him in person. She recovered the quickest, however, asking him, "Did you have a good flight?"

"It was fine, thanks. I kept finding myself leaning forward like I was willing the pilot to make it here faster, but it was good." With that, he reached back and gave Kat's hand a squeeze.

"That accent!" Jessica mumbled and then looked up completely mortified to have spoken aloud not only in front of him, but her mother-in-law too. Kat burst out laughing.

"Don't worry, Jess. Everyone seems to say stupid things around Ian at first. I think he's well used to it by now. But I do wonder if he ever thinks that Americans are a bunch of idiots?"

"Canadians, too!" he replied with a wink. "In all honesty, though, not at all. Though it still surprises and catches me off guard. I mean, I'm just me. I don't quite see what all of the fuss is about?"

Kat reached up and kissed his cheek and said close to his ear, "It's because you are so gorgeous." Ian just blushed slightly as he shook his head, a small, shy smile emerging.

The room was silent for a few uncomfortable seconds before Kat's mother said, "I've been stirrin' the stew. I'm not sure what you want to have with it?"

Ian's eyes lit up. "Could you make your biscuits?"

"Sure! Wanna help?" she asked as she moved to a cupboard and removed a big metal mixing bowl. He stepped up beside her and watched as she gathered the ingredients. Together, through a whole lot of laughing, they made the dough. Kat's mother and sisters-in-law were quickly enchanted by the easy familiarity and ease between the two of them, noticing the intimacy and stolen glances they shared, like there was no one else in the room.

After watching how Kat and Ian interacted for a while, everyone began to relax and started seeing Ian as a person, not a T.V. star, and soon they were joining in the conversation, enjoying stories of Ian's cooking escapades through the years. He told them that for about six months in his twenties, he gave up cooking entirely and lived off of Indian takeaway from down the street. He claimed he had stopped only when he began to smell like curry. In turn, Kat's mother regaled them with stories of Kat's kitchen mishaps throughout the years.

"So, did she learn her cooking skills from you, Mrs. Curtis?"

"Oh, no, Ian, but bless your heart! Aren't you sweet? No, she learned all of that from my sweet ol' mama. Cookin' is a genetic trait that seems to skip a generation in our family."

"Well, then, I intend to be the lucky beneficiary of that genetic lottery win for a long time!" he said, leaning over to kiss Kat on the top of her head.

Kat began to roll out the biscuit dough in order to start cutting them out. Ian, wanting to show Kat he had remembered what she had taught him during their time in the kitchen on location, asked to take over, but the rolling pin kept sticking and he was pushing flour over the counter's edge onto the floor. He threw his hands up in mock disgust and told everyone that he had better stick to acting. Kat snickered as she reached to take back the utensil. Wanting to kiss her cheek, he reached over and pushed some hair off of her face, leaving a white trail in his wake. When he saw what he had done, he chortled, causing Kat to seek out her reflection in the door of the microwave to see what was so funny. Her eyes widened with mock annoyance as she determinedly took her own hands and placed them on either side of his face, giving him a big kiss on the lips and leaving two floured handprints on his cheeks. Everyone in the room was laughing so hard by this time, no one heard Kat's dad and brothers walk into the kitchen.

"What have we here? What's all this commotion?" Kat's father's voice boomed. Everyone turned to look at him and his sons standing in the doorway.

"Oh! Hi, Daddy! We're just making biscuits!" Kat happily replied.

"I can see that," he said coolly. "Who's this?"

Ian stepped forward and went to reach out his hand. Realizing that it was still covered in flour, he quickly wiped it on the thigh of his jeans before extending it once more.

"Ian McGregor, sir."

454

"Ah, yes. The infamous Ian. Nice to meet you, son."

"Nice to meet you as well."

Kat could hear that Ian was nervous, but only because she knew him so well. With his years of acting and natural talent, he was able to hide it well.

"Thanks for watchin' out for my little girl out there in the wilderness so that she didn't get eaten by a bear or somethin'."

"It was my pleasure, sir."

"Well now, the boys and I were just about to grab a beer and go sit out on the deck. Would you care to join us?"

"Um, sure. That would be great. Just go on ahead and I'll be out as soon as I get cleaned up a bit." Ian rushed out of the kitchen, heading toward Kat's bedroom.

"So, that's Ian, then?" Thomas asked dryly.

"Yes! And y'all go easy on him, boys, ya hear?"

Kat gave them her sternest look.

"Yes, ma'am!" Christopher replied. The three men grabbed their beers and headed out. It wasn't too long before Ian ran back down the stairs and joined them outside. At first Kat heard only snippets of polite conversation, but after a few minutes they all started to get animated, talking about golf. Kat's father was holding court as he retold stories of his lack of prowess on the green, while the younger men laughed. Kat sat at the table with the women while the biscuits baked and eavesdropped, smiling to herself. Ian was fitting right in.

"So, tell us, Ian. Did you golf in Ireland?"

"No, sir. I didn't even pick up a club until I came to Los Angeles. I tried playing a few times with some studio people. Not surprisingly, it did not go well."

"I thought Ireland is where golf started?" Christopher asked.

"Common misconception. It was Scotland," Ian replied easily. "We don't really have a national sport, except for hurling, and maybe football. And by that I mean real football, too; not this running about and stopping every few seconds with the ball in your hands while wrapped in bubble wrap that you Yanks play. Oh, and drinking at the pub."

"Oh, no he didn't!" Christopher exclaimed. "Not only did he just insult our favorite sport, but he also called us Yanks!"

"Just calling it like I see it, lads! How do you say it? I'm sorry, but 'y'all' are Yanks on this side of the pond," he fired back, trying on a Southern accent for size. "Isn't that what I should say down here?"

All of the men began to laugh before continuing their conversation.

Meanwhile, the women continued to prepare the meal and dessert under Kat's supervision, while the girls set the table in the dining room. Jessica turned to Kat and said, "I cannot believe I said that! I'm so embarrassed!"

Kat smiled kindly. "Honestly, after what I've seen in airports, that was nothing. He might not be all that famous yet, but his fans are sure devoted, I will say that much. At least y'all didn't try to throw yourself at him, take a selfie, or try to get him to sign some part of y'all's anatomy."

"People do that?" her mother asked incredulously.

"That and more. It's insane. I haven't got a clue how actors deal with it, honestly."

"He's certainly easy on the eyes," Laura interjected and then quickly looked to her mother-in-law with a glint of fear in her eyes.

To everyone's surprise, Kat's mother just smiled and said, "That he is, sugar. I almost couldn't speak for a few minutes what with him standin' on my porch in the flesh. Made me feel seventeen again. He is actually better lookin' in person than he is on T.V., if that is even possible."

"Lydia actually described it perfectly to me once: he makes women swoon," Kat reported.

"That he does," Jessica responded. "No offense, Kat, but wow! I mean, how did you ever land a man like that? You're pretty and all, but he could get just about any woman in the world, I would think."

Kat sighed. "I know. It was a big concern of mine. But he's assured me time and time again that he isn't interested in a

Barbie doll. He told me that two actors rarely make a good couple; that because of the nature of the business, they have to be vain and too much of that in a relationship just doesn't work. And to be honest, I've never seen his eyes wander once when we're in public. He's always gracious and kind, but he's never a flirt."

"But what attracted him specifically to you?" Jessica asked incredulously.

"Thanks, Jessica! I think that was a compliment?" Kat laughed. "Anyway, he said that it was because I *didn't* swoon that he was attracted to me. He didn't know what grits were and he was giving me a hard time, feeling ornery, and said that it floored him completely that I didn't get flustered.

"He told me later it became a challenge to see how far he could push me before I broke. He never expected me to push back but when I finally did, Lydia stepped in, along with George, the producer, and he backed down. I guess having raised three teenagers prepared me well for some attitude. But to be honest, I felt flustered. I think I was just able to hide it well, partly because of shock, but mostly because of sleep deprivation."

"Well, whatever it is, hearts are breaking all around the world tonight!" Laura said. Kat beamed happily.

When dinner was ready, everyone came together in the dining room. By some mix up, Ian and Kat ended up sitting across from one another while Emily and Brooklyn were on either side of him. After the food was blessed, the din of everyone serving and talking overtook the room.

After a few minutes, there was a momentary lull in the conversation, and everyone heard Brooklyn's sweet voice saying, "What do you do with your horse when you aren't making the show?"

They all turned toward her and saw that Ian was completely engrossed in a conversation with the young girl, sitting sideways in his chair to face her and leaning down slightly; he hadn't even dished himself up a plate.

"He lives in a stable near Los Angeles. I go and ride him as much as I can."

"So, you are a horseman, then, are you, son?" Kat's dad boomed across the room.

"No, not really, sir; at least not in the beginning. I lied to get the part. I almost broke my neck several times filming the first season."

"Did you really?" Kat's mother asked.

"I did, ma'am. It was not pretty. I laugh now at how bad my seat was when I see the earliest shows. But after a while, I gained a real appreciation for the old boy. I found riding relaxing. We have come to an understanding of sorts now, and he does what I want almost without me having to tell him."

"I don't know if Kat has told you or not, but my mama and daddy owned a horse ranch in Kentucky."

"She did tell me that, sir. Her riding also shows it." He grinned at her.

"I used to ride all of the time, but I haven't been on a horse in I don't recall how long now."

"Kat was amazing. When I fell off my horse, she rode him back so I could have Lydia's mare, who is smaller and a lot less feisty. Buster's kind of a brute, especially with someone he doesn't know, but he was on his best behavior for her."

"So, Ian..." Kat's mother cut in "Kat tells me that your mother's movin' here from Ireland?"

"She is, ma'am. She arrives in Los Angeles next month."

"What's she goin' to do there?" she inquired.

"Hopefully, relax and take it easy for once. She has worked hard her whole life. She deserves a break."

"What did she do?"

"She was a nurse until just very recently."

"And your father?"

Kat looked up at him and caught his glance. He took a deep breath. "My father was a policeman."

"Was? Oh, bless your heart! I'm so sorry, sugar."

"Thank you. It's all right. It was a long time ago now. But my ma worked hard to provide for my sister and me. I'm looking forward to paying some of that back.”

“Will she live with you?”

“She will. I just closed on a house about… How long ago was it, Kat?”

Kat swallowed her mouthful and then responded, “It was about eight weeks ago now.” He smiled sweetly at her.

“Have you seen his house, Aunt Kat?” Brooklyn piped up.

“Yes, sweetie, I have. It’s very nice.”

“Is there room for your horse?” she asked Ian excitedly.

He chuckled. “Sadly, Brooklyn, there isn’t room for my horse. Even if there was, I wouldn’t be able to keep him there in the city. It’s against the law.”

“Oh.”

“But I promise you and your grandfather if you ever come to Los Angeles to visit, you can take a ride on him, okay?”

“Okay!” she replied gleefully.

With that, the women stood up and began to clear the dishes. Ian looked around and got up, too. “You all please sit down. I’ll take care of these,” he declared.

The family gaped at him. He looked at Kat with panic in his eyes. He hadn’t a clue what he had said or done to elicit such a response.

“Well, that’s so nice of you, Ian!” Kat’s mother cried. “I don’t think that kitchen has seen a man voluntarily wash a dish in the whole time this ol’ house has stood!”

Kat could tell that he was thinking of something to say in response that wouldn’t incriminate him in the eyes of either gender. She quickly grabbed his arm and called over her shoulder, “I’ll help him. Y’all just relax.”

When they made it into the kitchen, they placed the dishes they were carrying into the sink, and he took her into his arms. “Mmmm…” he sighed, inhaling the fragrance in her hair from her shampoo. “This feels so nice.”

Kat reached up on her tiptoes and gave him a peck. Though she was trying to be quick and playful, he placed his hand on the back of her head and pulled her in closer, deepening the kiss. Kat felt all of her senses go blank as she stood in his arms, their lips communicating everything they had been feeling for the last few weeks. Things were just about to cross into inappropriate behavior for a communal area in a house full of people, two of them minors, when Kat heard her mother say that she was going in to check on how things were going in the kitchen. Kat and Ian sprang apart just in time. Kat's mother walked in and looked around, observing that the sink was still full of dishes. She then saw the disheveled mess Ian's fingers had created in Kat's hair and noticed her swollen lips. Kat was sure she could hear their still rapid heartbeats and see their chests heaving. But, being a polite Southern Christian woman, she chose to not say anything before simply walking out to return to the living room. Ian and Kat looked sideways at each other and then started to giggle.

"Whoa! That was close!" she said.

"Why do I feel like I'm sixteen again and my ma just walked in on me and my girlfriend?"

"Because in a Southern household, as long as you are unmarried, any relations between a man and a woman have to be as clandestine as they are when you are teenagers, even if you're over forty."

"I'm not over forty," he said with a wink.

Kat let out a groan. "You just *had* to remind me of that, didn't you?"

"Sorry, not sorry!" He grinned at her. She smacked him on the butt with her dish towel in response.

They finished the dishes and cleaning the kitchen, just enjoying being together after so long apart. It was like no time had passed, as they immediately fell back into their comfortable routine of conversation and intimate touches. Ian put soap bubbles on Kat's nose at one point, garnering an indignant look of mock surprise, complete with her hands on her hips. She looked so adorable he could only laugh as he grabbed her and pulled her close.

They wandered back into the living room holding hands and joined everyone on the couch. It was getting late, and the conversation was dying down as the excitement of the day finally gave way to exhaustion. Ian stifled a yawn and stretched his arm over Kat's shoulder, pulling her closer into him. She responded by turning her face up to his, so he leaned down and gave her a kiss on the forehead. For just a few seconds, they forgot they weren't alone, and everyone could feel their desire radiating off of each other.

Kat's mother cleared her throat. "It's gettin' late. I reckon we'd better get Ian settled for the night." Ian glanced at Kat with a questioning look.

"I'm so sorry, Ian, but the house is just full up right now. What with Kat and the boys and their families bein' here for the graduations, I don't have another bedroom to offer you. But the couch in the basement is a pullout."

It clearly dawned on him at that moment that he would not be joining Kat in her double bed upstairs. His shoulders slumped just a little bit before he answered, "That will be fine, ma'am. Thank you."

"Just let me get it all made up for you, sugar," she told him.

"It's really all right, Mrs. Curtis. I'm just fine with making my own bed. Just point me in the direction of the linen cupboard."

"Nonsense! You are a guest in this house, and I won't have you doin' any such thing!"

Kat rolled her eyes. "Don't worry, Mama. I'll take care of it with Ian, so you don't have to."

She stood up and took Ian's hand, leading him to the basement door. They made their way down the stairs and together they pulled out the mattress from the couch after which Kat grabbed the sheets, blanket, and pillows from the closet.

"This is certainly not the way I imagined we would spend our first night together again," he told her quietly, a look of obvious disappointment showing on his face.

"Yeah, sorry about that. They're very old fashioned," she responded.

"I guess I'll just have to settle for being happy to be under the same roof as you after the last few weeks," he said and turned to kiss her on her cheek. Kat turned her head at the last second, catching his lips in hers and getting instantly lost in the intensity of it.

Just then, Christopher walked by. He looked at them and said, "If y'all are going to try and have sex down here tonight, at least do it quietly! Oh, and that bed squeaks."

"Christopher!" she heard Jessica exclaim from inside their room. "What a horrible thing to say!"

"Well, it does!" he responded indignantly. "You remember that time…"

Kat stuck her fingers in her ears and cried out, "Lalalalalala! I don't want to know this about you, big brother!"

Christopher shrugged as he walked into his room. "Just trying to save y'all some embarrassment based on personal experience," he called out over his shoulder before shutting the door.

"Don't let Mama catch y'all, either!" Thomas yelled out. "Also from personal experience…."

"So, I guess the only way to share a bed in the Curtis household is if you are married?" Ian guessed.

"That is correct. It hasn't really been an issue since I was almost twenty. But then again it wasn't too much of an issue then, either, because James and I lived in the same city and never slept together before we were married."

"What? Are you serious?" he asked her.

"Yes! I told you that before, remember? Times and traditions were different back then. Especially here," she said with a shrug.

"I'm thinking we may have to alter this arrangement sooner rather than later, then," he told her as he pulled back just a little to look into her eyes.

Kat gave him a strange look. *What did he mean by that?*

They shared one more intimate embrace before Kat reluctantly started to walk away. Ian grabbed her hand, stopping her, and stepped closer to whisper in her ear. "Want to test the squeaky bed theory?" he asked with a grin, giving her shivers down her spine.

"Yes!" she whispered back. "But I don't think we dare. There are too many people here. And Tom's right: we don't want my mother catching us. We would never hear the end of our 'sinful' behavior."

She kissed him lightly one more time and walked up the stairs. Ian let out a low whistle under his breath. She looked back over her shoulder, shook out her hair behind her and added a little more swing in her hips as she made it up the rest of the way. Just then, they heard Thomas call out, "Hey, that's my baby sister you're whistling at there!"

As she disappeared out of sight, Ian smiled and shook his head while he crawled under the covers. "Goodnight!" he called out, chuckling at the cacophony of Kat's family members responding to him.

Chapter Forty-Eight

Kat woke at daybreak the following morning and joined her father for a cup of coffee on the deck. They sat together in companionable silence, watching the cardinals fly around the backyard and listening to the mockingbirds call to each other in the trees. Finally, as the sun's rays peeked through the trees, Kat spoke.

"You're sure up early, Daddy!" she told him as she stood up to fold her legs up under her in the chair.

"Old habits die hard, baby girl. I was up and on the road to work way before the sun was up for over forty-five years. You on the other hand… Well, now, this is the real surprise."

"I have a lot to do between today and Friday. Ian's surprise visit, though very welcome, has put me a bit behind schedule with getting everything ready for Drew's party. I was going to go up to the old house yesterday, today, tomorrow, and Thursday, but somehow I don't think that I should bring Ian over there, out of respect for James. He really doesn't deserve much consideration after what he did to me, but, at least as far as I know, he never brought his mistress into our home."

"And that's what makes you a better person than he is, darlin'." Her father was quiet for a moment before continuing, "Speakin' of Ian, I like him."

"You do? Already?" Kat couldn't hide the surprise in her voice.

"Yes, I do. He was already more comfortable out here on this deck with your brothers and me after one afternoon than James was in over twenty years. What's better is that he wasn't tryin' to impress us none, either—he was just himself. He also wasn't conceited like I assumed an actor with some success might be."

"I'm glad to hear it," Kat told him.

"The boys like him, too."

"They told you that?" she asked incredulously.

"Didn't have to, sweet pea," he drawled. "I could just tell by how they were all banterin' back and forth."

"Yeah, I held my breath for a few seconds after I overheard him make that football comment."

Her father laughed. "Those boys didn't know which insult to attack first: the crack about *real* football or his callin' us 'Yanks'!" He shook his head at the memory.

"He does have a pretty good sense of humor." Kat grinned.

Her father looked up at her intently and reached over to take her hand in his. "But most of all, I like who you are with him. You're comfortable, relaxed. There's a level of intimacy there that you never had with James, at least that I saw."

"It's strange, Daddy… even though he's relatively famous and getting more so, I've never felt more relaxed around anyone. You're right about his not being conceited. He still seems genuinely surprised that people admire him. He has told me several times that he can't see what all of the fuss is about, that he is just himself."

"Still, he certainly has healthy self-esteem, which is good. He's comfortable with who he is, so he doesn't need to bring anyone else down to compensate. James has always been a little too demeanin', especially to you."

"Yeah, Ian really is just a nice guy. No hidden agenda, as far as I can tell. Just what he did to protect Lydia made me realize what a good heart he possesses."

"All I've ever wanted for all y'all was to have mates who made you feel loved and secure. I'm sorry you didn't have that with James. I hope that it continues with Ian, though." He stood up. "Well, I'd better get started on my day. The boys and I are goin' to the ball game later. Think Ian would want to come?"

"Not sure. I can ask him…."

"You do that, sugar. See you later." Her father kissed her on the cheek and walked back into the house.

Kat sat out in her chair until she heard movement and voices in the kitchen. She went in to find her brothers, their wives, and her nieces scrounging around for something for breakfast.

Thomas looked up as she came through the door and exclaimed, "There's my favorite sister! How about you whip us up some biscuits and gravy?"

Kat laughed and said she would be happy to after she checked on Ian. As she went down the basement stairs she heard Christopher call after her, "There's no need! He's alive; I checked. If you don't get to cooking though, we won't be!"

"Y'all will live!" she called out as she hit the bottom step.

Kat smiled when she saw Ian's sleeping form as she crept over to him. He was curled up on his side, facing away from her, his hands resting under his cheek. She couldn't help herself as she leaned over to kiss him. He surprised her by reaching up and grabbing her, causing her to squeal as he pulled her down over him. True to report, the bed squeaked loudly with the movement and they both burst out laughing.

"Good morning!" he said, raising his head up to give her a kiss.

"Good morning!" she answered, burrowing her face into the crick of his neck, from which his own intoxicating scent rose blended with that of slumber. "How did you sleep?"

"Better than I have in a really long time, honestly. What time is it?"

"A little after eight," she replied as she brushed the hair off his forehead and landed a kiss there.

"Is everyone else still asleep?" he asked.

"Not at all. They're all upstairs, impatiently awaiting my return to make them biscuits and gravy."

"Mmmm… that actually sounds really good. Grits?" he asked with a wink.

"You mean corn oatmeal?" she replied sarcastically. "Of course. No self-respecting Southern cook would have it any other way!" she continued, seriously.

Ian sat up and covered her lips with his. "Mmmm…" he moaned quietly. "This is what I'm really hungry for!"

"To be honest, I thought that you would come up to my room last night when everyone fell asleep."

"Believe me, I was very tempted. But I didn't dare disrespect your parents like that. This is their house, so their rules."

"I almost came down here at one point. Good thing I didn't though: the boys weren't kidding, this bed does squeak!" She leaned over and gave him another kiss before standing up and telling him where he could find towels and other supplies if he wanted to take a shower, since she was going to start breakfast.

The meal was a raucous affair with everyone laughing and talking over each other, the boys dishing it out to Ian and him handing it right back. They seemed truly enthusiastic to have him tag along to their baseball game later in the afternoon. Afterward Kat and Ian cleaned up the kitchen together, lost in their own little world, oblivious to what was going on around them. Watching them from the doorway, Thomas smiled before joining the rest of the family in the living room.

"I don't think I've ever seen Kat look so happy," he said to no one in particular, but everyone murmured their agreement.

In the kitchen, Ian and Kat were finishing up. "Are you sure it's okay, Kat, if I go to the game with your father and brothers?" he asked.

"Sure! Why wouldn't it be?"

"I know that you have to get ready for Drew's graduation party on Friday and I sort of wrecked your schedule by showing up here unannounced yesterday. I was wondering if you needed my help?"

She walked over to him and wrapped her arms around his waist. "I'd rather have you wreck my schedule for the next hundred years than not have you here," she said quietly.

He tightened his arms around her and kissed the top of her head. "I've never been to a baseball game. Anything I should know?"

"Nope. Just cheer for our team and you're good! As for Drew's party, don't worry. I'll head up to the house this afternoon while y'all are gone. I can get quite a bit done with Olivia there."

"Back up to your old house?" he asked, evidently surprising even himself with the hint of jealousy creeping into his voice.

"Yes, Ian. Back to my old house. Where my children still live. Don't worry, James is at work."

"It's fine. I just forgot that this wasn't your house, that's all."

"Regardless of what has happened, we still have three children together and need to do our best to work in their best interest. That means I'll have to deal with James in some capacity for the rest of our lives."

"I know. I guess I'm just insecure, knowing how much of a history you share together. I'm still worried that you're going to discover I'm not worth all the bother."

"Some of it isn't such great history, Ian, especially the last year or so."

Ian frowned. "He won't give you any trouble, will he?"

"He's already asked me a few times to come home to him and each time, I've told him no. It doesn't appeal to me in the least."

"I'm sorry. I know I'm being ridiculous. But now that we're finally together, Kat, I don't want anything to mess it up."

"It won't!" she promised, slapping him on the backside with the palm of her hand. "Go with my father and brothers and enjoy yourself. I'll see you tonight!"

A short time later, Kat set out in her mother's car.

She arrived at the house and, as suspected, Olivia was there, lounging in front of the T.V., enjoying her much needed time off from school. Olivia looked up, surprised, as her mother walked through the door.

"Hey, Mama! What's going on?"

"I'm here for a few hours to make some of the food for Drew's party. Want to help?"

"Is he here?" she hissed, looking down at her pajama pants and stained tank top.

"Who?"

"Ian Gregory!" Olivia cried.

"Oh! No. He went to the baseball game with Pawpaw and

your uncles. Why?"

"Look at me!"

"You look fine, sweetheart. He isn't even here."

"I cannot believe what he did, Mama! Daddy was fit to be tied. Came home madder than a hornet last night, slamming things around and hardly talking to Drew and me."

"Uh oh. I was wondering if he had found out and how he reacted."

"He's pretty upset, Mama. I think he really hoped that y'all would eventually get back together, especially after last week."

"I know and I am sorry for that. But I've been very straight forward with telling him that it's over. He just doesn't want to accept it," Kat told her sadly.

"Is Ian coming up here this week?"

"Yes, for the graduation and party. Other than that, no. I don't want to make this any harder on your daddy than it has to be. I know he'd be none too pleased to know that Ian was in this house with me."

Olivia nodded and started up the stairs before stopping and turning. "Mama, I know he's upset, but I'm glad to see you so happy. You've done so much for all of us; it's time you get to live for yourself a little."

"Thank you, baby!" Kat answered her, genuinely surprised.

Olivia ran the rest of the way up the stairs to get ready, while Kat got to work, baking cake tiers to freeze and making other dishes that would keep until Friday.

Olivia returned, and they worked side by side for several hours, talking and laughing with each other, catching up further about what had happened over the last few months and with Ian the day before.

"I can't believe it was just yesterday!" Kat exclaimed. "It feels like a lifetime ago already."

"So, when do we get to meet him?" Olivia asked eagerly.

"I'm not sure. Y'all could come down to Pawpaw and Gramma's house. That is unless y'all just want to wait until this weekend."

"I can't speak for the boys, but I'd love to meet him before the party."

"Why don't you come on down with Drew tomorrow night then, and I'll call Derrick and make sure he knows he should come, too. Sound good?"

"Sure, Mama."

Kat worked until around six at the house and then cleaned up and left. As she wound her way down the streets of her neighborhood, she passed James on his way home.

She waved at him as she drove past, thankful that she had dodged that bullet.

When she walked into her parents' house, laughter was coming from the living room. She was already grinning as she stopped in the doorway but burst out laughing as she caught sight of Ian. He had on a jersey and cap with the team's logo on it, and balls, flags, and bobble heads surrounding him.

As she walked in, Christopher exclaimed excitedly, "You need to start dating more celebrities! As soon as it got out that he was there, we all got the royal treatment. Free food, booze, swag, box seats. If I had known this would happen, I would have pawned you off on someone famous long before now!" He walked over and slung his arm around her shoulders.

"Ah, thanks! *Now* I understand my worth. My bride price is that y'all get free stuff at ball games!"

"Got that right!" Thomas agreed.

"It certainly was a nice perk, baby girl. We may just have to see if Ian can get us bowl game or World Series tickets," her dad added with a wink.

Kat shook her head and walked over to Ian, putting her arm around his shoulders. "So, how was it?"

"It was good!" he replied. "Much better than 'football'!" he added cheekily while making air quotes to get a rise out of her brothers. He leaned up and kissed her. "How'd it go for you?"

"It went well. Olivia and I got a lot done. The kids are going to come down here tomorrow night for dinner, if that's okay with y'all?" Everyone nodded their approval.

The evening that followed was pretty much the same as the one before, though Kat had to admit it was going to be much harder to leave Ian alone on the sofa bed this time as she had been away from him for the majority of the day.

After dinner, she grabbed his hand and pulled him out on the back porch. They sat in chairs opposite each other for a while and watched the lightning bugs twinkle among the bushes. Ian had never seen them before and was fascinated, particularly when Kat managed to catch one and bring it up to him in her hands.

"Ugly little buggers up close, aren't they?" he asked, clearly investigating it. "How can something that looks so beautiful from far away look like that close up?"

"They aren't quite as mystical in close proximity as they are from a distance, are they?" she asked. "My boys used to love to catch them and put them in jars when they were little."

"These things actually almost make up for those other giant, disgusting insects you have here," he told her.

"What's the matter, Ian? Scared of a little cockroach?"

"Ummm… I'm not sure what your definition of little is, but an insect the length of my thumb is not mine!" he retorted.

Kat placed the bug carefully on the railing and they watched as it took flight. As she stepped back, Ian grabbed her around the waist and pulled her down onto his lap. She looked up to kiss him and felt his hand glide up under her shirt. The touch of his warm skin made her tingle and she sighed as she relaxed into him. When he touched his lips to hers again, he was much demanding than before. Kat turned and began kissing down his neck to his shoulder, circling her tongue and nibbling his skin gently, feeling him shudder as he let out a small groan. He moved his hand around to cup her breast before maneuvering his fingers under her bra and slowly rubbing his thumb back and forth. Kat pushed herself even closer to him as she felt her body's response to him. Relishing in his nearness, she rolled her head back onto his shoulder and he smiled. Feeling his breath increase, she ground her hips deeper into his lap, enticed further by the growing evidence that he was enjoying her ministrations.

"I want you," she whispered in his ear.

"I want you, too," he said softly into her neck. "Can we go down on the grass where we won't be seen?"

Kat shook her head against his neck. "No. Fire ants."

"What?"

"Fire ants. We can't see if there are any mounds in the dark down there and we don't want to find them by accident."

He groaned in frustration as he rolled his head against the back of the chair. "What the hell kind of place do you live?" he asked her.

"Somewhere where the bugs are in cahoots with mamas to make sure their precious daughters aren't sullied in the shadows," she replied, giggling.

"It works. It's like nature's bloody birth control!"

She shook her head, giggling even harder at his comment. "It's dark out here and no one knows where we are," she told him, lightly kissing his ear.

"Are you suggesting out here, on the deck?" he asked her incredulously.

"No one ever comes out here at night," she told him. "We will go back inside quietly, turn off the lights, tell them we are going for a walk, and then sneak back around the side of the house."

"You are quite the risk taker!" he replied with admiration.

"You're worth it!"

She grabbed his hand and pulled him through the backdoor into the kitchen. She slammed a few cupboard doors before they walked out into the living room. "We're going for a walk," she casually told everyone, and they headed for the front door.

They silently skulked around to the backside of the house and crept their way up the wooden stairs.

Logistically, it was going to be difficult, but then Kat caught sight of the armless rocking chair in the corner.

"What do you think?" she whispered.

"Could be fun!" He sat down and she followed suit, facing

472

him, and draping her legs over his lap.

They fell into each other, and it wasn't long before they were deeply, messily involved, with hot, wet kisses and sweating bodies, craving more. Ian's hands on her felt like fire and she was aching to be with him. She bent forward, tickling his ear with her tongue, as he contentedly sighed. He ran his hands up and down her back, grabbing her bra and unclasping it, freeing her breasts. He lifted her shirt above her head as he unconsciously continued to gently rock them. It wasn't long before Kat couldn't wait anymore and stood up to take off her shorts. Then she bent over and unbuckled his belt, unbuttoned his jeans and, as he stood up slightly, pushed them down. She straddled him again and slowly inched her way down, eliciting a sharp gasp of pleasure from him.

"Oh, God, Kat! You feel so good!" he quietly moaned in her hair as his hands found their way to her back, his fingers pushing into the silky flesh, holding her tightly against him.

Together, the momentum of the chair kept increasing as their movements become more frenzied. Ian slid his hands down until they were firmly placed on her hips, guiding her as she pushed further into his lap, wanting to appreciate every last possible inch of him. As the incredible sensation began to build, Kat's moans began to raise in volume; Ian grinned like a naughty schoolboy before he covered her mouth with his in an attempt to quiet her.

"Good?" he pulled back and asked her. Mouth open in ecstasy, she could only nod in response.

Watching her, he was also quickly losing control and he knew that he wasn't going to be able to hold back much longer himself. When he could resist no more, with a low growl, he let loose, driving deeper, as Kat leaned back on his lap, whimpering quietly as her body tensed around him, before collapsing against him.

She leaned against his chest, listening to the reassuring thump his steadying heartbeat while he gently kissed the top of her head as he held her. They rocked slowly back and forth, enjoying holding each other close, delighting in their being together again at last. Eventually the afterglow of their lovemaking began to fade, and they realized they were pushing their luck. Kat quickly put back on her discarded pieces of clothing while Ian pulled up his own. Creeping down the stairs hand in hand and around the side of the house, they tried not to giggle. On the front porch, he held her back as she went to reach for the doorknob.

"Just a little bit longer," he begged her, pressing his forehead against hers. "Please?" She smiled at him, and they kissed again, conveying goodnight to each other as they would not be able to later.

When they opened the front door, they saw that her parents had gone to bed leaving only Thomas and Laura watching T.V. They looked up at them and then Thomas did a double take.

"How was the walk?" he asked them, clearly trying hard not to laugh.

"Good," Kat responded neutrally. "Why?"

"Because, my dear little sister, you put your shirt back on both inside out *and* backwards." He couldn't contain his laughter anymore as she looked down and gasped when she saw what she had done.

"Oh, God! Thank goodness Mama isn't still awake!" she cried.

"Yeah, y'all are lucky!" Laura agreed.

Having said good night again with a quick kiss, Ian reluctantly walked down the stairs away from Kat. He turned and looked at her from halfway down and mouthed, "Thank you! I love you!" Kat kissed her fingers in response and held out her hand as she blew.

Chapter Forty-Nine

Kat and Olivia worked hard the next day while Ian went out with her father and brothers to the golf course. Kat was thrilled they all seemed to be getting along so well, like they had known each other for years rather than just a few days. Her brothers kept texting pictures of Ian in the rough, sand traps, and standing next to the water. At one point Christopher also sent: *He wasn't kidding that he can't play golf. Great entertainment value, though. Didn't know he could also be a comedian, did you?*

Kat: *Y'all be nice! At least he's trying!*

Christopher: *Hey, no judgment here. The guy is willing to laugh at himself which is more than I can say about stick in the mud James!*

When Drew got home, he, Kat, and Olivia headed back to her parents' house. Olivia was talking a mile a minute, obviously very excited to meet Ian, while Drew was unusually quiet in the backseat.

"What's the matter, baby?" Kat asked him.

"Nothing," he replied sulkily.

Kat inhaled sharply as it dawned on her that just because her kids were older, it didn't mean they hadn't been deeply affected by the recent changes to their family. She realized then how naïve she was being, expecting that her children would instantly be okay with her and Ian's relationship, just assuming it would be fine because she never expected him to step into the role of "father figure" to them, especially at their ages. She was hoping instead for more of a relationship like Ian was developing with her father and brothers.

"Drew," she told him gently, "I know that there have been a lot of changes for you lately, with more still to come. But, please, try not to take it out on Ian. He didn't do anything to break your father and me up. I didn't even know him until I got to Canada."

"What do you mean?" he snapped back. "Because of him,

you divorced Dad, and now everything as we knew it is gone!”

“Drew, please understand, sweet pea, that everything as you knew it was already gone before I met Ian. Not to mention, everything you know was going change anyway, starting Friday when you graduate, go to work over the summer, and then leave for college. Even if Daddy and I had stayed together or I had never met Ian, your life would still be drastically different than ever before.”

“I know. But I hate the fact that whenever I come home from college, I’ll have to stay with Dad in the townhome he’s going to buy here or go to Los Angeles to see you.”

“So, do you think it’s reasonable to say that it’s more that your idea of home will be gone than that it’s Ian’s fault?”

Drew was quiet as he sat and stared out the window, contemplating what she said. Finally, he answered, “It’s just really hard, Mama, to think about how I’ll never come home again. I’ll still see you, but it’ll never just be us again.”

“I understand that, Drew. But, baby, you have to know that I can’t stay in a relationship with your father for the rest of my life just so that you have a house to come back to. What he did was not something I could just forgive and forget. I know this is hard for you, but you need to see me not only as your mother, but as a person, too. Aren’t I entitled to respect and happiness?”

Again, Drew was quiet, considering her words. “You do deserve to be happy, Mama. I just wish that none of this had ever happened.”

“I know,” was all Kat could say. What she could no longer say was that she wished it hadn’t happened, too. She hadn’t known what she was missing or how good she could have it until the mess with James had pushed her out of her routine, her comfort zone, and allowed her to explore herself as an individual, with her own wants, desires, and needs. She sighed before speaking again.

“Drew, you know that Ian has no intention of trying to be your stepdad, right? I mean, if we do end up together, he’ll just be my partner, not your pseudo-dad. Y’all are adults now, and while I'd like it if y'all could form some sort of meaningful relationship with him, it wouldn't be one of parent and child. I would hope it could be as friends."

Again, Drew was quiet as he looked out the window. Kat watched him through the review mirror and could tell that he was ruminating over what she had said and saw almost the exact second he became resigned to what she was telling him.

"Okay, Mama. I'll try. I'll try not to think of him as the reason why you and Dad didn't reconcile."

"He really is nice, Drew. He's funny, he loves to laugh, is passionate, and articulate. I think that you'll find him easy to be around."

"Everything I've read has said that he's about the nicest guy in Hollywood," Olivia added.

"It's true. He treated everyone on set, from his costars to the interns, with respect and kindness," Kat agreed. "Well, except for me when we first met," she chuckled. "But after that happened, he actually was really, really nice to everyone up there."

"Is Derrick meeting us down there?" Olivia asked.

"Yes. He had a job interview this afternoon, so he said he'd head down later, after he's done. He said he'll drive y'all home after, too."

Kat had hit the afternoon gridlock and concentrated on the traffic surrounding her for the rest of the trip. When she finally pulled up to her parents' house, she took a deep breath and thought, *Here goes nothing...*

She waited for Drew and Olivia and together they walked up to the front door. Kat put her hand on Drew's shoulder just before reaching for the doorhandle and gave him an understanding smile when he looked over at her.

Kat was relieved to see that no one was sitting in the living room, waiting to pounce on the kids. She hadn't really talked to Ian about how he felt about meeting her children, so she was glad that he wasn't hovering just inside the door when they came in, as it may have looked like he was trying too hard. Emily and

Brooklyn were on their iPads in the family room and barely looked up until Olivia said, "Hi!" to them. They uttered a few pleasantries and then went back to their devices without any fanfare.

Walking into the kitchen, Kat's mother stood up and moved swiftly to the kids to wrap them in her embrace. Kat had issues with her mother's ideals about how life should be, but those ideals also made her an excellent and affectionate grandmother.

"Hey, Mama. Where are the boys?" Kat asked her, as she leaned over and gave her a kiss on her cheek.

"They're out back on the porch, drinkin' their Cokes," she replied as she took Olivia's hand and led her over to the table, asking her about any recent developments with her engagement.

Kat looked at Drew and said, "I'm going out to say hi. Want to come with me or stay in here?"

"I'll stay," he replied tersely. Kat worried that perhaps he had already forgotten the promise he'd made to her in the car. She smiled at him, though, and opened the backdoor, stepping out into the warm, humid evening.

"Hey, boys! How was golf?" she asked as she moved over to where Ian was sitting.

"It was great fun!" Ian told her.

"It sure was," Thomas retorted. "Ian provided *lots* of comic relief!" he smirked.

"Yeah, I don't think I've ever seen anyone so bad at golf," Christopher laughingly added.

"But, it was okay, baby girl, because he made the rest of us look fabulous!" her father joked.

"Poor Ian!" Kat exclaimed. She looked down and saw that he was sticking his bottom lip out in a fake pout. She bent down and gave him a kiss.

"No, really, Kat… It was good fun! They got a hardy laugh at my expense, and I learned a lot from them. Maybe by the time I'm fifty, I'll actually not embarrass myself playing out there."

"Don't worry, sugar," Kat told him. "They would suck at soccer! Um… I mean… 'football'." She made air quotes around football and gave him a sly grin. He reached up and grabbed her around her waist, bringing her down hard on his lap.

She smiled and laid her head on his shoulder when he boasted, "Yeah, I could kick all your arses on the field, hands down."

Just then, Drew stepped out the door and looked at Kat and Ian, snuggled together in the chair. His eyes widened a bit at first, then narrowed, as he turned to his grandfather and said, "Hi, Pawpaw."

Kat waited for a few seconds to see what would happen next and then when he said nothing more, she stood up off of Ian's lap and said, "Drew, this is Ian McGregor. Ian, this is my youngest son, Drew."

Ian stood up and put out his hand, and to her relief, Drew grasped it with his own. Ian smiled and said, "Nice to meet you, Drew. I bet you can't wait until Friday!"

"Yeah, I guess," Drew mumbled.

"Happiest day of my life, finishing school," Ian tried again.

"Yeah," Drew responded, still refusing to engage.

Kat gave Ian an exasperated look that conveyed her apology about his behavior, but Ian only smiled back at her and gave an almost imperceptible shake of his head to let her know it was okay.

Kat cleared her throat and asked Ian, "Want to go help me inside?" completely forgetting that Olivia was in the kitchen.

She opened the door just as the realization hit her that he still had two kids to meet. She pasted a smile on her face and walked into the room. Olivia was talking to her Aunt Jessica and stopped mid-sentence when she saw Ian walk through the door. She gaped at him for what seemed like several seconds, before Kat figured she had better step in and save her only daughter from certain humiliation.

"Olivia, this is Ian," she said quickly.

Olivia continued to stare at him, still unable to say anything, so Kat continued slowly, "This is my daughter, Olivia," hoping to give her daughter a few extra seconds to pull herself together.

Thankfully, Ian, fully accustomed to having this effect, just stepped forward and said, "Lovely to meet you, Olivia. You are just as beautiful as your mother." Both women blushed at his compliment.

Kat recovered and asked, "What can we do?" "Nothin', sugar," her mother replied. "Daddy's makin' his famous pulled pork and we're just havin' a bunch of salads and fixin's from the market. The girls already set the table, so we're just waitin' until His Royal BBQ Highness decides the pork is done. It has been in the Egg since early this mornin'. Should be nice and tender."

Kat smiled and went to pull out a chair when Ian moved around to do it for her. She flashed him an appreciative look and motioned for him to join her. He sat down next to Laura and across from Olivia.

"So, Olivia, your mother tells me you're studying social work. It's not an easy job, but I admire all they do. My costar, Lydia, has lots of experience with them, and she had some good ones and some not so good ones. I'm sure if you're as kind and straight forward as your mother, you will be one of the good ones."

Olivia could only nod. Kat chortled and said, "Sorry, Ian. All the Curtis women seem to go mute when they first meet you."

"All but one of them!" he retorted, flashing her a cocky grin.

"Oh, yes. All but me and my big mouth in Canada…"

"That's why I love you!" he said.

Kat noticed the quick looks the women flashed each other; her family hadn't yet heard him openly declare his feelings for her in person. It was certainly in stark contrast to James, who would instead criticize Kat under the guise of humor rather than publicly expound on his love for her.

"Thank you!" she exclaimed happily, "I love you, too!"

Derrick came through the door then, apologizing for being so late and giving his mother and grandmother each a hug. He stopped for a second to look at Ian but then he shrugged and stretched out his hand. "I'm Derrick. Nice to meet you."

Kat could see Ian visibly relax when he realized that at least two of her children seemed okay with him being in their mother's life. He smiled as he stretched out his own hand and said, "Ian, and the pleasure is mine."

Kat didn't want to give Derrick a chance to second guess his acceptance of the situation, so she quickly asked, "How'd the interview go?"

"It went well, Mama. I think it's mine if I want it. Pay is decent, and if I find a small place in town, the commute won't be bad."

"That's wonderful!" Kat declared.

"Yeah, Dad'll be real happy if I get this one…" Derrick's words slowed and then stopped when he realized that he had brought up his father and worried it could make for an awkward situation.

Ian, sensing his discomfort, jumped in to say, "It sounds like a good prospect. I'm sure any father would be proud to have their son land such a good opportunity right out of school."

Derrick looked over at him and smiled, relieved that he hadn't made a huge faux pas.

Kat's father then marched into the house, proudly carrying his pork roast into the dining room. The family all fell into seats around the table and bowed their heads as Kat's father offered the blessing. Then, the racket of various conversations was deafening to anyone who wasn't directly involved in one of them. As the dialog swirled around them, Kat and Ian looked up and caught each other's eyes. He offered her a reassuring smile, which she returned before she saw Drew looking between them and rolling his eyes as he continued to talk with Emily. Kat sighed, hoping that the situation would get better, but knowing in her heart that it very well might not.

Honestly, given he was the firstborn, Kat had figured she would get more disapproval from Derrick than Drew. But then she remembered that Drew was the one she was closest to of the three and that he was also the baby who had the most to lose at this point. The other two kids were older and had experience leading their own lives.

Drew, however, was facing his entire existence changing, even without the upheaval of the divorce, and she could sympathize with how being unable to picture life at home the way he recalled it could make leaving for school seem even harder. She reminded herself to be patient with him and thought that she would speak with Ian about it later, hoping he hadn't taken Drew's snubs too personally.

As the evening progressed, Ian seemed a little more reserved and quieter than normal, and Kat grew concerned that he was re-evaluating his decision to get involved with someone who had so much baggage now that he had met her kids. He had grown extremely comfortable around her family over the past few days, like he had always belonged there, but she could tell he was much more self-conscious about saying or doing the wrong thing in front of her children.

When dinner was over and Kat's mother had gone to retrieve dessert, Kat overheard Ian ask Drew about lacrosse. Drew looked over at him and said, "Look, you don't have to talk to me, okay. In fact, I'd prefer it if you didn't."

Kat was mortified and was just about to say something when Derrick jumped in.

"Drew! Bro, that's no way to speak to someone! What's the matter with you? You knock that crap off!"

Drew bristled. "What's the matter with me?" he spouted off, "Mama's gone off and found someone to try to relive her youth with. She totally abandoned us for three months and then shows up with this guy, expecting all of us to form some new, big, happy family together." And with that, he stood up and stormed out of the room.

There was a stunned silence around the table before Kat's mother, ever the lady, tried to ease the tension by sweetly drawling, "Who wants pie?"

Kat angrily threw her napkin down on the table and pushed back her chair to go after Drew when Ian stood up and gently requested, "Let me. Please."

She wasn't sure how to respond. Grateful that he wanted to

try to smooth things over, she still felt an obligation to do it herself and worried that if he went, it might only make the situation worse.

Feeling defeated, she took a deep breath, looked at him, and simply replied, "Okay."

Ian walked toward the family room, where Drew had headed. Kat was torn between wanting to sit back, letting Ian know that she thought he could handle it, and wanting to make sure that Drew was minding his manners. She was deeply embarrassed by her son's behavior and only sat still in her seat for a few minutes before she couldn't take it anymore and walked out of the dining room herself. Not wanting to just march into the room, however, she hung back by the doorway for a few seconds, listening. They were sitting on the loveseat with their backs to her, so she could overhear them without them knowing she was there.

She heard Ian say, "I know, mate. I understand. After my father died, I didn't want anyone around my ma. There just wasn't going to be anybody else who was good enough for her. All I wanted was my father back and there was never going to be anyone who could ever take his place."

"Your dad died?" Drew asked him.

"He did. When I was seven. It was bollocks."

Neither said a word for a few minutes, seemingly lost in their own thoughts. Drew finally broke the silence. "I don't know, man. I just want my family to be back together again."

"I get that, Drew. Honestly, I do. I felt the same way. Hell, I still feel the same way."

It was quiet again for a bit, but then Ian spoke up once more, "You know, Drew, I met your father when he came to Canada. He seems like a good man. He didn't punch me in the face or anything," he added with a chuckle. "Seriously though, I can tell that he cares a lot about you… all of you, including your mother. It's not my intent to take his place in your life or make things uncomfortable for you. All I want to do is love your mother. I would also like for us to eventually be friends, but I understand if this is just too raw for you right now.”

“You met my dad?”

“I did. He came to Canada when we returned from Los Angeles, shortly after your mother had served him the divorce papers. You didn’t know?”

“No. He didn’t tell me. That must have been the weekend he left when I had a lacrosse tournament and was staying with a friend. I thought he’d just gone on another of his millions of business trips.”

Ian bristled a bit, knowing from Kat exactly what had happened on those business trips, but knew it wasn’t his place to tell James’ son, saying only, “He came to try and talk your mother into going back with him and trying again. He wasn’t too happy when she told him she wouldn’t and confirmed that we were getting to know each other better.”

“That must’ve sucked for you!” Drew said with a smirk.

“It did. But, honestly, Drew, I love your mother enough that if that’s what she’d wanted to do —to go back with your father— I wouldn’t have stood in her way. It would have killed me, but all I want is for her to be happy.”

“Really?” Drew asked incredulously. “Are you sure you aren’t just telling me this because she picked you over my dad?”

“I’m sure. I love your mother, Drew. Really, I do. I’ve never met anyone like her. But she has a long history with your father and you kids, and I wouldn’t get in the way of that if she decided it was what she wanted. The fact of the matter is, though, that it wasn’t what she wanted. She chose me, and I know that as difficult as it is to hear that, you have to understand that I tried very hard not to influence her one way or the other. She actually kicked me out of the room after your father and I had words, and she was so smooth about it, I didn’t even realize what had happened until I was standing outside with the door shut in my face,” Ian told him with a chuckle.

“Yeah, she’s pretty good at getting people to do what she wants and not messing around,” Drew smiled, in spite of himself. “Served you right, though. You had no business being in there,” he added defiantly as an afterthought.

"I realized that, which is why I didn't go back inside. I also gave her some space later. I know that you, your brother, and sister will always come first for her, and quite frankly, that is how it should be. I'm an adult; I'm not threatened by a mother's relationship with her children." Ian took a deep breath before continuing.

"The real truth, Drew, is that I can't make you like me. But I also can't help that your father made some poor choices that affected all of your lives. It isn't fair and it isn't right, but it happened. Your mother is a wonderful, caring, funny woman who is about the only person in the world to stick around and put up with me when I'm at my worst who isn't genetically obligated or paid to do so. She deserves to be happy. I'm sorry for you kids that your father isn't the one to do that for her anymore. But Drew, if it wasn't me, it would be someone else. She's an incredible woman."

Drew was quite for a few minutes. He didn't say anything, just looked out the window. Finally, he asked, "Did your mother ever date after your father died?"

"She didn't. But that was different. I've never seen another love like theirs. He didn't purposely disappoint her or hurt her, he just died. She probably would have dated, maybe even remarried, if she didn't feel like he was her soul mate. But I can guarantee you that I would have felt the same way you do. I probably still would, honestly."

"So, even if I hate you, are you still going to be with my mother?"

"I will as long as that's what she wants because I want her to be happy. I really hope that over time you'll come to not hate me, though, because I know it would make your mother happiest if we could all just get along. She loves you and she loves me. We're going to have to figure out a way to coexist in her world, even if we aren't close."

"So, I just have to put up with you and give up any hope of my parents getting back together?"

"If that's what your mother wants, then yes, that's what you will have to do."

Drew sat and contemplated for a while before responding. "I guess you really like my mother."

"I do, Drew," Ian agreed emphatically "I love her! Like I said before, I've never met anyone like her. She doesn't have any agendas or ulterior motives; she just freely gives love. Believe me, in my line of work, I could have my pick of women..." Drew turned his head to him and gave him a withering look.

"But," Ian hurriedly continued with a nervous chuckle, "everyone else always seemed to love what I looked like, what I did for a living, my money, my growing fame, or what I could do for them to break them into the business... Either that, or they were dithering idiots who I couldn't stand to talk to for more than five seconds, regardless of how beautiful they were. Your mother is the first woman I've met since I became an actor people actually recognize who likes me, just as I am. I feel like with her, I could walk away from acting today and never look back, and she wouldn't care. Do you know how rare that is in my profession?"

"No," Drew said simply.

"It's rare. Like non-existent, actually. Your mother had just found out where she was, who I was, and she still handed me my arse on a plate—politely, of course; she *is* a Southern lady, after all. But she wasn't in awe or intimidated by me, and believe me, I took that as a challenge. I knew from our first interaction that she saw right through me, and while she was nervous, she held her own. She was more worried about losing her job than she ever was about trying to impress me. In fact, for the first time in I don't know how long, I felt like I had to impress her."

Drew smiled, despite his best efforts not to. "She can be a bit of a hard ass, my mama. She can rip you a new one without you even realizing it's happening."

"You've got that right," Ian agreed. "I will tell you too, Drew, that even if you can't be nice to me, I'll be nothing but nice to you. You don't have to like me, nor do you have to pretend to be my best friend. All I ask is that you respect the fact that I love your mother, that she chooses to love me, and that I'll do whatever is in my power to keep her happy, all right?"

Drew thought for a few seconds. "Okay. I guess I can agree to that," he said. "But, if you hurt her, I'll kick your ass!"

Ian laughed. "That sounds like a reasonable accord and one that I don't think I ever want to break. You could do some serious damage with that lacrosse stick!"

Having heard enough, Kat sneaked back down the hall to the dining room and sat down, waiting for them to return. After a few minutes, the two men came in and sat down again at the table. Though they were obviously not the best of friends, they seemed to have cleared the air and come to an understanding.

Emily asked, "So, Drew, is Ian coming to your graduation?"

Drew looked at him for a second before answering. "If he wants to, I guess he can come." With that, Kat knew that Drew would eventually be okay with their relationship, and it made her heart sing.

"I'd be honored," Ian replied humbly.

Chapter Fifty

The day of Drew's graduation arrived, and just like the week before, there was a mad scramble to get everyone out the door on time. Thankfully, they had managed to score some extra tickets from Tom and Ashley, and Holly and her husband, as they didn't need all of the allotted amounts for their smaller families.

Kat was very uneasy about Ian and James meeting up for the first time since that day in Canada; it was sure to be an emotionally charged situation. Kat wasn't sure if one of the children had already told James that Ian was joining them, so she had texted him the evening before to give him a polite heads-up. Given he had not responded, she knew he was not happy about that development. James' parents would also be in attendance, making it even more uncomfortable, and Kat felt very awkward being there with her new love interest while their son was obviously still grieving. Kat realized she had never asked James if he had told them the whole story, but then she realized it honestly didn't matter; it was none of their business anymore what she did with her life.

James and his parents, Olivia, and Derrick were already waiting by the front doors when they walked up. Not wanting to make it look like he was claiming Kat, Ian was hanging back a little in an obvious effort not to touch her, which she appreciated. Even so, James' mother's eyes went wide for a second when she saw him with her, then quickly narrowed. She stiffened when Kat reached over to give her a hug and a peck on the cheek, responding only with "Kat" to her "Hello, Barbara." James' father wouldn't even look her in the eye as he shook her hand. It hurt her that they would be so callous after so many shared years together, but she understood. As a parent, you never really get over your child being hurt by someone.

Ian stepped forward during the introductions, politely extending his hand to James' parents, Olivia, and Derrick. When he got to James, James looked at Ian's hand, but didn't react. Ian then lowered his and simply said, "Hello, James."

As they entered the building, James pulled Kat aside by her elbow. "Did you really have to bring him to this?" he hissed quietly near her ear.

"No, I didn't. Drew asked him to come."

"Yeah, only after Emily opened her big mouth at dinner the other night, according to Olivia."

Kat took a deep breath and tried to center herself before speaking. "James, I'm here to watch our last child graduate high school. Please do not make a scene. I know you're unhappy with how things have turned out, but you couldn't really have expected that I wouldn't meet someone else, could you?" She had to fight incredibly hard to keep from saying, "You didn't even wait until you were no longer married!" She knew, however, that it would only generate more animosity in an already tense situation.

"Is he coming back to the house?" James asked her.

"Yes, of course. Where else would he go? That's where we're having the party."

"Kat, I don't want that guy in my house!"

She finally couldn't help herself and her anger bubbled over. "It's my house too, James, at least until we close, and I invited him. We aren't going to have sex on the couch, for God's sake." She saw his eyes widen in shock but continued, "There will be plenty of people around."

With that, she freed herself from his grasp and walked over to Ian, who had been waiting a respectful distance away to give them privacy, but because James had been acting so childishly toward Kat, had been unwilling to leave her completely to fend for herself in case things got nasty.

The situation got even more uncomfortable when Kat ended up sitting between James and Ian. Neither man acknowledged the situation, but Kat couldn't relax. She began to think about what had happened between her and James at Derrick's graduation and she was unsure of how Ian would react if, in the excitement of seeing their child walk across the stage, something similar happened again. Even though it would be completely reactionary and innocent on her part, it would still be an intimate moment between the two of them, privately rejoicing in the accomplishment of the son they had created together, but she didn't want to make Ian feel irrelevant or excluded.

As Drew's name was called, the whole family stood up and cheered. As predicted, Kat got caught up in the emotion of the moment but surprised herself when it was Ian for whom she reached out to embrace in her joy. When she stood upright again, she saw James watching her with sadness in his eyes, so she took his hand in hers and gave it a squeeze. She caught his eye, and he gave her a sorrowful grimace. Leaning over, she repeated what he'd said to her just the week before, "We raised another hell of a kid!"

He smiled tightly at her and squeezed her hand back. "We sure did!" he said quietly.

After the ceremony, things were chaotic as parents tried to find their students and exit the building, so Kat and Ian lost their group in the sea of people. He had pulled her off to the side to wait for a few minutes for the crowd to thin, when Kat suddenly realized that she had left her sweater at her seat. Ian graciously volunteered to retrieve it for her, leaving her standing alone against a wall. She wasn't paying much attention while she waited so by the time she saw Tom and Ashley come out of the auditorium, it was too late to escape. Instead, she uttered a silent prayer that they wouldn't see her, but quickly realized she would have no such luck.

"Oh, my!" Ashley drawled. "Look what the cat's dragged in."

"Hi, Ashley. Hi, Tom," Kat responded flatly, hoping to give the hint that she didn't want to speak with them. Of course, Ashley was never one to pick up on subtlety.

"My word, Kat. How are you? You look so sad standin' out here all on your lonesome!" Ashley remarked. Kat just smiled at her in response.

"Did James tell you not to sit with him?" Ashley's asked in a mock hushed tone. "Well, sugar, you could have come and sat with us instead of bein' all by yourself."

"As if..." Kat quietly muttered under her breath before replying, "That's okay, Ashley. I was fine, thank you."

Tom, feeling highly uncomfortable, tried to excuse them, but when that didn't work, he told Ashley that he was going to go get the car. He politely said goodbye to Kat and walked away.

"So, how you doin', sugar? So terrible to hear that you and James couldn't reconcile. I guess you slinkin' around with that actor sealed the fate of y'all's divorce." Again, Kat just smiled.

Ashley continued, "So where is that actor now? I reckoned he would drop you like a hot potato."

"Here it is, love!" Ian said, as he ran back, handing Kat her sweater. He turned to look at Ashley. "Oh, hello!" he said amicably.

Ashley turned a ghastly pale color and stared, her mouth hanging open. Kat took her opportunity to pounce.

"Thank you, sweetheart. Ashley here was just wondering if you had dropped me like... What was it, Ashley? 'Like a hot potato,' right?" She looked at Ashley who gave the slightest of nods in response.

"Nice to meet you, Ashley," Ian said distractedly, clearly wondering what was going on, not quite having it sink in yet. As he looked at Kat and saw her irritation, she could tell the exact moment recognition dawned on him. His eyes narrowed and an expression akin to thunder swept over his features for a split second before he composed himself again. He wrapped his arm around Kat's waist, pulling her in closer to him. Then he took a deep breath.

"So, you are Ashley?" he asked her coldly. All she could do, again, was merely nod.

"So, you are the opportunistic *wagon* who tried to ruin my career and Kat's reputation in one blow, then?" Ashley said nothing, her mouth hanging agape.

Ian continued. "You know, there are actually very few

things that leave me really fuming. *Gombeens* like you who take advantage of a situation for their own gain certainly rank right up there. Thank God rational people realized the gammy rubbish you were spouting was absolute shite… I guess it was the only way you could get anyone to pay attention to you, you good-for-nothing *geebag*! Do you realize how many people your antics could have affected? It's a good job that no one bothered to take your blathering seriously!" Ian's accent thickened significantly in his anger, and he had fire flashing in his eyes.

"I'm sorry?" Ashley asked, obviously not following everything he was throwing out at her.

"Oh, I'm sorry, Ashley," Kat said, her voice dripping with sweetness. "Did you not understand? Let me translate for you: Ian thinks you're a self-serving bitch, and quite frankly, I, for one, whole-heartedly agree. See ya later, *sugar*!"

With that, she grabbed Ian's hand and together they ran out the door before Kat doubled over, grabbing her stomach while laughing.

"Do you know how long I've wanted to say that to her?" she asked him, her giddiness apparent. "Every day for as long as I can remember that woman has put me down, and I could never say anything because James worked with her husband. I just swallowed her crap time and time again. Thank you for giving me the opportunity to throw it all back in her face. I'm so happy I don't ever have to deal with that bitch again!"

"Glad to be of service!" he said, grinning. "And the best part is that there weren't any witnesses!"

Getting caught up in her exuberance, Ian took her in his arms and swung her around, giving her a long, deep kiss on the front steps of the venue. Kat heard a door slam shut and opened her eyes. Her arms still wrapped around Ian's back and without even breaking the kiss, Kat caught Ashley's eye as she came outside, and lifted up her middle finger as the woman walked past them.

When they broke apart, Kat told Ian, "You got so worked up, it was like you were speaking a different language!"

"I guess I've lived in England and here long enough and played an American for so long, my colloquialisms from home are usually pretty suppressed. However, I have to say that you translated brilliantly!" He grinned.

"Honestly, it wasn't too hard to figure out," she teased him playfully as they walked down the stairs and into the parking lot.

A short drive later, they arrived at Kat and James' house. As Kat reached to open the front door, however, she sensed Ian hesitating; something was holding him back.

She looked back and asked, "What is it?"

"It just feels strange," he replied quietly.

"Strange? Why?"

"Because this is your house. This is where you lived and built a life with him for twenty-three years. You spent every day here together for your entire marriage. It's where you raised your family…"

"Ian, are you jealous?"

"I think I am a little," he said sheepishly. "Though I know it's ridiculous to be. I think I'm more just saddened that you had a whole life before me. It also makes me a bit sentimental. I'm seeing all I've missed, both with you and just in life in general. I can't help feeling like I'm the one with whom you could have shared these things if circumstances had been different."

"Well, again, you were only fourteen when I married James. I don't think it would have been appropriate or legal to be together with you then," she teased him.

"Oh, of course: the old 'I would have been with you, but you hadn't gone through puberty yet and lived on another continent' excuse, eh?" he quipped, the corners of his mouth twitching as he tried not to smile.

Kat laughed and looked down, shaking her head. "Something like that," she said. "But this house won't be mine and James' much longer. In fact, I wanted to ask you about that… I need to get my stuff from here to Los Angeles. I'm thinking I'll rent a truck and drive back. Wanna come with?" she asked flirtatiously, running her finger down the buttons of his shirt, stopping at his belt buckle. "I promise I'll make it worth your while," she added seductively, looking coyly up at him through her eyelashes.

"Road trip?" he asked. "Just you and me? Across the U.S.? With lots of uninterrupted sex?"

"Uh huh," she purred.

"You drive a hard bargain, my dear." He pretended to contemplate the decision for a second. "Okay," he impishly relented.

"Can you take that long to get back? You already haven't been back for this week after you finished shooting. Can you take another six days or so?"

"Kat, I'm an actor, remember?" he asked. "Right now, I may very well be an unemployed actor, actually. I guess I had better return my agent's calls and read my texts. But it isn't exactly like I'm expected back at the office on Monday. I don't even know if they have scheduled any ADR yet. Truth be told though, even if I was, I wouldn't give up this opportunity."

"Oh, God. That's right!" Kat exclaimed. "I've enjoyed having you here with me so much, I forgot about all you gave up."

He pulled her close to him and, after he kissed her ear, whispered, "I wouldn't change a thing.", causing shivers to run down her spine.

"I just hope you remember that when you have to become a waiter to pay your mortgage!"

"That's all right. You can support me with your catering gig. You will be my sugar mama," he quipped with a wink.

"Shall we?" he asked, putting a hand in the small of her back and opening the door with the other.

When they stepped inside, Ian quickly looked around. His expression was reminiscent of a child being caught with their hand in the cookie jar, and it was obvious he felt like he was intruding. Just then, James stepped around the corner and looked at the two of them. His eyes narrowed just a bit when he realized that the rival for Kat's affection, the man who had stolen her heart from him, was standing in his house. Kat held her breath for a second, thinking that this was very much like watching two animals pace around each other, waiting to attack.

Finally, Ian took a step forward and put his hand out. "Hello, James," he said simply.

"Hello," he answered, leaning over to give Kat a kiss on the cheek and leaving Ian's outstretched hand hanging for the second time that day. "Come in," he continued tersely, clearly trying hard to keep up his Southern gentleman demeanor.

They had been running a bit behind due to her forgotten sweater and their encounter with Ashley, so Kat was relieved to see that her mother, daughter, and sisters- in-law were already setting out the food and greeting guests. The house was packed with teachers, coaches, family, and friends all congratulating Drew, Kat, and James. Ian was causing quite a stir, too, especially with the women, adding to the pandemonium. Kat tried to stay with him, but the throngs of people vying for their attention eventually separated them. Every few minutes, she would look over and catch his eye, though, and he would flash back his famous dimpled grin, letting her know he was all right. He was graciously interacting with everyone, charming them all with his quick wit and dazzling looks.

Even James' mother eventually got caught up in his ability to draw people to him.

Eventually Kat found herself next to Holly after seeing her several times from across the room. She hadn't had a chance to get together with her since their canceled lunch date.

"Hi!" Holly exclaimed, quickly leaning in to give her a one-armed hug, holding her glass of Burgundy in the other.

"Hey! Can you believe these boys made it?"

"Sure, I can. They're great kids. How could they be anything less when we raised them?"

"I'm so sorry that we haven't been able to catch up. It's been such a whirlwind with the boys' graduations a week apart and then Ian coming."

"Yeah, about that… Girl, he is *fine*!" Holly exclaimed. "All he would have to do is smile at me like he smiles at you, and I wouldn't think twice about leaving my husband and kids to become his personal sex slave."

"He *is* pretty amazing!" Kat gushed.

"Amazing? Kat, he's perfection. They don't make them any better than that."

"I know, and the best part is that he's a good person, too! He's not at all stuck up or snobby. He's really down to earth and grounded. Come on! You have to meet him!" Kat grabbed Holly's elbow and brought her over to where Ian was standing.

"Ian, this is my friend, Holly," she introduced her.

"Ah!" he exclaimed. "You're Kat's 'Jen away from Jen', right?"

Holly giggled. "That's what Kat tells me."

"It's so nice to meet you! Congratulations to your son, as well. Kat told me that he and Drew have been good friends for a long time."

"Yes, since we moved down here," Holly replied, not taking her eyes off of him. After a while, though, she relaxed, and they all conversed as the crowd began to thin.

Eventually, after everyone had left, Ian and Kat stayed to help James clean up. They stood in the kitchen, Kat washing and Ian drying, laughing, and talking together. James would come in with more dishes and watch them for a few seconds before turning and leaving for more.

"Great party," James told Kat, after Ian had excused himself to find the washroom.

She turned to him with a conciliatory smile. "Yes, it was. Thank you for letting us have it here."

"Kat, I already told you, this is your house as much as mine until we close. In fact, I still meant what I said; you're still welcome to move back in at any time," he chuckled uncomfortably.

"Thanks, James, but I'm good. I appreciate it, though. Speaking of which, I'll come by on Monday to pick up my things, if that works for you?"

"So, you really are moving out there?"

"Yes." She could see the pain in his eyes as he realized this was truly it.

He took a deep breath and said, "Honestly, Kat, I've never seen you so happy. As much as it kills me to say this, Ian's a good man. I'm just sorry that I ever let you go. I hope that you can eventually forgive me and know it really wasn't about you; it was me and my own selfishness. As much as I miss you, you deserve to be this happy."

"Thank you, James," she said quietly, leaning over and giving him a hug.

By that time, Ian had returned and walked up beside Kat. She knew that he was still trying hard to prevent any further drama by not being overly demonstrative in front of James, but when she had stepped back from their embrace, she caught that he had started to stretch his hand out, then quickly pulled it back in again. It was obvious he was fighting a strong urge to reach out and draw her in closer, but he eventually settled on clasping his hands behind his back to ensure he could resist.

"Everything okay in here?" she heard him ask, looking between the two of them.

"It's just fine, Ian," James said. "I was just telling Kat that you're a lucky man."

"I know," Ian replied humbly.

"Just take care of her, all right? She will always mean a great deal to me." James' eyes began to mist over.

"I promise I will, James," Ian said seriously. "I know that you will always mean a great deal to her as well, as it should be." He stuck out his hand and James finally took and shook it.

"Ready, love?" Ian asked, looking toward her.

"Yes. I was just asking James if it's okay that we come by on Monday with the truck and pick up my stuff."

"Ah." Ian said, now understanding why the mood had been a bit uncomfortable when he had walked in.

"I guess this is it, then?" James said.

"At least until Olivia gets married, I suppose," Kat agreed.

"Well, I mean it, Kat. Thank you for giving me three beautiful children and a lifetime of memories. Take care of yourself."

"Thank you, too, James. They are great kids, and we made a good team. I'll leave the key under the mat when I leave. Good luck with the closing and I'll sign whatever I need to on my end—just let me know. Oh, and I'll keep my same cell number, so don't ever hesitate to contact me. Don't be a stranger. You will always be an important part of my life."

By this time, they had made it to the front door. Kat leaned in to give James a hug and kissed his cheek. "I hope that you find happiness, too, James. Please don't punish yourself for the rest of your life."

He smiled weakly at her, trying to keep the tears in his eyes from spilling out. "Goodbye. Be careful."

Turning to Ian, he said sternly, "I meant what I said. You take good care of her, ya hear?" Ian simply nodded.

As they got in the car and headed back to Kat's parents' house, Ian was contented to just let Kat quietly process what had happened. About halfway, her tears finally stopped, and she sighed, saying, "I'm glad it's over. All of it. I'm glad that I can start fresh."

Ian reached over and clasped her hand. "Me, too."

"Thank you for being there today and for being so nice to him," Kat said.

"I told you before that I had no intention of treating him poorly. He'll always be significant to your children and to you. I get that love comes in many forms, and that even though you don't share a romantic love for him anymore, you will continue to care for him because of the history you share and what he meant to you."

"I'm so lucky to have you, Ian. Many men wouldn't be so understanding."

"Kat, you chose me. For some unknown reason, you decided that I was the one worthy of your love. I don't know what I ever did to deserve you, but I'm confident in the fact that you decided to be with me."

"You're right," she said. "Thank you."

When they made it back, everyone ate leftovers from the party and sat together, talking and watching movies. As exhaustion from the day set in, people began to excuse themselves for the night. Kat's brothers and their wives were heading back on Sunday morning, so the fact that they only had one more full day together was weighing heavily on everyone's minds as they went to bed.

Saturday was full of packing and preparing food for one last family dinner before everyone went home, and they all spent the majority of the day in the kitchen or around the smoker in an easy, relaxed atmosphere. In the early afternoon, Kat's children also arrived, anxious to spend one more evening together with the majority of the Curtis family. As Ian helped Kat make the cornbread and biscuits, she teased him about how she would have never believed he would enjoy cooking the food he had thrown such a fuss about eating just a few months before. When it came time for the greens, he said, "I've got these!" with a cocky smirk. Under Kat's supervision, he fixed the greens exactly as she had shown him in Canada, much to his own satisfaction.

"Better watch out, Kat!" he gloated. "I wasn't kidding when I said I may just join you and Jen in the catering business now that I'm more than likely out of work."

Kat reached over and squeezed his backside, before raising up on her tiptoes and murmuring into to his ear, "I certainly wouldn't mind. But, like Lydia said, we would probably get in trouble with the health department at some point."

When they all sat down together at the table, Kat's father said the blessing and the food was passed around. Though the conversation was lively, there was a palatable undercurrent of sadness that came with the knowledge that their time together was quickly coming to an end. There was talk about everyone coming back for Thanksgiving or perhaps Christmas, but no one could say for sure if it would be possible. Kat figured it was as good a time as any to break the news to her parents that she was also leaving for Los Angeles on Monday afternoon.

"Mama? Daddy?" she said, hoping that having everyone around would help to keep her mother a bit calmer when she told them her plans.

"What is it, baby girl?" her father replied.

"Ian and I are also going to be leaving on Monday."

She paused to breathe deeply and brace herself for the fight she was sure would ensue. Thankfully, though, before her mother could respond, a young voice cut through the tension in the room.

"So, Aunt Kat, are you moving to Los Angeles, then?" Emily inquired.

Kat looked up at Ian and caught his gaze. The corners of his mouth turned up slightly and he nodded. "Yes, Emily, that is the plan. Your cousins don't need me to live here to be their mama anymore, so I want to go and work with my friend Jen."

"Where are you going to live?" inquired Christopher, his eyes twinkling mischievously.

Kat narrowed her eyes and pursed her lips, giving him a look that said she knew exactly what he was doing, and she wasn't happy about it. He couldn't help the little snicker that escaped his lips.

Kat took another deep breath. She wasn't quite sure yet what the answer to that question was going to be.

However, she was just about ready to respond that she was going to live with Jen, at least in the short term, when Ian jumped in. "She's going to live with me, Emily."

The table fell instantly silent. Ian looked up at Kat with a hint of panic in his eyes. He had anticipated some flak from her mother, but when everyone stared at him without uttering a word, he began to feel very unnerved.

"Over my dead body!" spat out Kat's mother. "There's no way a daughter of mine is goin' to be livin' in sin with a man out of wedlock. It's bad enough she's divorced!"

"With all due respect, ma'am, who said she would be living

with me out of wedlock?" Ian countered.

Kat gave him a double take before saying, "Excuse me?" obviously shocked at the comment and confused about what he meant.

Ian turned to her mother and smiled. "I have what is known as the Traditional Irish Mammy. She is a force of Holy Catholicism that is not to be reckoned with and can put to shame even the most devout Southern Baptist mother with her fits of objection, threats of eternal damnation for my immortal soul, and most importantly, inflicting guilt of Biblical proportions. I would never dream of living with a woman out of wedlock, as it would most certainly be the death of her."

Again, no one said a word. Kat was too stunned to form anything even resembling a coherent thought. She glanced over and saw that he was smirking, his dimples melting her heart.

"Excuse me?" she repeated.

"Kat, I know you think your mother is tough, but I guarantee you, my mother can out cry and out guilt the lot of you put together, all while continuing to pray the Rosary. She's moving in next month and, and as I said, she would never stand for her only son to be living in sin, especially in what will also be her home. So, we will have to get married," he said matter-of-factly, as though it was obvious.

"I'm sorry… What are you saying?" Kat was having a difficult time comprehending.

"What I'm saying—well, asking really—is, Kat, will you marry me?"

There was a collective gasp in the room. Kat was too flustered to speak. Finally, Christopher asked, "I'm sorry. Did you just ask my sister to marry you?"

"I did," he responded.

"But we haven't been together that long!" Kat exclaimed.

"So what? We're both adults; we can do whatever we want as far as I see it. What would we be waiting for, exactly?" he asked her with a shrug.

"Are you sure? I mean, it seems so sudden!"

"Kat, you sure know how to make a guy feel self-conscious about his proposal!" he laughed. "In all seriousness, though, I'm an actor. I'm passionate and make a living off of reading people's expressions and body language. Therefore, I know without a doubt that you love me, and I love you. Why in the world would we waste any more time playing at a game when we both know what the end goal is? I want us to be together for the rest of our lives. What does it matter if that happens a year from now or a week from now? I'm more certain about us than I have ever been about anything in my life. Aren't you?"

Kat could only stare at him, wondering how to respond. She finally just nodded.

"So, what do you say, then?" he asked, dropping to one knee, and taking her hand in his, "Kat Anderson, will you be my wife?"

Epilogue

A little more than one year later, Kat sat in a chair in Jen's back yard, relaxing as the reception following Jen and David's emotional vow renewal ceremony was winding down. Jen came over and plunked into a seat beside her, happy to get off of her feet for a while.

"So glad that it's over!" she exclaimed.

"It was beautiful, Jen. Simply amazing! I'm so happy y'all figured it all out and are back together."

Jen smiled. "Me, too! How about you? How are you holding up? How are the kids and James?"

Kat looked down at her arms crossed in front of her and said, "Everyone's good, thanks! Things seem to be progressing nicely and I'm happy to be off my feet for a while. Being eight months pregnant doesn't yield itself to standing all day, especially at my age."

"I still can't get over that you are pregnant!" Jen exclaimed.

"Yeah, most days I can't, either. But the swollen cankles and my enormous morphing physical form are making it easier and easier to believe every day!"

"And I've never seen a man so over the moon! He can't wait to meet his little boy!"

Kat smiled softly, looking across the yard at her husband, running behind a toddler in a white sundress, dark curls falling down to her shoulders. He finally caught the little girl and swung her up in his arms, giving her a kiss on her cheek, as she cried, "Again, Daddy! Again!"

"It certainly was a shock when we found out, especially after we had just had Isabella placed with us. I am just so glad he is healthy, and everything looks good, given that I'm forty-four."

"Have y'all decide on a name?" Jen inquired.

"Yes, we're naming him Daniel, after Ian's father."

"That's awesome! What's going on with Izzie? I never would have guessed that Ian would be so adamant about fostering and adopting."

"He says it's because of what happened to Lydia in the system. He wanted us to be the ones to make a difference in at least one child's life. Her birth parents agreed to terminate their rights fairly quickly, given their situation, and it seemed to make them more comfortable that the adoptive father is a bit of a celebrity. It helped ease their worries that she wouldn't be taken care of, I guess.

"Now just comes the adoption finalization hearing next month, and then she is ours forever."

Jen just shook her head and chuckled softly. "What?" demanded Kat. "What's funny about that? It's wonderful!"

"I'm not laughing about that at all. It *is* wonderful. She is one lucky little girl! I was just thinking back to that moment out in front of the trailer in the middle of nowhere Canada when I told you to just wait; that your life would be completely different, unrecognizable even, in a year, and that it would be a good thing!"

"Oh, yeah! I vaguely remember that…"

"I was right!" Jen declared smugly. "I was a friggin' fortune teller!"

"This year has been a trip, that's for sure."

"I can't believe you agreed to marry him that quickly. It was such a very unKat-like thing to do! And then to just elope in Las Vegas while y'all were driving back here? It continues to blow me away!"

"I figured he was right!" Kat declared defensively. "What would we have been waiting for, exactly? Though, to be completely honest, it's a little crazy that we got married in the same place my first marriage had imploded just a few months earlier. Ironic, yet apropos, I guess."

"You're right! I'm just surprised because you usually are so cautious and psychoanalyze everything to death."

Ian walked up to them, carrying Isabella on his arm. "Isn't that the truth," he interjected, leaning down and kissing his wife on her forehead, placing the little girl on her lap. "Here's Mama!

How are you feeling, love?"

"I'm good. Just tired," she replied. "I am so happy that the filming for the fourth season wrapped before I got this huge. I'm also very glad that your mother agreed to come up there with us to help with Isabella so we could be together and both work."

"My trailer was certainly a lot livelier than the first three seasons, that's for certain," Ian laughed. "Good thing you and my mother get along so well. Three months away from you would have been hell, especially knowing this little guy was on his way," Ian concluded, reaching down and rubbing Kat's baby bump. "Seemed to make the most sense that George just went ahead and hired your and Jen's company again, though," he said with a shrug.

"Yeah, like you had no influence over that at all…" Lydia said sarcastically as she and her fiancé, Andre, joined them at the table.

"Hey! I resent that insinuation, Lyds! You think after everything that happened, I would have that kind of clout? I simply told George that I'd become quite accustomed to grits in the morning, prepared by my personal Southern chef, and would appreciate it if he could make that happen on location." He winked as he said it, and he leaned over to give her a kiss on the cheek.

"Which I certainly appreciated!" Jen interjected.

"Well, you definitely scared the crap out of everyone when you told the world you didn't care if they fired you and marched off that sound stage. They never thought we would have the guts to walk away, but then they saw their gold mine get up and do just that," Lydia stated.

"People like me, but let's be honest, the majority of our audience is made up of middle-aged women hot for you! Add to that the success of the third season, and I don't think there was any way they were going to deny us anything. In fact, I'm pretty sure they will give us whatever we want from now on. Who would have ever guessed that by coming clean, we would generate even more buzz?"

"And how are you feeling, Kat?" Lydia suddenly turned her attention to Ian's wife, who was busy trying to prevent a squirmy toddler from sliding off her greatly diminished lap.

"I'm good, Lydia, thanks! More than ready for this little one to make his debut, but other than that, things are amazing."

"And how are your kids taking all of this?"

"In stride. Y'all know that Drew was furious when we got married, but he has gotten over it. The other two have always been fine, if we don't count Olivia's mortification that, how did she put it, Ian? 'It was gross that technically we could be pregnant at the same time,' wasn't it, babe?"

Ian laughed. "She certainly made it quite clear that she thought having a baby at forty-four was a bit over the top. But she has enjoyed following Isabella's case, given she's studying social work. They all think she's adorable, and they're right! She is!" he answered, as he reached over and took the little girl into his arms, giving her a hug.

"And they will think this guy is adorable, too, once he's here," Kat affirmed, rubbing her swollen belly.

"And how's James taking all of these changes?" David asked, having finally wandered over to the group after checking on Lucy, who was playing with friends.

"He's okay, actually," Kat replied. "He struggled at first, but the kids say he's finally seeing someone, and they like her. They say she's nice, so I'm happy for him."

"And I'm ecstatic he *finally* realized he wasn't going to get you back!" Ian told everyone.

"Yeah, my getting married to someone else kind of ended that possibility!" Kat replied, poking him gently in the side.

As the easy banter amongst their group continued, Kat looked around the table at all the faces of the people she loved. Jen was right: she had predicted Kat's future, and she wouldn't change it for anything in the world.

About Majken Selinder Nilsson

After a particularly difficult year, Majken (pronounced "My-ken") Selinder Nilsson started writing novels as a way to safely and legally deal with an extremely stressful period in her life, finding during the process that she really enjoyed and had a knack for it. Though becoming an author was never in her plans, it was not surprising, as Ms. Selinder Nilsson has always had a vividly active imagination, having not only one but two imaginary friends as a child. Even as an adult, her characters come to life in her head and their personal stories often flow out faster than she can type. In just three years, she had written three novels and had received publishing contracts for two of them. Her books are available for sale in print, ebook, and audiobook editions with a variety of retailers, from Amazon.com to BarnesandNoble.com, and even through vendors abroad.

A native Nevadan from a small town, who also spent some time living in her ancestral home of Sweden, Ms. Selinder Nilsson is now a transplanted Southerner, where she lives with her very understanding family who accepts that she stays up way too late writing, and all of whom are now used to calling her name several times to get her attention whenever she is in front of her computer. They are also accustomed to her bringing her laptop everywhere there could possibly be a few minutes' wait and have even stopped teasing her about her ever-changing facial expressions while she is writing dialogue.

Ms. Selinder Nilsson strives to develop a strong sense of place blended with complex characters with whom people can relate, while utilizing succinct, developed dialogue. Their personas become like close friends, often surprising her with the twists and turns in their lives as much as her readers. She connects with her characters on a deeply personal level and is known to mourn them when their stories come to an end.

Social Media

Facebook:
https://www.facebook.com/MajkenSelinderNilsson/

Website:
http://majkenselindernilssonbooks.com

LinkedIn:
https://www.linkedin.com/in/majken-selinder-nilsson-43b31112b

Twitter:
https://twitter.com/MNilsson_Author

Blog:
https://majkenselindernilssonwritesblog.wordpress.com/

If you enjoyed this story, check out these other books by Majken Selinder Nilsson:

Western Skies

Discover the story of the couple at the heart of Western Skies, the TV show featured in Majken Selinder Nilsson's debut novel, A Good Kind of Crazy...

When Sarah marries her childhood sweetheart, she expects that their life together will be perfect, happily raising a home full of children on their family farm. However, life doesn't go as planned as her world is turned upside-down and she loses almost everything.

In an attempt to escape the pain of her personal tragedy, Sarah and her young son travel to her sister's home in a small Colorado mining town. There she meets Joe, the dutiful but awkward town sheriff, full of disappointments of his own, when he comes to her aid. Each reeling from crippling heartache and believing that their unhappy courses are firmly set, Sarah and Joe forge an unlikely friendship.

Can Sarah and Joe overcome their disillusionment and stubborn pride long enough to risk taking a chance on finding a different "Happily Ever After"?